CODE NAME WALTER

A Novel

Enzo:
I hope you enjoy this diversion.
Roger

By: Roger B. Anderson, Sr.

the Peppertree Press
Sarasota, Florida

Graphic design by Rebecca Barbier.

For information regarding permission,
call 941-922-2662 or contact us at our website:
www.peppertreepublishing.com or write to:
the Peppertree Press, LLC.
Attention: Publisher
1269 First Street, Suite 7
Sarasota, Florida 34236

ISBN: 978-1-61493-072-3

Library of Congress Number: 2011943205

Printed in the U.S.A.

Printed December 2011

DEDICATION

This book is dedicated to Callie, whose strength and character in times of adversity are an inspiration to all who have met her.

ACKNOWLEDGMENT

I would like to acknowledge the perseverance and editing assistance given by my wife, Rachel, and my mother, Evelyn Anderson. Both read the first and subsequent drafts and provided recommendations on the structure and content, as well as enthusiasm for the story itself. I would especially acknowledge the assistance of Candace Daniels, whom I pressed into editing the first draft based on our friendship and long working relationship. Candace saw the manuscript at its worst and made significant contributions and editorial comments. Thanks also to Carol Butler for her editorial contributions and insight into the literary community in St. Petersburg, Florida.

I would also like to thank my many cohorts and friends in the field of environmental consulting. Thanks for the intellectual stimulation and exchange of ideas, as we explored numerous environmental issues and projects.

TABLE OF CONTENTS

CHAPTER 1

The Dispersal

He sat on the hot hangar floor, as the arid and dusty African wind began to cool with the onset of night. He levered the bolt of the 9mm sidearm and slipped it into the holster on his field pack. At 42 years of age, Quinn Wilson was a trim 6 feet 2 inches tall with a close military-style haircut that showed a touch of gray above his ears. He wore a frameless pair of glasses that gave him the bookish appearance of a college professor preparing for a lecture. He looked out of place in his desert combat fatigues with an M16 lying across his lap. Since the mission was about to begin, he took his glasses off and put them into one of the many pockets of the borrowed combat fatigues he wore over the hot body armor. He would not need reading glasses where they were going in the morning.

Elsewhere in the hangar, the small team of young marines were quietly checking their gear and trying to get some rest. A melancholy harmonica tune drifted through the hangar with the light breeze. The equally young captain stood at a table under the single glaring light bulb hanging from the ceiling, alternately talking with his sergeant and diligently going over the maps covering the table. Outside the hangar, an aging C-130 waited on the tarmac, a faint light casting shadows from its gaping cargo door. By 0400 hours, this small team would be winging its way north towards the southeastern Sudan border on a clandestine rescue mission. The captain had been adamant that he did not want an "old man" on this mission, and for reasons other than his age, Quinn had to agree with him. As a younger man, Quinn had served as a Marine Captain in Desert Storm, leading a Platoon of Marines against a Republican Guard stronghold in some of the heaviest fighting just outside of Kuwait. He had done his time in combat, but thanks to Agent Ken James with the Central Intelligence Agency (CIA), who had the final say on this rescue attempt, he was once again in full combat gear, armed to the teeth, and ready for a HALO jump from 25,000 feet in the dead of night over one of Africa's most troubled areas with a group of young, untested marines.

It was not supposed to be this way. Quinn was only a few months away from his environmental consulting job in Tampa, Florida, and his comfortable family life in northeast St. Petersburg. But all that had dissolved with incredible speed and seemed a lifetime ago. Quinn had thought he and his wife, Nancy, would travel and rekindle the spark that had been missing from their life for a long time. But that wasn't going to be the case. Upon arriving back home from a short business trip to Panama City one Friday afternoon, he found Nancy had left him and moved out of the house, leaving behind most of her personal belongings including her clothes and jewelry. She left a note saying she wanted more from life than what he was offering. Their daughter was enrolled in an out-of-state college and loving her new independence. It seemed that their daughter had been his wife's whole life. Now that she away was away from home and in college, his wife began to feel that her life had no purpose or meaning. She had attempted to turn back the clock to her young, more carefree times, with new clothes and a different hairstyle. Against his advice, she had plastic surgery to eliminate a few wrinkles and went so far as trying to restore a figure that was showing the first signs of being influenced by gravity. The results were striking, he had to admit, but at the same time she had become more aloof and secretive as her appearance had changed. Quinn had not understood and seemed helpless as they drifted apart. She was adamant that it was time to concentrate on what *she* wanted to do.

Since his wife had left him and his daughter was away at college, he sought a change of pace from his current position.

He loved the job and supervised a group of dedicated scientists. But he knew he had to make a change, in an attempt to outrun the empty house and broken heart that were all that was left of his former life. He called a former client with the National Science Foundation (NSF) and was invited to Washington to look at some possibilities. As luck would have it, there was an opening in the Foundation's Polar program for the upcoming winter in Antarctica. Quinn thought that this would give him a "cooling-off period" where he could reset his priorities and figure out what to do with the rest of his life.

While in Washington, his client introduced him to Alex Reager, the Pacific Operations Officer for the National Geo-Spatial Intelligence Agency (NGIA). NGIA managed the national satellite imaging system and provided current intelligence to U.S. agencies and friendly foreign governments throughout the world. Quinn learned that the U.S. military was the largest client of the NGIA, but others, such as the Department of Agriculture, National Ocean and Atmospheric Administration, and the CIA were also dependent on their services. He and Alex talked through lunch and much of the afternoon about the agency and its role in an increasingly complex world. Alex asked him to consider a position as field agent, stationed in Australia or New Zealand, to be the agency's eyes and ears on the ground. He further explained that satellite photographs did not always provide the details needed. Conditions on the ground were almost always different than what appeared on the aerial photographs. Quinn's job would be to fill in the blanks and provide greater intelligence by reporting activities on the ground. Alex was willing to wait until after Quinn's winter assignment with the NSF before beginning with the NGIA.

He also asked Quinn to attend a six-week course for field agents in St. Marys, Georgia, since he would be working independently through much of the South Pacific with minimal support. Quinn was to report to McMurdo Station in Antarctica in mid-March for the winter and would have time to participate in the course. "It could be very helpful," Alex had assured him as he had his assistant, Candace, reserve a slot for him in the six-week course.

He recalled Alex asking, "Before I forget, Quinn, all of our agents have a code name. Nothing fancy—it's in part, tradition from our early CIA days. But it serves a purpose, especially in this day of emails and passwords. Do you have a code name in mind that we can get into the system?"

Quinn thought for a moment and said almost tongue-in-cheek, "How about Walter?"

"Walter?" Alex had responded with a curious expression on his face. "Let me check and see if we already have a Walter on record," and turned to Candace, who was already checking the security system.

"Uh, let me see, we have a few Walters on staff, but none of them had selected Walter as their code names in the records," she said while staring at the screen.

"Well that does it. Welcome aboard, Walter," Alex said with his hand extended to Quinn. "We'll get it into the system and use the code for all communications in the future."

There had been stimulating conversations throughout the afternoon about Antarctica, the South Pacific and Australia. The adventurous-sounding assignments had reminded Quinn of a short story he had read in college, "*The Secret Life of Walter Mitty,*" by James Thurber. It was the hilarious short story of an old man who dreamed of adventure and performing heroic deeds, while his wife nagged him back to reality. That name had flashed across his mind when Alex had asked him about a code name. So within a few short minutes, Quinn had become "Walter."

Upon leaving Washington, Quinn had accepted both jobs. He would serve as the Director of Environmental Research with the NSF at McMurdo Station in Antarctica for the winter. After overwintering, he would settle into New Zealand or Australia and become the eyes and ears on the ground for NGIA. His life was about to change radically, so he left Washington with much to do in preparing for these new adventures.

The next few weeks were filled with activities of moving on. He quit his job, said his farewells, sold his boat and put the family home of 25 years up for sale. Since he did not know where Nancy was or if she would ever return, he left half the revenue from the sales of all assets in her name and left her favorite credit card open. Other financial accounts were placed on hold until he could call for the transfer from his new home base in New Zealand or Australia. Their daughter was convinced that he had driven her mother away, so she could have cared less that he was leaving, as long as he continued to pay her college expenses.

So on a cold January morning, he reported for the training course at a security facility outside of St. Marys, Georgia. It was called a "course," but Quinn soon learned that it was a military-style boot camp. Ever since his early days in the Marines, he had a recurring nightmare about being back in boot camp. Now here he was, living in a barrack, revelry at 0400, and running 5k before breakfast, all with the loud and boisterous admonishment of a drill instructor. The technical courses on intelligence gathering were lead by senior field agent, Ken James, from Australia. Since Quinn was at least 20 years older than most of the young recruits, Agent James paid special attention to his training. Most of the recruits were right out of college and entering a career as agents for the FBI, CIA, or Secret Service. By week three, Quinn was moving up in the morning pack and challenging some of the former college athletes. His roommate was a young graduate of Clemson named Steven Coates and the two developed a bond as they competed in hand-to-hand combat and small arms training. He also was responsible for giving Quinn the nickname of "Pops." By the end of the course, Quinn was physically fit and since he had little time to think of his broken marriage, he was feeling more confident than ever that he was making the right move.

Upon graduation, Alex Reager contacted him and asked if he would accompany a United Nation's humanitarian mission to Africa. Quinn was to be an observer assisting Hope Roberts, whose home base was out of Kingston, Jamaica, where she covered the Atlantic Region for the NGIA. He met Hope Roberts at the International Airport in Paris. She was a tall, athletic Jamaican with a delightful island accent. The most interesting thing about her appearance was her brilliant white teeth that flashed like a neon sign when she smiled and her startling deep green eyes that looked back at you from a beautiful brown face. Quinn soon learned that she was a former Olympic runner, who had won the bronze medal as the anchor on the Jamaican 440-meter relay team in the Year 2000 games. She had graduated from the University of the West Indies with a Masters in Geography and had been a high school teacher in Kingston to fund her Olympic track training until recruited for this position. Hope had been with NGIA for 2½ years now and admitted that things had been slow in the Atlantic region. She had covered a few tropical storms and hurricanes in the Caribbean, but not much else. She was glad to be making her first trip into Africa. Quinn immediately liked Hope. They were to meet the United Nation's team at 0900 hours and get acquainted over breakfast at a café in downtown Paris.

Anthony Aguirre was the lead scientist with the UN team. Tony was a portly man in his late 40s with a scraggy beard and unkempt hair. He cut quite a figure in his safari hat and vest. The many stuffed pockets on his vest attested to the fact that he was always ready for the field. He appeared to be a cross between Burl Ives and a shaggy Santa Claus. Quinn could tell that they would get along famously. Tony was an extremely outgoing jovial man who was able to make a joke and laugh at almost anything, including himself. The rest of the U.N. team members were task guys and bean counters, who seemed to have minimal social skills and no interest in getting acquainted. The team of eight headed for the airport for their flight into equatorial Africa.

The great continental African convergence zone lies to the south of the Sahara Desert. This portion of the continent was described by the noted climatologist, Glenn Trewartha, as being one of Earth's most problematic climates. The east-west expanse of the continent at this latitude was the longest on

Earth. No mountains, large water bodies, or notable variations in topography broke up the land features to interrupt the dry northeasterly winds that parched the landscape. During wetter years, the southern fringe of the desert blooms in an impressive display of diversity and color. The human population and wildlife of the region seems to optimistically migrate north during these wetter periods and renew their foothold at the edge of the desert, where they congregated in small villages and subsistence farms. Once the inevitable drought returned, the population first became stressed and then famine and disease caused either death or migration. During these drought years, the great Sahara Desert moved south and with it came the dry, dusty brown landscape. In prolonged droughts, the bleak landscape provides little support for the population that stubbornly occupies the area. To their credit, they are resilient people, skilled in survival in this dry climate. For generations they have tenaciously lived on the land. Still, prolonged drought brought hardship, famine, disease and even death.

It was just such a drought and impending human disaster that prompted the UN's visit. The objective was to get a firsthand evaluation of the conditions and develop a relief plan to reduce human suffering. It was a routine trip with a simple humanitarian objective in a harsh landscape. The NGIA had provided a series of satellite photographs documenting progression of the drought, but were not able to answer all the questions regarding the remnant population in the area or the effects on the North African wildlife. Hope's mission was to fill in these blanks and provide insight into the satellite photographic products that would best serve future humanitarian missions.

Three white Land Rovers with large blue UN signs on the doors awaited the team at the airport. The trip to the most stressed areas would take two and a half hours. Signs of third world poverty and the resiliency of the people were evident from the start of the trip. They broke from their daily struggle to stare as the small caravan rolled by. It was obvious to Quinn that Tony was well acquainted with third-world conditions. He was jovial in conversation, but very attentive to the living conditions and health of the people they passed. Outside the village of Banto near the Sudan border, Tony asked the caravan to stop. Here the group disembarked and fanned out across the landscape. Hope and Quinn walked north through the village, looking at the soils, vegetation, subsistence farm plots, and at any other resource conditions that would influence their report.

Shouts from Tony's group that were a half mile to the east caught their attention. Almost at the same time, they saw a small band of raggedly clad boys emerging from the brush carrying AK47 assault rifles. The main contingency of this band had surrounded the UN observers in Tony's group. Now Hope and Quinn had attracted the attention of the stragglers and their weapons were pointed in their direction.

Reports on the area had indicated human suffering, but not insurgency or rebel faction operations. The nearest reported uprising was in Darfur, two hundred miles to the north. Based on these reports, no security was considered necessary for the trip. Suddenly, things started to happen. The shouts from the distant group turned into screams of pain. Hope and Quinn found themselves surrounded by a small group of armed boys. Some of the youths were no more than twelve years old. They seemed intoxicated with the power of the weapons they brandished. They apparently had never encountered an individual like Hope. Dark skinned like themselves, but head and shoulders taller, it became obvious to both Hope and Quinn that the older members of the band intended on getting better acquainted. Quinn was pushed aside and one young rebel attempted to clumsily tie his hands. Two others crowded Hope. To her credit, she took the first action. A swift kick to the crotch sent one of the band members to the ground. Almost at the same instance, Quinn planted an elbow to the nose of his assailant and grabbed his weapon as he fell. Quinn then leveled a sharp blow to the back of the head of the rebel accosting Hope. Three down and Hope was on the move, taking full advantage of her Olympic training. Shots were being fired at them as they ran towards the vehicles. Quinn paused at a tree to assess the situation and trained the AK47 on the largest and loudest pursuer.

The recoil of the weapon came as a wake-up call to Quinn. *This was for real,* he thought as he continued to run towards the village. This disorderly group of armed men and boys were trying to kill them and he was forced to join in the fight. Quinn's shot took the man off his feet and left him writhing in the sparse grass, a cloud of dust rising from his death throes. Hope was farther ahead by now and shouting to him to catch up.

As they approached the village, they could see the handiwork of the advanced group of bandits. Claude, one of Tony's staff members, lay in the center of the village on fire. The rebels had necklaced him with a tire and set it on fire. It had been his screams that had alerted them to the danger of the situation. No time for formalities; the bandits had reorganized and were sending stray shots in their direction, firing haphazardly from the hip as they ran in their general direction. Quinn raked the truck keys out of Claude's smoldering pocket and turned to face the pursuers. Half out of anger, Quinn dropped the two leaders of the group with single shots. There was no sign of Tony and his group, as they reached the truck and managed to get the door open. Quinn gunned the truck into a tight spin and raced down the road. Out of the corner of his eye, he saw the bandits leading the group of hostages into the brush. Hope was on her satellite phone, reporting the incident, to whom Quinn had no idea. Distance gained them a margin of safety, but Hope, who had been brave during the incident, now sobbed over the horror of the situation.

She received a call advising them to go directly to the French Embassy and to await instructions. Once safely within the embassy grounds, they were treated nonchalantly by the French staff, who had become inured to the hardships of service in this part of the world.

Quinn and Hope stayed in the same room that night, two tortured soles haunted by the events and sights of the day. Towards the first light of the morning, a heavy knock on the door awoke them from their troubled sleep. After checking the peephole, Quinn opened the door to find Agent Ken James and a young military officer, looking like they meant business.

Agent James began talking before he entered the room. "Jesus, Wilson, I get you out of training and in two days, you are in the middle of an international incident!" Agent James was passing through Europe on his way back to Australia and had commandeered a seat on a CIA flight into Kenya to organize a rescue mission. The young officer was Captain John Dietz, the Officer-in-Charge of the Marine Guard at the American Embassy in the Kenya capital. They informed Quinn that there would be a rescue attempt and they needed answers, with no time to waste.

Quinn and Hope were interrogated regarding the incidents of the day before. How many men were there? How were they armed? Did they carry just AK47s or were there sidearms as well? Were they in uniform? Who appeared to be leading the group? What direction were they going? Did you see any transportation, especially armed pickup trucks, or were they all on foot? How were the captives being treated?

Agent James listened as Captain Dietz continued to search for details and finally raised his hand and spoke. "Okay. This is what we're going to do. Captain, you and your men are going to conduct a rescue mission and I want Agent Wilson to accompany you. He is an old Marine and fresh out of training, so you can use his assistance. Quinn, call Washington and get the best reconnaissance available and we'll see if we can locate their camp. I want you on the ground no later than sunrise tomorrow. If we wait any longer, we'll lose more people, any questions?"

The captain responded, "Damn it, sir, that's too little time to organize such a mission and I don't want this old man tagging along. I'll have enough to keep me busy without babysitting a senior citizen."

Agent James responded, "Don't recall giving you a choice, Captain. I know his capabilities better than I know yours. If he can't hack it in the field, I'm sure the rebels can deal with him. Now, let's get going!"

Quinn dressed and nodded goodbye to Hope as they left the room and headed to the airport. They were joined by the captain's squad of twelve men, a collection of young men from various missions in west-central Africa. They included Marine security guards from various American embassies, Army Rangers from military liaisons, and a couple of Navy Seals from the Indian Ocean fleet. All were well trained, but with little to no combat experience.

The day was spent in preparation—combat gear, helmets, body armor, sidearms, and assault rifles all appeared as if by some master plan. Quinn received word from headquarters that the satellites had observed a disorderly band of men traveling southwest from yesterday's site. They were moving at a leisurely pace, avoiding populated areas and by late afternoon, appeared to be setting up camp in the scrubs. By evening, the satellite infrared sensors revealed scattered campsites, but a small group, isolated from the main body, appeared to be the captives. The plan was to conduct a pre-dawn HALO jump from 25,000 feet and fall to within 1,200 feet of the ground before opening their parachutes. The element of surprise would make up for the difference in force that Quinn estimated to be approximately forty men and boys.

Captain Dietz addressed the group about their mission, "Gentlemen, we are authorized to use due force to rescue the UN captives that have been taken prisoner by this group of G…D… rebels. I would emphasize that we are not here to start World War III, nor are we here to kill these insurgents without cause. We have checked with the Sudanese government and they have no troops in the area. We are the only force that is available and capable of this rescue. You will use deadly force only if fired upon. Is that clear? Agent Wilson will be accompanying us—he is on his own as a member of this team. We are not here as his personal bodyguards. The mission is to secure the rescue of the UN team. If we can do this without bloodshed, then the mission will be a success. But gentlemen, we are well armed and by God, we will do what needs to be done to complete this rescue. We will embark at 0300 Zulu. Get some sleep."

As the men fell from ranks and sought a cool place on the hangar floor, the captain reminded Quinn, "Stay out of my way and let my men do their job. There is no place on this mission for you. If it were up to me, you would still be lounging back at the Embassy with your lady friend. Do I make myself clear?" Quinn nodded and settled down alone to wait sleeplessly for the departure. He had been a Marine captain in his Desert Storm tour of duty and knew how to bark with the best of them. It was part of the job, so he took no offense.

Give a surgeon a scalpel and he seeks a surgical solution to any medical problem. Give a man a gun and it becomes the chief means of resolving a dispute. Quinn had never imagined that a position as a natural disaster field agent for the NGIA would bring him into armed conflict with an unknown militia, yet the weight of the weapon on his chest was real, as well as the fear of death that he observed in their small attack force. The team's weapon was the modified M16 with a shorter heavier barrel, telescopic laser sights and silencer. The shortened stock and barrel gave the weapon a totally different feel from the M16 of the Desert Storm era. An M249 grenade launcher was mounted below the barrel as an added assurance that adequate force was available to address any situation.

With time to think and no sleep in sight, the old questions resurfaced amidst his anxiety. Why had she left him with only that short note? There was no time to talk, to understand her motives, or to have closure with her decision. How could he have missed the warning signs? Why was she so interested in her appearance? Was she having an affair? Was her preoccupation with her looks one of those signs? How could she leave and not call to let him know where she was or how she was doing? Had the last 23 years of marriage meant nothing to her? Did she hate him so much that she would not call to explain her actions? Was it entirely his fault, as his daughter had insinuated? Yes, he could admit he probably was a boring guy, not much in the looks department, and very much into his work and away from home on business several days each week. All these qualities are minuses in the world of romance. Would he ever get any answers to these questions? Since he would probably die in Central Africa by 0800 tomorrow morning, maybe it wasn't important to have answers—certainly it was not important to her, wherever she was ...time passed slowly and sleep finally came.

He awoke with a jerk.

"Gentlemen on your feet, time is wasting," came the roaring voice of Captain Deitz. "You will rise up and turn to. It is time to get this show on the road. You need to perform the final checks of your gear and file out to the aircraft." The captain's voice was filled with assumed authority and delivered loudly enough to mask the fear of the coming mission. They were undermanned and going up against an unknown enemy. Quinn had provided the only knowledge of the force and admittedly, he had not seen everything. The rebel band had been so spread out that the number of combatants could not be determined, despite repeated questions by the captain and Agent James.

The insertion was to be accomplished by a HALO jump. Truck deployment was considered out of the question, since the route would be through a number of villages and the dust plume could be seem from five miles away, even at night. The HALO jump would be swift and they counted on the element of surprise. Thirteen men would exit the C-130 at 25,000 feet, stay bunched together in two groups until approximately 2,000 feet off the ground, and then break up and open the chutes at 1,200 feet. Thirty seconds later, the entire force would be on the ground and in a defensive position ready to attach. Quinn's combat deployment in Desert Storm had always been by troop transport. Despite the captain's irritation at Quinn's participation in the mission, he and his sergeant had rehearsed Quinn on the jump. Timing was everything, both on deploying the parachute and then getting out of the rig and into a defensive position on the ground. The captain was sure Quinn would screw it up and confided that privately to the sergeant after the impromptu training session.

Quinn had forgotten about the mixed feelings of anticipation and fear before a combat mission. There is something enabling about being in full combat gear before dawn, with the drone of the aircraft engines in your ear as it warmed up on the apron outside the hangar. The power of the weaponry made you feel invincible, while the armored vest and helmet made you feel invulnerable to enemy fire. He knew these thoughts were dangerous and it would take experience to exercise caution once in battle.

The platoon walked to the aircraft through the early morning heat, some cursing at the vagaries of the mission, as combat veterans are likely to do. Inside the C-130, Quinn was sure it was the same plane that carried his company to Kuwait during the Desert Storm offense in '92. The engines revved and the cargo bay door began to close as the big plane began to taxi.

A forty-minute flight later, the intel from Central Command reported the latest satellite recon. The infrared images showed the camp still occupied, but the separate group of suspected hostages was no longer visible in the image. Just one scattered encampment of an unknown number of warm bodies. "Three minutes!" shouted the jumpmaster as the lights dimmed and flickered to red. "Lock and load," intoned the captain. "Two minutes," and the team were on their feet and grouped on either side of the plane ready for the jump. "One minute," and the rear ramp deployed over a jet black landscape. "GO! GO! GO!" came the captain's command. Quinn was the next to last out of the plane and he remembered the captain's firm hand on his back, making sure the old man did not interrupt the jump pattern.

Quinn's first impression on leaving the aircraft was that it was cold at 25,000 feet over the equator. There were only a few seconds to learn to maneuver during this freefall before Quinn began awkwardly moving toward the huddle. Of course, he was the last to link arms. Then the surrealistic fall as the sergeant shouted elevation changes…23, 20, 15, 12, and 11, in decreasing cadence. At five thousand feet, he counted down on his fingers, with his hand extended to the center of the circle, so that his voice would not be audible.

As the jumpers approached three thousand feet, they prepared to break from the group and clear before opening the chutes. Just before the break, the captain reached across the circle and pulled Quinn's rip-cord. Startled, Quinn found the team departing from him as his parachute opened. This would put him late to the ground and on his own when he landed. Two thousand feet lower, the other chutes opened in unison. Quinn flipped the night-vision glasses down and watched as the team spiraled to the ground. He was not sure when he heard the first guttural rattle of the AK47 or if it was the flash of weapon fire that he saw first. In any case, the battle lines were drawn and the engagement begun only seconds after the team hit the ground. Quinn could see increased activity to the right of the team as the rebels stirred from sleep in the main encampment. On instinct he pulled sharply on his steering cord and spun the parachute to the right, placing him to the far edge of the skirmish line between the platoon and the rebel advance. The landing was rough but at least he was not under fire before he could get out of the chute and into position. He had not been observed. From his right, a squad of men appeared amid the confusion. This group would flank the rescue team that currently had their hands full. Quinn flipped the safety of the M16 to automatic, chambered a single round into the M249 and cut loose with both barrels.

Both rebel bands immediately thought they had encountered a company of trained troops since fire was now coming from a completely different direction and it was coming with deadly force. As if on command, the rebels broke rank and ran for the darkness of the bush. Quinn moved fast to rejoin the squad, dropping two rebels that crossed his path. A rustle behind him sent his reactive instincts into hyperdrive. Out of instinct he did a forward summersault, with the benefit of the short barrel M16, and sharply rolled to the left as rounds kicked up dust next to him. From this defensive position, he scanned the dark in front of him and found the red targeting dot of his weapon trained on the forehead of a rebel. He fired two rounds, rolled and was on his feet running again in a matter of a few seconds. "This is just like in Desert Storm," he thought. There are some things you can never forget. The squad looked surprised to see their savior single-handedly taking command of the right flank. Quinn did not stop when he reached the squad, but continued on towards the main camp looking for the captives. He was soon joined by five of the squad … the captain was not among them.

The original resistance had quickly given way, when the rebels thought an entire army had fallen from the sky. There, in an opening by the campfire, were the bedraggled captives, looking fearful and tired from their ordeal. Mission accomplished at 0420. Since no one was taking action, Quinn said. "Get these men away from the fire and secure the area." Immediately the marines followed his orders and set up a parameter. Tony's bush jacket was stained with blood and crumpled, but otherwise, he looked relieved.

"Is everyone okay?" Quinn asked, as he scanned the darkness around the campfire.

"We survived a grueling night. They intended to ransom us off at the first opportunity. Thankfully, you have relieved them of that option," Tony said as he rubbed his free wrists. "You are about the last person I expected to see again and here you are leading the rescue."

"Yes, it is a rag-tag rescue team lead by the U.S. Embassy security platoon and I was requested to come along. I was glad to help," Quinn said, as he led the group away from the fire.

With the hostages safe and protected by the marines, Quinn returned to the battle lines and was relieved to find no fatalities. The captain had taken a round in the calf of his leg early in the fire fight and was obviously in pain, but out of danger.

"Smart idea I had to bring you in late," he said smiling sheepishly.

"So, that's what you were thinking?" Quinn said, feeling a small margin of fellowship with this commander, now that they were out of danger and the field was leveled.

The captain added, "I suggest we send three men out towards the rebel retreat route to make sure they don't regroup. Will you take the lead, Quinn?" His request was made without any "old man" remarks.

The advantage was all theirs, as they moved rapidly through the shrubs with night-vision goggles. Several shots were fired at retreating stragglers to keep the force from reforming. One hour later, he stood looking into the African bush as the first rays of sunlight cast a pale orange glow on the eastern horizon. The early morning light allowed him to remove his night-vision goggles. In the distance at about two hundred yards, he could see the shadows of the last stragglers from the marauding rebel band disappearing into the thicket. As he watched, one turned in his direction and fired several rifle shots from the hip. The squad members, standing on either side of Quinn, ducked for cover as the shots ripped through the trees overhead. Quinn stood his ground as his attention was drawn to a solitary figure standing away from the main group of retreating forces. Two more shots rang out and Quinn heard thuds as the rounds raised plumes of red dust not six feet from his position. Slowly, he knelt and raised his M16, as he flipped the telescopic sight into position. The shadowy figure in the distance took form as the scope found its target.

The image was of a relatively short stout man, dressed in jungle fatigues standing with a short-barreled assault rifle braced with both hands. His bearded face was framed by a gray-green turban and pair of gold-rimmed glasses with yellow lenses, the kind worn by marksmen on the shooting range to improve their vision. He calmly fired two more rounds, as if he was adjusting his aim based on the effects of his first shots. Quinn heard two more thuds close by. The rules of engagement were to free the hostages and not to kill indiscriminately, so Quinn shifted his aim slightly away from the figure and caught a glimpse of gold necklaces reflecting in the early morning light. This was not one of the young boys that Quinn had encountered in the last few days. Quinn fired two warning shots to the right and left of the figure, just to let him know he was in his sights and watched as the man slowly lowered his weapon and glared in his direction. Then, as if he was in no rush, he turned and walked into the bush. *Curious,* Quinn thought, *this man has had combat experience. He must be the leader.*

Quinn lowered his M16 as he stood and scanned the tree line. All the forces had disappeared into the bush. Quinn motioned to the young marines on both sides of him to move forward and keep the pressure on the retreating forces. As they moved rapidly into the open, Quinn pondered the circumstances that had brought him to this remote region of Africa and into an armed conflict. The events of the last few days ran through his mind, as he ran in a crouched position towards the edge of the bush.

Quinn brought his small detail back to camp, as the sun radiated heat into the dry and dusty battlefield. The captain was bandaged up, on his feet and back in command. He had called in the HH-53 for early retraction. The whip, whip, whip sound from the incoming helicopter was another reminder to Quinn of the battles fought in Desert Storm. By 0800 hours, the team was in the air, heading for the coast with the rescued UN team.

"Well, I guess you proved me wrong, old man. You carried your weight very well. Thanks for bailing us out back there. We were definitely in a poor defensive position when we landed," the captain said sheepishly.

"Next time, why don't we bring an entire company, instead of faking it? I think we can only fool them once," Quinn responded with a good-natured smile.

Agent James was at the airfield when the helicopter landed. During his debriefing of the team, he was particularly interested in Quinn's description of the encounter with the apparent leader of the rebel gang. "You got a good look at him?"

"I saw him clearly through the telescopic sight for 10 to 15 seconds. He was medium height, beard and mustache, gold-rimmed glasses, green turban and wore a gold watch. He was definitely dressed better than the young rebels. I assumed he was the leader."

"Shit, I think you had Caleb in your sights. His name is Kaleb Fusan or Caleb for short. Why didn't you shoot the son-of-a-bitch? I have been tracking him on two continents with no success. He is a member of al Qaeda and has been organizing factions to disrupt and destroy western influence."

"Well, I didn't shoot, because the captives had been rescued and the rebels were fleeing. So, I fired a couple of warning shots just to let him know he was covered."

"You would have done the world a favor if you had blown him away. He was probably heading into Kenya to blow up some western target. So if you have the chance again, do not hesitate to shoot the bastard."

"Hopefully, I won't be in this position again. You do recall, I am not with the Company, just the NGIA?"

"Yes I know, but you guys work for us and when you are on a mission like this, you are CIA. Listen, I have to finish this debriefing. Thanks for your help, Agent Wilson. I'll catch up with you in Australia when you get back from the deep freeze. Why the hell you want to go down there, I'll never know."

"Thanks for the encouragement," Quinn said as he collected his gear.

Quinn changed clothes and unceremoniously hitched a ride to the terminal from the UN to make connections for the next scheduled flight to Australia. There were a few nods from the squad as he left, as if to say well done, but no actual goodbyes. It was like a different world here. Australia was the next episode in this new life before departing for Antarctica.

CHAPTER 2

Lap of Luxury

Life was good! After her abrupt departure from St. Petersburg, Nancy and her plastic surgeon, Roberto, had taken the first plane to New York and stayed at the Waldorf. Their days were spent shopping, attending Broadway shows and making love. The need for a secret liaison was gone and they enjoyed the luxury of extended periods of time in each other's arms, without the fear of being discovered. She had left most of her personal belongings in St. Petersburg, since she knew that this was the start of a new life. So she shopped for a new wardrobe, for which Roberto had insisted on only the best. Saks 5th Avenue sales consultants gave her the personal attention usually reserved for celebrities. She had the presence of mind to grab her passport, during her hasty departure from Florida, and it became her only reminder of her past life. After three days in New York, she and Roberto departed for Paris. The plans were for an extended stay at the family villa in Nice. This was the world travel and attention that she had only dreamed about.

The villa had belonged to Roberto's father, who was also a renowned plastic surgeon. It was a seven-bedroom mansion overlooking the Mediterranean and the narrow road and quaint shops in the neighborhood became her passion and daily haunts. The days stretched into weeks as she became even more attuned to the luxurious lifestyle. After a month had passed, Roberto became increasingly involved with urgent phone calls and finally announced that he must return to the U.S. and pay attention to his practice. His partners could no longer cover for him and his patients were demanding his personal attention. He departed on Friday afternoon after a particularly passionate morning.

She enjoyed the solitude. Well, it was solitude, if you did not include the villa's three servants, who took care of her every need: Pierre, the butler; Madelyn, the chamber maid; and Rocco, the chauffer. All three seemed overjoyed having someone to attend. Her days were full of leisure, working on her tan, shopping and becoming more familiar with her surroundings.

Life had changed so completely that only rarely did she have thoughts of her former life, her husband, and her abrupt departure. She knew that Quinn had been a good husband and father and did not deserve the shock she had presented him. But she was not sorry for the changes leaving had brought to her life. There had been no communications between her and Quinn since, and so much time had elapsed that she could not just pick up the phone and call him. There was too much distance between their lives now to make that connection. No, the next communication would be by her attorney, as she asked for a divorce and her share of the assets from their former life. Divorce always favored women and she was sure that her attorney would be able to get the lion's share of the estate. Not that it mattered, she thought. She was into her new life of luxury with Roberto, who was a world-renowned plastic surgeon to whom money was not a problem. She had no intentions of returning to the ordinary existence she had known with Quinn. If she played her cards right, she would marry Roberto and continue enjoying this fairytale life between his lucrative practice in Florida and his villa in the south of France.

She looked forward to the daily emails and twice-a-week phone calls from her soulmate, Roberto. He always made them intimate and suggestive. One day around three o'clock, he called to say she would be having a house guest, a Dr. Frank Mallord, a fellow surgeon and friend, who would be staying for four days the following week. Roberto suggested that "he would like for her to do everything she could to entertain his guest."

She responded, "Well, do you want me to take him sightseeing or to the museum?"

"That is not exactly what I had in mind, dear. I have given you a beautiful body and I want you to make the most of it. You are now living in my house and I pay the monthly bills from your shopping sprees. As you are aware, life is not free. I want you to show my friend a good time," he said with a serious tone.

She was stunned. Her middle-American morals had surfaced and she was insulted by his implications. Still, she had already broken the moral code by having a satisfying affair with Roberto. She wondered what he was implying with his comment about giving her a beautiful body and making the most of it. She could not believe the latent meaning he was conveying. She sat pondering his call for several minutes and, for a fleeting moment, had a pang of homesickness. She realized that there was an ill-defined social structure around this new life and she had been so much enraptured with Roberto that she had refused to acknowledge it. This was a much more open lifestyle with the lines between fidelity and promiscuity blurred or even nonexistent. Perhaps she was free to experiment, freer than she had ever been or dreamed of being. Maybe, this was just another step along a path she had already chosen. She would think about it ....

CHAPTER 3

Home Port

Quinn sat on the plane from Kenya to Sidney pondering the events of the past few days. The rebel force had been just boys, some as young as twelve, from the most rural poor section of equatorial Africa. They had little or no training in the use of their armaments. They were following a leader and looking for a better life, a way out of the depressing poverty of the Sahara region. However, instead they died as combatants without a purpose. Some leader figure had sold them a dream and provided an AK47 as a way to meet that dream. Apparently, the kidnapping was an effort to extort ransom to fund their rebel excursion. The power of their weapons had gone to their heads and there could have been no other outcome. No reasoning, no negotiation, ceasefire, or diplomatic solution could have occurred, but still—they were just boys.

Only one day out of the improbable field of combat and Quinn found himself in a comfortable business class seat on a flight from Nairobi to Sidney, Australia. The haunting thoughts of the day before played over and over in his head. Even though he was only a few months away from his consulting position in Tampa, he would never have dreamed that his new life would require deadly combat and the necessity of killing young boys—even in self-defense. He was reminded that the scarcity of resources and natural disasters can provoke violence and even rebellion. With great deliberation, he forced his mind away from the tragedy in Africa and concentrated on the next steps in his new life. It was two weeks now before he was to assume his position with the NSF at the McMurdo Station in Antarctica. He needed to establish a home base for his new position as Natural Resource Investigator for the NGIA once his tour in Antarctica was over in the fall—or was it spring? Life in the southern hemisphere was going to take some adjusting. Once in Sidney, the plan was to head for the waterfront and see what opportunities might be presented. The house in St. Petersburg had sold while he was in boot camp in St. Marys, Georgia. He had dutifully put half of the proceeds into a separate account for his wife, if she ever did resurface and demand her share of their life. The other half was ample to establish a new life for himself—he was thinking of living aboard a sailboat.

It was fall in Sidney and the early morning chill reluctantly gave way as the sun rose higher above the horizon. He left his hotel to walk along the waterfront, trying to get a feel for the area. There in the distance was the famous Sidney Opera House and Harbor Bridge slowly emerging from the early morning fog. He had always heard that sailing was big in Sidney Harbor, and as he walked the waterfront, there were the familiar and heartening sights and sounds of sailboats gently rocking in their marina slips. The soft clanging of halyards on the masts had a reassuring sound of home. A stop at the Harbor Master's office at a few marinas revealed that there were slips available, but he could not answer the questions about the size of his boat, since he did not have one. At his last stop, the Harbor Master told him to go see Meg at the Archer Shipyard, if he was interested in purchasing a boat. After a brief lunch, he followed this advice and found the Archer Shipyard in a sheltered cove on the south side of the bay just east of the Harbor Bridge.

Meg Archer, the most recent member of the Archer family to manage the shipyard, was busying herself with a stack of paper in what was an otherwise very organized office. She appeared to be in her late thirties to early forties with blond hair that she wore in a short no-nonsense style befitting the outdoor marine environment of the boatyard. She wore no makeup, but did not need any on her suntanned face that would light up with a shy smile. She was about 5 foot 6 inches tall and as trim as an athlete. Her manner was friendly but businesslike and, as Quinn would later note, she knew her boats. The walls and window sills of the office were filled with generations of photographs and memorabilia of the business and family. Her grandfather had founded the shipyard and worked it for more than forty years before turning it over to her father and uncle to run. Meg had grown up around the shipyard and learned the business from the ground up. The Archer Shipyard was renowned in the Harbor, southeastern Australia, and apparently worldwide for their marine services.

Quinn introduced himself to Meg and asked about the availability of a sound sailboat in the thirty-five to forty-two foot range. Meg was more than happy to show him what was available. There were all kinds of boats in the basin: large and small, new or old, and cheap and expensive. After looking at several boats, Quinn noticed an older boat moored in the basin. Its deep-blue hull seemed to match some sailor's dream that he had carried with him for some time. Meg said that it was a 37-foot Sabra, probably built in or about 1987, a stout boat that had taken a real beating in the Indian Ocean crossing from South Africa. Its owner had a falling out with his wife and abandoned it here about six months ago. "Let's take the skiff over and have a closer look," she said.

Quinn could imagine the problems that occurred on that crossing. The standing rigging had been strained to the breaking point and there were a number of hurried "jury rigs" evident. The radio and radar antennas hung dangling from the masthead and the wind speed indicator and steering rudder were broken. The interior of the boat showed significant wear and the diesel engine looked like the original equipment that came with the boat in 1987. Still, the hull was sound and tight and the boat had the romantic feel of a world traveler. Meg said the owners were asking $100 thousand. "Will the owner consider an offer of $65,000?" he asked.

"If you would like to make a formal offer, I'll call and let him know in the morning," she responded. "The owners are back in the states, so I would have to contact them after 10:00 P.M. this evening." Quinn spent the rest of the afternoon talking to Meg about his plans for the boat. He would like to do a total refit, new standing and running rigging, new sails, diesel engine and spruce up the interior. He left the shipyard late in the afternoon excited about the boat and hoping he had found his first friend in Australia.

Upon returning to the hotel, he was surprised to find a visitor waiting for him. It was Steven Coates, his former roommate from the boot camp they both had attended in Georgia. "Glad to see you again so soon, Quinn. Here we are less than a week out of camp and already you have developed a reputation. Good work in Africa, by the way."

"How did you ...?" Quinn began.

Steven laughed and interjected, "You forget, we are in a position now to know these things. When I heard it was you, I volunteered to be your welcoming party. Is there somewhere private we can talk? You don't want to look too American these days," he relayed with a surprising good Australian accent.

Quinn studied Steven for a moment. He was now in his new post at the CIA in the Sidney office and was rapidly growing into his new role. His boot camp crew cut had already begun to give way to an unkempt casual style that fit in well with the two-day's growth on his chin.

He presented Quinn with a casual briefcase and together they inventoried its contents. It contained a laptop computer, ID badge, satellite phone, GPS, code book, and a Walther PPK 9mm handgun, for business purposes, of course. Quinn had no sooner turned the phone on when he received a call from Alex Reager, his new boss with the NGIA. Alex stated he was calling to give him an update on the Sudan incident, as it was now called among international agencies. Tony and his crew were recuperating in Paris and doing well. "Thanks for your work there in Sudan—even the captain speaks favorably about you now," he said with a laugh. There will be some hazardous duty pay in your next paycheck. Alex explained that the briefcase dropped off by Steven was to remain in his possession even during the months at the McMurdo Station in Antarctica. They would stay in touch via email and satellite phone, but understandably, any missions would wait until after he returned to Sidney. Alex surprised Quinn by asking about Meg and mused that the Sabra 37-foot sailboat would make an excellent home base. Quinn had no idea how this information had gotten back to Washington, since he had left the Archer shipyard only a half hour ago. He silently vowed to be more observant to those around him. It seemed to Quinn that life would indeed be different.

Steven, who had heard most of the conversation, said that he would be in touch when Quinn returned from the icebox. He would be serving as his contact with the greater closed net United States security apparatus in the South Pacific. He departed with the trained saunter of an invisible man who drew no attention to his passing. Quinn thought, *I have two prospective friends in Australia.*

At 9:00 A.M. Pacific Central time, Quinn called Meg. The boat owner had counter-offered for $75,000. Quinn offered seventy and by noon, he was back in Meg's office as a proud boat owner. He and Meg negotiated a work order to rehabilitate the old world traveler. The restoration projected cost with a new auxiliary engine was $35,000.

Meg turned all business when it came to the question of money. She could broker the sale and would need assurances of a continued draw to pay for the restoration. No credit. Quinn trusted her and the Archer reputation enough to pay for the renovation and leave an additional $10,000 on account for the miscellaneous repairs that had not been budgeted in the work order. She responded rather coolly to Quinn's suggestion of closing the deal over dinner, stating she preferred to do business in her office or at the bank. "It is just business, of course," he said, echoing her exact words. He could only surmise that she had been seriously burned before—but so had he.

Disappointed by the mild rebuff, Quinn returned to the hotel near the Harbor and called the NSF Center regarding the flight to McMurdo Station in Antarctica. He was informed that he was already behind schedule and should report to the center as soon as possible for orientation and outfitting.

The next morning, Quinn reported to the bustling NSF office near the Sidney Airport. He was given a handful of forms and asked to sit in a corner and complete them. He waded through the usual questions of nationality, passport dates, addresses, next of kin, and contact information should he freeze to death. The next-of-kin question gave him pause. *Who should he list*, he thought, as he erased Nancy's name from the sheet. His thoughts went to his daughter, but she might never speak to him again and probably would celebrate his demise. Still the question made him feel isolated and alone in this new life.

The NSF staff was friendly and pleasantly disorganized. They typically administered to a family of scientists and technical support staff that annually spent time in Antarctica. He was the new kid on the block with the title of NSA Director of Environmental Research, so they took time to explain the basics that were common knowledge to the veterans. He learned that he was bunking with Dr. Mark Raulson, a PhD marine biologist from—of all places—Florida. Dr. Raulson headed up research on seawater. Like most of the scientists who would be in Antarctica for the winter, Mark was a university researcher who had written a long-term research proposal that was funded by the NSF. Quinn's job was to oversee the grant program and to coordinate the research that would be conducted this season.

After a four-hour orientation, Quinn left the office with a list of clothing and supplies he would need to survive. Each staff member was responsible for his own wardrobe, personal equipment and hygiene items. He was told (ordered) to follow the instructions to the letter, with threats of bodily harm in the frigid climate of Antarctica, if he departed from the approved list. There would be many long cold nights and he wanted all the protection from the cold he could get. After all, he was born and raised in Florida and got a chill when the thermometer dropped below 50°F.

With departure time drawing near, there was still one housekeeping chore that had to be done. With his shopping completed and his duffle bag full, Quinn began stopping at marinas around the bay, looking for a slip to moor his 37-foot Sabre in the spring. After a number of inquiries, he found a slip at a small marina at the head of the bay that would be available in the spring. He paid the first and last month's rent to hold the slip in preparation for the start of the next big adventure in his new life. The plane would leave in three days from Wellington, New Zealand, heading for Williams Field, 18 km from McMurdo Station. He would have just enough time to bone up on all the rules and requirements for overwintering in Antarctica. A call home made his heart beat faster, but there was no news about Nancy and his daughter still was not speaking to him, indicating again that it was *his* fault her mother had left. He should have known Nancy was unhappy. "Men are so insensitive," she had said and promptly hung up.

McMurdo Station is the largest of Antarctica's research stations and the most southern seaport in the world. With the active seaport and three airfields, the station does the heavy lifting for the continent and serves as a supply base for all American and other nation's bases under various agreements and contracts. Williams Airfield, located on the shelf ice approximately 18 miles from base, handles the heavy LC-130 cargo planes, while wheeled aircraft used the Pegasus site, with a harder, smoother runway on sea ice during the southern hemisphere winter and spring months in October, November and into December before the sea ice breaks up, usually in summer. There are over 100 structures in the small city of McMurdo. During the summer months, the population rose to a little over 1,000 to include not only the administrative staff and research scientists, but logistic specialists, engineers and construction workers. Winter population would be more like 250 persons. Those wintering over would be isolated from the outside world between March 1 and October 1, weather pending, of course. McMurdo Station had evolved throughout the years into a cosmopolitan place, where people of different backgrounds met and worked.

CHAPTER 4

On to the Ice

The scientists are the elite members of the staff, so Quinn was looking forward to meeting and working with them. He was on one of the last planes into the continent that year. Many of the winter staff members were already at the station and involved in their work. His role would be largely administrative and would include the review of ongoing work under contract to the NSF. His office would be in the chalet along with the U.S. Antarctic Program (USAP) offices and their primary contractor, the Raytheon Polar Services Company. In addition to the administrative offices, the chalet had a conference area and meeting rooms for presentations and official functions. The main communications facility was also located in the chalet, with satellite and single-sideband radio connections to the South Pole Station and field parties.

The NSF supports a wide range of research at the station, including marine and terrestrial biology, biomedicine, geology and geophysics, glaciology and glacial geology, meteorology, agronomics, and upper atmospheric physics. Research contracts were awarded to teams of scientists usually associated with arctic research programs with major U.S. universities. Some teams of scientists return yearly to the continent to continue their research. The veterans were the intellectual leaders of the station and, as Quinn would soon discover, they sometimes did not appreciate the NSF's oversight role, especially with new and inexperienced administrators, such as himself.

Much of the research was carried out at the A.P. Crary Science and Engineering Center, which was dedicated and began operation in 1991. The center contained state-of-the-art instrumentation to support the advanced science and technical work. The Crary Lab had five pods with a total of 4,320 square meters of working area. Even with the amount of room available at the Crary Lab, the scientists were constantly in competition for space and facilities to support their research efforts. Quinn's job was to make sure all needs were met, as well as research deadlines.

There were eight scientists and support crew making this flight to McMurdo Station on this last incoming flight before winter closed the vise on the continent. The outbound flight would undoubtedly be full, as the last of the "summer crew" scrambled for warmer climates. Dr. Mark Raulson, Quinn's assigned roommate, was among those aboard. Dr. Raulson was a tall authoritative-looking man with a balding head and a mustache that looked like he was born with. He seemed to be in a perpetual state of distraction, as if the immediate circumstances were far less important than the truths that lay just over the horizon. Once his attention was drawn, he seemed to emerge from a fog and was quite engaging. It was not long before he was discussing his golf game with a notable measure of intensity. He was the only staff member to bring his golf clubs to the station. There was a reason Dr. Raulson was on the last flight into the base—because it *was* the last flight. Quinn would soon hear that Dr. Raulson was late for everything, be it meals, meetings, or social events—he was truly undiscriminating. Mark, as he preferred to be called, held a PhD in marine biology and would be supervising the seawater research project during this season. He was accompanied by his chief scientist, Dr. Randall Worthington (Randy), a systemic ecologist and former Woods Hole alumni. Dr. Worthington was an intense and energetic man in his early 40s with a large round face and a booming voice that was easily heard over the drone of the turbo prop engines. When not loudly expounding on some key point of statistical analysis, Randy was engrossed in crossword puzzles, which he devoured with remarkable speed and much muttering.

Dr. Pamela Laystrom and two of her assistants made up the balance of the flight. Dr. Laystrom (Pam) would be the senior scientist at the station this year, having returned for her eighth winter. She and her staff were continuing their ongoing research, cataloging life on the continent. Her team included Ellen Ragland, a marine biologist and science diver, along with Amy Stark, a terrestrial ecologist with a minor in palynology.

Pam was a slim, athletic-looking female of indeterminate age, somewhere between thirty-five and fifty-five. Her jet black hair and brown eyes conveyed a measure of authority. It was obvious that her staff held her in high regard, as they peppered her with questions of life at the station during the flight. Quinn was soon to learn that Pam was very much a dedicated feminist. She was absolutely convinced that females were the superior gender and that anything remotely associated with male dominance, including male NSF managers, were open for attack. Her demeanor was totally void of normal female traits. She wore no makeup, never fussed with her short hair, and dressed in jeans with hiking boots while not in her polar garb. She was also a self-described "flaming free spirit" who did not want to be told what to do, nor how or when to do it. When not in the Antarctic, she lived an almost hippy existence with her northern hemisphere roommate, a white water rafting captain during the summer on the Snake River in Wyoming and who made kites during the winter months. Another interesting thing about Pam was that she violated the station's rule and brought along a coffeemaker with a winter's supply of Starbucks coffee. The entire administrative staff turned their heads at the violation, in part because of her seniority, and partly in the hopes of being offered a cup.

Amy Stark was in her twenties, and like Quinn, would be overwintering for the first time. She appeared to be a bright young lady and only a few years away from the giggles of girlhood. Her outbursts of laughter would be a delightful addition to the cold winter nights of Antarctica.

Ellen Raglan was a contradiction. She was a hearty soul in an apparent fragile female body. At about one hundred and ten pounds, fully dressed, she was the lead diver, who would explore the marine environment under the Ross Ice Shelf in the dead of winter. Quinn shivered just to think of being outside, let alone diving through the ice, but admired her tenacity.

Royce Lynch (Roy) managed the largest group of scientists at the station. He, like Quinn, did not have a PhD behind his name and was held in somewhat lower regard by the scientists wintering at the station. With 24 staff members under his direction, he was more of a politician than a scientist. His well-groomed gray hair and mustache portrayed him as somewhat vain and opportunistic. He seemed to have a different personality with every person at the station, especially with the female members. He immediately saw some advantage in being friendly with Quinn, based on his administrative position with the NSF, and went out of his way to get acquainted. His intent was so transparent that Quinn was almost embarrassed by all the attention. Still, it would have been a lonely first few weeks early in the winter, if Roy had not been so attentive. "Sure thing, buddy, anything you say," he would call at the slightest comment from Quinn. The program Roy administered was the largest at the station this year, with glaciologists and climatologists working on climate monitoring and ice core borings. He demanded much of the resources available onsite.

It was not long before Pam and Roy were involved in a "major" conflict and came to Quinn's office asking for a resolution. Pam contended that Roy was hogging all the room at the Center and forcing her staff to work in a small section isolated from one another without the resources to perform their studies. Roy's position was that he was there first and if she wanted better accommodations, she should have gotten to the station earlier in the season and secured it, just as he had done. After some investigation, Quinn found that Roy was indeed hogging space. His 24 members were occupying almost 600 square feet each, while Pam's small staff was closer to 250 square feet and not grouped together. In spite of Roy's blustering, Quinn put the situation straight by stating that each individual would be allowed 400 square feet. His business-like response was, "Give Dr. Laystrom's staff a consolidated space of 1,600 square feet for her four staff members. Take care of it between you two right now or I will come over and rearrange the work areas for you both." Roy was not his friend for a full three days. Dr. Laystrom could have cared less that he found in her favor.

After several weeks, the station was running well. There had been no more problems among the scientists and Quinn was having no trouble sleeping, but as an early riser, he enjoyed the solitude of the station. On one particular morning, he ran across Pam making coffee in the Crary Center area.

"Good morning," Quinn said with his best baritone voice.

Startled she remarked, "Good morning. I thought I had the station to myself this morning. Would you care for a cup of coffee?"

"Wow" he said, very chipper, "I am indeed honored. Does this mean I am finally accepted into the scientific community here?"

"I know what you're thinking," she replied. "Don't even go there. I know what you men have on your minds and the answer is NO! I will not be sleeping with you now or in the future."

"Excuse me!" Quinn said, a little on the defensive side. "How did we go from a cup of coffee to your not wanting to go to bed with me?"

"Go ahead and admit it. We both know what you had in mind. It was written all over your face."

"Can we just drop the subject and get back to the coffee question?" Quinn asked, feeling uncomfortable and a little embarrassed at her outburst.

"Oh sure, avoid the question, but I just want to make it clear to you up front, that I have no intention of sleeping with you or anyone else under any condition. You are not good-looking or interesting enough, so don't think you have any privileges, just because you are Science Director."

"I think I'll just get a cup of coffee from the cafeteria," he said, as he quickly turned and walked away.

"Fine," was her only response as she turned back to her coffee machine.

Quinn knew a little about her background. He knew she was divorced and a single mom. The conversation had gotten way to personal ...and he had to admit to himself, there could have been a little truth in what she had said. He had awakened with thoughts of Nancy on his mind. He had been so depressed when she had left without a word. He would not let this encounter with Dr. Laystrom affect him. He picked up a cup of jet-black coffee in the cafeteria and headed back to his office. It was one of the few places where he could be alone with his thoughts. He had just sat down at his desk facing the door when Dr. Laystrom appeared.

She walked into his office, cradling her Starbucks coffee cup. "Okay, that was a rather awkward exchange. I think I owe you an explanation."

"Well, I really don't want to rehash that discussion, if you don't mind. I think your point was well taken."

"You do recall that this is my eighth year at the station, don't you?"

With his composure back in check, he answered, "Yes, I've reviewed your resume, along with the other scientists on staff."

At this point in the conversation, both Dr. Laystrom and Quinn became aware of a glow coming through the window in Quinn's office. The dark of winter was replaced by the soft light, which quickly increased in brightness. Quinn saw it first on Pam's face, then spun around in his chair towards the window. Both were transfixed by the stream of light crossing the southeastern sky. After a few seconds, the stream disappeared behind the Crary Center and for a second, the sky brightened, followed by a blinding flash that forced both of them to turn away from the window. A sudden hard jolt caused them to lose balance and grab the desk for support. Both cups of coffee spilled and crashed to the floor. The lights at the station flashed off and in the distance, alarms began sounding a plaintive and repetitive warning.

"My God, what was that?" Pam exclaimed.

"I think it was a meteor. It was either very large or extremely close to the station or maybe both. Hopefully it was a meteor—nothing else should be within the atmosphere over the continent this time of year," replied Quinn. "That flash of light had the strength of a nuclear explosion."

Roy Lynch fumbled along the corridor to the door and shouted, "What the hell was that? Someone took a shot at us?"

The lights flickered on and off. Shouts could be heard from various locations, "Earthquake," while the alarm continued to sound. They started down the corridor towards the voices, as Roy continued, "This kind of seismic event is not supposed to happen here. The station is located on bedrock with no fault lines or tectonic plates anywhere near here. Shit, if it is an earthquake, it may be followed by a tidal wave."

They stumbled down the hall to the Crary Center and found it in confusion. There was at least some light from the computers that were still booted up on battery power. Quinn attempted to take charge of the situation, "Listen up! We need to do damage assessment of all the buildings and facilities in the station. We need runners. Can someone go to the power station and find out the status? Someone else needs to go south and check each building as you go. Come back here to report any damage especially to the power grid. Okay, let's go!"

"Pam, find the maintenance staff. We need to see if there is any breach in the roof and walls. Also, before you go, has anyone written an emergency management disaster plan for the station?"

"Yes, but no one ever thought about an earthquake. We are basically on our own."

"Well, if we are on our own, let's get the damage assessment going and start taking care of the problems, one-by-one. Power first."

At that moment, Quinn was surprised when his satellite telephone linking him to the Central Geo-Spatial Intelligence office in Washington rang. He answered with his code name, "Walter here!"

"Walter," inquired Pam with a puzzled look on her face?

"What is going on down there?" asked a familiar voice on the other end.

"That's what we're trying to figure out," Quinn responded.

"The phones lit up here at the office a few minutes ago. The United States Geological Survey (USGS) in Colorado says there was a seismic disturbance in your neighborhood. The center was approximately 125 miles southwest of the McMurdo Station."

"Yes, we saw what we think was a large meteor crossing the southern horizon, just before we felt the impact. There was also a very bright flash of light. The jolt was strong enough to move the furniture around and cause things to break. We do not know the extent of damage. The lights are still off and we can hear alarms in the distance. Hold on, Alex, someone is shouting for everyone to suit up."

"A meteor! How big do you think it was?"

"Hard to say, but it gave us quite a jolt. Do you have any recon satellite coverage over the continent?"

"Unfortunately, there was no surveillance satellite coverage, nor will we have any coverage until we can relocate one in orbit. We need some intel. Everyone is calling us for answers and it just so happens that I have you as a resource located close to the event. Can you help us with some answers?"

"You do recall that it's the dead of winter down here, don't you?"

"Hopefully it was a meteor, but if some rogue nation wanted to test their nuclear weapon in a remote corner of the world, Antarctica would be the place. Do you think you can reach the site over-ground from your location?"

At the far end of the center, urgent calls were being issued. There had been a breach in the wall and -35 degree cold air was flooding the building. "Suit-up now, it is going to get cold fast," came the repeated call. Still only the emergency lights provided illumination, as people ran in both directions in the hall.

"Alex, can I call you back? We have to deal with the emergency here. It is getting colder by the second."

"Yes, I heard the warning. Call me when you can."

Quinn and Pam both joined the race down the hall to their respective quarters. They passed through extremely cold areas near the south wall of the center and could now hear alarms from the outer buildings. The smell of diesel fuel became stronger the further they ran.

"I hope the nuclear reactor in the power center is okay. The diesel fuel powers our backup units and without the reactor, I doubt we have enough fuel to get us through the winter. If it is damaged, it will be cold for a long time," Pam said between breaths as they ran.

Mark was in their quarters throwing on his parka when Quinn burst through the door.

"Do you have any idea what is going on?" he asked.

"Apparently, there has been a meteor impact close by. Pam and I saw it through the window of my office." Quinn stated as he grabbed his bib overalls off the hanger.

"If we go more than a half hour with no power, this station will be as cold as a tomb," Mark said as he headed out of the door.

It was well into evening before things at the station started to settle back to normal. Over a cup of coffee, Quinn called Alex to continue their discussion.

"How are you doing down there?" Alex asked.

"Better. The biggest problem was the jolt ruptured a fuel line and shut down the reactor powering the station, while it sprayed diesel all over a hot engine. We were lucky there wasn't a fire. We also had breaches in five of the buildings. Everyone has just started getting out of their polar gear. So where were we before I had to run?"

"We were talking about getting answers," Alex said. "Would it be possible to get to the impact site and take a look?"

"If we can get there, which is a big if, what would we be looking for?" asked Quinn.

"Well, let me put it this way. If this is not a rogue nation testing a nuclear bomb, then this could be one of the largest meteor or asteroid impacts in modern times. It's dark down there and we can't get satellite photographs to look at the impact site, but we don't want it to go uninvestigated. Quinn, let me get back to you. Candace tells me the Pentagon is calling and the President wants an update. Check around the station and see if it's possible to launch an expedition."

"Ten-four, let me check with the staff and I'll get back to you."

Dr. Laystrom heard the last part of the conversation. "I'm going with you …and by the way, who is Walter?"

"I'm not at all sure anyone is going anywhere, let alone who."

"Let me get Hank Tobias up here ASAP and we'll have a quick conference," Dr. Laystrom said, as they rushed down the hall toward the geo center.

"Hank…?"

"Yes, Tobias. He's our facilities manager for the station and the guy that brought the power back on. You have met him. He has more time on the ice than anyone, including me, and he is also in charge of the tractor fleet."

"Okay, I'll check with the geo-tech guys, while you round him up," said Quinn.

Quinn was on the phone, as Pam ran from the room with girlish enthusiasm. Quinn's call rang into total confusion in the Crary Center. The geo guys had been busy with damage control and were just getting back to their instruments. They had barely taken over from the night shift in the morning, when their instruments went wild—they thought some kind of a trick was being played on them. Quinn asked if Mark Raulson was in the area and was relieved to hear his collected voice.

"Mark, it looks like we've had either an atomic bomb blast or a meteor strike southwest of the station."

"What? Who is saying that?" He asked.

"Well, Pam and I think it was a meteor, since we were in my office and saw the trail of light outside my window. Then, a few seconds later, the flash brightened the sky just before the jolt. Also, I received a call from Washington about its impact and they are paranoid that it may have been some kind of weapons test by a rogue nation."

"Washington! I'm surprised they remember we are down here."

"I'll tell you about that later. Can you collect as much data as you can and come to the NSF conference room? We need to figure out what we're dealing with and maybe, go take a look."

"Will do, meet you there," exclaimed Mark.

Ten minutes later, about twenty people collected in the NSF conference room. News had traveled fast in the hallways and everyone was looking for answers.

Quinn began the meeting, "This is what we know for sure. At approximately 0647 Zulu this morning, a celestial body of unknown size entered the atmosphere southeast of the station and impacted at a point approximately 125 miles southwest of here on the plateau. I received a call from Washington and the Defense Department is viewing this as an unexplained suspicious event in one of the most remote corners of the planet. So far, they have not ruled out a weapons test of some kind. They think some rogue nation may have launched a nuclear device. Whatever it was, they want answers. Washington views this as a potential risk to national and world security. Does anyone have additional information?"

Randy Worthington related the details from the station's seismograph, "It was a single impact that registered approximately 6.4 on the Richter Scale. We are triangulating its impact with the Chile National Station and will have an exact location within the hour. Since it was a single impact, we can expect it to be either a bomb of unknown origin or a large meteor that did not break up on entering the atmosphere. In either case, it looks like a big one."

"Hank, we have been asked by Washington to go take a look. Is that possible? If so, how dangerous will it be to send a mission?" asked Quinn. Hank Tobias was a quiet man, who spoke in very measured sentences. Those who knew him listened closely to his few words, since they included both knowledge and experience.

"The temperature is 30 to 50 below and would present some danger, but yes, we could do it."

"Can the equipment take the temperature?" asked Quinn.

"The tractors can withstand the cold, but even a small breakdown can put the crew at risk."

"We need to deploy a team, if at all possible," said Quinn.

Hank stated, "Two of our newest tractors pulling crew trailers with extra fuel and emergency equipment will be the safest."

"Are there any other observations, concerns, or comments? If none, do we have any volunteers?" asked Quinn.

Hank was the first to speak up, "I'll go, but you will need another tractor driver. Tom Thorton has the most experience."

"I'll volunteer," said Tom from the doorway, followed in unison by Pam, Randy and Mark.

"Okay, we are going. The two tractor pilots will handle the logistics of the expedition and navigate the tractors with Drs. Laystrom and Worthington making up the scientific portion of the team. Mark and I will serve as leaders/observers and be the third team member in each of the tractors."

Hank had been running some numbers on his calculator. "From my quick calculations, I think we can be ready for departure as soon as 0600 Zulu tomorrow." Everyone was in agreement, so the flurry of activities began in earnest, as the team made the necessary preparations.

Since the station had settled into the winter routine, the rare expedition onto the ice cap was receiving a lot of buzz. The preparation involved almost everyone. Hank prepared and provisioned the tractors and the crew cabs that would be pulled by each tractor. Pam oversaw the food for the trip and assisted Randy in organizing the scientific equipment. Each tractor would be equipped for a ten-day expedition, even though the trip could be accomplished in three to five days under ideal conditions, which would leave a five-day safety margin. Randy and Mark packed insulated cameras, survey equipment, precision GPS units, parachute flares, and ice-coring equipment. Hank arranged for each crew trailer to carry an all-terrain vehicle (ATV), especially equipped for work in the harsh climate of Antarctica. Quinn coordinated the expedition with the NSF in Washington. He received more refined coordinates for the impact site and a considerable amount of advice and recommendations for caution.

The plan was to set a direct course toward the impact area at maximum speed of about 12 knots. The expedition would hold this speed for 10 hours and then slow to 5 knots, employing sonar to watch for crevasses that may have been created around the impact zone. After 14 hours of travel, the expedition should be in the vicinity of the impact. They would stop for a rest break of 12 hours at that point to eat and get some sleep before pushing forward to the impact site. The course through the mountains and onto the ice cap was well-charted, as it was used during the summer months to transport equipment to the South Pole Station. Once on the ice cap, the expedition would chart a course to the west into areas that were less well-known and seldom traveled. Visibility for the trip was anticipated to be good, considering the 24 hours of darkness. There would be a 15-minute period of light glow on the northern horizon as the sun reached its zenith in the northern hemisphere. Observation of the impact area would be timed to coincide with that period. If the weather closed in and observations were not possible, the team would hold up and wait for better conditions. If the going was good, then they would proceed to within one mile of the zone and use the fast-moving ATVs to investigate the impact site. The plan was to deploy emergency flares to illuminate and photograph the site, confirm its location and configuration with the GPS system, and document the observations for further research back at the station. Onboard scientific equipment would be deployed to measure for any magnetic or radioactivity anomalies. If time permitted, ice samples would be taken from the debris field to analyze for metals and organic material. The return trip would be done at top speed and the real work would begin once the team was back at the station and had time to examine the data and photographs.

After a flurry of activity, the tractors departed the station at 0623 Zulu. Everyone not on duty turned out to see the expedition off. It was the most exciting thing to occur at the station so far this winter. The weather reports were encouraging with -30°F, winds out of the south were moderate at 5 to 7 mph, and the polar skies were clear. The long-term forecast was less promising with increased winds and colder temperatures by day three. All the more reason to push forward as fast as possible before the temperature and wind chill factor went below -100°F. Even at -30°, there was a +90° difference in temperature between the outside and the highly desired 60° in the cab. The rumble of the diesel engines and the whine of the heater fan were only small reassurances that the cold was going to remain at bay. Still it was cold—cold beyond Quinn's wildest imagination, a hostile predatory cold that threatened to hunt down and destroy any skin that the unwitting person was foolish enough to leave exposed. *What was a Florida boy doing on a trip like this anyway?* he thought as he watched the mountains grow closer.

The expedition made good time. Five hours later, they were up on the ice cap. Eight hours into the trip, the tractors departed from the South Pole supply route and headed west towards the impact site. Randy, riding in the lead tractor, had brought a CD and had the stereo cranked up as loud as possible, so loud that Dr. Laystrom was calling on the radio complaining. It seemed that Randy's music was keying the VOX transmission on the radio. Still Randy continued conducting an invigorating rendition of Beethoven's Ninth Symphony with enough arm-waving to warm the cab. Quinn could feel the energy. There was something about Beethoven that fit in really well with the ice expedition.

Ten hours into the trip, Hank slowed the tractors to five knots and began paying even closer attention to the crevasse monitoring equipment regularly. The wind had increased and forward visibility decreased to 30 yards. Tension began to build in the lead tractor. There was an unknown feature on the landscape that could hold some danger for the small expedition. It was Quinn's job to assess the risk and ensure the safety of the team. Out of concern for the changes in the weather and the uncharted ice conditions ahead, Quinn called an early halt to the expedition. Out of caution, the tractors would remain at this station for 12 hours. During this period, the team would get something to eat and sleep. The next day, the expedition would push forward another ten to fifteen miles and reassess conditions.

Working in an extremely cold climate burns a lot of calories just to stay warm. Dr. Laystrom was well aware of this metabolic condition and had packed enough food for a small army. The crew braved the short sprint to the rear crew cab and settled in for a hot meal of steak, mashed potatoes and broccoli, topped off with chocolate cookies and hot coffee. The moral of the crew unit was high and the jokes and laughter created a festive mood.

In more serious moments, they discussed the schedule for tomorrow. The expedition would get underway again at 1300 Zulu. The tractors would continue forward at a reduced speed until the first signs of the impact zone were encountered. These first signs could be small secondary craters or uneven terrain along the route that would warn of impending crevasses. At these first signs and, if the weather permitted, the team would proceed forward on all-terrain snowmobiles. Each tractor carried one. Within the last few hundred yards, the team would proceed on foot, tethered together with floodlights and flares to shed as much light as possible on the impact crater.

With the final plans laid out, it was time to get some sleep. The one crew cab where they met only had bunks for four, so Quinn took a spot on the floor and drifted into a hazy and fitful sleep. His thoughts took him back to Africa, where only a few short weeks ago he had done battle with a group of young insurgents. There was both pride and sorrow over his part in that event. Taking a life was only slightly more palpable when your own is at risk. These were boys with dreams and hopes for a better life. The thought of his wife floated in and out of his dreams …where was she, what was she doing? Was there ever going to be any closure to these open emotional wounds? Every movement in the quarters would rouse him from his fitful sleep. Both Hank and Mark were sound asleep and snoring with gusto. Pam hit the bunk after complaining about men not helping with the dishes and she had not moved. An increasing wind buffeted the quarters and Quinn worried about the safety of the crew, as every leader before him had done in this hostile environment. Would they be able to successfully complete the mission and return to the safety of the station within the next few days?

After what seemed like an eternity, a brash and raspy buzzer told them it was time to go. Hank was up and reviewing the weather conditions. While everyone stretched and climbed back into their parkas, Hank reported that the winds were still up past 15 knots, gusting to 25. The windblown snow obscured visibility and the temperature was now -45°.

"We could continue forward with the tractors, but visibility would be too low for extended outside work. We would have to wait that part out, once we got closer," was Quinn's best advice. After energy bars for breakfast, the tractors got underway again. They had progressed only a few hundred yards, when they encountered the first secondary crater, an eroded indentation, approximately six feet across, lay just to the right of the route. Tom brought the second tractor up close and jumped out the door with the Geiger counter. He reported no elevated radiation was present and then brushed the ice from the bottom of the crater. With an ice arguer, he probed the bottom for fragments of the projectile. This was a process that would be repeated a number of times, as the craters became more frequent and larger in size. Finally Tom scored with a six-inch chunk of the meteor. It was indeed a metallic nodule that showed signs of being melted in the heat of entry into the atmosphere. They were definitely dealing with a large iron and nickel meteor that had wandered through space for millions of years before coming to its final resting place here on the Antarctic ice sheet. Washington's concerns of a rogue nation testing an atomic weapon were laid to rest.

It was time to stop the tractors and transition to the ATV snowmobiles, but the weather was not cooperating, so the expedition again went on hold, awaiting a better weather window. Quinn was able to communicate with the station, informing them everyone was okay and that there had been one fragment retrieved, but they had not reached the main impact site. The ice cap was stable with no signs of fissures or crevasses.

By now they had been on the ice cap for 36 hours.

Once again, everyone crowded into the aft crew trailer. Tom was the appointed chef and, although the food he prepared was not quite as good as Pam's shift, there were plenty of calories and lots of companionship. Randy expounded at great length on the oriental poetry haiku, explaining that it was text lines of five syllables, followed by a line of seven, and then another of five syllables. There was no need to rhyme the words. The rhythm of the text established the poetic sound. It seems that it was common practice to communicate around the station with emailed haiku. This was a surprise to Quinn. He had not received any haiku. Apparently, Pam was in the loop and one of the chief authors of haikus. Randy and Pam excitedly demonstrated their skills by speaking in haiku. Mentally, Quinn gave it a try and came up lacking on every attempt.

In a lull in the conversation, Quinn asked, "Randy, you're so good at haikus, maybe you can answer a question for me?"

"Sure, if I can't, we know Pam can. What do you want to know?"

"How come there isn't any Antarctic music?"

"Antarctic music," Randy retorted with a puzzled look.

"Yes, every continent, country and culture has music. Just listen to the continent talking to us through the wind outside. But I have not heard any attempts to capture the character of this continent in music. You've heard Hawaiian music and the way it seems to capture the rhythm of the wind and the waves. Why hasn't anyone attempted to capture the magnificence of Antarctica in music?"

"Huh, very interesting. Of course, Hawaiians have something to sing about. There have been a number of documentaries done on Antarctica. Many of those dub in a soundtrack that usually misses the point. I'd never thought about it, but you're right," Randy said somewhat amused.

"Could it be that scientists have no sense of rhythm?" Pam inquired, inserting herself into the conversation.

"Are we talking about male and female scientists?" asked Tom.

"Oh, no, don't get her started on male-bashing again. That is all we have heard since we left the station," said Mark.

"Well, if there is going to be any Antarctic music, it's obvious that it would have to be written by a woman. You men are not that sensitive to refined arts, like music," she retorted with her usual conviction.

"Boo! Boo!" was the resounding response from all the guys.

"Are you challenging us to show that we do not have two left feet and we can dance and sing with the best of them?" asked Randy.

"Yeah, right, like that's going to happen," laughed Pam.

Randy responded with conviction. "Guys, I'm now talking to the Y chromosomes. Are we going to sit here and accept this abuse or are we going to rise to the challenge and become Antarctic rock stars? Hell, the rest of the world might like to hear from Antarctica—we could become famous."

The exchange had lightened the mood and everyone had a good laugh.

"I hate to be the wet blanket on this party, but we had better get some rest," suggested Hank.

"Okay, this time I want you guys out of my bedroom. Go back to your own cab! There was too damn much male testosterone to suit me and that goes for the snoring as well," Pam added.

With those parting remarks, Quinn, Hank and Mark dressed for the ten-yard run to the other crew cab amid some speculation that a real man could make the run without being in full Antarctic dress. Yet, no one was seriously thinking of attempting the transit in less than full gear. Hank put an end to all speculation with a warning about what -50 degrees would do to the human body in very short order. The run was short and brisk. "Dammm it'ss cooold out herrre," mumbled Mark through a double scarf wrapped around his face.

Once in the cab, Mark spoke in a more philosophical tone. "You know, this expedition reminds me of some of the horror movies we watched as kids. Do any of you remember, *It Came from Outer Space*? It started with a spaceship landing in a rural area and people gathering to see what happened. The next thing you know, people were disappearing and strange creatures were being spotted all over town. Then there was, *The Body Snatchers*—I think that was the one where an alien race was replacing people by growing duplicates in a vegetable patch. The truth is, we don't know what is out there. So Quinn, tell me, why were your friends in Washington are so interested in having us come take a look?" asked Mark.

"You're starting to spook me out, Mark. Those movies were total fiction designed to scare the crap out of little kids. This is reality and we are all adults, right?"

"Well, of course, we are all grown-up adults, but there is a pretty big unknown out there, from deep outer space to boot, and we just might be very surprised. What if someone knocks on our door during the night? What are you going to do then?"

"You're scaring me, Mark!"

"I'm scaring myself!"

"Good night, Mark," chimed two voices.

"Okay, okay, I get your point. Good night, everybody. But if there is a knock at the door, I'm not answering it."

Twelve hours later, the winds were subsiding. Hank ventured out and fired the first flare due west. It illuminated the impact zone so that the team could see numerous craters scattered across the visual range of sight. "Call Tom and tell him it is time to hit the road. The visibility is as good as it's going to get." Thirty minutes later, the snow mobiles were ready to go. Randy and Pam would take a southerly route and Quinn and Mark would go north. Everyone would keep their radios on and report any findings. Hank and Tom would stay by the tractors and serve as emergency backup.

"Remember," Hank warned over the crackle of the radio, "You only have 15 minutes on the ice before you need to be back here and in the crew cab. No more than 20 minutes at the most." "Understood!" was the response from all and the snowmobiles took off as if in a race. Two hundred yards to the north, Mark and Quinn encountered a crater that was approximately 100 yards across.

"It's pretty big," observed Quinn with a muffled voice. "Do you think this is the main impact area?"

"Don't know, but I have a GPS reading, so let's keep going," came Mark's reply.

Flares were illuminating the sky from the south. "Damn, will you look at those flares light up the ice! Give me one of those." Each team carried about a dozen flares and it was time to put them to use. Mark fired the first and both marveled at the light displayed all around them. "It looks like a dark area straight ahead," observed Quinn. "Let's connect the tether and walk in. Leave the snowmobile facing in that direction for the tractor headlights."

Quinn immediately radioed the other ATV, "South team, south team, come in!"

Immediately a reply came, "South team here. How's the hunting going?" Randy inquired.

"We have what appears to be a large depression directly ahead of us and are walking to it. Have you made any contacts?" asked Quinn.

"We have seen small depressions and one large crater, but … wait a minute …Pam STOP!" Randy yelled.

"Randy, what is it?"

"Christ, it's the Grand Canyon and Pam almost drove us into it," replied Randy.

"Back up from the edge, Pam. Can you fire a flare so we can see where you are?" Seconds later, a single flare was lofted into the darkness, lighting a vast depression.

Quinn and Mark could see for the first time that it was the same crater they were approaching, yet the teams were almost one mile apart. "More flares," shouted Mark. "This is the real thing, let's give it some light!" They sent up two flares and then four more to light up the night. Blue ice materialized from the walls of the crater, as the flares passed into the mammoth hole in the ice.

A crack in the radio brought Hank's voice to the teams, "Take pictures and get back here. Your time is running short."

Quinn and Mark both fumbled with their cameras and fired another round of flares to get the maximum light. Randy and Pam on the southside were doing the same. "Look at that fresh melt at the bottom. That must be where the meteor landed and the residual heat melted the ice," observed Quinn.

"You're right and there is no way we can get down to it. Those walls are almost vertical and it has to be almost three-fourths of a mile deep," replied Mark.

"Time to get back to the tractors, I'll radio the south team," said Quinn.

"South team, we are returning to camp."

"Yeah, yeah, what a couple of wimps!" came a notably female voice.

"Pam!"

"Okay, okay, we are coming, but it sure is beautiful. The ice is pale blue, almost iridescent. We are looking at a cross-section of ice that is millions of years old."

The north team was the last to get back to the tractors and Quinn and Mark excitedly entered the aft cab to compare notes. Randy and Pam were still in their parkas. For a full ten minutes, there was a flow of descriptive words from both teams, "Huge, deep, wide, majestic, ominous, spectacular, foreboding, gigantic, unbelievable."

"Okay, we have got to do a better job documenting these observations. These superlatives will get us laughed out of the scientific community. How big do you think it is?" asked Quinn.

"It has got to be well over a half-mile wide and 500 meters deep," volunteered Randy.

"I'd say a mile wide and 750 meters deep," said Mark.

"Do you realize that both of those estimates are larger than the biggest recorded impact crater on the planet?" asked Hank.

"Seriously, Hank, it's huge. How can we confirm its size, short of driving the rim of it or deploying survey equipment?" Randy asked.

"Is driving the rim out of the question?" asked Pam.

"Yes, my guess is that the direction of the impact would have thrown a mountain of ice into the ejecta blanket and would be impassable," replied Hank.

"I think you are probably right. We could make a few more trips to the edge to get a better estimate. Hank, why don't you and Tom make the next trip and then, we can compare notes and see exactly how we will handle this information," suggested Quinn.

With a big grin Hank looked at Tom and said, "There's still plenty of gas in the snowmobile, let's get suited up. Oh, before I forget, Quinn. I keep hearing someone keying a microphone over the radio. It's that click, click sound you hear just before someone calls. I thought it was one of your radios, but a couple of times, I heard it when you both were talking."

"That's strange. Do you think it was the station's radio?"

"No they come in with a lot of power. This was a weak signal. Listen for it, while we are on the snowmobiles and see what you think," Hank said as he pulled on his parka.

"It could be a radio frequency bounce off the stratosphere, possibly someone off-continent tuned in to our frequency."

"Pam and I will listen for it while you are out."

Pam was listening in on the conversation as she downloading the camera to the computer and started looking at the photos.

Quinn checked the reception on the satellite phone and suggested that a few of the images be forwarded back to the station and Geo Spatial Center with the explanation that the details would come later. As the cameras were downloaded, the team was relieved to see that everything had worked. Also they had some time to study the photos.

Meanwhile Hank and Tom were on one of the snowmobiles heading back towards the crater.

The images revealed a yawning crater whose size could

not be determined with snapshots from hand-held cameras. The transmission back to the station went well and the radio was crackling with explanation remarks. Still the lingering questions remained: how big is it and is there a remnant of the meteor at the head of the crater? Several of the glaciologists from the station offered suggestions for analysis of the crater, while the team was still at the impact site. With their input, the next phase of the expedition was planned.

After another 12-hour rest period, the two teams would again approach the crater. First one team would install a survey laser station at the leading edge of the crater and return to base. Then both teams would drive the rim for a measured distance of one mile. Each team would use laser survey equipment and determine the distance from one another and the base station. Since time on the ice was limited, this survey would have to be accomplished within 15 minutes. If more time was needed, the process would be repeated, after a rest break. All outside work was, of course, dependent on the weather.

Hank and Tom returned to the tractors with new photographs and a fresh batch of adjectives to describe the crater. Before removing their protective clothing they prepared the snowmobiles for the next expedition. Once all were back in the crew cab, it was time to eat again and get some rest.

By this time, the expedition had been away from the station for 68 hours.

The team was notably restless after the first trip to the crater and had difficulty in settling down for the rest period. Hank and Quinn stayed up, checking weather with the station and refining the plan to deploy the survey equipment the next time out. The process was not complex, but had to be done quickly to get the data and return to the safety of the tractors. The good news was that the weather was holding and possibly improving. The team would see a calm, clear -85° tomorrow at 0600 Zulu tomorrow. The low wind conditions were also favorable for the survey.

"There certainly is a lot of chatter on the radio," observed Quinn.

"Yes, we are hearing from everyone," said Hank in his usual understated tone. "The NGIA from Washington seems particularly excited. Who are those guys? Their acronym sounds like some intelligence agency."

"That is the National Geo-Spatial Intelligence Agency, my employer," Quinn said.

"Oh! I thought you were with the NSF," replied Hank.

"I'm on loan to the NSF for the winter here at the station. Then I will be home-based out of Australia, conducting research," replied Quinn.

"What kind of research are you talking about?"

"The Agency is primarily responsible for providing quality satellite surveillance photographs to other governmental agencies and friendly nations, but not everything is discernible from photographs. So basically, I will serve as their eyes and ears on the ground to fill in some of the holes."

"Will you be returning to the station next winter?"

"I don't think so. From what I hear from a certain scientist, I doubt I will be missed."

"If you are talking about Dr. Laystrom, I know what you mean. Your problem is that you are the wrong gender."

"She just does not like men?"

"I can't say that she dislikes us, it's just that the female is so much more superior. She views men as beasts of burden and if we stay in that role she likes us fine. We have all had a run-in with Dr. Laystrom."

"Before I forget, Hank, I have not heard anymore of those random clicks you mentioned earlier. I know it is not possible, but the ones I did hear sounded close-by."

"That is what I thought as well, but with the atmospheric conditions and the amount of radio use going on, it could have been anything."

"Yes, we may never know. I think it's time we sign off the radio and settle in for some rest," replied Quinn.

Hank nodded his head and yawned.

"McMurdo, McMurdo, this is Crater Station, come in."

"This is McMurdo, over."

"Yes, Roy, I hear you have the watch."

"10-4, Good Buddy, what can I do for you"?

"All preparations for tomorrow's survey expeditions are complete. We are closing down for the evening to get some rest."

"Understood, Crater Station. I'll keep the news hounds away from your door. If you need anything, someone will be here monitoring this frequency."

"Thanks and goodnight, Crater Station signing off."

"Goodnight and stay warm."

"Hank, do you remember what warm felt like?"

"Ha, I plan to sail in the Caribbean during the summer months just to feel warm again."

"You sail? I just bought a 37-foot Sabra back in Sydney and will be using it as my home base," said Quinn.

"Sabra builds a great boat. We will have to talk more later on," Hank replied in a sleepy voice.

"Yeah, I'll talk sailboats anytime. Goodnight,"

The chatter on the radio faded way and was replaced with the constant guttural rumble of the diesel engines and circulation fans.

By this time, they had been on the ice cap for 83 hours.

Quinn and Hank awoke at the same instance. There was the yawning sound of ice bending, followed by multiple cracks that sounded like pistol shots. The window was obscured and Hank was the first to be in gear and out of the cab door to investigate. Quinn waited and wondered how Mark could continue to sleep through the noise. Also, there was no sign of lights from the other crew cab. After what seemed like an excessively long time, Hank returned.

"It looks like we lost a sizable section of the rim right in front of the tractor. It just calved off and left a clean edge on the rim. It took me a while to figure out that we were another 50 meters closer to the edge than we were last night," Hank offered in an uncharacteristic excited manner.

"Do you think we need to move the tractors back?" Quinn asked.

"I think we are safe, but I was not expecting to be 50 meters closer to the rim either. So let's move them back another 500 meters just to be sure," replied Hank.

After rousing Tom in the rear tractor, Hank slowly put the tractor in gear and moved the small expedition back along its original course by 500 meters. Quinn was asleep again before Hank brought them to a halt.

Quinn was the first to wake the next morning and just had to wake up the group like from his military days. "Reveille, reveille, you will fall out and turn to! We have scientific history to make today and no time to waste," Quinn's booming voice proclaimed. Quinn enjoyed using the old military wake-up ritual he remembered from his early days in the Marines. He had enjoyed waking his daughter to old military chant, much to her displeasure, of course.

"Oh crap, he is one of those neo-Nazi types," groused Pam as she jumped from the upper berth. "I've got the bathroom first and you he-men can go outside.

There were a lot of elbows and zippers being pulled in both crew cabs, as the teams prepared to deploy the survey equipment. This time Mark and Randy would set the laser station and return to base camp and remain at the tractors as backup. Tom and Pam would take one of the snowmobiles south along the crater's rim. Quinn and Hank would travel the north rim for one mile. Both teams were to be back on station in 15 minutes. They would have only a few minutes to set up the instruments and take the readings before returning.

"Is everyone ready?" Quinn asked.

"I'll be ready as soon as I finish my coffee. Give me another 15 minutes," joked Pam.

"I want to give a few words of caution. The crater's wall calved last night and dropped about a 50 meter section of the wall. Let's stay harnessed together, just in case another section calves while we are out there.

"Wait a minute. I like Tom fine, but I don't want to be tied to him!"

"Yes, I know what you're going to say, Pam. A 50-meter piece of the crater wall gave way last night, so wear the harness and be as careful as possible in picking your station along the rim. Tom, I am putting you in charge of that job."

"Yes, sir!" Tom responded with a half-serious military salute.

"Okay team, this may be our last shot, so let's make the most of if it!" Quinn said with a salute.

The rumble of the diesels was punctuated by the high-pitched whine of the ATVs as the two teams sped into darkness. Mark and Randy lit the floodlights of both tractors to provide as much illumination as possible, which only made the tractors look even more isolated in the vast darkness of the ice cap. Hank and Quinn reached the place to deploy the base station. Both were breathing hard as they fought to unfold the tripod that was not cooperating in the -75° temperature. Soon they were underway again along the north rim. To their left and seemingly a long way apart, they could see the lights of the other snowmobile speeding along through the darkness.

"Just one mile, just one mile," Quinn kept repeating to himself as the bitter cold from the mobile's apparent wind seem to be boring though every seam of his clothing. After what seemed like an eternity, Hank slowed the ATV and stopped about 10 meters from the edge of the crater. Both men jumped off and began to deploy the survey laser. The chatter over the two-way radio system told them that the southern team had their equipment in place and were standing by. Once the tripod was in place and Hank was leveling it, Quinn fumbled with the on/off switch and brought the instrument to life. First, each team was to survey back to the base station, secondly, across to each other, and thirdly, down on to the crater's floor. Their heavy gloves and face masks made the precision measurements slow, but step by step, the information was collected and confirmed.

Now came the fun part. With all the measurements completed, it was time for the last photographic effort. Each team had again brought parachute flares and the plan was to fill the darkness with as much light as possible. Mark and Randy were standing by at the tractors to unleash the artillery of large emergency flares.

"North Rim station, ready to go," announced Quinn.

"South Rim here, let's get the show on the road. It's getting cold out here!" shouted Pam.

"Light the fires! Light the fires," was the enthusiastic response.

What followed next felt more like a combat mission. The large emergency flares from the tractors were awesome. They were followed by a series of flares from both sides of the crater. Each team bracketed the flares on about ten degrees, so that the light would cover the maximum amount. There was only a 15-second period when all the flares were in the air and for the first time, the entire crater was illuminated. The northwestern end of the crater was ringed by a mountain of ice thrown up by the impact. At the bottom where the meteor would have come to rest was a green pool of ice. Apparently the meteor had melted the ice as it cooled and created a pond that rapidly froze.

"Oh, my God, would you look at that!" came the radio chatter with a female voice.

"Holy crap! It's much bigger than I thought it would be!" was Hank's unscientific response.

"Keep those cameras rolling. No one is going to believe this unless we bring them proof," admonished Quinn.

"Quinn, look at the rim," warned Hank.

"What?"

"The rim is calving and we can see it clearly in the full light. We are well within the fracture zone and are in danger," said Hank with concern.

"Uh, yeah, you're right, Hank. South team, did you hear Hank?"

"Yes, we heard and the conditions are about the same on our side. We are breaking camp and heading for safety."

"10-4 south! The flares are fading. We have the pictures. It's time to head home everyone. Mark, do you read?"

"Copy that. We are on the move."

"Can you and Randy be ready to pick up the base station

when we get back to the tractors? We have been on the ice too long and it's starting to take its toll," said Quinn.

"Affirmative, Quinn, we will be in gear and ready by the time you're back," came the reassuring answer.

Once again the roar of small engines filled the Antarctic night, as the two teams raced back towards the distant pool of light. Hank hesitated and examined the ice carefully before leaving the crater. The fissures and calving were showing up with increasing frequency and the crater was getting more dangerous to be near. The south team was already there when Quinn and Hank made it back to the tractor. They had been on the ice for 47 minutes. Mark and Randy where suited up and raced back to retrieve the base station and take one last series of photographs with the remaining flares. Pam was warming her fingers and getting ready to download the cameras to the onboard computer.

"Those fissures are getting more pronounced and the walls are calving much more frequently. If we had not come to see the site, the scientific community would never have seen the actual impact crater. By spring when the satellites can see the surface again, the crater will have deteriorated," Hank observed.

"Do you realize what we have just seen? It's like we were the first to see the Grand Canyon or Victoria Falls. One of the largest impact craters in modern times and our expedition was the first to reach the impact site. From what Hank says, we may be the only ones to see it," Quinn offered philosophically.

"I have the pictures from my camera on the computer. Hand me your camera. Also, do you want me to send the photos back to the station?" Pam asked.

"That is affirmative! Send them back as soon as you get them into the computer. Did we get some decent shots?" Quinn inquired.

"Oh, yes! These will be seen all over the world by this time tomorrow."

"Hey, guys, we just lost another section of the rim. Let's get the hell out of here," Hank said with some urgency.

Hank and Tom revved the engines and grounded some

gears out of exuberation, as they turned the tractors around and put them on the return course towards the station. Once again the familiar rumble of the diesel engines combined with the gentle rocking of the cab, the tractor got up to speed. Pam, Hank, and Quinn were in the lead tractor. Once all the photographs were sent to base, Pam did what she could to get some hot coffee and food going.

"We never got to finish our conversation back at the station," Pam said to Quinn as the tractors began to move away from the crater.

"Oh, really, I thought we had."

"Well the first part, yes. I would really like to know more about you. For example, are you married? I noticed you do not wear a wedding ring."

"Married ...that is a hard question."

"What is hard about it? Either you are married or not. Don't you know that?"

"Let's just say ...I'm separated at the moment."

"You left her alone to come to Antarctica! Shame on you!

"Well, that is not quite it either. I would rather not talk about it, if you don't mind."

"Oh, she left you! Ha! Whichever way, it was your fault. It's always the man's fault. Males are such morons."

"Thanks for clarifying that for me."

"Do you have any kids?"

"Yes, a daughter, 20 years old, in her sophomore year at Berry College in Georgia. How about you—any kids?"

"Yes, I also have one daughter. She lives with her father while I am on the ice. She is a very precocious 13-years-old. I've been divorced for two years now. The only good thing that came out of that marriage was my daughter. Some people were never meant to be married," she added.

An incoming radio message interrupted their conversation, much to Quinn's relief. Roy Lynch was on the radio requesting one of the scientists on board to give an interview with NPR. The breaking news was too good to pass up as part of their Radio Expedition Series. As a senior scientist and the only scientist in the front tractor, Pam was the selected spokesperson.

Quinn settled back with a cup of coffee, while Pam excitedly relayed the impressions of the crater over a relatively clear radio connection. They had truly been lucky. There had been only minor frost bite and no lost fingers or toes. There were no lost equipment and the team had taken numerous photographs and measurements of the crater.

Oh, yes, the measurements, Quinn recalled. Once Pam was off the radio, Quinn contacted the station and relayed the digital survey data from the base station and two transits. Hopefully, they would have it plotted out by the time they returned to the station.

They had been on the ice for 123 hours.

Unbeknownst to Quinn or the team, their expedition had aroused worldwide interest. The impact had been routinely announced on public airways. But it was the NPR and BBC reports of the intrepid explorers launching an expedition from McMurdo Station in the dead of winter that had stirred public interest. The news outlets had followed their progress along with the hardships endured by the expedition and now that the pictures were being broadcast, the team had reached celebrity status.

CHAPTER 5

Realization

FRANCE

Two weeks after the infamous phone call from Roberto, the guest arrived—Dr. Jack Fargo, a young associate of Roberto's. He had just finished his residency and was taking a break before entering the practice. He was tall with dark brown hair and an athletic built, but pale and tired-looking. She assumed the fatigue was from his long hours as a resident doctor. Nancy introduced herself and smiled appropriately, all the while wondering if he had received the same message from Roberto. Nancy played the hostess and showed him to his room and had Rocco bring in his luggage. She suggested that he get some rest and come down for dinner at 6:00 P.M. He thanked her with a show of good Midwestern manners and Nancy departed thinking that her imagination had run away with her. This was a nice young man, maybe six or eight years younger than herself. It would be interesting to entertain a house guest and she was looking forward to a little company. Certainly with the difference in age, there would be no romantic interest.

The conversation she had with Roberto two weeks earlier had played over and over in her head. Although she had attempted to discuss it with him on later phone calls, he had only laughed and said to let her hair down and enjoy herself. She wasn't in Kansas anymore and no one was watching or keeping score, but this only added to her confusion. She had always loved one man and that affection had been transferred to Roberto. Now he was suggesting that monogamy was no longer a prerequisite or a requirement of their relationship.

Dinner was delightful. Jack was a good conversationalist and it was great to catch up on the news from home. Even the servants seemed to enjoy the visit. They were very prompt to meet all of their needs. After dinner, they retired for a drink to the balcony overlooking the Mediterranean. As the sun slowly set, Thomas commented how romantic the village looked as sun descended to the sea and with a slight change in position, he brushed her arm. It was a casual, even innocent move, but enough to convey the message to Nancy that he knew what was expected …it was decision time for her to make up her mind. Part of her was repulsed by the overture, while another part was excited by the possibility of acting outside the Victorian moral constraints that had governed her past life. That was it, she thought, her past life! Things were different here—this is where she was going to spend the rest of her life—no constraints, moral expectations, or accountability existed. She was free to experiment and answered to no one.

This time it was she who reached out and touched his hand and with a smile, she brushed the back of her hand against his cheek. "Yes, it is very romantic," and then she heard a voice that sounded like her own say, "Why don't we make the most of it?" His response was instant and affirmative, as he swept her into his arms and kissed her long and passionately. Like two experienced dancers, they waltzed for a closer position, all the while caressing one another. Now the sunset was truly intoxicating and she knew there would be no turning back.

Passion overwhelmed both of them, as they had made love on the balcony before retreating to his room for a very passionate night. The next morning, Nancy could not explain what had happened the night before. There was an unleashing of passion of which she did not know she was capable. Here was the perfect young male body that was starved for a woman's touch. There was no morning-after guilt—only anticipation for the rest of his visit. It was love without any commitment, no baggage or long-term relationship—just plain unadulterated going-out-of-your-mind sex.

Over a cup of morning coffee, Jack turned on the television to check the weather. Both were captivated by a reported meteor impact in the Antarctic. It seemed that some intrepid poor souls were going out in the winter cold to investigate. Nancy was half-listening to the report until the names of those participating in the expedition were announced, when her attention was jolted by the name, *Quinn Wilson*. She could not believe her ears. Surely this was not …no it could not be … her husband. The recognition that he was indeed still her husband sent another jolt through her system, bringing her back to her past life and her completely abandoned moral standards.

"What's wrong?" asked Jack.

"I ... I know …I know one of those scientists," she hesitatingly volunteered.

"Which one?"

"Quinn Wilson, the expedition leader …he was …no is … my …my … husband!"

CHAPTER 6

Back on the Ice

Quinn received a call from Roy Lynch at the station that the media frenzy was beginning to disrupt operations. It seemed that every newspaper, magazine, radio, and television network was clamoring for an exclusive. Since none could send reporters, they all were requesting a link to the team or news conference broadcast, under their control of course, so that the news could be extracted and broadcast.

"Oh, boy," chortled Quinn, "this is going to be interesting. Let's see if we can take control of it by offering a news conference and a written statement of the findings. We will start working on it here and, Roy, you start telling all the reporters that we will televise a conference once we are safely back at the station."

"10-4 that. When do you think you will be back?"

"We are only seven hours out, if we can maintain speed. Hank is concerned with the weather, as we have pneumatic winds off the ice cap from the south. Once we reach the mountain pass, we will have to make a judgment call and see if we can make it through or have to wait it out. Ice expedition out."

"Understood, expedition! The winds are rising here at the station as well, so let us know what you encounter. We received a call from the French, who launched an expedition from the Dumont D'Urivlle Station two days ago and are heading to the crater. They could have been close to your position yesterday. Did you get a call from them?" McMurdo out."

"No call, but we did hear someone keying a microphone. It sounded close by, but we attributed it to atmospheric conditions and the amount of background chatter we were hearing from all over the globe. What frequency is the French team operating on? We need to pass on some warnings. The crater was deteriorating when we left and they should be very cautious approaching the rim. Ice expedition out."

"They are monitoring 186.5 MHz, but they are probably targeting the western end of the impact area, away from your position. Give them a try and I'll send a message to their station with the warning. McMurdo out."

"Just talked to Hank again and the winds are picking up. We are definitely stopping at the pass. Our fuel is running low, but he thinks we have enough for another 24 hours. With a 6-hour run back to the station that gives us only an 18-hour hold time. We will be shutting down and conserving fuel once we get to the pass."

"Understood. We will keep you posted with the latest weather report every hour. McMurdo Station over and out."

"Ice expedition out."

Quinn switched to the intercom to contact the rear tractor. "Hank advises that we hold at the pass, due to high winds and low visibility. We will need to go into fuel conservation mode as soon as we stop. I suggest that we collect here in the lead tractor and get organized for the return to the station. We should be coming into a sheltered area within the hour, so you may want to get suited up for the run between tractors. It's still 60 below out there, so no hot dogging without your gear on. 10-4."

"10-4, Fearless Leader."

"Mark here—Tom wanted to make the run in his birthday suit, so you burst his bubble. Give a shout when you are ready and we'll make the run."

"Hank is formulating some fuel conservations measures. Looks like you will idle down and turn off all non-essential equipment. Leave the life-support heaters at absolutely the lowest levels. Understood?"

"Understood!"

"Stand by."

Then Quinn turned the transmitter to 186.5 MHz and hailed the French team en route to the crater. "Ice team, ice team, come in. This is the American Crater Expedition—you need to turn back. I repeat turn back now." After several attempts, the radio receiver crackled with a response.

"This is Major Dumas at the D'Urille Station. We have not been able to contact our expedition. They are currently en route. Please....zeeezee … crackle …respond. Over."

"Major! This is Quinn Wilson, leader of the American Crater Expedition. We are en route back to McMurdo Station. What is your team's position? Over."

"They last reported in yesterday approximately 35 kilos north of …crackle … en route …crackle …to …buzzz."

"Major, you are breaking up. We want to caution your team about approaching the crater. Repeat, be cautious approaching the crater—it is deteriorating rapidly. Over."

"Zzzt …crackle …crater …route …."

"D'Urille Station …. D'Urille Station, come in, please!" Repeated calls brought no reply. "It looks like we lost radio contact with the French station and they apparently have lost contact with their team. Let's hope they were able to get the warning through to them."

A call from the other tractor team came on, "Hey, we have reduced power over here and it's getting cold fast. Make room, we are coming over." Within seconds, the three bundled-up team members were at the door and jumping into the crew cab. The wind was rising and with it, the chill factor was plummeting. It was time to hunker down and wait it out, as Antarctic winds blow off the ice cap with near hurricane force. This weather phenomenon could last for days and is fatal for anything or anyone exposed to the elements. While all the crew was safe in the crew cab, low fuel limited their ability to wait indefinitely.

With everyone on board, Quinn briefed them about the media frenzy that they were likely to encounter with the return to the station. "We need to do a press release and designate a spokesman—excuse me, Pam—a spokesperson, to meet the press demands. We have some protection from the onslaught, since the press can't physically get to the station. However, the satellite channels will be maxed out with demands for interviews. First, who will be our spokesperson?"

"Why don't you do it?" responded Mark.

Quinn had anticipated the question and the real answer was that an effective intelligence agent avoided direct exposure to the media. As they taught in the intelligence courses a few short months ago, agents worked best when they moved freely below the radar. An international spokesman for a major scientific event was not a role he either wanted or could afford to take at this point in his new career with NGIA.

"I think that one of you scientists would be much better suited to be the spokesperson. There would be far more credibility. So, Mark, I think you or Pam should be the spokesperson," Quinn suggested.

"Well, I think I speak for both of us. Usually the administrator would seek to grab the spotlight and take all the credit for a scientific discovery. So, we thank you for stepping aside and allowing us to talk about the sciences. Right, Pam?"

"I think ...that there are probably other reasons that you don't want the exposure, but yeah, we can do it. Thanks," replied Pam.

"Okay! We will need a press release, so let's work one up," declared Quinn. The team huddled around the laptop computer and comprised a short press release that would be eagerly received by almost every news outlet on the planet.

PRESS RELEASE

> On May 14th at approximately 7:13 A.M., an asteroid of indeterminate size entered the atmosphere over Antarctica and impacted in an area called Wilkes Land, approximately 110 kilometers east of the Transantarctic Mountains and 1,200 kilometers north of the North Pole. The impact is near latitude 77 degrees north and longitude 133 east.

An expedition of six scientists, including glaciologists and astronomers, from the American McMurdo Station on the Ross Ice Shelf were dispatched on May 15th and were the first to arrive at the impact zone 18 hours later. Observations made at the site revealed multiple secondary impacts from decaying fragments of the meteor, some as large as several football fields. One large impact crater roughly measured 1.3 miles in width, approximately 2.0 miles long, and 800 to 1,200 feet in depth. A large unstable ice mound was observed on the crater's northeastern rim. This ice mound was thrown by the impact due to the low trajectory of the meteor. These observations confirm that this is the largest meteor to have impacted earth during recorded history. While the impact was observed on seismographs worldwide, the remote location of the impact area spared the planet of any human impact. Photographs of the crater taken by the expedition team are transmitted with this news release. The expedition experienced extreme cold and high winds, typical of the Antarctic winters that limited their observation time at the impact area to less than a few hours. The team safely returned to the station after spending 156 hours on the ice. We are told that a French team from Dumont D'Orville Station on the Indian Ocean is currently en route to the impact zone.

Fragments of the meteor retrieved from the secondary impact craters indicate that the meteor was predominantly metallic with nickel and iron suspected to be the primary components. This was not, we repeat, not a decaying satellite or rocket of human origin. No remnant of the meteor was evident in the crater. Green ice was at the head of the impact zone and revealed signs of extreme heat where the ice had melted, water pooled and frozen in place. The crater's walls were observed to be unstable and deteriorating, much like the face of a glacier, by calving large sections of ice onto the floor of the crater. Further expeditions to the site should exercise extreme caution in approaching the crater's rim due to this condition.

The expedition, lead by National Science Foundation supervisor, Quinn Wilson, successfully returned to McMurdo Station with only minor injuries from exposure to the harsh environment. Other scientists on the expedition included: Dr. Mark Raulson, MS meteorologist; Drs. Randy Worthington and Pam Laystrom, glaciologists; and Thomas Thorton and Hank Tobias, engineers.

"Hey, we need to name the crater!" Randy said with enthusiasm.

"You're right, our name will stick with it forever, so let's make it a good one," Mark added.

"Of course, we have to call it something. Aren't craters usually named after the person who discovered them or the region of impact? In this case it would be either name Laystrom Crater after me or the Wilkes Land Crater," observed Pam.

"Neither name has any pizzazz! We need a name that will catch the magnitude of the event and the imagination of the public," Mark offered.

"Steady now, people, we have departed from the sciences and started talking public relations. That is not the kind of thing scientists are good at," stated Quinn.

"Well, do you see any PR people here?" Pam asked. "Randy is right! We need a name and we have to come up with it fast. This is our crater and we should name it."

"Okay, what are you suggesting?" asked Mark.

"I don't know …Randy?"

"Me?"

"Yes, it was your idea and you are always working on those crossword puzzles. Give us something to work with."

"Huh …"

As the high winds buffeted the crew trailer, the team unleashed their collective energies and brainstormed. Hank broke out a bottle of Crown Royal that he had hidden for emergency purposes, so the whiskey further loosened their mental processes.

"Forget about it, forget about it! There is just not any place names that we can use," shouted Pam over the six-way discussion among all members in the cab. "I think you should name it after me. I was the first person on the planet to see the asteroid because I was sitting in Quinn's office facing the window. As you know, there aren't many windows at the station and practically no reason to look out during the winter, so it's my meteor and my crater and I want to name it Laystrom Crater …anyone have a problem with that?"

"They name comets after the person who discovers them and hurricanes have women's names. But, meteor impact craters …I don't know," mused Mark.

"How about just calling it the Ice Crater?" volunteered Tom.

"Well, there is the Barringer Crater in Arizona and the Chicxulub Crater in the Yucatan Peninsula. Chad, Africa, has the Aorounga Crater and …" Quinn speculated drawing on some past data source that he had almost forgotten.

"When did you get so smart? You have obviously been holding out on us!" Pam snapped.

"I'm just drawing on knowledge from one of my geography classes a quarter of a century ago. I'm sure all of you had the same course material in geology," Quinn responded.

"Not in my memory banks," said Mark.

"Nor mine!" exclaimed Tom.

"In lieu of a place name, how about an impacted formation? That jives with some of the names," Quinn suggested.

"Yeah, it impacted a billion years of ice," said Mark.

"How about that green pool of ice at the bottom of the crater? I thought that was a very distinctive feature," added Tom.

"Hey, you're right, Tom! That was very noticeable and quite unusual," said Quinn.

"Not many people have seen an ice crater. They deteriorate much more rapidly than a terrestrial impact, as they are extremely ephemeral. This crater will be largely gone by midsummer," Tom said.

"The Ephemeral Green Crater?" Pam put in.

"I'm in favor of Wilkes Plato Crater. We cannot escape the standard geological approach to the identification of this phenomenon. We can use all of the adjectives and description we conjured during these discussions, but the crater will be identified and named after the impact site. So that would be Wilkes Plato Crater, Antarctica," Quinn offered to a now silent crew.

"Hey, I hate to be a spoil sport, but I think we need to get something to eat and rest before the final push into the station. The weather has not cleared, fuel is getting low and we may have to make the run in the wind just to survive," Hank said in his longest speech of the expedition. All eyes were on him as he spoke and the stress was obvious on his face. In the excitement of discovery, they all had taken the logistics of the trip for granted. Now it was time to pay attention to the basics.

Hot soup and stale bread were the order of the day and no one complained. The crew cab was now being buffeted by the strongest winds of the trip and the moan and shrieks of the gusts put everyone's nerves on edge. Quinn radioed the station to let them know the team was holding up on the Plato near the pass. There was considerable static, but the connection was good enough to relay their intent. Everyone settled down in full gear and filled all horizontal space in the cab and the winds blew stronger. To Quinn's surprise, he went to sleep immediately with no dreams whatsoever.

He awoke with a start when a cold blast of air hit his face. Someone had just exited the cab and woke everyone with his departure.

"Somebody shut the damn door," screamed Pam from the bunk.

"That wind froze my nose off! It must be 125° below," complained Randy.

"Well, I'm awake, so who went out?" asked Mark.

"Huh …Hank's not here, so it must have been him checking out the other tractor," replied Quinn.

"What time is it?" Pam asked.

"Time, what is time but an arbitrary quantification of this feeble dimension," said Randy.

"Don't start with me. I can see you've been reading too much Hawkings and Greene," admonished Pam as she peered out of the bunk.

The door flew open and another blast of cold air jolted the cab. Hank stood looking at the crew for a moment, then offered this ultimatum. "We have got to go now, if we hope to make it back to the station under our own power. Our fuel gauge on the lead tractor shows that we have 7 hours of running time before we are dead on the ice. The temperature outside is well below -100° and our survival time would be limited. We could stay here and count on the second cab to keep us warm until a rescue party could arrive. But we don't know how long that would take."

"How high are the winds?" questioned Quinn.

"They have diminished some, but we are still getting gusts of over 50 knots. I won't kid you, no one has ever navigated the pass in these conditions."

"Is it possible?" asked Quinn.

"If it can be done, this crew can do it," replied Hank.

"Oh, crap! We are going to freeze to death and that is not the way I want to go!" Pam moaned.

"Okay, guys, what do the rest of you think?" Quinn asked.

Everyone raised their hand in agreement.

"Okay, Hank! Light the fires and let's get out of here!" commanded Quinn.

"Yes, sir," replied Hank. "Tom, you drive the second tractor and stay on the intercom. I will be going very slow to make sure we are on the path. Let's hope the wind falls and we can see the route."

"I'll be at the wheel in just a few seconds," Tom replied. The next few minutes were a blur of activities, as the tension of the long delay gave way to action and gear was stowed in preparation for the hazardous run down the mountain pass. The crackle of the intercom and the conversation with Hank indicated that the number two tractor was reluctant to start in the cold, but finally came around. Hank was visibly concerned as it came time to start down the mountain.

"We are ready to go! I've made this run a number of times during the summer, but never in this kind of weather. The wind keeps a constant cloud of ice six feet off the ground and makes it difficult to see the trail," exclaimed Hank.

"What is the downside, Hank?" Quinn asked, knowing the answer before he spoke.

"We could lose our traction and slide down the mountain. If the fall did not kill us, we would probably freeze to death before we reached the bottom. At 100+ degrees below zero, our life expectancy would be a couple of hours without the protection of the crew cabs. Not a pleasant thought and if we don't leave now, we would be marooned here out of gas." Hank speculated.

"We trust you, Hank. We all know what is at stake here, so let's get underway!" Quinn announced.

The Transantarctic Mountains rose sharply from the Ross Ice Shelf to 4,000 meters in height. During the summer months, supply caravans regularly navigated the mountain pass en route to the Amundsen-Scott South Pole Station. These supply trains were the main support for the South Pole mission in the transport of heavy equipment and building materials that would be difficult to transport by plane. In the summer, the trail through the pass is well marked and frequently used. During the winter months, ice drifts obscure the trail and the darkness makes travel extremely hazardous, if not impossible.

These facts were well-known and mentally reviewed by the crew, as Hank navigated into the pass while being buffeted by 30 knot winds. The steepness of the slopes reminded the crew that this route would be dangerous. There was silence in both tractors as the vehicles inched down the slope.

Pam broke the silence with a proclamation, "Just keep in mind that I would rather die falling off a mountain than freezing to death for lack of action. Think about the obituary! 'A group of intrepid scientists dies attempting to traverse the Transantarctic Mountains in a winter blizzard.' How cool is that? Does anyone here want to die in bed of old age?"

"Thanks for putting everything in perspective for us, Pam, but if it is okay with you, I would like to defer that spectacular violent death to some point in the distant future ...that is, if you don't mind." Hank said. The exchange brought horse laughs from the second tractor and the tension was broken.

"Hang on to that bravado! We are going to need it," Quinn said.

Foot by foot, Hank navigated down the frozen trail, stopping every few hundred feet to get his bearings. The winds continued to diminish on the lee side of the mountain and slowly the conditions improved. Four hours of jolting down the pass and they were at last on the Ross Ice Shelf and picking up speed.

"I've been told that the gas gauge on these tractors were the most accurate in the industry. Right now I'm hoping that some engineer built some conservation into the system, because we have two hours to travel and only an hour's worth of fuel." Hank observed.

"Steady as she goes, Hank, every foot counts in our favor," Quinn responded.

"What do you mean, calling the tractor a 'she'?" asked Pam.

"Not now, Pam, this is serious." Hank said, not wanting a feminist discussion at the moment.

Quinn called the station and told them the good news that they had traversed the pass and were on the Shelf and heading home. "We are two hours out, but are not sure that we have sufficient fuel to bring us in. Please have a contingency plan worked up, if we have to call for an assist."

"An assist?" responded Roy. "We call that a rescue where I come from."

"Either way, Roy, we will let you know if we need a tow, over and out."

Hank seemed to be energizing the tractor with his intensity. His white knuckles gripped the wheel and he checked the fuel gauge every few seconds. Twelve miles per hour seemed like light speed compared to the slow descent from the pass. With increasing momentum, the small expedition ate up the miles to the station. At long last, the station lights came into view.

"Looks like we are going to make it," Hank said, after a deep sigh of relief.

"We never doubted you, Hank. If there was a way, you would find it and you did. Have we got enough fuel to make the last three or four miles?' asked Quinn.

"We ran out of fuel twenty miles back! I don't know what is keeping this thing running. If I wasn't so happy about this, I would call the manufacturer and complain about the so-called accuracy of the fuel gauge," Hank said with a smile.

"There is time to complain later, but right now, let's get our butts back into the barn."

"I hope no one has gotten into my coffee stash," Pam said after a long and uncharacteristic silence.

"How about that cup of coffee when we get back to the station?" Quinn could not help to ask.

"Yeah ...well, forget it. I've been cooped up with all this testosterone for almost a week and I do not want to even see you guys for the next month. You understand?" she said with good-natured bitterness.

"Huh ...Okay," Quinn relented, as Hank chuckled at the wheel.

Everyone should have a homecoming like the one experienced by the expedition team. It was a June day in the dead of Antarctic winter when the tractors approached a seemingly deserted station. As the doors to the motor pool building opened, the entire 250 residents of the station were waiting. Floodlights and shouts of welcome filled the air as the tractors came to a halt and the teams opened the doors. Someone had put a John Phillip Susa marching medley on the intercom and the effect was festive.

Quinn noticed that the video cameras were still running, so he lingered in the cab until the cameras were following the team. Then he stepped out and quickly mingled with the crowd. A hand on his shoulder caused him to turn and see the somber expression on Roy Lynch's face.

"Welcome back, good buddy! We just got word that the Durmont D' Urville Station lost radio contact with their team. Last GPS transmission put them within thirty-five miles from the crater, when both the radio and GPS went out."

"Oh, no! Didn't they get our warning about the deterioration?" Quinn asked.

"They got it, but I am not sure they took it seriously. They seemed hell bent to get to the crater and make some observations for themselves—just like we were when our team started out for the crater. If you don't mind missing some of the festivities, let's go to the communications room and see if there is any news."

No one but Pam noticed as the two men worked their way through the crowd and exited the garage. As they left, Mark and Pam began their roles as spokespersons by reading the prepared statement and for the next hour, they answered questions that had been radioed to the station by the world news media. It was their moment in the spotlight. No one missed Quinn and that was the way he preferred it.

Once in the communications room, Roy contacted the French team's director via shortwave radio. "Durmont D'Urville, Durmont D'Urville, this is McMurdo Station. Over."

Sssssth ...crackle, "Durmont D'Urville Station here. Please go ahead."

"We wanted to report that our expedition has successfully returned from the crater. What is the status of your team? Over."

"We have received no word from the expedition and fear the worst. There has been no radio, GPS, or transponder signal from them for the past twenty hours. May we speak to someone on you expedition about the conditions they experienced at the crater? Over."

"I have Quinn Wilson, the expedition leader, here with me and I'll put him on."

"Quinn Wilson here, how can I help?"

"Welcome back, Mr. Wilson! We have followed your progress with great interest. We received your warning about the crater and passed it on to Major Dumas. However, our last contact with him was 35 miles from the lat-long bearings your team transmitted. We fear that he had yet to employ due caution due to his distance from the crater. Over."

"We observed a number of rim fissures and calving while at the crater. Some major fissures were observed one-half mile of the rim. The conditions seemed to be worsening as we departed; but there was nothing that would have indicated a problem two miles from the rim wall. Over."

"Can you describe the fissures you observed? Over."

"The walls of the crater were almost vertical and the fissures were much like those occurring on a glacier head, where it meets the ocean when the ice fractures eventually calve away from the ice flow. The ones we observed covered very large areas, enough to cause us to move an additional half-mile back from the crater for safety reasons. Over."

"Can you tell us more about the secondary impact craters you reported? Over."

"There were numerous secondary impact craters, some as large as 100 to 200 yards—excuse me—meters across and 10 to 20 meters deep. However, we did not observe any fissures around these smaller secondary craters."

"Were these secondary impact craters easily observed and avoided in transiting the area?"

"At slow speeds and by using the spotlights, they were easy to spot and avoid."

"Were there any unusual phenomena in the area that you have not reported?"

"I'm not sure what you mean, but the answer is no. All observations indicated that this was an impact crater from a large iron and nickel meteor. It was unusual only in its size. At an estimated 2.3 kilometers long, we believe it is the largest crater experienced in modern time. In a few hours, we should be able to transmit photographs and survey data that may assist in your recovery effort."

"Thank you. The photographs would be appreciated ...but we are not sure there will be a recovery effort. If we do not hear from the team soon, it may be spring before we can dispatch a recovery team. We fear that conditions are too hazardous to send a rescue team. Over."

"Please keep us informed and let us know if there is anything we can do to help. McMurdo Station, over and out," Quinn said with a heavy heart.

The Antarctic community is always ready to help anyone in distress. Much like mariners of old, they would go to extremes to help anyone in need and expected that same treatment regardless of nationality. The thoughts of someone stranded without the possibility of rescue was very disturbing, especially when you have just spent a week on the ice. Still, no rescue was possible from McMurdo, since it would take a week to launch another expedition to the crater.

Quinn found the team in the mess hall enjoying a hot meal. Their moment in the spotlight was short-lived and it was time to settle back into the workday patterns of the station. Quinn told them about the French team.

"Wow, I'm still too close to it. One wrong turn and it could have been us," noted Pam.

"You say they're not planning a rescue mission?" Tom asked.

"Apparently not."

"Well, I'll volunteer," said Hank. "Just get the tractor gassed up and re-supplied and I'm ready to go."

"That's pretty big of you, Hank. I guess if anyone is qualified to navigate the crater again, it would be you."

"Just give me the word and I'll start the preparations," Hank added as he left to tend to a neglected physical facility problem that had come up in his absence.

Hot coffee sounds real good, Quinn thought, as he eyed the cafeteria line. It was nice to have a choice and everything's hot.

The team was departing as he reached the table. Mark had another news conference with CNN. Pam was doing a video link with a European television consortium. Randy was anxious to get to his computer and run some statistical analyses of the crater. He had also enlisted Tom's assistance in conducting some water quality analyses of the ice samples collected from the ejecta blankets around the secondary craters.

Quinn sat and enjoyed his lunch by himself. While it was nice to have the fellowship of other scientists, it was also very nice to be out of the cramped crew cab and have some solitude.

A jingle of his satellite phone brought him back to reality. Alex Reager was on the line welcoming him back to civilization.

"I heard you were back and had sent pictures your team had taken. All pretty impressive, Quinn. I assume you have heard about the missing French team?" asked Alex.

"Yes, I spoke to the D'Urville Station 15 minutes ago and offered our assistance on the search party. Hank Tobias wants to launch a rescue party now," Quinn added.

"I wanted to let you know that we have repositioned one of our polar satellites for a better look at the area. Even though it is in the polar night, our infrared can pick up some images."

"What do the images show, Alex?"

"We are seeing a rapidly decaying impact zone. Just as you reported, the calving has increased. We noted some residual heat at the head of the crater. We think the meteor was hot enough to melt the ice and form a lake before it froze over. That makes sense, but we are not seeing any temperature zones or spikes now."

"Where do we go from here?" asked Quinn.

"The glaciologists are eager to analyze all the data from the expedition, including things like the ice samples for trace metals, the onboard spectrographs and Geiger Counters. We need to see if anything surfaces. After that, we just wait out the winter and look at the site in the spring."

"Any thoughts about a rescue mission for the French team?"

"We will honor any request for assistance we receive from the French. As I mentioned, we spoke with them just 15 minutes ago and they are still trying to contact their team on the radio. If we were to launch a rescue mission from here, the earliest we could be there is three days and that may be too late. The French have the best chance of reaching their team from their station." Quinn added.

"Keep me informed, especially if we get a request for a rescue mission. On a personal note before we lose our satellite connection, how is your new boat coming along?" asked Alex.

Taking his mind off all that happened the past ten days took effort on Quinn's part. "Oh, my boat …I don't know! I haven't thought about it very much for the last couple of weeks. I've not even checked my emails to see if there is a message from Archer Marine. I'm sure it is in good hands and will be ready when I get back to Sydney. Are you still going to come down and sail with me sometime?"

"You can count on it. Thanks for the offer. I plan to work your butt off, as soon as you stop hiding out on the ice. I can guarantee that any assignments I give you will be in a warmer climate than the one you're in now. Good talking to you, Quinn."

"Same here, Alex. Warm would be very nice. There's only two months until spring. Keep that in mind. McMurdo Station out."

Mark and Pam took their expedition spokesperson roles very seriously. The request for interviews poured into the station for weeks. They spent extended periods of time in the media center doing radio interviews and video conferences with the media. Mark even did a technical conference presentation to the British Geological Society in London, a notable career achievement.

Pam, in true professional fashion, was busy writing grant proposals to study the impact zone in more detail. It was this pursuit that brought her to Quinn's office late one afternoon.

"Quinn, I want your opinion on this grant application I have been working on. I am seeking an NSF grant to study the impact zone and obtain some core borings of the meteor impact crater."

"That sounds ambitious. What are you proposing?"

"There is a possibility that the meteor is still partially intact and I think it would be a good—no—a great opportunity to investigate it and the impact zone at the same time. Actually, it's like two expeditions operating side by side. One would concentrate on the impact zone, ejecta blanket, and secondary craters, while the second expedition would drill at the head of the crater in search of the meteor. We would document the entire expedition as the official scientific record of the event. It would be a comprehensive analysis of the impact, size of the meteor, trajectory, site conditions, and composite samples of the meteor itself. What do you think?"

"Well, it's definitely needed. All you have to do is look at the amount of scientific and public interest we've had in the event. What about the logistics and timing? Would the expedition be conducted in the spring? How big of an expedition would be needed and where will you get a drill rig to do the coring? My first impression is that it is too comprehensive to pull off in one season."

"So, I have your support, if I can answer those questions to your satisfaction?"

"Not so fast …in concept, yes, I support your proposal. In practice, however, it has big logistic problems that we would need to talk through. I can't speak for the NSF in Washington, as this would take a substantial portion of their annual budget at the expense of other research projects."

"Quinn, it *should* take most of their budget! An event of this magnitude does not happen that often and if we don't make a commitment, we will either miss some important scientific finding or concede our role to the French or the Russians. You can bet they are having the same conversation there," she argued with some force.

"All good points to consider, Pam, but I am wondering if you have a draft for me to look over yet?"

"Not yet, but I should have a draft ready by Friday. Oh, what day is it today?"

"I think it is Wednesday. It would definitely help if the sun would come up and provide a division to the night. Then we could figure out what day it is."

"Okay, Friday, I'll bring a draft over for your review. Would you like that cup of coffee now?" she asked hopefully.

"Are you talking about a cup down at the cafeteria or your private stash?"

"I'm talking about my Starbucks!"

"Huh …honestly, I don't know what to say!"

"It's just a cup of coffee, Quinn."

"That thought occurred to me the last time you asked and apparently I was wrong then. So I'm going to pass this time, but thanks for the offer."

"Suit yourself. I'll see you, Friday," she said as she pushed indignantly from her chair and headed for the door.

As she left, Quinn could not help but think how much he would really like a good cup of Starbucks coffee and some good conversation. Was she being friendly or was she offering a bribe?

Roy Lynch stuck his head in the door seconds after Pam left. "Hello, good buddy! Was Dr. Laystrom in here hawking her research grant or was this a personal visit?"

"As a matter of fact, she was talking research," Quinn responded.

"It's just like her to be on the ball, where there is some grant money involved. What is she proposing?"

"Roy …I do not think that I am at liberty to discuss her proposal with you. After all, next year's NSF grants will be competitively awarded. Why don't you talk to her directly? I thought you two were friends?"

"You're probably right. I'll talk to her and see if there is a piece of the action that I can help with," he stammered and then added, "I stopped by to give you an update on the French expedition. I was by the communications center and overhead a discussion. There is still no sign of the French expedition. They did dispatch a rescue team and followed the same coordinates, but as of yet, they've not found a trace of the team. By now, they would have exhausted all their fuel and supplies, so they are assuming the team is lost."

"Sorry to hear that. Did the rescue mission approach the crater's rim?"

"They made it to the point of our last communications with the expedition and were nowhere near the rim. If the rim had decayed further, it still has not reached two miles from the impact zone."

"So …the last GPS coordinates were on open ice?"

"Apparently so!"

"Huh …no secondary craters in the vicinity?"

"None were mentioned in their communication. The route was along a relatively level portion of the ice cap, so there should not have been any crevasses. If the French are interested, let's coordinate a radio call to the station and talk to them in more detail. I think it would be good to have Hank and Mark sit in on the call."

"Okay, I'll give them a call and see if we can set it up. By the way, did Pam offer you a cup of Starbucks coffee?"

"Why do you ask?"

"Ha, ha, just curious that's all. A cup of Starbucks coffee is worth its weight in gold. You accepted, of course?"

"Let me know when the call is set up."

Quinn turned to his computer as Roy left the room and dashed out a message to Robert Murey at the NSF headquarters in Washington. It read:

Rmurey@nsf.com:

The scientists here at the station are developing grant applications for research on the impact crater. Please advise me on the role I should take in this process. I am being asked for advice on the research program and available funding. Also how do we address competing proposals? We will probably see more than one application for the same funding.

Quinn Wilson
NSF McMurdo Station

Quinn glanced at his watch and did a mental calculation of the time in Washington DC. *Probably 3:45 AM*, he thought. *I will not get a response until tomorrow morning at the earliest.*

Quinn found Mark in the gym, hitting golf balls up against a net. The familiar sounds of golf seemed strangely out of place here at the station. Mark was too engrossed to stop his practice while he talked to Quinn.

Whack … "Being away from the golf course is the hardest part of these winters—I miss it terribly. What's up?" Mark asked between swings.

"The French rescue team has returned to base. They had no luck finding the expedition. The strange thing is that they approached the last transmitted GPS coordinates and were nowhere near the rim. So we have a mystery. We are trying to schedule a conference call to the French team and I would like you to sit in," Quinn explained.

"Sure, count me in. When is it scheduled?"

"Roy is setting it up. I'll let you know the time."

Quinn left Mark and heard another whack as he left the gym.

While heading back to his office, Quinn found Randy and Pam in the computer center.

"Come look what Randy has come up with," said Pam.

Since their return from the crater, Randy had been engrossed in data analysis. No one had been paying much attention to him, because he always sat mumbling at his computer screen doing statistical analysis. The difference this time is that he had been modeling the meteor's impact.

"Based on the data I have been able to collect, I can project the meteor's size and angle of impact. It entered the atmosphere at a 37° to 39° angle from the southwest. This angle gave it a prolonged exposure to the atmosphere, causing it to burn away approximately half of its bulk."

"You used the word, 'approximately,'" gasped Pam in disbelief.

"Yes, Pam, I have not completed the analysis, so it's approximate at this time. Don't give me any crap about my work until I'm finished—okay!" Randy retorted in half jest. "As I was saying, the meteor lost half its bulk on entry, and then fragmented due to gravitational and atmospheric pressures at about ten miles above the earth. This tells me that it was a very solid piece of rock. Had it been a comet, it would have dissolved into a billion pieces. Instead, we have a couple of hundred relatively small fragments separated from the main body. We observed the resulting secondary craters in the field, and luckily obtained a fragment from one of the craters," Randy noted, pointing to a dark brown chunk of rock in a specimen jar on his bookshelf.

"Now here is the interesting part. At the point of impact, the meteor was as big as a truck. Had it entered the atmosphere at a sharper angle, it would not have burned away as much bulk and would have been as large as an 18-wheeler, say 5 to 6 tons. I'm working on the tonnage and will have more for you later on, but applying a logarithmic function to the size and angle, I can tell you that for each degree of declination, the impact would have increased 10-fold! Had it come through the atmosphere at a shorter 60° angle, we would have experienced an impact equal to a 50-megaton nuclear bomb. So, in other words, we lucked out, with the longer burn the 37° angle of descent gave us!"

"Now at the point of impact, I'm working on a model that will tell us how many cubic yards or tons of ice was vaporized, based on the angle of impact, size, and the projected temperature. This vaporized material is in addition to the ice that was thrown up into the ejecta blanket we observed in the field. Right now I can say the vaporized ice was on the order of 25- to 35-million cubic yards. When ice goes instantly to vaporized steam, it generates a hydrothermal explosion that would exacerbate the actual impact. That vaporized material refroze rather quickly in the -100° temperatures and most of it fell back to the ice cap within a 100-mile radius, predominantly downwind of the impact site. However, I think about 10 to 20 percent of the ice reached the stratosphere and is probably still in suspension. Some materials may have made it back into outer space. The impact was that powerful! This material will remain in the stratosphere and be circulated into convergent zones worldwide. This means more moisture at higher altitudes, more sun reflection back to space, and less sunlight reaching the surface. In other words, it will change the world weather patterns for a number of years to come."

"The good news is ...You do want to hear the good news, don't you?" he chided.

"I hope it is *really* good news," responded Quinn.

"The good news is that the meteor impacted ice in Antarctica in the middle of winter!"

"Okay, tell me something we don't already know."

"Had it impacted land, the resulting plume of soil and debris would now be circulating the globe! It would obscure the sun and significantly reduce solar radiation. We are talking about a major disaster here. We would be talking about major climatic change for decades to come instead of changes in weather patterns for three to five years. Isn't that good news?" Roy said with a smile.

"I still need to digest this a little more before I'm as happy as you are. Are you putting together a report on this modeling effort? Also, have you had any correspondence with some of the leading climatologists stateside?"

"Not yet, but that should be the next step after I have finished the model," Randy responded.

"Contact them now. I am willing to bet they are in the process of doing the same forecast modeling and you have far more information than they do. Okay?"

"You're the boss!

"Pam, after hearing what Randy had to say, are you sure your proposal is going in the right direction?" Quinn asked.

"Yeah, that is a good point ...did you tell Roy to talk to me about my proposal? He tells me that he needs to be the project manager for the work I am proposing," retorted Pam.

"Well, he was asking me about your proposal and I suggested that he talk to you. I did not want to give him any details without your knowledge."

"That is good to hear. I thought you were part of the 'Good Ol' Boy' network trying to steal my work."

"Not me, Pam. Your work will speak for itself. We are trying to get a conference call set up with the French station. Do you want to sit in on the call?"

"Oh, thanks for asking. Roy was acting like it was his idea and we were not invited."

"Hmm ...am I detecting a little tension among the scientists?"

"No ...it's just that Roy is an SOB and he pisses me off!"

"Okay, if that's all it is, we should be fine. I would like to have you and Mark in on the conference call. Randy, your information is very interesting, but I think the French team is more interested in finding their lost team. So, can you stick with the modeling and get in touch with the climatologists stateside to discuss your findings?"

"I'll do it. Tell the French for me that I am sorry for their loss and we are here to help if needed."

"I'll do that, thanks."

Quinn stopped by his office and found an email from NSF:

QUINN:

> A grant application to investigate the impact crater will be well-received here at NSF. Work with the scientists as much as you can to get a defensible application together. Most of the top scientists are already on the continent, so a single unified application would be preferred, over a number of competing proposals. Funding should be ample, given the interest in the impact shown by all levels of government. Be advised that other scientists have expressed interest and are preparing grant proposals. Most are from the astrosciences with little or no experience on the ice.
>
> Get them to work together if you can. We have tried before and failed, so good luck. Also remind them that this research effort should not interrupt any ongoing programs. On many of these, we cannot have a break in the data.
>
> Robert Murey
> NSF Director

Later that day the team gathered in the communication center and contacted Durmont D'Urville Station.

"Durmont D'Urville, Durmont D'Urville, this is McMurdo Base calling. Come in, please," Roy chanted into the transmitter microphone.

"D'Urville Station here. Go ahead, please," came a tired-sounding voice with only a touch of French accent.

"This is Quinn Wilson, NSF supervisor at McMurdo Station. I am here with the members of the McMurdo expedition. We all offer our sincere regrets over the loss of Major Dumas and your expedition. We thought it might help to contact you to discuss the conditions and findings of our expedition, in the hopes it may help with the recovery effort. McMurdo Station out."

"Thank you for your concern Mr. Wilson. I am here with Major Douyon who led the rescue mission. Perhaps your input would help us resolve the mystery. D'Urville Station out."

"Major Douyon, may we ask about the conditions you encountered near the crater? McMurdo Station out."

"Major Douyon here. I was in command of the four-man rescue team that departed the D'Urville Station at 1300 Zulu four days ago. Travel conditions were optimal during the entire trip with light winds and temperatures no lower than -30° F. We observed an unusually thick layer of fine snow and ice along our travel route, but it was passable and offered no constraints to our progress. We followed the continuous GPS readout recorded from the expedition, slowing to just over one kilometer per hour as we approached the last recorded coordinates of their transmission. Transect time was 13 hours. We reached the site and observed nothing out of the ordinary. No crater, secondary impact zones or fissures. After an extended search of the area, we continued northward to the crater. There we observed the ejecta blanket and mounds of up to 30 meters in height, as well as the fissures along the edge of the crater that you had warned us about. This section of the crater had not decayed substantially, so we could approach the rim. We took a number of photographs, but did not observe any signs that the expedition team had been in the vicinity. D'Urville Station out."

"Major Douyon, how high were the ice drifts you encountered en route? McMurdo Station out."

"They ranged from half meters to 3 or 3.5 meters in height. We traveled on hard-packed ice and easily avoided the higher drifts and penetrated the low drifts without slowing our progress. D'Urville Station out."

"Just before our call, we reviewed a model of the impact that revealed a plume of ice ejected from the crater, approximately 80 percent precipitating in the first 100 miles from the point of impact," Quinn explained. "The remaining 20 percent of the ice would have reached the stratosphere and will circle the globe, causing broad weather changes. McMurdo out."

"Yes, yes, that does explain the loosely packed ice along the route. D'Urville Station out."

"That deposition is the only plausible lead we have

encountered that would explain the loss of the expedition without a trace. McMurdo out."

"Can you elaborate on this theory? D'Urville Station out."

"We know that there is a blanket of unconsolidated ejecta covering a thousand square miles with isolated piles reaching up to 3.5 meters or more. We also know from our expedition that there are numerous secondary impacts in the area. Now our two expeditions approached the crater from different angels. We observed the secondary craters and had to navigate around them. You observed the ejecta blanket at the head of the crater. We would speculate that there are secondary impacts in your area that were rapidly filled with ice and snow. We think that your expedition inadvertently drove into one of these craters. Once they were under the weight of the ice, it was like an avalanche. They were unable to exit their vehicle or extract themselves from the crater. The diesel would have stalled for lack of air and the team ....you can imagine the final outcome, with limited air and little or no heat .... McMurdo out."

After a long silence, "Your theory is plausible ...we are unaware of any secondary craters, but you are correct in saying that they must be out there if you observed them on the other side of the crater. D'Urville Station out."

"Have you plans to continue the search? McMurdo out."

"We are a small station, with only 40—excuse me—only 37 men now, and limited resources. Unfortunately, we have exhausted our surplus winter fuel supply and will not be returning to the site until the spring. We ...have given up hope of finding survivors, since their fuel and resources would have been exhausted a week ago. The loss of the team is a tragic chapter in the history of this station. D'Urville Station out."

"Once again, our condolences to you and the families of the missing team. We will research our records and contact agencies that may have been monitoring the area and let you know if we uncover any evidence. In the meantime, if we can be of any further assistance, please give us a call. McMurdo Station out."

The team sat in silence for some time after the transmission. The Antarctic was a hostile environment and the few hundred winter residence of the continent formed a close bond. So the loss of three French team members was felt strongly by all the McMurdo Station.

"Randy, were there any satellites over the continent that may provide some evidence of the French expedition?" Quinn asked.

"I'll check with the Energy Research and Development Administration. Perhaps ERDA has further details."

"Okay and I will check with the NGIA."

"Who is the NGIA?"

"The National Geo-Spatial Intelligence Agency or NGIA."

"I've never heard of them. Will you coordinate with them?"

"Sure, let's meet on this tomorrow morning and see if we have any additional information to pass on to the French."

Quinn returned to his office and emailed Alex Reager.

Alex:

We just communicated with the leader of the French rescue mission. Their rescue team has returned to base and found no evidence of the expedition team. They have asked for our assistance. Can you tell me if there was any satellite coverage over the continent a week after the meteor impact? We are looking for any clues regarding the disappearance of the French expedition from Dumont O'Urville Station. The date they lost contact was June 26th, a clear moonless night. The expedition's GPS, radio and environmental monitoring system went out. Therefore, any satellite images and/or infrared heat signatures could be very helpful.

Quinn Wilson
NSF McMurdo Station

With that email Quinn was ready to call it a night. It had been a long day and mental demands had taken their toll. When Quinn reached his room, Mark was already asleep and snoring loudly. Still Quinn was asleep by the time his head hit the pillow. His troubled sleep conjured up some dark dreams.

He was alone back on the hot African savannah, in full military gear, running through the intense heat, dry sand, and brown scrub, exchanging fire with insurgents. He could see the faces of the boys as they fired their AK47s. They showed fear as if being chased by a monster. They should have been on a little league baseball or soccer team, rather than brandishing weapons on a field of battle. They would fire their weapons indiscriminately and Quinn would follow with precision shots, dropping them one at a time and in his dream he was enjoying it like a Sunday outing. The images and thoughts awoke him with a start. He realized he was sweating and a little disoriented from the power of the dream. It had been so vivid! Why was he dreaming this? How could he be taking lives so casually, even in a dream? Those boys were seeking a better life, only to have encountered a mass murderer in their path. Yes, he thought, under any other circumstances he would be considered a murderer, responsible for taking a dozen, maybe two dozen lives. He was stirred from his anguish by Mark.

"Hey, are you okay? It sounds like you're fighting a battle over there!"

"I was—sorry about that. I was apparently having a bad dream or some form of post-combat trauma."

"Combat? When were you in combat?"

"A few months back, I was involved in skirmishes with some insurgents in Africa. Once again, I'm really sorry about waking you. I think I'll take a short walk. You go back to sleep." Quinn pulled on his jump suit and shoes and left the room. The station never really slept, but it was quiet in the hallways and the mess hall was empty. Slowly, he was able to wrestle his mind out of Africa and back to the Antarctica over a stale cup of very hot coffee. He could not believe how much his life had changed these past months. He wondered where his wife was and what she was doing. Was she okay? He missed her. How was his daughter doing? He missed her too. So much of his former life was out of his control, leaving him feeling disconnected. After a lonely cup of coffee, he meandered down the corridor to his office. The computer and the satellite link were his only connection to the outside world.

There was the message he had expected from Alex:

Walter! Walter!

Please stand by to receive a series of images in a zipped GIS file, via satellite link. These images containing all the information we have on the Wilkes Land area of Antarctica. Unfortunately, there were no satellites over Antarctica at the time of impact. We are sending the most current photos of the area taken at 'last light' over the Continent. We are also forwarding the infrared photos taken over the past week. We repositioned the Polar Explorer satellite after the impact to see what we could find. The first series appear to be obscured from the impact plume. The later series are somewhat clearer and could be useful. We may even have an infrared signature from the French team just hours before their disappearance. See Photograph 6 and let me know what you think.

By the way, we are damn lucky to have you down there. Having an asset on the continent puts NGIA at the forefront of discussions here in Washington. For a young intelligence agency, that is not a bad position to be in. The CIA is calling us for data and status reports. The bastards are paranoid and have not given up on the conspiracy theory that some foreign power was testing a weapon of mass destruction. So keep us in the loop.

Alex Reager,
Director NGIA

Quinn picked up the telephone after reading Alex's note and called Randy Worthington's extension to leave a message. He was surprised when he answered. "Randy, we have zipped images coming in from NGIA. Can we receive them on your machine?"

"Sure can, but tell me again who is NGIA and why are they screwing around on my continent? In regards to my computer,

I can make this machine sing Dixie while scratching its crotch! Just give me the link and get the hell out of my way!"

By 1500 Zulu, Randy had retrieved the aerial photographs and zeroed in on the crater area. As expected, there was little infrared imagery on the aerial taken one week after the impact. The crater itself loomed as a dark shadow against the white ice field. Quinn was not surprised when Randy started his data analysis.

"This confirms our observation! It's a damn big hole! My calculations make it about 3,584 acres or about 1,500 hectors. The entire impact field is roughly 2.5 miles in diameter—much larger than the field estimates we made during the expedition. Definitely, we are dealing with the largest impact crater in modern times. There are several hundred secondary impact craters visible. I have not done all of the calculations, but they range in size from mere dimples to hundreds of acres in size. Almost all the impacts are trailing the meteor's flight path, with the exception of a cluster on the right flank here." Randy gestured as he and Quinn poured over the imagery.

"The ejecta blanket is very large and difficult to define. I will have to spend some time with the imagery to define its extent. Of course, I cannot tell if there are secondary impact craters at the head of the impact zone because of the blanket, but it looks like there should be none or relatively few, based on what we can see on the satellite images."

"That fits with what Pam and I saw. We were in the station office near one of the only windows in the center when the asteroid entered the atmosphere. I recall that it was burning very evenly with almost no fragmentation when we saw it. But it was probably in our field of vision for only a few seconds," Quinn observed. "What about the areas between the crater and the Dumont D'Urville Station? Let's see if we can plot the route of their expedition and see if there are any anomalies along its path. I'll send a message to the French telling them what we have and what we are looking for."

"Okay, but keep in mind that these are satellite images and they are not rectified or registered to known fixed points. As a matter of reference, there are damn few known points on the ice sheet. You do recall that it is a relatively unpopulated and seldom traveled region of the world?"

"Randy, are you okay? Of course I remember that we are in Antarctica in the middle of winter. I also recall that there are only about 1,500 people on the continent at this time. Keep in mind that we are dealing with a major event and there is a lost expedition we are trying to help locate. So detailed sciences aside, we need to do the best we can to define the event and hopefully help the French in their search. Okay?"

"Yeah, I guess I am getting a little antsy. I didn't mean to lecture. Thanks."

"I'll meet you back here in ...say four hours. If you see Mark and Pam, please ask them to join us. I'm sure they would like to see the imagery."

Pam was waiting in Quinn's office with the latest draft of her proposal when he walked through the door. "Good morning! You're up early." Quinn volunteered.

"I am not up early! I was up all night working on this proposal and I want to talk to you about it, while it is still fresh on my mind. I ran into Mark on the way down here. He tells me you had a rough night yourself. What is this about Africa and being in combat with insurgents?"

Shaking his head he said, "Things really get around fast here. I had a rough night last night, that's all."

"Would you like to talk about it?"

"Thanks for the offer, but no! Not to change the subject, but before we get started, what is going on with Randy? I just left him and he was ...about to climb the walls. Has he been drinking way too much coffee or what?"

"What did you mean about not wanting to change the subject?"

There was silence on Quinn's part.

"Okay, I get it, you don't want to talk about it. As to the other, don't pay any attention to Randy. He gets that way every winter. It's just the polar anxiety that comes from the confinement here and the lack of sunlight. He'll be okay."

"Well, that's what I thought. I know he is a super-intelligent guy, but it sure looked like he was ready to blow a fuse. I wouldn't be giving him anymore Starbucks coffee."

"Oh no, my Starbucks coffee is only for special people."

"Huh …okay, what have you got for me to look at?"

Pam began organizing a stack of paper in her lap when Roy Lynch knocked on the door.

"Good morning, good buddy! Oh, I didn't know you were having a meeting. Say, if you two are going to be talking about the proposal on the impact crater, do you mind if I sit in?"

Pam stopped rustling her papers and shot Quinn a look that would stop a train. It was obvious that she did not want a third party in these discussions.

"While I have both of you here, I wanted to let you know that Randy is downloading some satellite imagery on the crater from the NGIA. Can you both be available at 1100 to review the data? In regards to this meeting, Roy, I think it best for Pam and me to meet alone. We have a number of things to talk about …okay?"

"Oh sure, good buddy. I didn't mean to intrude. I'll see you at 1100," Roy replied after a rather exaggerated smile towards Pam.

"That son of a bitch, I could scratch his eyes out. He has been skulking around the center all night trying to see my work."

"It seems that Randy is not the only one suffering from long polar nights."

"Don't you start on me! Roy is a snake and is trying to weasel in on my proposal and I resent it. I know that you two are great buddies and I am only a female in need of assistance from you big strong guys with your deep voices …."

"Pam, slow down. Roy and I are not exactly friends. We work together, just like you and I. Don't assume we are fast friends, just because we are both male. I still have some ability to measure a person's character, capability and intentions. So let's talk about your proposal."

"Okay …okay, I may have overreacted a little to that intrusion. Sorry for the outburst. But I still think he's a bastard!"

"Yes, I think I understand your point. What have you got?"

"I have roughed out the proposal to investigate the impact crater. It will include extensive time in the field this summer. I broke it down into three parts that include a survey of site conditions, an analysis of the ice and debris collected, and a deep boring to obtain remnants of the meteor."

"Did you think through the logistics? We would need to explore logistics, like crew quarters, tractors, drill rigs, snowplows, and snowmobiles. Then there is the human component. How many scientists and support personnel will be needed? Also how do we support them for an extended period of time in this remote area? You will need to include shelter, fuel, food, water, sanitation and transportation. Also we can't interrupt the transportation of supplies to the South Pole. Most of the equipment will be needed for those supply trips."

"Slow down. Now it is you who is going too fast. I'm trying to define the scientific objectives of the expedition. Then we can give it to someone like Hank to fill in the blanks on the logistic and besides, who is this 'we' you speak of? I am the scientist. You are administration. I will be on the ice. You will be in the office …if you even come back for another year."

"Regardless of who goes where, it will be a team effort. Call it a collective 'we' okay? Now, getting back to the scientific objectives, how would you define them?"

"The objective of the program is to investigate and characterize a large meteor impact on the Wilkes Land area of Antarctica. As we talked earlier, this is the largest impact crater in modern times. It needs to be thoroughly investigated. My proposal defines a program to do just that."

"Have you talked further with Randy about the modeling of the impact area that he is doing?"

"Well, not since we spoke yesterday."

"You need to! The modeling information he is developing quantifies the amount of material displaced by the impact and the volume that is deposited in the ejecta blanket versus the volume that remains in suspension in the upper atmosphere. Now that is a critical area of research. You know, Pam, I just thought of something."

"What?"

"You and I may have been the only people on the planet to visually see that meteor enter the atmosphere. There are only a few windows on the entire continent and we were sitting next to one of them. I was telling someone just yesterday that it seemed to be burning very uniformly. You don't remember seeing any fragments in the tail, do you?"

"That is strange—I never thought of it that way. I guess you're right. We may have been the only ones to see it. There were no reports of visual sightings from other stations were there? I remember that it looked rounded like a basketball, but very large in size."

"What color was the flame? Do you remember?"

"The color of the flame …let me think. As I recall, it was orange, trailing to blue against the black sky."

"Do you recall the way it was burning and whether there was any fragmentation?"

"Oh, I have to process those thoughts! What with the expedition and the busy week doing interviews since we got back, I have not thought much about what we saw. It only lasted for a few seconds."

"Yes, but you saw it for a few seconds longer than I did. I first saw the light …and the look in your face before I turned around and saw the asteroid. See what you can remember. There may be some clues to its makeup. Sorry, we seem to have gotten off the subject of your proposal."

"I guess I need to touch base with Randy about his modeling. As you say, the modeling will be a significant part of the research."

"Well, I have him busy right now, downloading those satellite images. We need to meet with him in a couple of hours. Why don't you leave me your proposal and let me read through it and we can discuss it further after we look at the satellite images?"

"Before you read it, remember it is a draft. It is based on field recon of the impact site. What you just told me about Randy's work sounds very interesting and maybe should be part of the effort. I will talk to Mark and Randy about it."

"What about talking to Roy?"

"You know how I feel about him!"

"He is still one of the most prominent Antarctic researchers I know. Don't you think there is a role for him here?

"Yeah, like when hell freezes over!"

"I think that pretty well describes our current situation. It was 50 below zero in the station's weather report this morning."

"So, you think I can't handle it!" Pam said defensively.

"No, I did not say that. I think we need an open and comprehensive discussion of the objectives with all knowledgeable individuals. This will be a one-time research effort and we need to get it right. That includes research and the logistics to get it done."

"And you think Roy can do that?"

"I think we need as much experience and as many hands as we can get to develop a feasible program and conduct the research. Roy may be a part of that. Just keep an open mind about it would you? I am not going to talk to Roy about any research until you are ready, but remember, we need a defensible unified approach to get a grant. Also there is one other thing."

"What?"

"I got an email from Robert Murey at NSF headquarters. He recommends a comprehensive application from the scientists here at the center rather than competing and overlapping applications. He also indicated that ample funding was available for the right approach. I think his comments establish the playing field for next year's program. Now I don't want to be a dictator, but can we make a unified application work?"

"I see! You are pushing for a comprehensive approach, with me being a good little team player."

"Comprehensive, yes …the size of the team and the role played by each is to be determined."

"So, all this work I did last night was for nothing! I just throw it away and let someone else make the decisions …is that what you are saying?"

"Pam, I think you are further along than anyone on the

approach. Who best to direct the preparation of the grant application? You know you're going to need researchers. You cannot do it all by yourself. Who is better than the team here at the station? I don't know who should lead at this time, but you should be in charge of the scientific effort. Will you at least think about a broader program?"

"Well, I don't like it but will think about it. I don't want to get in the way of the precious grant funds."

"I suggest we—you—call a meeting to discuss a comprehensive approach to the study. I would call it myself, but my role is to review and recommend approval of next year's research program. I cannot lead or even participate in the development of the program. I guess you all could go with separate applications, which I would have to review and recommend one over the other. That will be my job and I'll do it based on the scientific merits of the proposals. It is up to you researchers to decide what to do."

"Okay, okay, I get your drift. You want us to team up and provide one proposal."

"It's your choice. But, I think the impact crater will need all the talent available. You still have the option to go separately, if you wish. NSF tells me that they encourage a comprehensive approach, but admit that they typically get competing proposals. They think this is a very important and time-sensitive research topic and they have ample funding. So, the option is yours."

"So you won't even attend a meeting if we have one?"

"Yes, I will attend. I just cannot lead. I would probably state my role and that of the NSF at the start, so that we know what the playing field looks like."

"That's a bummer! I'll talk to Mark …."

"Don't forget about Roy."

"Yeah, I'll get with Roy, Mark, Randy, Marisa, Tom and even Hank and see if we can't agree to team up on this proposal."

"Remember, NSF does not want to interrupt ongoing research programs to concentrate efforts on the impact. Also, their message hinted that there was considerable interest in research from scientists off the continent. So, you can expect some competition."

"I remember you said that. Yes, I know there's always competition. I'd better get going."

It was now August at the station and the first faint glow of sunlight appeared on the horizon. Everyone was talking about it and beating a path to the few windows in the science center to see this phenomenon. Quinn was amazed at how beautiful it was. This was more than just the return of the sun. It was hope, inspiration, passion …life itself returning to the world …, his world. Soon aircraft would be returning to the station. New people, supplies and news would be circulating—it would be a celebration. It was almost time to start the next episode in his life, so he had better check on his boat to make sure it would be ready when he returned to Sydney.

There had been a series of cheerful and reassuring messages from Meg Archer about the restoration and commissioning work being done on his boat. Having owned a boat for years, Quinn was not surprised at the additional repairs that surfaced during the commissioning. Meg had regularly sent notes about the mast and boom being replaced, sails being delivered, the diesel engine and water maker installed, the stuffing box on the drive shaft replaced with the new oil-filled type. She also had recommended that the cutlass bearing be replaced and there was a leak around the starboard chain plate and forward hatch that needed repair. Then she recommended that the alcohol stove be replaced with a combination electric/propane system for a token price of only $2,300. The bright work was being attended to by the top guy in the yard, but the interior wood was in bad shape and costing more than expected. Quinn had agreed with all her recommendations. The boat would be both a home for him and a certified world cruiser when she was finished. Quinn was also encouraged by the cheerful tone of her messages. She seemed very friendly and possibly …well, it was premature to speculate, but maybe she could be more than a friend. He would have almost no acquaintances once he settled into Sydney.

While walking through the station heading to the cafeteria, he was gratified to see Pam, Roy and Mark talking intently in the library.

"Is everything okay here?" Quinn asked in passing.

All three looked up with a smile and Mark announced, "Just keep your checkbook handy, Quinn. We'll be coming to see you soon with a comprehensive proposal," Mark said.

"You're talking to the worldwide experts on the Wilkes Land Crater," shouted Pam from the table.

It would be two weeks before the planes began running on schedule. Quinn planned to depart the continent by August 28th and then fly from Willingham, New Zealand, and on to Sydney via a commercial flight he had set up on the Qantas Airline Web. The winter had gone by fast with the impact and crater investigation taking up the largest amount of time. Still, there was time to do his job of reviewing the reports of this year's research and getting the future grant applications ready for submittal. There was plenty to do. After several all-night sessions, Pam had presented a comprehensive grant application for research on the meteor and impact event. Its emphases had evolved to favor Randy's impact and climatologic model. There were several on-site field inspections planned, but Quinn noticed that the drilling effort to locate remnants of the meteor was no longer in the scope. Instead there was a sub-task to collect fragments from the secondary craters. The team included just about everyone on the ice this year, plus scientists from the National Center for Atmospheric Research (NCAR) and the Climate Systems Research Center (CSRC) with the University of Massachusetts. The proposal was very creditable and staffed by the best team of polar researchers available on the planet.

Quinn forwarded the proposal to NSF with his recommendations to review and approve immediately. Work was to commence as soon as the days started to get longer. No sooner had he transmitted it than Pam and Roy knocked on his door.

"Hey, we wanted to touch base with you and see if you have any questions on the proposal?" Pam offered.

"Thanks for stopping by. I reviewed the proposal and just forwarded it to NSF Washington with my recommendation. I asked them to move fast, since you plan to start work in about two weeks."

"That's great news! Thanks for the support. We thought it was a pretty tight research effort and we know we need funding to get it started," Roy observed.

"The question now is how to keep the ongoing research programs running, while all the scientific muscle is researching the impact. How do you propose to do that?" Quinn asked.

"We talked about that and think we have an answer. We are promoting Marissa and Tom Thorton to senior scientists and putting them in charge of the ongoing programs. We will then recruit some new heads to fill the staff scientist's slots here on the ice," Pam said.

"Are there enough scientists interested in coming to the continent to fill those slots?"

"Yes, we checked the NSF resumes and a number of candidates are crazy enough to want to work for a year or two in Antarctica. We have already contacted some of them and it looks like we can easily fill the slots. Did you notice that we even had the cost for a new dormitory in the proposal? The next three to four years are going to be intense, with a lot of scientists working at the station," added Roy.

"Are you staying through the summer, Quinn?" Pam asked.

"No, I have another engagement awaiting me. How about you two?"

"Well, I'm flying out on the August 28th flight and will take two weeks off to go back to the states and see my daughter. Then I will come back and work through the summer. This will be my longest period on the ice, since I'll be staying through next winter. Roy is staying over. He will be serving as project manager for the program and I will be chief scientist. We would really like for you to stay. You're a part of this too."

"A very small part perhaps, but I am sure you will get along just fine without me. After all, as you once said, I am not a scientist—just a ubiquitous geographer."

"Yeah, ha, ha, I did say that, didn't I?" retorted Pam.

The three fell silent as their attention was directed towards the station's window. A faint glow on the horizon began showing a ting of orange.

CHAPTER 7

Disillusion

Nancy was transfixed by the news report. A portion of her old life had surfaced half a world away and it was haunting her. She had not thought about him for the past few months. Seeing him on television brought a lot of guilt to the surface. Here she was delving into her new life in a county and culture far from home and her husband intrudes. "The bastard," she thought as she remained glued to the television report. Quinn seemed to have disappeared and now here he was on international news about some crater and the expedition. The news reports kept mentioning Quinn Wilson as expedition leader … and she had seen him—or had she imagined that she saw him? No, she was sure that was him getting out of that tractor and walking through the crowd.

Thomas finished reading the paper and was observing Nancy as she stood in her bathrobe, intently watching the news report. She was a very attractive woman, sensual and willing! So, this was one of the perks that a plastic surgeon could expect from the women who sought his services. He felt a surge of longing drawing him to her. He rose from the breakfast table, crossed the room and stood in back of her, massaging her shoulders. At first, she seemed not to notice his presence. So he ran his hand down the front of her robe and kissed her neck. Her response was immediate, as she leaned further back into his embrace. So much for the guilt. Passion filled them both, as Nancy forgot about her husband's untimely intrusion back into her life. Now there were only two people in the world ...and there were things to do ...important things!

Thomas' visit was over before they knew it. It had been six luxurious days of sex. It was a honeymoon without the long-term commitment and responsibility that followed. Nancy had never known such unbridled and uninhibited passion. She saw Thomas off at the curb and had just returned to the house when Roberto called.

"Well, how did it go?" he asked.

"What do you mean, how did it go?" she retorted, somewhat flustered by the question.

"Cut the crap, Nancy. We both know what I'm talking about. How was the sex?"

A little shocked by his rude boldness, she muttered, "It ... it went fine! He was a very nice young man and we had a good visit."

"Nancy!"

"All right, all right, the sex was great! We made love all over the place. Is that what you wanted to hear?"

"I knew it! It's about time you let your hair down and learned to enjoy yourself, Nancy. That is what life is all about ...'if it feels good, do it,' I always say," Roberto responded with a smug self-righteous tone.

"Thank you for that philosophy lesson," she said coolly.

"Are you up for some more company? I will be coming over next week with some colleagues for a conference in Brussels. We can spend a few days together. Are you up for it?" he asked.

"Well, of course Roberto. I would love to spend some time with you. You know that," she gushed.

"We have to spend the first part of the week at the conference. On Thursday, we will take the train down to the coast. We should be in by about 4:00 PM, local time. Can you arrange things on your end? We will need to be picked up at the station and ask the staff to have a dinner ready for about seven people. We will need three bedrooms ready," he dictated, as if talking to his hired staff.

"Okay, I can have things ready on this end. Who is coming with you?" she responded as she jotted down some notes.

"Two of my long-term colleagues from New York will be joining me at the conference and I have promised them a visit to the Mediterranean, if they ever made it across the pond. You will like them …and Nancy, we will want to show them a good time."

Once again, Nancy was flustered by the tone in his voice. It was the same phrase he used when he told her that Thomas was coming and she was to provide entertainment. What was he getting at this time?

"I will have things ready for you and your friends, you can count on that."

Her misgivings over Roberto's tone of voice gave way to the excitement of seeing him again. She would make the most of it. After a meeting with the staff to tell them of the impending visit and discuss the menus for the weekend, she busied herself in preparation. Everything had to be just right. Of course that meant an extended shopping trip to buy a completely new wardrobe all the way down to the sexy lingerie. She was sure Roberto wouldn't mind. It was only a few thousand dollars. He would want her to make a good impression on his friends.

As the weekend approached, she received short messages from Roberto regarding his schedule. He was to fly to New York and meet with the conference committee, have dinner with his colleagues and then catch a charter flight to Brussels. He was to give the keynote address during the luncheon on the first day of the conference. On Thursday, he and his friends would board the train and be in Nice by 3:00 P.M. that afternoon.

She met regularly with the staff to discuss the accommodations for each of the guests, transportation, tours, menus, wines, and entertainment. She was the perfect hostess and she felt at home coordinating the visit in what she would have once considered to be the world of the rich and famous. Everything was coming together as she planned and she was sure Roberto would be so proud of her.

The day finally arrived, so she got up early. She spent a long moment looking at her reflection in the mirror. Standing there in her nightgown, she studied her face, complexion, and figure. Yes, she thought, I look rested and beautiful. I am ready for a visit from the love of my life. With confidence and anticipation, she began the last-minute preparations for the visit.

In the early afternoon, she dispatched the chauffer to the train station in plenty of time. In efficient European fashion, the train arrived right on schedule. Roberto and his friends were in a festive mood when they arrived at the château. Nancy's excitement of seeing Roberto again was quickly dispelled. While he kissed her and briefly introduced her to Harry and Stan on arriving, he seemed more intent on his friends and showing off the chateau. She told herself that her disappointment was ridiculous. Just wait until she and Roberto could have some private time and things would be different. But the private time did not come that afternoon. Roberto and his guests got settled in, unpacked, dressed for dinner and then gathered in the study for cigars and drinks. She could hear the boisterous laughter coming from the study, as she finally knocked on the door and announced that dinner was served.

She was largely ignored during dinner, as Roberto and his guests told stories about their patients and laughed.

Men! She thought. *They are so delightful when you are alone, but in a group they act like adolescent boys, so crude and so much sexual undertone in their conversation.*

On the third round of after-dinner sherry, she excused herself to freshen up. Roberto asked her, with an air of urgency, to join them in the study when she returned. All eyes were on her as she left the room. *This is not going at all like I had envisioned*, she thought. Thomas was a delightful guest, so attentive, and she assumed that all of Roberto's business friends would be—after all, these were doctors and surgeons. She took her time freshening up and returned to the study about an hour later. Upon entering the study, she was surprised to see two other women. She first thought of introducing herself, but was caught short by their expressions. These were exotic females with disinterested expressions, pouting lips, and painted faces. They sat nursing their drinks and did not make eye contact with her. Nancy turned to

Roberto and was about to ask, when he just waved his hand and said, "Don't pay any attention to them, they are just local women I recruited to escort our friends. Here have a drink."

A sense of uneasiness welled up in Nancy as she took a sip of her drink and again looked at the women. Roberto and his friends were continuing to make fools of themselves, while ogling the women. She had to admit they were sexy creatures, dressed to the nines with short, short hemlines, bleached hair, and dangling ear rings—the works. *These were …working women,* she thought!

Roberto's friends continued to drink and make sexual overtures to the women. Nancy could see where this was leading as they began to sprawl on the couches and remove layers of clothing. Roberto seemed to be enjoying the show as he laughed and drank repeated shots of bourbon. His eyes were bloodshot and his voice slurred when he turned his attention to Nancy and began groping her and attempted to unzip her dress. She protested and pushed him away. He grew angry, grabbed her arm and pulled her toward the closest couch. Again she fought him off and tried to run from the room. He stopped her at the door and she could see it coming, as if in slow motion. He cursed as he drew back his arm and his open palm headed towards her face. The contact sent her to the floor in shock. Her disbelief turned to reality and she knew that she could no longer stay in this place. Roberto was not the man she thought he was.

She ran to her room, locked the door and sat crying on the bed, as she tried pulling herself together. Downstairs she could hear the joyful laughter of the women as the party continued. As the evening drew on, she decided to take action. Hurriedly she changed out of her party dress and packed a small bag. She searched the room and found her old handbag with her passport and wallet. While at the villa she had not needed it since she was living on Roberto's ample resources. There were five one-dollar bills and several credit cards still in the wallet from her past life and she whispered a prayer that the cards were still active, as she came quietly down the stair and headed for the front door. No one was stirring as she passed the study, with its mass of repugnant fat naked male bodies. Finally, she was on the street and walking fast but to where?

She found a café that was just opening its doors and took a seat. She was strangely reminded of a short story that Ernest Hemingway had written during his years in Paris. He had a refuge that he often sought and referred to only as "a clean well lighted place." How simple and reassuring to sit and collect her thoughts in such a place. She was still not clear what had happened, but she knew her trust had been violated and she shuddered to think how trusting she had been. There were bruises on her cheek and arms as evidence to his everlasting love. She had been such a fool to be drawn in by his charm.

She panicked when it occurred to her that she was going to have to pay for the coffee and croissant she had ordered. She only had five dollars in cash. Her only resources were the credit cards and she had no way of knowing whether Quinn had closed all accounts. After all, she knew from her daughter that he had sold the house, quit his job and was in Antarctica of all places. She would go to an ATM and see if the cards were still open. The check at the café was $4.87, so she left a 13 cent tip and walked briskly back into the early morning darkness, searching for a bank or ATM. Panic was beginning to rise and her heart was beating rapidly. At times she just walked in a daze. There was no way she was returning to the villa and facing Roberto after what he had put her through. How gullible she had been …she had called him the love of her life! She had given up Quinn for this! Boring, predictable, practical, steady, and loving Quinn!

At last, an ATM! Her hands trembled as she withdrew the cards, dropped them on the ground and collected them in near panic. She was almost sobbing as she inserted the first card and waited for the response to the password. Failed! The second card also failed. The third card was a Master Charge card to the leverage line she and Quinn had set up with an $80,000 limit. She remembered that the password was "sailboat," one of Quinn's boring pastimes. She inserted the card and entered the password and waited. After what seemed like an eternity the ATM flashed the message "English, Spanish or French," and then, "Withdrawal or Deposit." Her face flushed as she realized that old methodical Quinn had apparently left the card open, just for her. He had saved her from long distance and she cried openly. "Dear sweet dumb Quinn" she thought! "I love you, I love you!"

Withdrawal—$2,000! And the cash rolled out as if she had discovered salvation. Once the travel agencies were open this morning she would book a flight back to Florida! But first she would need a new wardrobe and luggage. She was not returning to the villa for her belongings.

CHAPTER 8

Back to Civilization

The plane lifted off from the McMurdo Station Airfield heading for its home base in New Zealand. Everyone was in a festive mood. Ahead of them was civilization, family and most importantly, warm weather and sunshine. Quinn sat looking out the window at the ice fields as if he had never flown in an airplane before. The sun was now slightly above the horizon and the few degrees of solar radiation were showing their effect on the continent. The edges of the ice field were giving way to open water in this primordial climatic dance that had gone on since the beginning of time. Large sections of the ice sheet were calving off and drifting into open water where they would last for decades in the frigid sea as they slowly melted. Still the process seemed to be speeding up, as indicated in the debate of global warming, which continued in the scientific and political world. To see this firsthand was an absolutely magnificent experience.

Pam and Roy sat across the aisle from him chatting and laughing as if they were old and fast friends. Quinn was glad to see that they had mended fences and would be working together on the impact crater study after a short vacation in warmer climate. *Scientists are just like the rest of us, protective of their turf*, he thought.

They flew for seven hours, with broken cloud cover, over the dark and foreboding Indian Ocean north towards New Zealand. The first green land they saw was Stewart Island, and next, the South Island and the majestic Southern Alps. Then the plane flew over the rural communities of Invercargill, Dumsden, Cromwell, and Timaru. All eyes were now looking out the windows, as they approached Christchurch. The green landscape was intoxicating and a cheer went up as the plane touched down back in civilization.

Quinn thought to himself that his life was taking on a rather episodic existence. Each episode either began or ended with an airplane. This flight was the beginning of the next chapter. The trip to Africa had been the shortest and most violent of these episodes and Quinn lowered his head and moaned under his breath, as the events of that operation came chasing back into his memory. It took him a few minutes to force the memory of those days out of his mind. He never wanted to experience those life and death trials again.

He spent three days in Christchurch performing administrative cleanup on reports from the winter stay, grant applications, invoices, university inquiries, and an interview with the prospective new NSF director for next winter. He was an archetypical professor, with a resume full of publications, a serious attitude, and a desire to manage the NSF program much like he managed his classroom. It would be his first time on the ice and Quinn thought that the scientific team was in for a serious shock.

Now it was time for the long-awaited trip back to Sydney. He had received an email from Meg saying his boat was ready and he was anxious to see her again, both the boat in her feminine context, and Meg Archer in the flesh. Her emails had been increasingly personal and he had begun reading between the lines. He considered her a friend and allowed his imagination to explore a more intimate relationship. He hoped for a closer friendship in his new home base.

The flight was eight hundred miles and the plane seemed to be going in slow motion, the seat was hard, and the peanuts were stale. *Good Lord, get me back on the ground and into my new life.* Once on the ground, he shouldered his bags and made a short stop at the immigration desk. As he walked out of the terminal, he was surprised to see Steven Coates, his old boot camp buddy, waiting for him.

"What a surprise! Nice of you to come welcome me back to civilization," Quinn said somewhat elatedly.

"Don't mention it. I heard through the grapevine that you were coming in today, so I thought I would stop by. There is someone I want you to meet. You remember Ken James from our training. He's back as our senior field agent here in the Sydney office."

Ken James was dressed in tattered blue jeans, a faded Hawaiian shirt and boat shoes with no socks, even though the spring temperature in Sydney was more than cool. He had a mane of hair with streaks of gray that spoke of neglect rather than style and was pushed back into a ponytail. Quinn noticed that he walked with a slight limp, but otherwise appeared to be in good shape.

"Well, it's good to see you again, Quinn. Your reputation precedes you," Ken said.

"I have no idea what reputation you're talking about," Quinn responded.

"That little incident in Africa is well-known throughout the Company, to say nothing about your activities in Antarctica."

"Antarctica?"

"I am a student of human nature and, once in a while, I find a person who seems to always be present at notable events. I think you are one of those people and I just wanted to let you know, I am watching you to satisfy my curiosity. If I am right, I will be seeing more of you. Remember that up until 1998 the NGIA and the Company were the same agency. We still work closely out here in the field," Ken observed. "We are flying out in about an hour to Indonesia. Maybe we can look you up in a week or so. Where are you staying?"

"I pick up my boat tomorrow morning and will be berthing it at the Double Bay Marina until I can find a cheaper—excuse me—more cost-effective alternative," Quinn responded.

"The Double Bay Marina is quite a decent facility that's run by Jake Varn. I used to keep my boat there until I sold it a couple of years ago. Are you power or sail?" Ken asked with interest.

"Definitely sail!" Quinn said.

"What kind of boat do you have?"

"I have been refurbishing an older Sabre 37. Right now it is sitting at the Archer Marina ready for me to sail away."

"I know the Sabre line. They are great boats and 37-foot is just the right size for these waters. I'd like to come back by and check it out one day. But right now, Steven and I have a plane to catch. So we've got to run. It was really great seeing you, Quinn, but as you know, work calls," as they shook hands and headed for their plane.

Quinn spent his first night in a hotel downtown near the harbor. After a restless night, he arose early and walked to the Double Bay Marina. The newspaper said that the weather was unseasonably cold. Quinn looked up at the blue sky of the early morning in the hopes of getting reintroduced to sunshine. He observed a sky, streaked with high cirrus clouds streaming out of the south. Quinn's first thought was of the meteor and the ice that was lofted into the stratosphere. Surely there was going to be climate changes from that impact.

The Dockmaster was already in his office when Quinn arrived at the marina to inquire about his slip. Jake Varn looked comfortable in his tan Columbia fishing shirt with his sunglasses dangling from a lanyard around his neck, a blue baseball cap pulled down tightly onto his head. He had a well-kept gray beard and a look of satisfaction in his eyes, like a man who had found his life's work and enjoyed doing it every day. Even though the weather was still in the 40s, he wore a pair of tattered shorts over bronze legs that looked much younger than his weather-beaten face.

"Been expecting you mate. I'm Captain Varn, but everyone calls me Jake. From the beard and pale complexion, I assume you have either been in prison or Antarctica? To really get along good with the crew here at the marina, I hope it was prison," he said laughingly.

Quinn laughed too. "Well, I think you're right on both accounts. They lock you in, so you don't get out much to walk around on the ice." They both laughed that comfortable laugh of kindred spirits.

"Your slip is ready for you, mate. You're on Dock 4, Slip D109. The boat is under 40 feet, correct?"

"Yes, it's 37'6" to be exact. I've got full service at the slip?" Quinn added, just to be on the safe side.

"All of our slips are full service with three-phased electricity, telephone, intranet connection, cable and, of course, water. That is why I get top dollar for the accommodations. I see that you have paid three months in advance and plan to live aboard. There are a few rules you will need to follow. You know the basics, no crap or oil in the bay please, no loud music after 10:00 PM, and only small pets. Also, Maggie's Diner across the park is a good place for lunch. Almost everyone from the marina goes there at least once a week. Her shepherd's pie is especially fine. That's about it. If you have any questions about the facilities here at the marina, just stop by. Be prompt with your slip fee, mate, and we will get along just fine!"

"Thanks, for the information and warning. I'll have the boat in the slip by this afternoon."

Quinn walked to the slip enjoying the warmth of the sun and the cool breeze in his face. Cool was really nice after the frigid life and threatening winds on the Continent. He installed the new mooring lines he had picked up the day before and anxiously headed to Archer Marine to see Meg and pick up his boat. He didn't know which one he was looking forward to seeing more.

A 45-minute taxi ride through the city brought him to Archer Marine, just as the staff was taking a midmorning break. No one spoke to him as he walked out on the dock looking for his boat. He hardly recognized her with the gleaming decks, new standing rigging, and dark blue hull. The last time he had seen her, she was a bedraggled, beat-up survivor of a traitorous Indian Ocean crossing. Now she was completely restored and proudly waiting in the slip ready for more adventure. His admiration was interrupted by Meg's voice.

"Good morning! We had expected you yesterday," she said with a smile.

Quinn wheeled around with open arms and gave her a hug.

He noted at once that it was a one-sided hug that was not accepted nor returned by a stiffened Meg. Her hands were firmly planted on his chest pushing him back as she also took a step back from the embrace. It was not the reception he had hoped for. Both he and Meg struggled to regain their composure by discussing the cool weather.

"She is ready to go. We have given her a shakedown cruise. All systems are functioning. You have a one-year warranty on the labor we conducted, along with the various manufacturers' warranties on the equipment and parts. We did not spend all of the contingency funds you had entrusted with us and I can give you a check for the remaining amount," Meg said in a very business-like manor.

Quinn listened intently to the impersonal details, but it was not the conversation that he had hoped to have with Meg. Her emails had been so friendly …he had hoped for more.

"We need the space, so your boat will have to leave the dock by 11:00 o'clock this morning," she was saying. He thought he would be bold and salvage the meeting by asking her to join him for a cup of coffee.

"Thanks for all the work you have put into the boat, Meg. I really appreciate your attention to detail. It looks great! Why don't we keep that account open until I have had a chance to really check her out? I may want to install some additional equipment to get her cruise-ready. Can we talk more over a cup of coffee?"

The question lingered as Meg looked out over the harbor. "No thank you, Mr. Wilson," she finally answered, "I have a very busy day ahead of me and I am sure you will want to get acquainted with your boat," as she hurriedly walked away.

Quinn had mixed feelings as he stood at the helm of the boat leaving the Archer Docks. He glanced back, hoping to get a wave from Meg (make that Ms. Archer), but she stood with her back to the water, talking to her foreman. It was just business after all. He guessed that the loneliness of the ice had caused him to read between the lines of her emails. A man can hope.

He forced his mind away from such lonely thoughts and concentrated on his new boat. It was moving smoothly through the water with a steady and reassuring hum resulting from the new 29-horsepower Yanmar diesel, doing 6.5 knots at 1800 rpm. That was very promising. He slowed the engine to an idle and shifted into reverse. This boat was much larger than his old 27-foot Ericsson and he wanted to test its maneuverability before he reached the marina dock. Many sailboats tracked one way or the other while in reverse and he wanted to know that *before* he reached the slip and made a fool of himself. It was going to be hard enough to bring a boat this size into a slip alone, without causing some physical or emotional damage. However, the boat tracked well and was very maneuverable in reverse. Back into forward gear, he pushed the throttle and was rewarded with a burst of speed up to 7.5 knots and then an 8.0 hull speed at 2400 rpm. That was a very respectable speed. The boat had a 56-gallon fuel tank. However, there was not enough information on fuel consumption on the new Yanmar engine to calculate the boat's range. He would have to do that once he knew his fuel consumption rate. He knew it had a whole lot more range than he was used to. Now he idled back and pointed the boat into the wind and engaged the autopilot, which functioned properly. His confidence in the boat and his ability were increasing. With the boat headed into the wind, he unfurled the foresail, a 130 Genoa, and fell off the wind to put the boat under partial sail. Switching off the engine, he felt the boat respond and gain speed under sail. For a moment, he felt like a kid again at the helm of his Optimus Pram, feeling the blush of freedom that comes from being in command and under sail. This was what he had dreamed about. The Pacific Ocean—no—the entire world was within his reach.

He remained under sail for a couple of hours as he made the transit up the bay. He was in no rush—he had all day.

It was late afternoon when he approached the dock, furled his Genoa and prepared to bring the boat into its slip. There was no one on the dock to lend a hand, so he was on his own while dumping the speed and slowing the boat down to just barely make headway, as was standard docking procedure. He checked the pilings to see current movement and looked again at the wind speed and direction from his new gauges. There was a five-knot wind out of the northeast. He glided just past the slip and pulled the gearshift into reverse. After a brief delay, the boat responded and began a slow reverse into the slip. Out of his peripheral vision, he was surprised to see someone standing on the dock. It is common courtesy to assist a boat coming to a dock by grabbing a line or fending the boat off the pilings. However, Quinn was surprised to see a very attractive woman standing by to give him a hand. She was so attractive that he momentarily lost his concentration.

Then she spoke, "Swing her to starboard, mate, and throw me the stern line!" As if on autopilot himself, Quinn followed her directions. "Cut the engine and go forward with the boat hook for the port bow line," she shouted. Quinn was already on his way as she knelt and slipped the stern line on the dock cleat. Then she stood with her hands on her hips, watching his progress with concern.

"Thanks for the help!" he managed to say, once the boat was secured in the slip.

"Don't mention it, mate," she said with a beautiful Australian accent. "My name is Betsy Valentine. I own the Oyster across the way," she said pointing across the dock.

"It is nice to meet you Betsy. I'm Quinn Wilson and it looks like we may be neighbors. I plan to be here for a while."

"I thought you may be one of those world cruisers with that beard," she said with a laugh.

I'm just off an overwinter stay in Antarctica, but don't worry. I clean up nice and I am not as dangerous as I look," he laughed in return.

"Well, welcome to the dock. I'm off to work. I hope to see you around," she said as she headed down the dock towards the clubhouse. Quinn noticed that there was a limo waiting with the chauffer standing by for someone. Was it for her? In spite of himself, he indulged his male prerogative and watched her walk down the dock. Sure enough, the chauffer opened the door for her and she got in. He realized he had been on the ice way too long. She was one very attractive lady and she was his neighbor. Things were looking up.

CHAPTER 9

Paris

Nancy was at the door of the local travel agency when it opened for business in the morning. She was looking for the first available seat on any flight back to the states. She impatiently waited for the travel agent to get a cup of tea and boot up her computer.

"It is late in the season, no? The tourists are all returning home and I do not know what is available on such short notice. Why have you not made reservations in advance? You wish to fly from Paris as soon as possible, yes? Ha, here we are. Now let me see what is available. I see there is nothing on Air France for six weeks. There are a few seats on American in a month and the same with National Airlines. Oh, wait here is a first class seat available on Virgin Air next week, but it is an $8,000 fare!"

"I'll take it!

"Very well, I will book that flight for you. May I see your passport and how will you be paying for the flight?

Nancy rummaged in her purse and produced her passport and Visa credit card. There was a momentary wave of panic as the card was swiped and the approval delayed as the computer did the credit check. Finally, the screen flashed approval and Nancy hoped the agent did not see her sigh of relief. In fact, she was near tears as she realized once again that Quinn had a hand in her salvation.

With the transaction completed, she stood outside the travel agency with the ticket in her hand. She felt a wave of revulsion, as her thoughts strayed back to the night before and Roberto's violent outburst. She shuddered and forced her mind away from the images of his angry face and the slap that sent her to the floor. She touched her cheek and felt its swollen tenderness. *Thank goodness for makeup,* she thought. She had been blind to Roberto's motives and thus, was treated like a call girl. Is that what Roberto thought of her—just a sex object?

She had to get herself under control. She would need luggage, clothes and makeup. She would also require a place to stay and transportation to Paris! It was too much! She had always had Quinn and then Roberto to make all of these arrangements for her and now she was on her own.

It was back to the clean well-lit place of the Hemingway short story to sort out her course of action. There, over a European breakfast of hard roles and yogurt, she plotted her next moves. Shopping, yes, but she would buy sparingly here in Nice and then shop more in Paris. After all, she had a week left before the flight and needed something to occupy her time. She would skip the expensive shops where she had gotten her current wardrobe when she was spending Roberto's money. No, she would be practical and shop for inexpensive slacks, shirts and a jacket ...that is, until she reached Paris. Then she would take advantage of Quinn's generosity.

By that afternoon, she had boarded the train to Paris. She did not want to stay in the city where Roberto and his friends might be looking for her.

CHAPTER 10

Sydney

Everyone in Sydney was talking about the unseasonably cool weather. Since this was his first spring in the southern hemisphere and he had just come from an overwinter in Antarctica, he had no frame of reference. However, natives were saying that it was very cold, uncomfortably bone-chilling cold. One seemingly knowledgeable individual said that the National Weather Service was forecasting temperatures 5 to 7 degrees below normal, speculating that the meteor impact in Antarctica was probably the cause. Quinn smiled to himself as one news reporter quoted Mark Raulson and the news release prepared while they were still on the ice. *I wonder how the team is doing*, he thought.

Later that evening he stood on the dock admiring his boat. The dark blue hull looked great as it reflected the lights of the harbor. Everything was in order. The mooring lines were holding the boat away from the dock during the tidal changes, the sails were properly covered, and the deck was clean. He boarded the boat, opened the companionway, and climbed down into the cabin. *Home at last*, he whispered as he settled into the starboard bunk. *Tomorrow I will get reacquainted and get her away from the dock for a sail* were his final thoughts before he drifted off to sleep to the gentle rocking of the boat.

The next morning, a call from the dock brought him back up on deck. It was Betsy Valentine, dressed in a baggy sweat shirt and jeans rolled up to her calves. “I wanted to ask a favor,” she said.

"Sure, what do you need?" he responded.

"I have to take my boat over to Archer's Marine tomorrow for her annual bottom job and I wondered if you were available to crew with me."

"I would be happy to give you a hand," he said with a smile. "I was going sailing anyway, so I would enjoy it."

"Thank you! Would 8:00 A.M. be too early for you?"

"Not at all, I'm usually up much earlier than that. Just call over to the boat if you don't see me on the dock. Would you have time to give me a quick lesson on your running rigging before we left the dock? Your boat is a lot more complex than mine."

"Sure, we can do that. I'm assuming you're a quick study," she added.

"Hopefully, I'll catch on quickly."

"Okay, I'll see you tomorrow morning."

"I'll be there," Quinn replied.

Back on the boat, he fixed himself a bowl of cereal and began to plan his first full day at the marina. After cleaning up, he settled down to enjoy the gentle rocking of his boat in the slip. There was always something relaxing about being on the water. In addition to the boat's movement, there were the sounds of the harbor and the smell of the sea wafting down the companionway. Of course, the smell of the ocean was tempered by the smell of the boat's new paint and varnish, but it all smelled like the marine environment, which he loved.

After a while, he checked his email accounts. There was nothing from NGIA and nothing from home. He had some anxiety regarding his daughter. No communications from her for some time. Usually she would have contacted him for financial assistance for something by now. He looked at his watch and mentally calculated the time difference back in Florida. It was too early there to give her a call. Next he checked his bank accounts. The winter on the ice had proved profitable, mostly because there was no place to spend money. The money from the sale of the house was safely in a brokerage account and earning money. He had not used a credit card for six months now, but he checked the account to make sure everything was in order. At first, he was surprised to see a series of withdrawals from France. There was approximately $11,000 on the Visa account to date. Was he experiencing identity theft? He picked up the phone and called the 24-hour Visa information line to ask about the charges. After wading through the ubiquitous call options, he got a young representative on the line with a distinct Indian accent. He asked her to check on the charges and after a few minutes she returned and stated, "Yes, we show that the charges were a cash withdrawal from Nice, France, on October 3rd and a first class airline ticket on Virgin Air from Paris to New York on the same day. The charge for the ticket was signed for by Nancy Wilson. Can I answer any more questions for you?" She asked.

"No, thank you for the information, everything is in order," he responded. Nancy, he thought as his mind raced. She was in France and trying to get home. A first class ticket seemed a little excessive. She was always so economical during their marriage. Oh yes, they were still married. But, it must mean that she is well. How can I get a message to her? Instinctively, he reached for the phone and called his daughter. He didn't care that it was too early—this was important.

A sleepy voice answered after a few rings.

"Hello, honey, this is Dad. Sorry for calling so early. How are you?"

"Ooh, what time is it …and where are you calling from?"

"I am calling from Sydney, Australia, honey. Have you heard from your mom?"

"No …not for a month or so. She's in France somewhere with that doctor friend of hers."

"I just saw a charge on the Visa card. She apparently is heading home and I wanted to get a message to her. If she calls, could you give her my contact information? I will email it to you shortly. Give her the account information I gave you before I left and tell her that her half of the proceeds from the sale of the house are there for her. Will you?"

"Sure."

"What about you? How are you doing?"

"Okay."

"Is school going well?"

"Yes, Dad, school is going well. Do you want to see my report card?"

"Actually, I would love to see your report card."

"Yeah, right! Look, Dad, it's early. I am going back to sleep. Goodbye."

"Goodbye, honey. Take care of yourself. I love you!" He was in mid-sentence when the phone was disconnected.

The short exchange with his daughter left him unsettled. It was obvious she still blamed him for the breakup. Still, I am her dad and would like to have a role in her life, other than a banker. He sat thinking about the call for a long time, when he realized that it was very quiet. He had no broadcast radio or television to take his mind off his worries. So, he turned on the Marine VHF radio to the International Emergency channel 16. There was no traffic on the channel. Apparently all was well on the waterfront and coastal areas around southeast Australia. Next, he turned the channel to the marine weather station on Channel 9 and heard the melodious voice of the forecaster. Just like in the United States, the Australian National Weather Service had computerized voices giving the weather. This gave them an "other world" sound, as they droned out the basics in a monotone of broken sentences.

"The marine weather forecast for 8:30 P.M. PST for the southeastern coast of Australia from Newcastle to Jarvis Bay, including the offshore waters: Winds southeast at 12 to 15 knots, gusting 18 knots, seas 5 to 8 feet offshore and in unprotected coastal waters. Inshore waters in protected areas, a moderate chop. Winds shifting to east and increasing to 20 knots, gusting to 25 by midmorning tomorrow, barometer at 30.19 millibars and falling. Temperatures for tonight will be a low of 38 degrees F, rising to a high of 45 degrees by midafternoon tomorrow. The dew point is 56°F. Fog is predicted in the early morning with visibility one-quarter to one-half kilometer. Fog will dissipate by midmorning as the sun increases temperatures. Partly cloudy conditions persist with high cirrus clouds over the forecast area continuing to moderate seasonal temperatures. No rain anticipated for the next three days."

Quinn listened to the forecast with curious interest, in part because it was his only distraction, and because the weather was much more important to him now that he was living on the water. He had noted that the marina was exposed to winds out of the east, so tomorrow would be a good opportunity to see how the boat would ride in a moderate breeze.

He logged back on to his computer and sent his daughter the contact information. While he was still online, he transferred money to cover the Visa bill. Nancy was trying to get home and he was sure she would need the support.

It was 8:00 P.M. and with nothing else to do, he decided to call it a day. He slept through the night in his Antarctic long johns with the gentle rocking of the boat and the waves sloshing against the hull.

He was up early the next morning and managed to get a pot of coffee brewing, thanks to Archer Marine having enough forethought to fill the propane tanks for the stove. *Another minor detail that slipped by me*, he thought. He was not even sure where the propane tanks were located. There were still things to learn as he settled into home on the water.

There was no sign of Ms. Valentine on her boat, so he left the companionway open and fixed a bowl of cereal. The weather report was correct. It was foggy with limited visibility. Since he was new to the harbor, he would have been reluctant to leave the dock and he was not sure that Ms. Valentine would be comfortable with the fog obscuring the harbor.

He sat in the companionway with a hot cup of coffee and listened to the sounds of the marina. There was the gentle sloshing of the waves against the dock and the clanking sound as the halyards tapping on the aluminum masts that were so common, and reassuring, around sailboats. In the distance, some seagulls gave their plaintive calls as they looked for their first meal of the day. Just out of sight, someone cranked repeatedly on an outboard motor and muttered in a distinct Australian accent when it would not start. Even further out in the harbor, a large diesel engine emitted its deep baritone rumble, as it moved down the channel in the fog.

Betsy stepped out of her cabin and surveyed the weather. She wore a long-sleeved blue denim shirt and a loose fitting pair of blue jeans. Her blond hair was pulled back into a ponytail and threaded through the back of a red baseball cap. It occurred to him that she had done everything she could to cover up her remarkable good looks. *Despite her efforts, she had failed*, he thought.

She hesitated for a moment when she saw him and then waved a greeting, "Good morning! I see you're up early."

"Good morning. Yes, I'm a morning person. What do you think of this weather?" he asked.

"Not a problem, mate. I have radar and the fog should burn off as soon as the sun gets up. I should be ready to shove off in about half an hour. Let me get some tea and we'll take a quick tour of my boat. Okay?"

"No rush, I'm enjoying myself. Just give a call when you're ready," he replied.

His thoughts lingered on the harbor and current weather conditions for a few moments, but then loneliness began to resurface again. "There is no one to share this with, no one to come home to, or even to call on the phone," he thought. He was not even going to have the companionship offered by fellow workers in an office. This was going to be very different. Ever since he left Florida, he had been working with a team—first in the training camp at St. Marys, then Africa, and finally in Antarctica. Now his only contact was going to be by email and with an occasional telephone call. A few friends here in Australia would sure help out a lot, especially female ones.

He rinsed out his coffee cup, just as Betsy called for him to come over. He grabbed his foul weather jacket and closed his companionway. Betsy was wiping down the cockpit seats as he approached her boat. "Permission to come aboard, captain," he called with proper seafaring etiquette.

"Permission granted, mate. No need to salute or stand at attention while on board. I run a tight ship, but not tight-assed," she responded with a laugh. "Now let me show you the running rigging," she said with an authoritative tone. "All my wenches are electric and operated either by the foot pedals or the pressure switches there on the bulkhead. She carries two jibs in a full cutter rig. Today we will probably just run on the 130 Genoa on the forestay. Here is the roller reefer line. You just release it and then deploy the Genoa with the sheet around the wench. We will probably leave the dock on a starboard tack, so if I can get you to prepare the lines, I'll get the auxiliary up and running. Oh, yes, the mainsail! It is a roller reefed main in the mast. I can deploy it from the helm with the electric wench in the boom once we are underway. The boat is very easy to sail and with the autopilot, I can almost sail it single-handed. But, it's 62-feet long and it is nice to have another set of hands aboard. Let me get the diesel started and we'll get underway."

"Okay, I'm going to throw off the spring lines," Quinn volunteered.

"Good show, mate! It is nice to have another sailor aboard. I hate having passengers onboard who know nothing about the water or sailboats," she said from the companionway.

Quinn worked the lines on the deck and heard the reassuring sound of a large diesel engine starting up and rumbling to life. He uncoiled the jib and main sheets and threw off the spring lines and was ready to get underway, when Betsy returned to the deck. "Ready to cast off the bow lines, captain," he called from the bow.

Betsy made a quick inventory of conditions and shouted the order. "Cast off the bow lines and stand by to fend her off the piles." She in turn threw off the stern lines and slipped the engine into gear. From Quinn's position on the bow, she looked small behind the large wheel, but her demeanor told him that she had everything under control. The boat responded slowly and began to move out of the slip. She deftly handled the wheel, so there was no need for Quinn to push off the pilings as the boat left the slip.

He walked down the deck to the cockpit as the bow cleared the slip. Betsy had a smile on her face. "God, I love this boat! There is nothing quite like being at the helm of a well-founded ship with the Pacific Ocean in front of you."

"Believe me, I know what you mean," responded Quinn.

Not 50 yards from the dock, Betsy surprised Quinn by turning the boat into the light breeze and deploying the mainsail. The sail emerged from the mast, as a small car on the boom traveled gingerly toward the stern. "Get ready to launch the Genoa," she calmly called out to Quinn. The electric wenches worked effortlessly and Quinn had the multicolored Genoa out in a matter of minutes. Betsy made a slight course change and, as the sails fluttered in the breeze and filled with wind, she promptly turned off the engine. Silence engulfed them as the big boat gathered speed and moved down the harbor in the fog.

"You certainly wasted no time getting her under sail," Quinn noted.

"Well, it is a sailboat after all," she said with a smile that rocked Quinn back on his heels. "I love to sail. It's in my blood. I am always happiest, when I'm at the wheel and under full sail. Can you pull the jib sheet in a little to trim the Genoa?"

Quinn obliged as she watched the tell-tails closely. "That's it, cleat her off," she shouted with a measure of glee in her voice. "Now that is properly trimmed and pulling nicely." Quinn admired the huge sails and settled into the starboard cockpit seat in front of the helm. "How long have you been sailing?" he asked.

"All my life, I suppose. My dad was a captain on the MacGregor Lines, so I have been sailing and at sea since I could walk. This is my third boat and the largest that I have owned. I like the Oyster line of boats. This one was built here in Australia."

"It is a magnificent vessel and makes mine feel like a dingy. What is the beam?" He asked.

"She has a 16-foot beam and only draws six and a half feet of water. It's a wing keel and it works very well here in the coastal waters. I don't think I have given up any performance offshore either. It handles rough weather very well," she said with a measure of pride.

"Do you get offshore much?"

"I get out as much as I can with the usual pressures of my job. I plan to enter the Sydney to Hobart race in the fall if I can muster a crew. Would you be interested in that?"

"Sydney to Hobart?" He responded with a measure of shock. "That is one of the most grueling offshore races in the world! As I recall, it is 800 nautical miles across the Tasman Sea, a very turbulent stretch of ocean! Of course, I'm interested, but to be honest, I have never raced in that class of offshore competition before. All my sailing has been in the Gulf of Mexico off the West Coast of Florida. In comparison to the Tasman Sea, the Gulf is a lake. You should consider me a novice when you are selecting your crew," he responded with a measure of humility.

"All right then, I shall consider you. So far I have been impressed with your knowledge of sailing," she responded with another one of those breathtaking smiles.

"Thank you, but we are less than one kilometer from the dock. I suggest you reserve your judgment until at least the end of this voyage," he said with a laugh.

"Well, you don't know me yet, but I am an incredible judge of men and so far you are rating fairly high."

"Gosh, thank you! Now you see, you have embarrassed me …I have not said 'gosh' in at least a decade," he said, as his face turned bright red.

They laughed and fell into a comfortable silence as they both surveyed the fog-shrouded harbor. After a few moments he asked, "You mentioned work pressures. What line of business are you in?"

"Ohmmm …hospitality! How about you?" she said with some hesitation.

"I'm …an environmental consultant," he answered with an equal amount of hesitation. This had been the first time anyone had asked about his work and he was pretty sure, no one would understand if he said that he was a field agent for a resource intelligence agency.

"Hospitality? Is that with a specific hotel here in Sydney?"

"I work at a number of hotels, mainly with businessmen. It pays well and supports my sailing habit," and then she quickly changed the subject. "Would you be a good mate and bring me a cup of tea. There's a pot brewing on the galley stove. Just help yourself to one as well."

"I would be happy to, captain. That is definitely part of the skill set I bring to sailing," he responded as he headed down the companionway.

The interior of the boat was magnificent and spacious, everything in its place. In spite of himself, he couldn't help but comment on its beauty. "Below deck is absolutely gorgeous," he said aloud.

"Yes, I love to sail, but I also like my comforts. I had it custom-designed, since I planned to live aboard," she responded from above. "The tea cups are in the cabinet to the right of the stove. Do you see them?"

"Yes," he said, standing at the base of the cabin stairs looking up at her. "How do you like your tea?"

"Black is fine with me" she responded. "If you need cream or sugar, they're in the cabinet to the left of the sink."

Quinn returned to the cockpit with two cups of tea. The wind had increased slightly and the fog was beginning to break up, so that now they caught brief glimpses of the harbor and the city.

"When we first met there on the dock, you said that you had been in Antarctica?" she asked.

Quinn took a sip of tea and had a momentary recollection of the Starbucks coffee offers from Dr. Laystrom. "Yes, I served as director of the science program last winter for the NSF."

"Were you down there when the meteor hit?"

"Yes, I headed up the expedition to the crater."

"Oh, I think that is so interesting! I didn't know you were a celebrity," she said in a delightful way.

"Hardly! I had some very competent scientists on the team who deserve all of the credit. Still it was remarkable to see that impact crater in the middle of an Antarctic winter."

"As I recall, the expedition had trouble making it back—wasn't one team lost?" she asked.

"The French team that was approaching the crater from the south disappeared while en route. There was still no sign of them in my last communication. It was very tragic. We got caught in a blizzard and had to lay over two days, before we could negotiate the pass through the White Mountains. That ran us short of fuel and it was touch and go getting back safely to the station."

"Wasn't there a woman with you?"

"Yes, Dr. Pam Laystrom was on the team. She is a veteran of Antarctic winters and a hearty soul. She kept us all in line. I was just thinking of her, as a matter of fact. She kept a stash of Starbucks coffee that was very much in demand at the station. She only shared it with her favorite people. Needless to say, I never got a cup."

"Oh I see—in other words, no coffee for the boss?" she teased.

Betsy's attention quickly returned to the water. They were approaching the Harbor Bridge and there were increased shipping activities in the channel. A cruise ship was departing and it looked like they would arrive at the bridge at the same time. "I'm going to do a series of tacks to give us a little more clearance around the bridge. Will you stand by the jib sheet and let me know when you are ready?" she asked

"Ready when you are, captain," Quinn called back after he straightened the sheets on the cockpit seat.

"All right, ready about!" and the big boat responded immediately. As the Genoa lost its wind and began the process of changing sides, Quinn got confused on the electric wenches and was slow to sheet it on the port tack.

"Well, we're certainly going to have to do better with that aren't we," Betsy said in a half-serious voice.

"Sorry, I forgot about the electric wenches. I'm used to doing everything manually. It won't happen again, captain."

"Let's hope not. As I said earlier, I run a tight ship. I am going to stay on this tack for two minutes and then jibe back to starboard. Remember the foot pedals this time. The Genoa is much too large to muscle in, no matter how much of a he-man you are.

A jibe is when the sailboat comes about by passing the prevailing wind to the stern of the boat. It can be a difficult maneuver, if the wind is up or the crew inexperienced. This time, they handled it with ease and were back on the starboard reach towards the bridge. The cruise ship was now abreast of them and they could look up and see the people standing on the deck ten stories above them.

"There, that was much better. I shall put you back on my potential crew list for the Sydney to Hobart race," she laughed.

"Thanks, captain! It does take a little training to operate a boat this size efficiently," he responded. "Would you like me to take a turn at the wheel?"

"Thank you, but no. I don't get enough wheel time as it is, so let me take it under the bridge while you do all of the work," she said half-jokingly. They both settled in for an enjoyable tour down Sydney Harbor with a delightful 15-knot wind blowing steadily from the northeast. The boat moved well and held a steady 7 knots over the course.

As they approached Archer Marine, Betsy pressed the button and began furling the mainsail. "Quinn, will you furl the Genoa and get the bumpers out of the cockpit locker, please?"

She started the auxiliary engine and placed it in gear as soon as the Genoa was doused. Quinn returned to the cockpit to retrieve the bumpers and was surprised to find that they were as big as garbage cans. "You'll need a crew of at least four just to handle these bumpers," he said.

"We are only a few hundred yards from the dock. Let's put those bumpers on the starboard side. It looks like that side of the dock is clear to accept the boat." Betsy grabbed the marine radio and hailed Archer. "Archer Marine, Archer Marine ... this is the sailing vessel, Valentine. Come in please. In a few seconds, the cockpit speaker boomed with a response. "Sailing vessel, Valentine, this is Archer Marine, please go to channel 62." Quinn knew the voice and was looking forward to seeing

Meg again. Hopefully, he would get a better response than he did on his last visit. Betsy had changed channels and was informing Meg that she was approaching the outer dock for her scheduled maintenance at the yard. "Valentine out," she said as Quinn could see the activities on the dock.

Betsy reduced speed as the big boat approached the dock. Meg and her foreman were now standing by to offer dock lines and secure the boat. Meg looked curiously at Quinn standing on the deck. When they drew closer she said, "It's a surprise to see you so soon."

"Just helping out a fellow sailor," he said in response. Still Meg looked puzzled.

Betsy brought the boat up to the dock with skill and Quinn made some adjustments to the bumpers to make sure there was no impact to the hull. Meg and Betsy were already discussing the maintenance program for the boat when Quinn's satellite phone rang. He turned his back on the two women, and walked towards the bow to answer the call.

"Hello, Walter here!" Alex Reager's familiar voice boomed over the line. "Walter, old man, I've got a job for you. I told you I was going to work your ass off. Wouldn't you say that you've had enough time off?"

"Well, it is a beautiful day here in Sydney, Alex. With the sun and the wind in my face, this is what dreams are made of, but what can I do for you?"

CHAPTER 11

Coral

"I need you to go to Tahiti and check out some reports about coral bleaching. I'm not sure of the science, but I'm told that this is a serious problem and has not been seen in the Solomon Islands yet. Are you familiar with the problem?"

"As a matter of fact, I am. Coral has been bleaching in the Florida Keys for some time now. Scientists are not sure what's causing it, but it's a serious problem for the tropical reef ecosystems."

"Pack your kit and head on up there and send me a summary of your findings."

"I'll see what I can do, but remember no two scientists agree on what is causing the bleaching, so don't expect any answers."

"Understood, understood. Just get me the spatial location and an order of magnitude and that will help."

"Email me what information you have and I'll get underway tomorrow. Do you have a specific deadline?"

"We always have deadlines, but let me know how long it will take once you get to the island. I'll see that it is sent immediately. Keep up the good work, Walter."

Quinn turned to see Betsy walking down the dock and Meg standing at the wheel looking in his direction. He would have loved to give her a hug, but was not going to make that mistake again.

"Where do you know Ms. Valentine from?" she asked.

"I just met her the day I picked up my boat. She moors her boat across the dock from me and asked if I could help her bring the boat over for service. Why do you ask?" he said curiously.

"Do you know who she is?" she asked.

"What do you mean? I know her only as the owner of this boat."

Betsy had returned from the office and stepped onto the boat as Meg and Quinn talked at the helm. "Excuse me for interrupting, but our ride is here."

"Okay, let me get my jacket," Quinn said as he looked questionably at Meg. "I hope to see you later, Meg. I don't suppose an offer for dinner would be appropriate? I still feel that I owe you for all the work you did on my boat."

"Thank you, but you already paid us well for that work on your boat. We are in the business of providing marine services, so no additional thanks are needed." She said this with such cool efficiency that Quinn was sure it was all business on her part.

"Okay. I hope to see you again," was his only lame response. He wanted to indicate that he was interested in seeing her socially, but was too rusty to get his point across.

He caught up with Betsy near the office. She smiled at him and said, "I didn't know you knew Meg Archer. She and I go back a long way. We went to high school together. Don't you dare ask how long ago that was!"

"I had Archer Marine refurbish my boat and Meg and I became acquainted over emails while I was on the ice. In fact, I can still feel the chill around here."

"Ha, ha, I thought I noticed something between you two. She likes you, you know."

"I wouldn't say that. In fact, I can assure you that you are mistaken. She has been extremely short with me in our last two meetings. She says it is just business and I have to believe that."

"Quinn, here you are an educated man and a scientist and still don't know the first thing about women."

"That sound familiar and you are *not* the first one to bring that to my attention."

Following Betsy's look down the dock, Quinn noticed the black limousine he had seen before, parked in front of the marina office.

"This is our ride," Betsy said casually.

"A limo? Is this yours?"

"Uh, let's just say that I have access to it for my work. I'm sure you can catch the bus, if you don't want a ride," she said with a mocking tone.

"No, I will gratefully accept your hospitality." He said as the chauffer opened the door and Betsy slipped into the back seat with a smile.

"Can I offer you a Foster's?" she asked as she opened the refrigerator to the rather well-appointed mobile bar.

"Thank you! That would hit the spot," he said.

"What was that phone call about?"

"My home office called and asked me to check out a report about the reefs in Tahiti," he offered, making sure not to blow his cover. He also wondered if he had a cover to blow. After all, this was only a natural resource investigation, not a matter of national security.

"Oh, Tahiti, that sounds interesting. So, you will be leaving soon?"

"As soon as I can make some travel arrangements."

As they neared the marina, Betsy reached out and touched Quinn's hand and said, "Thank you for the help today! It was a very enjoyable sail and I will keep you on my list for the Hobart race."

"You are entirely welcome. I enjoyed the sail and the company as well. Where will you be staying while your boat is on the way?"

"I'll be staying at a resort hotel on the coast. It'll be a hardship, being off the water, but I'll survive. Meg has promised me that she will be finished in a week. So, I may even be back in the slip by the time you return from your vacation."

"It is hardly a vacation, but it is not hard work by any means. I'll see you around the dock," he said as he stepped out of the limo. He could still feel the warm touch of her hand as the door of the big automobile closed. He watched it merge into traffic and then turned towards his dock. As he rounded the corner of the office, he was surprised to see Ken James sitting on the bench outside the Harbor Master's office.

"Mr. James, are you looking for me?"

"Here you are, in town for only a few days, and already you are sailing big fancy yachts around, riding in limos and, with beautiful women, I might add."

"Ha, you know I haven't looked at it like that. I guess you're right and I was feeling lonely for no reason." They both laughed, and then Ken added, "I understand you are heading for Tahiti. Would you like some company?"

"Is there some official Company business that I should be aware of?"

"Hell, no! I was thinking about doing some diving and heard through the grapevine that you would be on a dive mission, so I thought I would horn in on the mission."

"Since I have only known about that trip for a half hour, my curiosity is up. Where did you hear about it and how did you know I was sailing today?"

"You forget who I work for, my man," he said with a laugh. "Also, when you weren't on the boat, I asked Jake and he told me that you were sailing with the lovely Ms Valentine."

"Okay, are you up for some lunch and at the same time, we can talk about Tahiti?"

"Are you buying? I left my wallet in my other pants."

"Okay. I think I can cover you. There is supposed to be a good place right across the park, even though I haven't had a chance to try it yet. Let's just head over."

They sauntered across park to Maggie's Café. Upon entering, Quinn was surprised when Ken hugged the first waitress he saw, much to her delight. They were seated with giggles and smiles from several of the ladies.

"You've been here before?" Quinn asked.

"I think I have eaten in just about every restaurant or bar in the city, since I never cook for myself. Actually, I used to come in here quite often when I kept my boat at Jake's Marina."

"So you know the waitresses?"

"Not really, but I don't see any of the old timers," he said while looking around. "But we'll be best friends before we finish lunch, just watch. Women just love me. I haven't been able to figure it out—it must be a curse. They all have such bad taste in men that I am a shoe-in."

The waitress Ken had hugged brought water to the table and stood smiling with red cheeks. He began his order with, "How about a couple of Foster's for me and my friend and keep them coming when you see that we are below half-full. Also, give us two of your daily specials ...You don't mind if I order for you do you, Walter?

"No you're on a roll, go ahead," Quinn laughed, enjoying the take-charge attitude. However, he was surprised that the CIA knew his code name ...and used it in public.

"Now we don't want the ordinary specials. We want them huge with all the sides. Tell the chef that we are the most important customers he will have today and my friend here is a big tipper. Now you can see that my beer is almost half empty already." Ken turned to watch her as she retreated to the bar with her hand over her mouth to cover a constant stream of joyful giggles.

As she departed, Ken looked at Quinn with a surprisingly somber look. "How well do you know Betsy Valentine?" he asked in a low voice.

"Not well at all, why do you ask."

Ken looked at him steadily for a few seconds, as if the judge the truth of the response. "That is one foxy lady and I was hoping for an introduction," he said with a less serious tone.

"She asked for help getting her boat over for maintenance and I couldn't refuse."

"As one agent to another, you need to be cautious. She knows a lot of very important people and they tell her all kinds of things. And besides, I want to meet her and sail on that boat. She came to the marina after I left and I always thought that my timing was terrible."

"Well, I don't know her all that well, but I'll introduce you when we get a chance."

"Hey, where's my beer?" he said when he saw out of the corner of his eye that the waitress was coming. Once again she was flustered and all smiles. “Thank you, honey, you’re one of the best.”

A few more slugs of Foster’s and Ken said, “I’m serious about the Tahiti trip. I need some time off and I love to dive. A Company plane is heading in that direction, so if you don’t mind the spooks, I can get you a seat—interested?”

“Sure! That would beat an island hopper with Pacific Air. When does it leave?”

“The Company plane always leaves before first light. With the time change, we should be there by 1330. Can you be at the terminal on the south side of the airport by 0400?”

“The 0400 doesn’t trouble me, but I have no transportation yet and taxis are not running that early in the morning.”

“Okay, I’ll pick you up then. Be out at the end of the dock at 3:30 A.M. and I’ll swing by to get you.”

“You’re sure this is a vacation?” Quinn asked as the waitress brought two giant sandwiches to the table piled high with pickles and onion rings. “Wow, it’s a good thing I’m hungry!”

“Thank you, love. Tell the chief to make them bigger next time.” As the waitress left the table, he returned to the conversation. “Yes, it is a vacation, but just like you, we are always watching and collecting information. Hey, beautiful, my beer’s getting low over here!”

Quinn didn’t have an alarm clock yet, so he decided to put the wake-up time on the dial of his shortwave radio and planned to watch it closely.

Since most of his clothes were for cold weather, packing would be easy, just underwear, shaver, and toothbrush. He would have to buy some tropical clothing once he arrived in Tahiti. He was up at 3:00 A.M., had a quick bowl of cereal and then headed to the end of the dock to wait for his ride. He was always early. He couldn’t help it. Ken arrived to pick him up at 4:15 A.M. He was always late; he couldn’t help it either.

“Will they hold the plane for us?” Quinn asked.

“Oh yeah, I know the pilot—he won’t leave without me,” he said with a smile.

The terminal was a rundown building located on the back

side of the International Airport runway. Security seemed lax to Quinn, but on entering the building he could see that there were a number of people actively involved monitoring radios and radar screens. Steven was there and greeted Quinn when he entered the room.

"I understand you are on the Hawaiian flight with a stopover in Tahiti," he said with a smile. Steve was dressed in blue jeans with a faded tee shirt and boat shoes, which was pretty much the same uniform Ken James was wearing. "I was hoping to talk to you about James, before you worked with him in the field. He is a very interesting person and an excellent field agent. However, you do have to put up with some quirks, but there is no one else I would want nearby when trouble starts."

"Hmmm, I wish you had time to catalog those traits for me. Unfortunately, I will have to learn on the fly. He said that this is a vacation for him, so I don't think we will be having any trouble."

"Vacation, is that what he told you?"

Ken approached with a tall man in his early fifties. "Quinn, this is Elliott Greene, our pilot for this trip. Elliott and I go way back to Viet Nam and he is one of the most resourceful pilots I have ever flown with and an asset to the Company."

"You gentlemen ready to go?" he inquired, cutting Ken off from the last part of the introduction that he had apparently heard before. "You're the only two on the flight this morning. The rest of the cargo is already loaded."

The plane was a Cessna Citation 5, a twin engine jet that carried seven passengers. The main seats in the cabin faced each other, with a couch to the rear. Ken flopped into the couch like he had done this a thousand times. "Let's get this crate in the air. I need to get some more sleep," he shouted up towards the cockpit.

"You should have gotten your sleep before you got here, Agent James. You're on the Company clock now," Elliott calmly responded from the pilot's seat. "Fasten your seat belts, gentlemen. There is a typhoon in the Pacific and the air currents are likely to give us a rough ride."

The copilot was the last to enter the aircraft. She was young and good-looking, dressed in what could be called a uniform of black slacks and white shirt open at the neck. Her brown hair was pulled back into a bun. She shut the cabin door and locked it in place, then turned and locked eyes with Ken. The two did not say a word. After a significant pause, she turned and entered the cockpit.

"I guess we're ready to go now," he said with a look of exasperation.

"I take it you two know one another," Quinn observed.

"Oh, yes, we know each other, maybe a little too well."

The little plane came to life and taxied to the north-south runway. The airport was silent in the early morning hours as the nondescript little jet gained speed and took off into the predawn sky. Ken slumped against the bulkhead and pulled his baseball cap down over his eyes. "Wake me up when we get there," he said, leaving Quinn to stare at the lights along the eastern coastline of Australia as they made their way north northeast toward Tahiti.

After about an hour of flight, Quinn made his way up to the galley, looking for something to drink. He opened a few cabinets and caught the attention of the copilot. "May I help you?" she asked.

"I was hoping to find some coffee and maybe something to eat," he responded.

"I'm sorry, I did not introduce myself. I'm Heather Summers and you are ...?"

"I'm Quinn Wilson with the NGIA. I'm just a passenger this morning heading for Tahiti," he said with his hand extended.

"You are a friend of Agent James?" she asked, while looking back to the cockpit instruments and ignoring his extended hand.

"We are traveling together, but I have only known him for a few months," Quinn said somewhat defensively.

"Coffee is in the cabinet to the right of the sink. There are some breakfast packs below the microwave. Can you get me a cup as well?"

"Sure, how do you like it?" Quinn asked, as she responded to a radio message and spoke to the pilot.

Quinn found the cups and the decanter of coffee. He was pouring a cup when she finally responded, "Agent Wilson, I need you to return to your seat and buckle in. There is some weather ahead and it is going to make things a kind of rough for a little while. I'll take that coffee though, black please, with a lid." Quinn handed it up to her and asked Elliott if he wanted a cup. It was obvious that he was preoccupied. So, Quinn poured another cup and went back to his seat. Ken was still asleep and snoring loudly. Make that *very* loudly. A few minutes later the plane, began experiencing turbulence. Ken seemed to be able to sleep through anything. Then when Quinn least expected it, Ken rose from the couch in mid-snore. He looked at Quinn, took a swallow of a stale beer and said, "Tahiti is experiencing some very real political problems. We are expecting almost anything and very soon. An economic problem with the tourist industry could put the situation into a tailspin. There are also reports of problems in the dive industry. What you call *reef bleaching* could create just that situation. The tourists on the islands could be in jeopardy, even in physical danger. So, don't think that you're just on a resource recon mission. It's much more serious than that. Keep it quiet and low key. Instruct your guys in NGIA or whatever its name is to do the same. My job is to keep this government from committing suicide. Do you understand what's at stake here?"

"I suspected there was another reason you were coming along on this trip. Tell me, who are they at odds with? Is it internal or a foreign power?"

"It's internal. Just small-town politics played out on a national scale for the hearts and minds of a small army."

"Thanks for telling me. I will modify my approach to the problem. So, you're not planning to dive with me?"

"Oh, yes," Ken said with a fake show of certainty. "I really am on vacation. I'm just preventing a civil war as a sideline. After college and before I joined the Company, I was a dive master in the Bahamas. We had a pretty good business going on Andros

Island near the Tongue of the Ocean. Are you familiar with the area?"

"I have never been there, but I am familiar with the Tongue of the Ocean," Quinn responded.

"We would dive every day the weather allowed. Everyone was fascinated by the tongue with its shear walls descending straight down to over 7,000 feet. You could see the ecosystems changing with the depth of the water as you floated down the wall. You never knew what the sea was going to bring to the walls. I'm talking about deep sea life, white sharks, whales and schools of pelagic fish. I miss it and when I heard about your mission, I signed up for vacation and here we are."

"Just how did you hear about the trip? I got a call on a secured satellite phone line and, within minutes, you drop by to say you were coming on the trip."

"Let's just say I have some trade secrets and like I told you at the airport when we first met, I've got this feeling about you. Things happen when you are around. I had to go with my gut instincts on this one. I did not want to be sitting on my ass back at the office when you brought down the independent nation of Tahiti single-handedly," he said half-serious.

"Now wait a damn minute," Quinn started in self-defense.

"Ha, ha, I got a little carried away there, didn't I? But I do plan on being around to see if my instincts are right about you." With a final laugh, Ken pulled his baseball cap back down over his eyes and once again was snoring as if nothing had been said.

Quinn, on the other hand, had a lot to think about.

After a very rough flight of approximately eight hours, the plane landed in Pupate, Tahiti and taxied to a small FBO along the runway. They were met by a tour bus that was specifically operated by the Company's field office. Elliott and Heather were staying in Tahiti. A fresh crew would be taking the plane into Honolulu after refueling. The tour bus would take the four of them to the Company's safe house just outside of the bustling urban center of town. "You go ahead and check in," Ken said casually. "I have some expatriates that I need to meet with. Quinn, you do your thing to arrange the dive boat and I'll catch up with you later. Francis at the front desk can direct you to the dive shop for setting up arrangements. Look up Curley Carswell at Sandman's Divers at the marina and he can set the trip up for you. We did talk last night about things, didn't we?" Ken asked as if trying to remember their conversation. Quinn nodded his head in agreement. "Good, I'll talk to you later," said Ken as he sauntered off towards town as if he was a native.

Quinn was slightly confused by the accommodations. It had all the feel of a small hotel, with a desk clerk, room service, a small bar and a swimming pool. Francis was indeed helpful, once Quinn had passed a battery of questions about the NGIA. He threw his small bag into the room and headed for the CIA-approved dive shop. He needed to get his dive gear, but he also wanted to buy some tropical clothing. A bathing suit, some Hawaiian shirts, a baseball cap and boat shoes seemed like the order of the day. He also bought a light wetsuit with swim mask and vest. The proprietor was very pleased to have a customer like Quinn, who obviously had not been in the sun for quite sometimes. Since Quinn spent over a thousand dollars, he threw in a bottle of SFP 45 suntan lotion for free.

Quinn changed in the store into his new shorts and shirt. He then walked through the town to the docks. He hoped that his appearance and the dive bag over his shoulder would allow him to blend in with the crowd as much as Ken seemed to. Unfortunately, the ultra white legs were a dead giveaway. There were some things you could not do in Antarctica and getting a suntan was one of them. Francis had given him directions to Curley's dive boat. Quinn found the skipper cleaning his boat after an afternoon charter. Captain Curley came highly recommended by the Company. He was a well-known and respected dive master. As Quinn would soon find out, he was a native Tahitian, of a Polynesian mother and a Portuguese sailor, so he was at home in the culture, as well as on the water.

"Good afternoon, skipper!" Quinn hailed from the dock.

"And a good day to you, mate. Any day here in the Society Islands is a good day," Captain Curley was also a member of the Chamber of Commerce and never missed a chance to promote tourism.

"I'm looking for a multi-island dive charter, can you help me?"

"Multi-island you say? You have come to the right place. Come on board and we'll see what we can do. How many are there in your party?"

"Just two," Quinn responded. "This is more of a scientific dive, so we will need to access some areas away from the usual dive sites."

"Ha, scientific dives are my specialty. You work for a university?"

Once again the issue of employment caught Quinn unprepared. "No, I am an environmental consultant," he said, opting to respond as he would have during his years in the consulting business. "I work for a variety of private and governmental agencies. I want to access some areas to inventory the species present and the diversity of habitat. Are you familiar with the worldwide biodiversity inventory?"

"Biodiversity! I think we have some of that in the bars down on Poota Street!" They both laughed. Quinn had gotten by the first obstacle, with his own ability to lie. "So where is this biodiversity you're looking for?"

"We haven't plotted all of the monitoring stations yet, but there are some areas that we would like to look at around here. We were planning on two sites around Tahiti and several others in Bora Bora and in the Tuamotu Archipelago. Can you help me schedule a series of dives in those locations?"

"No problem, mate. I have contacts on all the islands and can set up the whole expedition. When would you like to get started? I've got a charter tomorrow, but then I am available for the rest of the week."

"We really need to get on the water as soon as possible. Is there anyone else who can take us out tomorrow?"

"Oh, sure man. I have a brother-in-law who is almost as good-looking as me. He doesn't have a charter tomorrow. Just don't offer him a beer and you'll make it back to the island," he said jokingly.

"Does he have tanks and compressors on board?"

"Yes, sir, he comes fully equipped and my sister will love you for hiring him."

"Would you set it up for me for tomorrow? We'll be down here tomorrow morning at 7:30 your time," Quinn said, feeling good that tomorrow had been taken care of.

"Seven-thirty it will be then. My brother-in-law likes to sleep in."

"You sure give him a great sales pitch. I hope he appreciates your efforts on his behalf," Quinn said with a laugh, as he headed back to the hotel. With business out of the way, Quinn had time to look around in the late afternoon. In spite of its tropical location, Pupate had the feel of a third-world town. There were a lot of men hanging out on the corner drinking beer and watching as people passed by. The houses were crowded together and many of the lawns were bare dirt with shirtless boys playing in the mud, while large Polynesian mothers watched from their porches. Goats and chickens were common and seemed to wander free with no indication of ownership. Traffic was fast and the Tahitian drivers used their horns frequently. Pedestrians were at risk, as hotshot taxicab drivers impressed their fares with their driving skills.

Back at the hotel, Quinn made his way to the bar. There Elliott and Heather were lounging over a beer. "May I join you?" he asked cheerfully.

"Sure, come on over and have a beer," Elliott responded as he motioned to the waitress and pointed at his glass. "You both look like you know this place really well," Quinn observed.

"We have been making this milk run for …as long as I can remember. Tomorrow afternoon, we'll pick up the incoming flight and take it stateside," Heather said. "By the way, where is Striker?"

"Striker?"

"Agent James," said Elliott. "That is his chosen code name and pretty well describes what he thinks of himself," added Heather.

"Striker, huh. It does seem to fit, although I haven't known him very long."

"Don't get me wrong—he is the best field agent in the Pacific field office. However, socially he is a hyperactive little boy who never grew up. He can find a political conspiracy at a pajama party," Heather offered with a measure of exasperation. "But let's not talk about him. I understand that you are not with the Company?"

"No, my job is far less exotic. Just natural resource data collection," Quinn said, not knowing how much to divulge even to fellow intelligence agents.

"Can't talk about it, huh? It sounds just like the standard agency double-talk that we use all the time," laughed Elliott. "Heather and I come up with all kinds of explanations of what we do for a living. Our standard line is that we are corporate pilots for a big American engineering firm and fly company executives back and forth to the U.S. You get used to lying."

"Ken said that you were in Antarctic. How was that?" Heather asked.

"That's right. I've only been back a couple of weeks."

"This must be quite a contrast, being here in Tahiti after a winter in Antarctica," pondered Elliott.

"It certainly is, but I'm not complaining."

"I remember now! You were part of that expedition to the impact crater weren't you?" Heather asked excitedly. "Now that was interesting. I listened to every report and got concerned when the team was out of contact. What was it like?"

"Well, the trip was arduous, but the crater was unbelievable. There was a huge gaping canyon in the middle of an ice sheet. We believe that it is the largest impact crater to hit earth in centuries. We all were lucky that it landed on the ice sheet. If it was a few hundred miles to the north, it would have impacted in the Pacific Ocean and caused a tsunami that would have devastated coastal areas. If that had happened, we probably would not be having this beer or this conversation. There would have been a very destructive tidal wave."

"Amazing, that it would have been so destructive," Heather observed leaning forward and enjoying the story.

"You know, it is interesting to hear that people were actually listening to the expedition's progress. We felt totally isolated. Our world was reduced to the six of us and the two tractors. Of course, you heard that the French team was lost en route to the crater. No trace of them has been found."

A noisy intrusion caused all of them to turn and see Agent James entering the bar with his usual fanfare. The energy in the entire room increased as he shouted greetings to the bartender and hugged all the waitresses.

"Oh, crap, here comes Striker," Heather muttered.

"Hey, gang! I see you are getting acquainted," he said as he approached the table and then turned to Quinn, "I hear you set up a dive trip tomorrow with Curley's brother-in-law."

"Huh, yes! How did you ...?"

"That is my business! Get used to the fact that I know everything," he laughed as he kissed Heather's reluctant hand, which she pulled away, while cutting him down with her eyes. He didn't seem to notice. "What reason did you give for the dive?"

"I thought you knew everything," Quinn responded, while Elliott and Heather laughed.

"Well, maybe not everything—you got me there."

"Biodiversity inventory is our objective," Quinn stated, feeling vindicated.

"I bet you think that I don't know what that means," Ken chided. "I suspect that is a safe enough answer to keep us under the radar. Sports diving would not have worked, given the out-of-the-way areas you wanted to dive. Have you mapped them yet?"

"I have the coordinates and will put them on a nautical chart I picked up today. I'll have them ready by tomorrow morning to guide us to the dive sites. The dive boat leaves at 0730, you going to be there?"

"If I do not show up at 7:30 A.M. sharp, just leave without me. I may want to sleep in and will catch up later," Ken responded smiling in Heather's direction.

"Is anyone up for dinner tonight? I had a light lunch and I'm about to starve," Ken asked. Elliott and Heather just shook their heads in disinterest without saying a word.

"I know of a place over on the waterfront that serves the best snapper on the islands. They wrap it in banana leaves with plantains and cook it under coals," Ken said with some enthusiasm. "Come on, you guys have to eat, and you know what the food is like here."

Elliott and Heather exchanged glances, "Okay, but we have to be back here by 0900. We have a long flight tomorrow and have to be rested."

"Yeah, yeah, you pilots are such nerds! Sleep is so overrated and gets in the way of the mission too often," Ken said. "We'll leave here in 20 minutes."

Dinner was interesting as the three friends jockeyed around old relationships and avoided discussions of business, since there was a non-Company guest at the table. Ken was right about the snapper. It was served up in a little restaurant with tin walls and a roof of palm fronds, located on the commercial end of the waterfront but with little tourist traffic. The food was 100 percent Polynesian, prepared for the islander's taste and served on a bed of brown rice—delicious! Of course, Ken knew the proprietor and spent a few intense minutes discussing island issues with him at the bar. He was wandering around the tables like some host at a wedding party when we waved goodbye and told him we were heading back to the hotel. Ken waved back and continued to talk to some local fishermen.

Quinn spent the next few hours charting dive sites and getting all the tags off his dive gear. Sleep came slowly and the sun rose early over the island. It rained just before dawn, so the streets were wet, as if cleaned for the new day. The tropical trade winds were starting to build as Quinn walked through the town heading for the docks. The merchants were just opening the shops and the noisy taxicabs were not yet on the road. It felt like Key West back in his home State of Florida. He stopped and bought a cup of coffee from an island vendor and was feeling back in his element as he arrived at the docks. He was always early—he couldn't help it.

Curley's brother-in-law was not as bad as he had feared. An islander by birth, he was a short man with a barrel chest and broad shoulders but he also had a warm smile and a very strong handshake. Quinn reviewed the map with him and addressed concerns for the locations of the dive sites. The islander ventured, "I've never been to those sites, man, much prettier reefs over here and here. You sure you want to go to these sites?" he asked.

"Yes, these are the control sites for the program," Quinn responded. "Let me call my partner and see if he is on the way." Quinn rang Ken's cell number and was a little shocked to hear Heather's sleepy voice answer.

"...Hello."

"Uhh, this is Quinn, I was calling for Ken."

"Quinn, he is still asleep," she said without hesitation. "Do you want me to wake him?"

"No, I was checking to see if he was joining me for the dive today."

"No, I don't think he is in any shape to dive after last night."

"Huh. Okay, just tell him I called." After a few puzzled moments starring at his cell phone, he said to the captain, "It looks like I will be the only diver today."

"Not safe, man, always two divers minimum. You need a buddy, in case of problems."

"I appreciate the concerns, but let's go. I'll take full responsibility." Quinn said, knowing the captain was right. But the job needed to get done.

Within 45 minutes after leaving the marina, they dropped anchor at the first dive site. The water was clear and the sandy bottom next to the reef below the boat was a beautiful shade of light blue. Since it was only 25 feet of water, Quinn dispensed with the scuba and decided to free-dive the site. The plan was to document site conditions with a camera, do a quick inventory of bleached areas and move on. A half hour per site was all that was needed. By early afternoon, Quinn was sitting in the deck chair taking notes after diving on the fifth site of the day, when a call came in on the satellite phone. Quinn answered, expecting to hear from Alex in Washington.

"Walter here," Quinn answered.

"Striker, here. I need you back here at the dock as soon as possible."

"Striker? How did you get this number?"

"Let's just say I have my ways. We have an emergency and I need you back here, pronto. Do you read?"

"An emergency? What's up?"

"I'll give you all the details when you get back to the dock."

"Okay, Striker, I'll be there in 30 minutes." Quinn disconnected the call and shouted to the captain who was standing on the flying bridge with his binoculars, "It looks like we are done for today. Can you take me back to the dock?"

"Man, you pay for a full day of diving, no discount for returning early."

"I will pay for the entire day and I have Curley's boat tomorrow. There is some kind of an emergency and I need to get back to the dock as quickly as possible."

"Sure, mate, you pay full day, we go back to the dock now. No problem."

A half hour later as they approached the slip, Quinn saw Ken pacing the dock. He swung aboard before the boat was in the slip. "Listen, we have a problem," he started without further discussion. "A group of university types landed today and have been talking up the reef bleaching problem. They have already caused some problems and we need to shut them down before their big mouths get themselves killed."

"You think it is that serious?"

"Hell, yeah! I want you to go talk to them with me …and bring your weapon."

"My weapon!" Quinn said with surprise as he looked around to see if the captain heard his comment. "You want me to bring a gun to talk to a university professor and some graduate students?"

"Listen, trust me on this, all right. I'm not saying you have to shoot anyone. Leave that part to me!"

"Leave it to you!"

"All right, I was kidding. The weapons are there to make a point. University professors can be very self-righteous and I want to get their attention fast. Are you with me on this?"

"First, let me call the main office to see if I can join forces with the CIA on this."

"No need for that. How do you think I got your number, Walter?"

"Okay, okay, let's go …my weapon is in my sea bag."

"Put it on! Put it on! You can't scare the shit out of college types if your gun is not showing. Trust me, I have been doing this for a long time. We have been informed that professors Hank Swick and Marlene Luwinski from the University of Arizona landed at Pateate shortly after 1:30 P.M. They and five graduate students are apparently here to study the increasing threat of reef bleaching. They were also proclaiming their research objectives at the airport, in the taxi, and at the hotel. Word of their arrival was already circulating within the upper levels of city government and economic vigilantes were discussing how to silence the problem.

Ken and Quinn arrived at the hotel to find the professors and their students out by the pool. The grad students included two young men in their early twenties and three young women. Four of them were acting like teenagers, frolicking around the pool. The fifth one appeared older, possibly a professional who was returning to the university for an advanced degree after working for ten or more years.

"Oh God, look at these kids, playing while they bring down a government," Ken muttered under his breath as he approached the two people he intuitively recognized as the professors.

"Professors Swick and Luwinski?" He asked in his official voice. "I am Agent James and this is Agent Wilson. We need to talk to you in private."

"Agents? Agents for whom?"

"The CIA. Now is there a place where we can talk?"

"You say the CIA? I will need to see some identification."

Ken reached for his wallet in his coat pocket and in doing so, revealed the Smith and Wesson automatic in his shoulder holster. As predicted at the dock, the presence of a weapon had the intended effect on the professors, as they got much more serious.

Ken showed them his ID and said, "Now, is there a place we can talk?"

Professor Swick motioned towards a secluded area at the end of the pool, as one of the female graduate students ran passed squealing with laughter.

"What is this all about?" Professor Swick said as they settled in around a metal table under a palm tree at the end of the pool.

"We understand that you are here on a research effort. Is that correct?" Ken asked.

"That is correct. We have a grant to study reef bleaching here in the Society Islands. We plan to be here for about two weeks."

"Professor, the way you have been announcing your research, there is a chance you will not be alive in two weeks," Ken said for the shock effect.

"What are you talking about?"

"There are forces on these islands that will do anything to avoid the economic impacts that your effort may have on tourism."

"That is preposterous! I have a solid grant and I intend to conduct my research."

"Professor, you are going to conduct yourself in a manner that I tell you or you will not remain on this island. Is that clear?"

"Now just a God damn minute, you cannot talk to me in that manner. I am a respected professor and president of the Society of Marine Biology, and I intend ..."

Quinn saw Ken unbutton his coat and decided it was time he jumped into the discussion. "Excuse me, Agent James," Quinn said while placing a hand on Ken's shoulder, "Let me talk to the professors about this a moment, if I may."

"What is this—good cop, bad cop?"

"This is no joking matter professor. I'm getting a drink. Quinn, you see if you can talk some sense into him," he said as he rose and sauntered off towards the bar adjusting his jacket and scanning the pool deck for locals who looked familiar.

"I am sorry, professors. It appears that we have gotten off to a bad start."

"You damn right you did. We are here for a very valid research project and we intend to fulfill the contract."

"I understand, but as Agent James hinted, there is fear of economic problems if reports of degraded reef conditions should slow tourism here in the islands. Apparently, there are individuals or organizations that would go to extremes to avoid that kind of a problem, even going so far as silencing the source." Quinn waited to see if the message was sinking in. Both professors were silent and they looked at one another as Quinn continued, "I'm actually not with the CIA, but rather the National Geo-Spatial Intelligence Agency and I am here on the same mission as you. To see if the reef bleaching problems experienced in other tropical reefs have found its way to the Society Islands. Agent James accompanied me on this mission out of concern for the island's government. He tells me that the government is shaky and would be adversely impacted by bad economic news. Furthermore, he tells me the impacts could be violent and jeopardize the lives of tourists. For that reason, I have continued my work under the guise of the worldwide biodiversity inventory.

"Christ, I am a professor and I am used to dealing with the facts, a habit that I plan to continue."

"Would your truth be worth placing your students in harm's way?" Quinn asked. Seeing that his message was sinking in, Quinn continued, "Now this is what we suggest. First, you and your students tone down your rhetoric about your research. If the worldwide biological diversity inventory does not work for you, then come up with another topic that does not have the apparent fear factor that reef bleaching does. I have already scheduled a series of dives throughout the islands. You can join me and Agent James if you like. The benefits are that you will get free charter to each island and a measure of protection by having an observant agent along. Interested?"

After some moments he said, "If we were to go along with this charade, I want it understood that Marlene and I have the lead role of the research protocol. We chose the stations and structure the monitoring efforts. Is that understood?"

"Professor, I have information from a series of satellite imageries that would assist in targeting areas of concern. If you are willing to consider this data, then we may have a deal."

"Did you say your name was Wilson? You're not related to the scientist who led that expedition in Antarctica are you?

"That was me."

"Good God, man! That was an amazing piece of work. What in Christ's name are you doing here in the tropics after conducting landmark research in the Antarctic?"

"I am a natural resources troubleshooter. I go where the problems are," Quinn offered with a faint smile. "So do we have a deal?'

"Very well, we'll go along with this charade for now."

"Great! The first thing we need to do is talk to your grad students and tone down the discussions of your field work and secondly, you need to mend fences with Agent James."

"Mend fences—what on bloody earth for?"

"Because he has the gun!"

"Right! Right!"

CHAPTER 12

Connections

By early afternoon, Nancy was on the train heading for Paris. After shopping for necessities, she had been cautious getting the first train out. She thought that Roberto might come looking for her and she did not want to be found. She had made another stop by the ATM before leaving town. It generously produced an additional 2,000 Euros of security money for the trip home. She would have five days in Paris and had decided to take advantage of the time by exploring the city. She and Roberto had passed through the city on their way to Nice, but had not visited any of the sites. She had always enjoyed reading about the history of Paris, Rome, Venice and the movies that were filmed there. She remembered as a young girl seeing the movie, *Three Coins in the Fountain,* which was filmed in Rome. Maybe she could visit there too before she headed back to the States. After all she thought to herself, "Quinn owes me for all those boring years I put up with him. I deserve a little excitement."

The events of the night before remained a blur. However, some images kept popping into her head. She did not like what she was remembering. Roberto had been degrading, humiliating, and abusive. She touched the bruise on her cheeks and remembered his angry bloodshot eyes just before he hit her. She also recalled the other women squealing with contrived pleasure—that was part of the degradation.

As she tried to look forward to returning home, continued pushing those images and thoughts from her head. Once aboard the train, she found herself seated across the aisle from a rather studious-looking gentleman, who was occupied writing in his journal. He would pause for a moment in deep thought and then return to vigorously writing notes. Since they were both traveling alone, she thought it would be interesting to get acquainted.

"Excuse me for interrupting, but are you an American?" she asked.

"Why, yes, I am!" he exclaimed, surprised by her overture.

"So nice to meet you. My name is Nancy Wilson from St. Petersburg, Florida."

Taking her outstretched hand he said, "I am Thomas White. It's nice meeting you as well. I'm an attorney from New York. I am here in Europe on an extended vacation."

"I thought you might be a writer, considering the notes you were taking," she said with a nervous laugh.

"Just some travel notes about Nice and the Mediterranean. The journal is a hobby of mine. The notes help me remember the areas I visited better than photographs. I can read these years later and the feel of the place comes back to me. It is such a beautiful area, don't you think?"

"Oh, yes, I have enjoyed my stay here very much so far. But now it is almost time to return home. I have just five days left in Paris before I must go back to the States, so I plan to enjoy every minute of what's left."

"Well, I have a four-day layover in Paris myself. Perhaps we might join forces?"

This is just too easy she thought as she smiled in response. "Oh, that would be splendid. It is so difficult to be a female alone in Paris. Now tell me some of the places you have been." Within a few short sentences, she had established a liaison with a very handsome man on a train bound for Paris. It sounded more like a romantic novel than real life, but here she was, chatting away and enjoying herself tremendously.

Thomas was an athletic-looking man in his later 40s to early 50s with reddish blond hair and a touch of gray at the temples. He wore a pair of rimless glasses and had a habit of looking over the top of them as he spoke. His posture was straight and purposeful, reminding her of a military man. He was dressed casually in a blue denim shirt and khaki pants and boat shoes. He wore no distinguishing jewelry—she had checked earlier for a wedding ring and found no rings at all. His watch looked like the kind a marathoner would wear to keep track of his vital statistics. The blue journal was never out of his hands. A large rubber band separated the entries from the blank pages. He made entries into the journal with a fat fountain pen. While she could not read the notes, she could see very orderly handwriting interspaced with some sketches of buildings and landscapes. It aroused her curiosity.

He told her that he was on a sabbatical from his law firm in New York and that twice a year, one of the active partners got a six-month paid sabbatical to pursue other interests. So every five years he got the opportunity to travel. He was recently divorced. His job kept him away from home, so his wife had lost interest in their marriage. There were two kids still at home, but apparently they did not miss him very much.

She in turn said that she was divorced with a daughter who was in college in the states and that she was recovering with an extended stay in the south of France at her family doctor's residence. How grateful she was for the good doctor to help her recover from her loss.

"Where are you staying in Paris?" he asked.

"I don't have a hotel reservation," she said innocently.

"Why don't you stay at my hotel? It is a small out-of-the-way place that I discovered during my last trip over. I'm sure they would have a vacancy," he said with some anticipation.

"That sounds very charming. I think I would like that," she purred in response.

They were a couple by the time they reached Paris and needed only one room at the hotel.

CHAPTER 13

Reefs

Quinn's negotiated settlement with the professors was paying dividends. His first day of diving was by himself. By the second day there were nine divers in the water. So many, that they needed both Curley and his brother-in-law's boats. Agent James was in a jovial mood and dove with them three days straight. He particularly liked the graduate students whom he charmed with stories of his early days as a dive master in the Bahamas. The reef bleaching problem seemed to be widespread, but not as severe along the many reef formations and atolls of the Society Islands. Surprisingly enough, the outbreaks were typically occurring in isolated areas away from the anthropogenic influences of city life on the islands. There were those who were quick to point fingers at wastewater discharges, oil spills, or storm water runoff from developed areas as the primary cause of the bleaching. However, Quinn's observations and research indicated that the cause appeared to be a natural phenomenon, perpetuated by changes in temperature or water chemistry. At some monitoring sites, the coral near the surface was affected less than the same species at deeper depths. These were not isolated incidents, but rather a worldwide pandemic affecting all reef systems. Large numbers of coral reefs worldwide had died suddenly, leaving once thriving marine communities barren.

Quinn had first observed this in the Florida Keys during recreational dives in the early 1980s. When he had returned from Desert Storm and wanted to wash away the grime and sweat of the Middle East in his boyhood haunts on the reefs along the Florida Straits, what he found was disturbing. The bright reef colors and biological diversity he had known in the early 1980s were gone, with bare limestone left in their place. Also, gone was the vast assemblage of sea creatures that congregated around the reefs. At that time, no one knew what was causing the reefs to die. It was feared that overpopulation of the Florida Keys was causing the problem. The most likely suspect was the infamous wastewater treatment plant in Key West that had discharged raw sewage to the open waters of the Florida Straits. A political witch hunt had occurred, with carrying capacity studies, grants for waste water treatment system upgrades, and stricter land development codes, but still the problem persisted. Quinn reflected on these thoughts between dives, nearly two decades after he first learned of these problems. The scientific community had filled in some of the answers, but still no cure. From all indications, the cause was climate changes causing increased sea water temperatures or the more politically correct term, "global warming." Quinn began his report to the NGIA.

REEF BLEACHING IN THE SOCIETY ISLANDS

Sporadic reports of reef bleaching in the Society Islands have been investigated during the two-week period of October. Methodology of the investigation included reconnaissance dives on suspected areas identified from recent satellite images with documentation of conditions done by on-site inventories and photographs, and control dives conducted on healthy reefs in the vicinity to identify changes in diversity and assemblage of marine species. NGIA was assisted in this effort by a team of biologists from the University of Arizona, College of Marine Science. This report is based on over 200 hours of dive time recorded by this team around the islands of Tahiti, Bora Bora and in the Tuamotu Archipelago.

Overview:

Coral bleach is not isolated to the waters of the Society Islands, but rather is a problem observed with increasing

> frequency on tropical reefs throughout the world. Severe outbreaks can result in the widespread death of both the fast growing Pocillopora, as well as the slow-growing Porites coral. The skeletal reefs remaining after bleaching events are slow to recover and may not return to their pre-bleaching level of diversity for more than one hundred years. The loss of these bio-diverse communities is likely to have a profound and far reaching impact on the marine ecology, as well as the economy of areas vested in dive tourism. The marine assemblage of fish and crustaceans in bleached areas was notably less than the healthy reef systems viewed during control dives. Coral reefs are recognized as some of the most diverse and productive ecosystems on the planet and long-term impacts to these reefs would cause a ripple effect throughout the ocean communities.
>
> The body of research indicates that extreme temperature and increased solar irradiation are the main causes of coral bleaching. El Nino events in the South Pacific re-enforce this theory by documenting record rising sea-surface temperatures by as much as 1°C, a fifty-year high for that region.

Quinn's thoughts strayed back to the meteor impact back in Antarctica. It felt like a lifetime ago, yet it had only been a little over a month since he left the ice. He wondered to himself whether the huge amount of ice ejected into the stratosphere would moderate or exacerbate the global warming effect. More moisture in the stratosphere would reflect more incoming solar radiation back to space, but the increased cloud cover would trap more heat in the lower atmosphere. Climatologists always viewed climate change as a very slow process that moved in 10,000-year cycles. Yet, could a cataclysmic event such as the meteor impact change the earth's climate in a matter of weeks or months?

CHAPTER 14

Journey into Hell

Quinn was jolted back to the present by his satellite phone ringing. Once again it was Candace in Washington asking him to hold for Alex. She was also curious about the mission to paradise and how things were going. "Hello, Walter! Alex here. "I was wondering if you could possibly handle another crisis for us on short notice?"

"Well, everything seems to be under control here, so what have you got in mind?"

"We have another situation developing this morning. The Hibok-Hibok volcano on the island of Mindanao in the Philippines has apparently erupted. I say apparently, because Hibok-Hibok is on a small island off Camiguin on the western side of Mindanao. This eruption appears to be on the mainland approximately 25 miles from the parent volcanic cone. It is either a new volcano altogether or a vent of the existing one. There has been no eruption in this area since 1953, so this is a major event and volcanologists from all over the world are heading for the area."

"Wow, with that much coverage where do I fit in?"

"First, we want you looking at the human element around the impact area. Apparently, one of the earlier eruptions had casualties. Records say that 326 people drowned, attempting to escape the ash clouds. Apparently, this volcano erupts every 75 years, plus or minus a decade, and there have been people living around it for centuries. What we can't see from the satellite images is how they are responding to the eruption.

Let the volcanologists do their thing. We would like you to go and check out the evacuation efforts up to 100 miles from the eruption. Can you leave the coral expedition for a few days? It sounds like everything is going along pretty well there with the CIA's assistance and all."

"Yes, the CIA has been a big help on this one. The graduate students particularly appreciate Ken's involvement. I'll check the airlines and see what is available for Mindanao and get back to you."

"No need, I was able to call in a favor from the CIA. They have a plane heading in that direction tomorrow morning. You should be able to make connections at the safe house. I already have your name on the flight list. They can put you on the ground 100 miles from the event."

"By the way, Quinn, we have some trouble back on Antarctica. But first let's concentrate on the mission at hand. I'll talk to you later about that one.

"What kind of trouble are you talking about, Alex? Is everyone okay?"

"Yes, no one is in any physical danger, at least we hope not. It's just that the scientists are up in arms over management. The usual stuff, but it sounds a little more serious, due to the intensity of the impact research. The NSF was over this morning asking about your availability to help iron out the kinks. But as I see it, the volcano is much more urgent at the moment, so we will talk more about ice after you have reconned the volcano. You know, as a side issue, the tectonic plates seem to be on the move. We are getting increasing reports of minor earthquakes and tremors in all parts of the world and now a new volcanic eruption. Do you think the meteor impact had anything to do with it?"

"I would say that it is very possible, but almost impossible to prove. We'll just have to keep an eye on it and evaluate the evidence in a few years. That goes for the climate as well."

"As usual, travel with full gear and give the desk a call daily on this one, since there is a little more danger involved with this assignment."

"I'll get back to you once I arrive at destination."

Quinn talked to Ken and Professor Swick about his departure. They confirmed that he would not be missed for a few days. That evening back at the hotel, he made connections with the Company's pilot. The plane was scheduled to depart at 0400 Pacific Time.

There was little time or inclination to sleep that night, so Quinn was waiting in the lobby when the sleepy crew came down for the trip to the airport. As was typical on these Company flights, the passengers were cordial, but there was little conversation other than comments on the weather. Quinn stayed glued to the window of the plane through sun rise and the emergence of the emerald-blue water of the Pacific from the gray of dusk. In the distance, the water would turn a deep purple where the deeper water ran between the islands. The plane flew due west from Pipette and made a brief stop in Fiji to drop off a field crew. After refueling, the plane headed northwest past New Hebrides, Solomon Islands, and the Bismarck Archipelago off the coast of Papua, New Guinea. The pilot reported that a pesky typhoon was still churning westward through Micronesia and diverted the flight further to the west over the islands of Indonesia before turning north towards the Philippines.

As the plane approached its destination, an event began to take shape that would threaten this routine data collection effort. Far out in the Pacific, east of Guam, a seasonal thunderstorm began to increase in intensity, fueled by the heated surface waters at twelve degrees latitude, as it stubbornly persisted and grew in strength. Weather forecasters would first call it a local disturbance that moved from a tropical wave to a low-pressure trough, then a tropical storm, and finally a class-one typhoon. This newly formed storm began its westerly track as a minimal storm event, typical of the southeastern Asian summers, with little fanfare or long-range warnings. However, as it moved across the warm waters, it continued to grow in strength.

After what seemed like a very long time, the plane circled the airfield in Butuan on the island of Mindanao and prepared to land. Quinn could see the ash plume from the eruption to the southwest of the airfield as they began the approach. It was impressive, even awe inspiring. The sight reminded Quinn of the true power of nature once it is unleashed. His only exposure to a volcanic landscape had been on the big island of Hawaii during a vacation he and his wife had taken years ago. The lava flows had been beautiful. In comparison, Hibok-Hibok was an ash eruption, violent and very destructive. There is a reason for caution—the evacuation of the population around the volcano is a matter of life and death.

The local terminal was packed with people. It appeared that the eruption had not interrupted daily life for the locals, but there was evidence that spectators and scientists were flocking to the island to view and study the eruption. Quinn was delighted to discover that the powers of the U.S. government were at play when he found a Suzuki SUV reserved for his use at the Hertz rental counter. The young lady who waited on him was very pleasant and efficient. She was dressed in western attire and showed no concern for the eruption—after all it was over 80 miles way. She spoke English with only the slightest accent.

Butuan, a regional center on the north shore of Mindanao, was a city of 250,000 people and a mix of modern and traditional, with the relatively western-style downtown business district giving way to the traditional commercial and residential suburb as he drove through town. The streets were full of pedestrians, slow trucks and fast-moving cars with horns blowing and motor scooters all in a hurry to get to some important destination. The Filipino people appeared to be very industrious as they went about their daily activities, with no obvious concern for the eruption. Like the city itself, the people were dressed in a mix of western and traditional clothing. Quinn's geography background meant that he was always doing "socio-economic analyses" whether he wanted to or not. Here in Butuan, the people looked healthy and prosperous. There appeared to be a mixture of cultures. Some of the people appeared to be Polynesian who would be right at home in Tahiti, while the majority was Filipino and others appeared to be oriental or of mixed race.

The roads were well-paved and, after some momentary disorientation, Quinn was on what he thought was the right highway leading southwest from the city. The traffic flow coming from that direction was very heavy and many of the vehicles were loaded to the top with personal belongings and livestock. Goats and chickens in small cages were a common commodity. Traffic back to the west was light and Quinn made good progress towards the looming ash cloud that he could see at some vantage points along the road. His plan was to make it to the city of Lunao and then follow the coastline to Medina. Once there he would evaluate conditions and possibly head inland to see how the residents were responding to the eruption.

The Hibok-Hibok volcano was on Camigun Island in the Bohol Sea off the northwest coast of Mindanoa. This eruption appeared to be a major vent or a new volcano that was actually off the island and closer to the mainland. While Hibok Hibok had erupted every 50 to 75 years through recent times, this was the first event to occur off the island. The eruption was now thirty-six hours old and from Quinn's limited vantage point, it appeared to be getting more intense. The ash clouds rose an estimated ten to fifteen thousand feet off the coastline. The tropical tradewinds were taking the plume along the coast and generally out to sea. Still, the vehicles Quinn passed were covered with a layer of red volcanic dust. As he got closer to the region, traffic slowed as the roads became clogged with traffic that overflowed into the westbound lanes. There were more pedestrians, motor scooters, and bicycles, now all carrying huge bundles and, in some cases, entire families on a single scooter. There seemed to be a lot of babies in their mother's arms and young children clinging to their legs. Quinn could not help but marvel at the resilience of these people and the sturdy little urban machines that could carry a family of four.

Quinn had been in several hurricane evacuations back in Florida, but he could not help but note some differences in this Philippine evacuation. First, the eruption was a far more menacing threat than hurricanes had been. You could see the threat clearly on the horizon, with dark-gray to black clouds churning through the sky. Quinn was not sure whether he was imagining things or actually heard the rumble of the eruption twenty-five miles away. The second thing he noticed was the profound look of urgency on the faces of the evacuees. They were fleeing for their lives, unlike the Floridians, who appeared much more inconvenienced than threatened. There were also notable cultural differences. Floridians would pack suitcases and fill coolers with soft drinks and beer. The Filipinos brought their belongings bundled in sheets with garden vegetables and livestock for their immediate needs. He wondered if this was the kind of information the agency was looking for back in Washington.

At that thought, he picked up his satellite phone and checked the reception. *These new phones are incredible*, he thought. He was rarely out of communications anywhere in the Pacific Ocean or even Antarctica, for that matter. The situation desk answered his call immediately.

"NGIA," came the voice of a young female operator.

"Hello, this is Quinn Wilson on assignment in the Philippines calling to check in."

"Yes, Agent Wilson, please give me your code name."

"Walter!" Quinn could hear the sound of rapid typing.

"Very well, Walter, this call is being recorded and upon completion, will be forwarded to the appropriate destinations here at NGIA. Whom do you wish to receive the report?"

"Alex Reager for starters. He will distribute internally."

"Go ahead, Walter."

"This is Walter. I landed at the Butuan Airport at approximately 1430 Pacific time and I am en route to the Hibok Hibok volcanic eruption. The ash plume is fully visible from the Butuan area eighty miles from the event. The evacuation of the area around the volcano seems to be occurring currently, with the coastal roads operating at full capacity in an easterly direction. Judging from the bundles carried by the evacuees, it appears that they are carrying enough food and clothing to last for a week or more. Some are carrying livestock. The evacuation appears to be orderly so far, although the threat is still some distance away. This may change when I get closer to the eruption. My plan is to make it into the city of Gingoog on the coast of the Mindanao Sea before nightfall and assess conditions there. Then I will use that area for home base and recon out from there, depending on conditions. I will report back once I have reached that destination. At this time, the eruption is thirty-eight hours old. Walter out."

Quinn hung up the phone after receiving confirmation and concentrated on his driving. As he got closer to the eruption, the intensity of the evacuation increased, along with the strain on the faces of the people leaving. Cars and scooters were jockeying to get ahead and people were shouting at each other and waving arms to emphasis their need to make progress away from the menace that was becoming even more visible along the coast. It occurred to him that the throngs of people leaving the area were more like a controlled panic rather than an organized evacuation. Since Mindanao was an island, much of the travel throughout the area depended on ferries. As he drove the coastal highway, Quinn could see a number of boats large and small heading away from the eruption. While he could not see the passengers, he could imagine that these boats carried the same mix of evacuees that he was seeing on the roads. He recalled from his background reading that the majority of those killed in the last eruption drowned while escaping by water. The paved highways on the island generally paralleled the coastline with the main Pan America Highway running south of the mountainous center of the island, then north along the eastern coastline. He decided that he needed to see how the evacuation was going on this main road system.

The traffic continued to increase as Quinn drove further to the west. The urgency of the evacuees also seemed to increase as they jockeyed for space on the single two-lane road leaving the eruption. Quinn was often brought to a stop waiting for eastbound traffic to clear the road. A fleet of black jeeps approached from the rear and with a deft display of driving, they passed Quinn on the sharp shoulder of the road, just inches from a thirty-foot drop to the beach below and continued to plough into the oncoming traffic. Quinn followed as the lead cars simply forced their way through the crowds with repeated blasts from their horn. The vehicles were definitely not local and Quinn assumed that he was either following a government caravan or a research team making its way to the eruption. He smiled to think that it was only westerners who were heading towards the eruption, while the local population had the good sense to evacuate. His progress was slow but steady so long as he remained behind the caravan. It was well after dark when they approached the city of Gingoog. To the northwest, the dark clouds on the horizon were glowing orange with flashes of red as the volcano expelled magma. Quinn followed the fleet of black jeeps through the nearly abandoned streets of the city to what appeared to be an abandoned hotel near the coast. Four men in western attire exited the vehicles and the drivers made their way cautiously back to Quinn's vehicle. It occurred to Quinn that he may have represented a threat to the occupants of the jeeps. After all, he had been following them for two hours now and they had no idea who he was. The driver of the first jeep took a step back when Quinn opened the door and stepped out of his vehicle.

"Hi, I'm Quinn Wilson. I hope I haven't caused you any concern by following you through the evacuation."

"Well, maybe a little. My name is Scott Styles from the Volcanic Research Laboratory. It nice to meet you," he said with a handshake. "Things can and usually do get a little dicey during these eruptions. The criminal element always seems to capitalize on any disruption. We are here to measure and record this eruption."

Quinn felt an immediate affinity to Scott, a fellow scientist. His accent was American with a slight southern drawl. Quinn guessed that he was from the coastal areas of South Carolina. He was an athletic-looking man in his mid-thirties, about 5' 9" in height, with a closely cropped haircut and a pair of sunglasses on a lanyard around his neck. He wore a Columbia fishing shirt with multiple pockets and worn-out pair of blue jeans and running shoes. He spoke with an optimistic smile on his face that seemed to increase now that he knew that Quinn was not a threat.

"It is good to meet you, Scott. Are we in any danger here? The eruption seems to be increasing or is it just because we are getting closer?"

"You are right on both counts. You would expect that the eruption would seem stronger as we get closer, but it does appear to be increasing in intensity. At first light, we will be making our way towards the eruption and set up some instrumentation. Once we do that we can tell more about the event. This, for all practical purposes, is a new volcano, so we don't really know what to expect. To answer your first question, yes, there is danger. We can try to stay out of the way, but volcanoes are the most unpredictable and violent natural event on the planet," Scott said as if lecturing his college class.

With a quizzical look on his face, Scott continued, "What is your area of interest here?"

"I'm with the National Geo-Spatial Intelligence Agency. I'm here to fill in some of the blanks that cannot be documented by the agency's satellite imagery. I will be looking at the damages to the surrounding area and the evacuation."

"Okay, the NGIA! I am familiar with their satellite photographs. Would you happen to have any recent shots of the area?" Scott asked with anticipation. "We looked at the images two days ago before we started the trip, but have not seen anything since."

"Yes, I can access all the recent photographs of the area, assuming I can establish a computer connection to the satellite. Would you like me to give it a try?"

"Sure! Hey, guys, come on over and take a look at this! We may have access to the most recent government satellite coverage." Scott's team had been looking for the proprietor of the hotel with no success. The facility was deserted and locked up tight. The hatchback of the jeep was open and Quinn could see the glow of a computer screen and the green and blue indicator lamps from an array of electronic equipment.

Quinn booted up his laptop and was happy to see that he

had at least a tenuous satellite connection. He entered his password, "WALTER," and navigated to the secured website for the satellite imagery. The results were not disappointing. The most recent photographs already in the file were taken less than two hours before. Scott's team gasped at what they were seeing. The caldron had broken the surface approximately three quarters of a mile off the coast and a significant ash cone had emerged. The wispy smoke and ash they had seen two days ago had given way to a solid black plume of smoke and ash that was raising high into the atmosphere.

"Oh shit! This looks like a category three eruption and it has come to stay," one of Scott's team members volunteered. "We had better get a message out to the lab and a warning on the Worldwide Network. This fucker is dangerous."

"Can we connect your computer to our printer and run a copy of these images?" Scott asked.

"You have a printer?" Quinn responded.

"We are self-contained and very compact. Let me show you." Scott walked to the back of the jeep and retrieved a thin black carrying case. He plugged the machine into a power pack and connected it to Quinn's computer and as if by magic, an aerial photograph emerged. "How often do they update that file?" Scott asked.

"It is updated after every satellite pass, usually every ninety minutes. We can check it again later to see the next set of images."

"First things first, boss," one of Scott's team members said. "We have to get secured for the night. It would be good to have a roof over our heads—the only way we can do that is by breaking and entering. These thunderstorms are not good for the equipment. We have got to get them under roof!"

"Send Thomas to check on the other hotels and see if we can find one that is open. Have you got the walkie-talkies fired up yet?"

A young assistant, whom Quinn assumed was Thomas, was on the road almost immediately. A radio check came back before he was out of sight, "Home base, home base, this is a radio check, come back."

"This is home base, you're coming in five by five. Let us know if you find accommodations. Over."

Scott turned back to Quinn and asked, "Tell me again what your objectives are?"

"I am here to fill in the blanks that cannot be seen from the satellite photographs. There is particular interest in the evacuation process away from the event. The information I provide will be part of the narrative that accompany the images," Quinn explained.

"You are welcome to team up with us if you like. In the morning, we will be pushing closer to the volcano to take some measurements and set up our monitoring gear."

"Thanks, I may take you up on that offer. Eventually I have to range out into the foothills to see the impact and whether everyone is evacuating."

A small police car rounded the corner and the officer turned on flashing lights when he saw a group of men congregating in front of a deserted hotel. The single officer got cautiously out of his vehicle with his hand on his weapon. "You must leave immediately, as it is getting more dangerous by the minute," he announced in halting English.

"Officer, we are a scientific team here to monitor the eruption. We have permission from your government to be in the area. We take total responsibility for ourselves," Scott reassured the officer.

"I have my orders. You must leave now!" the officer relayed again with his hand still on his gun.

Scott pulled a water proof envelope out of his vest and spoke in Filipino. After reviewing the paperwork intently, the team was relieved when the officer began to shake his head affirmatively. Scott immediately took the opportunity to ask about accommodations. As so often happens in the Orient, the officer's brother-in-law was the proprietor of the hotel and within minutes, keys were provided and the team moved into the second floor bank of rooms, which offered a better view of the eruption. There was no electricity or air conditioning, but Quinn felt fortunate to have a roof and a bed. From his room, he could hear Scott's team securing their gear for the morning trip.

"Hey, has anyone heard from Thomas?"

"Oh shit, I forgot about him. No, he hasn't called in. Give me the walkie-talkie."

"Mobile one, mobile one, this is home base, come in, please!" There was static on the line but no response.

"Mobile one, mobile one, come in!"

"Home base, this is mobile one. I'm probably ten clicks northwest from your lat. The city is still teaming with people. A few bars are open and some girls working, but I have not found a hotel."

"Mobile one, you need to return to base camp. We have gained entry here at this hotel. So stop the sightseeing and get back to camp. We have a busy day tomorrow, home base out."

"Ten four that. I am returning to base but I must say it's still pretty interesting out here."

"We will take a look tomorrow, home base out."

"Roger that, returning to base," came the reply.

Quinn took some time to write a short report back to headquarters.

I have reached the city of Gingoog, approximately 25 to 30 kilometers from the eruption. The latest satellite photographs show intensification and the rumbling of the eruption can be heard at this distance. I have teamed up with a group of scientists from the Volcanic Research Laboratory and will accompany them towards the eruption tomorrow morning to assess conditions there. Afterwards, I will drive concentric arcs around the area to assess the damages and evacuation.

Conditions here indicate that most residents are either indoors or have evacuated. The roads were at capacity throughout the day, with evacuees heading east away from the area by any means available. However, there are unconfirmed reports of commercial establishments remaining open in town. The streets are passable, but electrical service is off to most, if not all the city. There are police cruisers on the streets warning residents to evacuate. Other than a light dust, there are no damages at this distance from the eruption. Aside from the eruption, the area is experiencing periodic and intense thunderstorms. While no weather reports are available to us, I estimate that the area has received 3 to 5 inches of rain since I arrived at Butuan. This is a tropical summer here in the Philippines, so summer rains can be expected, but the combination of an active volcano and summer showers could cause mud slides along the coastal areas and foothills.

Quinn transmitted his report and foraged in his backpack for some vegetables he had picked up from a streetside vendor along the highway. He noted that he was much less prepared than the scientific team, who looked like they were used to field work and were carrying the provisions they needed. Quinn made a mental note to pick up more supplies at the first opportunity. Luckily, he was invited to join the scientists for their sumptuous meal cooked on a propane stove. After dinner, he and Scott enjoyed a cold beer together.

"Wilson ...that name rings a bell. I recall recently that one of the scientists in that Antarctica expedition was named Wilson—any relation?"

"I am surprised at how closely the scientific community was following that expedition," Quinn related somewhat surprised.

"You mean that was you!"

"Yes, I lead the expedition and had a crack team of scientists who did the work."

"Hey, guys, we have a celebrity with us. Quinn here is the guy who recently led that expedition to the Antarctic meteor impact crater."

"Far out, man! I would have given my first-born to have been a part of that team," one of the young volcanologist said with enthusiasm.

"It got pretty lonely out there. At the time, we had no idea that anyone was interested in our progress until we returned to base." Quinn said with a little humility.

"Wasn't Dr. Pam Laystrom on that team? I heard one of her interviews on public radio. As I recall, she was a visiting professor at the university when I was in grad school," asked Scott.

"Yes, Dr. Laystrom was on the team and proved to be quite an asset. She kept us all on our best behavior with her feminist jabs at manhood."

"Quinn, that had to be the biggest scientific story of this century and you were in the middle of it, so what are you doing here?" Scott asked as he reached for another beer.

"Hey, watch that beer now—we may have to ration. There are some things you just don't want to run out of while investigating an eruption," one of the team members joked.

"You know, on all of the eruptions I have been on, you could always find beer. You may have had to drink it warm, but you can find it. Just because you brought it up, I am putting you in charge of the beer brigade. You mentioned someone saw some commercial establishments open, so plan on getting us a good supply tomorrow."

"There was more than beer flowing at those bars down the way. If I go into one of the bars, there's no telling when you will see me again," laughed the young volcanologist.

Guttural laughs resounded throughout the room.

Quinn was one of the first to retire from the festivities. Out on the walkway in front of the rooms, he stopped to marvel at the eruption. At night, you could see the flashes of orange at the base of the ash plume with periodic bomb-bursting theatrics, like a Fourth of July fireworks display from the ash cloud. It was an awesome sight and Quinn could not help but feel overwhelmed at the sheer size, power and majesty of the eruption. As he stood on the walkway, another squall front passed over the hotel. It was intense, even measured by Florida standards with which Quinn was so familiar.

Sleeping was rough with no electricity, fan, or air conditioning. It was hot and muggy in the room. Quinn kept peeling off clothes until he lay in his shorts on top of the sheet. The frequent thunderstorms provided some short relief, but the heat and humidity would quickly return. He was thankful when he finally heard the team stirring in the adjoining room. The rain showers had persisted throughout the night and the streets were flooded with standing water up to the hubcaps of parked vehicles. He was already dressed and loading his gear into the truck when Scott called from the second floor walkway, "Any chance of checking the satellite images this morning? It looks like it has grown larger overnight."

"Yes, there should have been a satellite passing over about two hours ago. We can check the infrared scans and see what it shows." Quinn booted his computer as he climbed the stairs and joined Scott gazing at the eruption in the early dawn. What they saw surprised them both. The heat from the plume was being carried aloft and showed as a green boiling caldron on the infrared photograph. "Tell me what we are looking at?" Quinn asked.

"Hmmm, we are looking at a major eruption. It seems it's becoming more intense with every hour. I am hesitant to take the team any closer then we are. There could be a caustic flow with this intensity."

"I think I know what that means, but can you give me the scientific definition?" Quinn asked.

"With a major eruption in an ash volcano, a huge cloud of ash and hot gases will race down the face of the volcano at over 500 miles an hour, killing everything in its path."

"And you think this eruption may produce a caustic flow?" Quinn asked with deepening concern.

"No one really knows. Hibok-Hibok has never exhibited this kind of intensity before. This looks like an entirely different volcano. We just don't know what it's going to do. That is the main reason we're here," Scott said with a measure of pride in his voice. "We must get our instrumentation in the ground as soon as possible to see if there's a magna chamber. Turning to his team he announced, "Guys, lets get cracking! We are missing valuable data."

Quinn could see now why the people had crammed the highway. This thing looked ominous. He fell in behind the last jeep as it raced through the streets of Gingoog and out into the countryside. The evacuees were once again shouldering their belongings and moving away from the eruption with stoic looks on their faces. There were no cars now and only a few scooters.

Most were walking or leading farm animals with small children hanging on for dear life. Still the caravan raced on and the plume got larger until it seemed to fill the whole sky.

Tropical rain showers skirted the area as the field crew set up their monitoring equipment. The rains washed the light dust out of the air and coated the green landscape in a dirty brown, which increased the depth of mud on the landscape. The ditches ran red with turbid water carrying the ash towards the sea. The showers reminded Quinn of Florida summer rains that could be quite intense with noisy thunderstorms that came and went within 15 minutes.

Scott came over and stood by Quinn as he watched the preparation. "We are about done. I'm leaving one team member here with the equipment and the rest of us are going back to the hotel. We will receive data by telemetry from the field equipment. Once this eruption settles down, we will make some insertions closer to the cone. Right now, this is about as close as I think we can get for safety reasons. You're welcome to come back with us and review the data as it comes in."

"Thanks, but I think I had better get on with my mission of filling in the blanks around the aerial photographs. According to this map, I can continue down this road and then circle back to the south. Eventually I want to get up into the foothills where the evacuation notices from the government may not be as prevalent. Hopefully, I can find some clear air to get a satellite connection and transmit my reports."

"Oh yes, I almost forgot the satellite connection. Can you see if we have a new aerial photograph of the eruption?"

"Sure, if I can get a connection but first let me see what we have." Quinn booted his laptop again, but found the ash cloud was interfering with the connection. "No, sorry, there is too much interference. I hope to be back at the hotel this evening and we can try again then."

As Scott and his team loaded up for the trip back to the hotel, Quinn typed a progress report that he hoped could be sent when conditions were better.

FROM: WALTER

Subject: Reporting from approximately five miles from the Hibok-Hibok eruption

The ash plume is continuing to grow in intensity. I am still with the Volcanic Research Laboratory scientists, who are installing monitoring equipment and initiating data collection at this location. I will be departing towards the south and evaluating conditions along the western side of the peninsula, the Trans-Philippine Highway, and further into the interior foothills. Attached are a series of photographs taken in Gingoog and en route to this base monitoring station. As noted in these photographs, there are still people moving along evacuation routes away from the eruption. At this point, most are traveling by foot. The volcanologists from the laboratory rate the danger as high and note that the volcano is not exhibiting the same characteristics as the Hibok-Hibok volcano. A new ash cone has risen from the sea and the eruption is continuing to increase in intensity. Local weather conditions include squall lines with intense and short-term thunderstorms. Local flooding is occurring with streams overflowing and the rudimental storm-water facilities along the roads are clogged with mud. Between storms, the weather is partly cloudy with continued trade winds from the northeast at fifteen to twenty miles per hour. These winds continue to carry the plume along the southwest coast of Mindanao and out to sea.

As he concluded his report, Quinn sat the laptop on the passenger seat and waved to the one remaining scientist, who had turned the jeep around and pointed it away from the eruption to make a fast departure, if needed. Quinn's route took him closer to the eruption before he could turn south on the next connecting road. The windshield was coated with the billowing ash plume before he reached the intersection. From this distance, he could see the volcanic bombs being hurled from the cloud and falling back to earth. Some looked larger then an automobile. Quinn became increasingly nervous as the road continued towards the eruption. He was relieved to finally make the turn south and almost involuntarily accelerated down the road, hoping to gain a little more breathing room. The amount of ash on the ground increased with every kilometer towards the volcano. Now on the western side of the peninsula, the ash and mud were six to twelve inches deep on the road. Still most of the ash plume was offshore. Quinn could only imagine the amount of material being deposited in the coastal waters.

Geology professors had always preached that changes in geological formations happened over eons of time. Now at the heart of a major geological event, Quinn questioned their observations. If this plume was over land, it would deposit a large amount of material and change the landscape significantly as the rains continued to sweep through the area.

The western side of the peninsula had been impacted extensively by the eruption. While most of the plume was offshore, the shifting winds had brought the ash over land and it had been washed from the atmosphere by the summer rains. Still Quinn found people in the area trying to protect their homes and fields from the destructive elements. As he drove through the rural areas he could see farmers valiantly trying to shovel a sea of mud away from their rudimentary dwellings. After all, these were their homes, their livelihood—all they had.

Further down the coast, Quinn turned inland towards the foothills. Soon the eruption and devastation along the coast were partially shielded from view by the heavily forested hills. As a result, there were more people carrying on their daily lives, apparently unaware of the events taking place nearby. Schools were still in session and troops of elementary students dressed in crisp uniforms walked on the shoulder of the road heading to class. There were farmers working their fields and ox-drawn carts lumbering along the road, heading for the local markets.

The rain was coming in pronounced squall lines now and Quinn could not help but recognize the pattern. He stopped at the crest of one of the hills and concentrated on contacting the home office in Washington on the satellite phone. Reception had been spotty and he was not sure his reports were getting through. Also he was receiving nothing in return from the home office. It was time to check in. Apparently there was atmospheric disruption, because Quinn could not secure a solid connection. As he sat in his vehicle thinking, he noticed a pay phone at a small market just outside a rural village and decided to try a landline. Residents of the area looked on with curiosity as this westerner attempted to use their local telephone. He was lucky enough that it was working and he even found an operator who spoke decent English. After a prolonged delay, the phone crackled and Alex Reager's voice was heard on the other end, "Walter, is that you?"

"Yes Alex. I've not had clear satellite connections for several days, so I'm calling on a landline," Quinn shouted into the phone.

"You have got to get out of there now! There is a tropical depression heading in your direction, which the weather wonks say will be a category 1 or 2 typhoon by the time it reaches the islands. Head back to Butuan immediately and give me a call when you get clear air. I'll arrange transportation off the island as soon as …." The phone crackled and hissed static, as the connection was lost.

Quinn stepped away from the phone and looked into the faces of the people watching him. Other than curiosity, there was no obvious concern for their safety, but how could he tell them? "English?" he asked, "Does anyone speak English?" No one answered. Quinn walked across the muddy lot to another group of natives standing at the edge of the commercial area, looking very stoic. Once again, he asked, "Do any of you speak English?" A young teenager stepped forward and said, "Yes, little English."

"Can you tell everyone that a typhoon is coming this way?" He asked and the young boy translated to the people around him. There was no response. "Tell them that the volcano eruption on the coast, combined with the typhoon can be very dangerous." Again there was no response from those around the boy. "Please go home and tell your parents that there is danger." The young man nodded his head, but continued to look at Quinn. Having done his best, Quinn returned to the truck and got out a map of the island. His route back to the main highway would take him closer to the eruption and based on what he had seen, that was not something he was willing to risk. There was a rural route across the foothills to the eastern side of the peninsula that connected to the paved road back to Butuan. Quinn couldn't tell the condition of the road from the map, but thought it offered the best opportunity for evacuation.

He checked his gas and saw he still had a half tank, so he cranked up the truck and headed down the road toward Butuan. He had been on the island for two days now and felt that he could make the eighty miles to Butuan by dark. The road was muddy but he could maintain about forty miles an hour without undue risk. About an hour into the trip, the truck began to bounce violently. Quinn immediately hit the brakes and slowed to a near stop, but the bucking continued. He was puzzled over the action of the truck, when suddenly he realized that it was an earthquake. The trees were swaying and mud from the hillside fell onto the road in front of the truck. Before he could unbuckle his seatbelt and open the door, the road caved in around him sending the truck careening down the mountainside in an avalanche of mud. There was the sound of metal scraping against the trees and shrubs, while mud and debris slammed into the windshield as the truck spiraled down the mountain towards the valley below. After what seemed like an eternity it came to rest with the hood submerged in a swollen stream. Quinn was thrust against the steering wheel in a daze. While he was trying to collect his thoughts and assess the situation, the truck shifted as the rushing water pushed the front end down the stream. Water began pouring through the bottom of the doors. Quinn unbuckled the seatbelt and slid into the backseat. He grabbed the satellite phone and put it back into its water-proof case and secured it and his computer into its knapsack. The truck shifted again and Quinn knew that it was only a matter of minutes before it would fall into the stream and be carried off in the current. His mind was working feverously, as he assessed what would be the best way to survive this situation. Since the world around him was rapidly filling up with water and mud, he grabbed his dive bag that he still carried from the dive trip and pulled out his wetsuit and dive vest. It might look funny to the locals, but this might well be the best survival gear available to him.

Getting into a wet suit was never easy under the best of conditions. Quinn braced his feet on the back of the driver's seat and stripped off his soggy clothing. In record time, he was able to get into the wetsuit as the truck continued to shift and fill with water. With the wetsuit and vest finally on, he tried to exit the vehicle on the dry side, but found the side doors blocked by debris. As he slid over the back seat to try the rear door, the truck rolled into the stream and began to sink. The weight of the engine caused the trunk to right itself, as it began to sink front first. With the rear window clear of the water, Quinn braced his back against the seat and kicked at it with both feet. After the third attempt, the window gave way and a wall of water entered the truck as it sank beneath the muddy water. Quinn grabbed his survival knapsack and crawled from the truck, as it began to cartwheeled through the current.

Now he was caught up in the current and moving swiftly downstream. The swollen stream was full of trees and rubbish, all being swept along in the strong current. Quinn grabbed onto a tree and was able to pull himself partially out of the water. There he inflated his vest and put both arms through the straps of his knapsack. He knew that the security of the tree would not last long. In a progression of events that were to be repeated numerous times throughout the day, the tree snagged and catapulted Quinn back into the current. He continued to fight to keep his head above water as another squall racked the area with heavy rain. The swollen stream snaked its way through the valleys and the amount of debris seemed to increase with every turn.

He knew that the approaching storm had probably intensified to a category one typhoon by now and felt that the winds had to be at least seventy miles an hour. It wasn't a strong typhoon yet, but given the combination of earthquakes and volcanic eruptions, the area was experiencing unprecedented destruction. Just as Quinn thought things could not get any worse, the counterclockwise winds began to push the ash plume inland and the skies darkened further as the rain turned into mud and the visibility fell to a few meters. He was almost blind to the obstructions in the stream as the current carried him even faster. Red ragged lighting ripped through the ash clouds seemingly only a few hundred feet above his head as he was carried downstream towards the volcano in a torrent of mud.

Death was becoming an ever-increasing possibility, either from drowning or being impaled by debris. His efforts to reach the shore were unsuccessful, given the crushing current and visibility now being down to near zero. By this time, he couldn't even see the shoreline. His mouth and nose were full of mud, so he coughed and sputtered just to breath in the mud-filled air. He kept his feet heading downstream, with his legs held tightly together, as he had learned on the family whitewater rafting trips several lifetimes ago. So, this is it, he thought as his survival options continued to diminish. This was not the way he thought his life would end. He would probably be lost under tons of mud and his body would never be found. His thoughts ran morbid—it would be a very lonely death.

Still the current raced along.

After what seemed like an eternity, he rounded a bend, in what was now a roaring river of mud and debris, just as a large tree uprooted by the winds fell from the banks in front of him. He hit the main trunk with enough force to partially knock the wind out of him and was immediately dragged under the tree by the current. His feet wedged into the snags below the fallen tree and he was trapped, unable to reach the surface. In his younger days' diving in Florida waters, he prided himself on his ability to hold his breath. He had a reputation with his friends for free-diving deeper and staying longer than any of them. Now twenty-five years later, he drew heavily on those skills and knew he was losing the battle and prayed silently, *Dear God …*

this is it ...I ...I ...can't breathe. He struggled against the snags as the strong current pushed him heavily against the tree trunk once again. There seemed to be no escape from this death grip. Then just before he lost consciousness, another tree pushed by the strong current smashed into the pile of debris that held him prisoner and the force of the impact rolled the massive tree downstream. By clinging to the branches, his head and then his chest emerged from the river as he gasped for what little air was left in the torrent of falling mud. Released from his tomb, Quinn pulled himself from limb to limb trying to reach the shoreline. A gust of wind seemed to clear his vision, as he caught sight of what might be solid ground. Without thinking, and ignoring the pain in his legs, he leaped towards his only salvation. His body landed partially in the water and he could once again feel the current pulling him downstream. "Ahhh! Jesus ...please!" he yelled aloud. One small tree after another ripped from his grasp, as he struggled to gain a handhold on the bank. Another snag came into his vision downstream, extending from the bank. He hurled his body at the tree and was able to get one leg over the log before the current impinged him again. Breathing heavily, he crawled along the trunk and grabbed onto the roots of the fallen tree. At long last, he felt the stream bank and began to crawl up the slope. Higher and higher he climbed, commando style on his belly, grunting in pain as he pulled himself forward. Still the winds and the torrent of mud cascading down the slope made progress and breathing difficult. "I need to find shelter out of this mud," he lectured himself, "someplace where I am not exposed and forced to breathe mud." He found such a place under the trunk of yet another fallen giant tree. Here under the six-foot-wide trunk, he found a margin of protection from the wind and driving mud and rain. He immediately passed out from exhaustion.

Hours passed as Quinn lay unconscious on the river bank. The day faded into night. The typhoon slowly passed north of Mindanao and into the Sulu Sea. The resulting change in wind direction moved the ash plume to the east and then north away from the heart of the island. Quinn awoke to a brownish-red world with no hint of green in the jungle that surrounded him. The river from whose rushing current he had risen the day before was only few feet from his shelter. Debris filled the river from shoreline to shoreline. Buildings and cars floated by and the river thundered with the sound of wrenching collisions as these battering rams collided with the debris dams. Quinn looked closer at some of the brighter colors and found that they were clothing on bodies of people, who were not as lucky as he had been to escape the grasp of the current. He was disoriented and it seemed that it was morning. Could he have been out all night or was the sun just setting? He didn't know which way was north. As he rose up on his elbows, he couldn't even recognize his own legs, so covered with mud were they. The rips in his wetsuit revealed only a muddy surface that he did not recognize as part of a living body. His attempts to move caused him to wrench in pain. A quick inventory revealed a number of bruises and cuts on his body. He had a laceration along his jawline that was the apparent source of the bloody mud on his chest. His left leg seemed to be the worst of his injuries. Thank God, it wasn't broken but the scrapes and bruises did not fully account for the pain in his knee. Unzipping his wetsuit he found that the rips to the neoprene corresponded to the wounds on his chest. His ribcage was very sore and on inspection, Quinn found several sensitive areas that he diagnosed as cracked ribs. Some of the worst injuries were to his thighs and buttocks. Since he had floated downstream with his legs in front, they had taken most of the direct hits from the snags. His left leg was still very painful. On examining it, he concluded that he had wrenched his knee in the one big pile-up that almost killed him. Overall, there were a number of cuts, scrapes and some puncture wounds that needed immediate attention, but no injury that was life-threatening. He knew that if he was not mobile, he could die of thirst within a few days. He had to get out of here …wherever here was.

"I am alive!" he shouted, which caused him to cough and gag on the mud he had breathed.

As the winds continued to abate and the low cloud layer

began to break up, Quinn took inventory of his situation. He opened his backpack and found that his computer had been smashed and his GPS was waterlogged, but his satellite phone appeared to be intact. He removed it from its waterproof case and turned it on. While it was searching for a satellite connection, he continued the inventory. His automatic pistol was clogged with mud but serviceable if he could clean the mud from the barrel. Its ammunition was also waterlogged, but salvageable, and the Swiss army knife looked God-sent. The last item in the bag was a sunhat that he had stuffed into the pack some time ago and promptly forgotten. First he used it to wipe the mud from his face and then strapped it on, pulling the lanyard tight against the wind.

Back in Washington, the operational section of NGIA was elated to see the GPS signature from Quinn's phone blink on the screen. He had been missing now for over 24 hours. Reports from the island revealed almost hellish conditions with earthquakes, typhoons, and the volcanic eruption. The duty officer had reported the news to Alex Reager the night before, stating that there was little chance of survival, if he was exposed to the environment. NGIA had reported the catastrophic events to the president and U.S. Naval ships were being diverted to the area to assist with the rescue and recovery. CIA agents were also heading towards the island, including Agent James, who had to cut short a vacation in Tahiti to fly to the island.

Quinn tried his satellite phone with no success. He told himself that he was too deep in the valley to get any kind of reception. He looked up into the muddy slopes in back of him and thought, "If I could get to the top of this hill, the satellite connections would have to be better." Looking back over the river gave him no hope that escape was possible in that direction. So, with much pain, he rolled out from under his refuge and began the laborious crawl up the steep slope, hoping there would be something other than more mud and jungle when he finally reached the top.

Hand-over-hand, he scaled the slope, crawling under fallen trees and over deadfalls of brush towards a summit that was always just out of sight. At long last, the slope became more moderate and he was finally able to stand and test aching joints under his full weight. "Everything works, it's just a matter of overcoming the pain," he reassured himself. He picked up a straight limb from a pile of debris to use as a walking staff. Gripping it with both hands and taking his weight off his left leg made him even more mobile. He was getting thirsty now and he could not even remember when he had last eaten.

Luck was with him when he finally crawled out of the jungle. He was in a muddy clearing that continued down the slope. *This may be a road of some kind*, he surmised. It was thigh deep in mud, with no human or animal tracks, but he could stand upright and the ground visible under the sluggish mud was level. In the distance to his left, he could see the ash cloud from the eruption, but it looked much smaller and the path or road he was on led away from the volcano. He made some mental calculations of his position. He had been driving the back road toward Butuan when the earthquake had occurred. No telling how far he had driven or the distance covered in the river current, but it seemed like a hundred miles. If he had traveled maybe thirty miles by road and river, then he still had five to ten miles to go and he knew he was in no shape to cover that distance without help. Still he had to keep moving. The sun was climbing into the sky and it was one of those lulls after the storm, when the heat and humidity would combine with the mud to make conditions unbearable. Several hours later, he was shocked to see trails in the mud that were unmistakably human. Someone else had survived the holocaust and was walking in the same direction toward the coast. Other footprints joined the parade. Gradually, people came into view, all moving slowly, looking like bronze statues or terracotta soldiers marching to some sluggish cadence. Soon, Quinn was walking among them, just one more bronze refugee, struggling to make it to the coast. No one spoke or took their eyes off their feet to look at the surrounding area. They had seen all the mud they wanted to see.

CHAPTER 15

The Rescue

By noon, after hours of forced march, the band of bedraggled survivors was out of the foothills and within sight of the coast. In the distance, Quinn could hear a car engine and was happy to see a pickup truck round a bend about a half mile ahead. He was even more surprised when the horn sounded. When it drew abreast of him and stopped, Agent James stepped from the passenger's side.

"Christ, Wilson! Earthquakes, volcanic eruptions, and a typhoon! They're bad enough one at a time, but you had to take them on all at once!"

"You only know half of the story! It is so good to see a familiar face. Do you have any water?" Quinn asked as his fellow travelers congregated around the pickup truck, hoping for a handout.

"Yes I have water, but I am not done with you yet. They should lock you up in a cage and not let you loose in the environment. You are a magnate for disaster! I told you I had a feeling about you, didn't I," Ken kept ranting.

"It's nice to see you as well, Agent James," Quinn responded as he gripped his makeshift staff a little tighter. "How about that water before I just collapse from dehydration right here in front of you?"

"Okay, okay, I have a few cases of water. I'll leave some for your traveling companions," he offered, as he opened a cooler in the back of the pickup. The mob pressed a little closer in desperation at the sight of a bottle of water. Ken shouted something in Pilipino and everyone took a step back as he began throwing bottles to the crowd. Quinn drank two bottles, then dumped a third on his head and wiped his face with his utility cap.

"We have been tracking you for some time. The GPS and satellite phone indicated to Washington that you were either dead on the river bank or somehow alive. They gave us a call when the signal started moving. You sure were moving awful slow, Quinn. Why didn't you call?"

"I forgot all about the phone. I just saw myself as one of these bronze refugees, trying to get out of the jungle," Quinn responded between gulps of water.

Ken was on his phone now, reporting the rescue. "Yes, sir, we found him. He's a little beat up and dirty, but I think he'll survive. I can't bring him in without a bath or you would just send him away to live in a cave. Yes, sir, give me a couple of hours and I'll have him there."

"Let's see if we can get this truck turned around. There's a safe house in Butuan where you can get cleaned up. They can get you on a computer, if you need to file a report with the NGIA. Then we'll see if there is a commercial flight back to Sydney. The disaster preparedness boys, along with the Navy, have landed and they can clean up your mess."

"Thanks, Ken, and just to set the record straight—this was not my fault."

"Yeah, yeah, you just keep telling yourself that, if it helps with the guilt," Ken responded half-seriously.

Being close to death had given Quinn a new feeling about living. It was an unbelievable luxury to sit in the back of a pickup truck and ride through the passing landscape. While it had only been a day since he drove himself, he was lost in the joy of sitting and feeling the wind in his face. They stopped at a closed gas station, where Quinn turned the water hose on himself and stripped the remnants of the wetsuit off. Ken had some spare clothes and Quinn was feeling almost human again as they resumed their trip.

As they approached Butuan, they could see the U.S. Navy setting up tents and offering food, water and first aid to the many refugees. Ken spent most of the trip on his satellite phone, discussing security and logistics. Butuan looked like it had come through the storm with only minimal damage. The wind had not brought the ash plume over the city. Ken dropped him off at the safe house, an unassuming two-story stucco, in a residential suburb of Butuan. "I'll catch up with you later this evening," he shouted as the truck pulled away.

Quinn watched him pull away and then walked up the steps of the safe house. The inside of the home was tastefully decorated but somewhat austere. A middle-aged Philippine woman entered the room, wiping her hands and said, "Hello, my name is Maria. You must be Mr. Wilson," she said in refined English.

"Yes, I'm Quinn Wilson."

"Agent James called ahead and said to expect you," she responded with a kindly smile. "We have some extra clothes in the back room, if you would like to take a look. I think we can find something in your size." Pointing to the stairs, she continued, "Your room will be up the stairs, second door on the left. Here is the key. We have a full house tonight. There is much activity after the storm. I understand Agent James and his fellow agents will be returning later this evening. Dinner will be served at 6:00, but I can fix you a sandwich if you are hungry."

"Yes thank you I would love that. I have not eaten since … since I can't remember when."

"Very well, it will be ready in about 30 minutes. You will have enough time to get cleaned up."

The shower water ran brown as Quinn washed his hair. He had no idea where all the mud was coming from. I guess if you sleep in a foot of mud, it's going to be in every pore of your skin, so it might take several showers to get it all out. Then he had the chance to check his injuries. He knew he had taken quite a beating in the torrent and needed medical attention. His legs and thighs took most of the abuse, but one laceration on his right jaw looked particularly nasty. He would ask Maria if a doctor was available.

Clean towels, underwear, pants, tee shirt and socks all felt like such luxuries, as he walked down the stairs to the dining room some thirty minutes later. "Maria, is there a doctor nearby?"

"Please forgive me, Mr. Wilson, but I have already taken the liberty of asking our local doctor to stop by. I noticed the blood on your shirt and pants when you came in and thought it would be wise."

"Thank you! That was most considerate of you." Quinn replied.

Maria had made some chicken salad sandwiches as a light snack before dinner. Quinn could not believe how hungry he was and tried to remember his manners and eat them slowly, when what he really wanted was to swallow them whole. He thanked Maria half a dozen times for those sandwiches.

While he was eating, the doctor arrived and spoke to Maria in Chinese. He seemed to be a humble young man in his early thirties, who spoke with much bowing and smiling. He was dressed in a short-sleeved white shirt with a brown-striped clip-on tie. His jet black hair was long and fell into his face each time he would bow. He and Maria would cast glances at him as they spoke and he knew he was the primary topic of discussion.

As he approached Quinn, he bowed deeply before speaking in broken English, "I am Dr. Chin. Please come to examination room."

Quinn rose stiffly from the table as the doctor bowed and motioned the way to the examination room. He was surprised to find a well-equipped medical facility that looked more like a small emergency room. Once seated on the examination table, Dr. Chin was all business. "Yes, this wound on your thigh does need stitches," he said half to himself. With Maria's assistance, he cleaned and disinfected the wounds and busily stitched away like a tailor. When they were done, Quinn was feeling more like an invalid, as he tried to get his clothes back on. Maria smiled graciously and helped him pull up his pants.

"Thank you very much, Dr. Chin, and you too, Maria, for your help. I am guessing that this is not the usual services you provide," he said in an effort to show his appreciation.

Dr. Chin seemed very humbled and said, "You are very welcome, Mr. Wilson. I am happy to be of service."

Maria also smiled and said "You are most welcome. I serve many roles here, but I am also a trained nurse. You have no idea of the trouble these boys around here can get themselves into. Our other guests will be returning shortly. In the meantime, we have beer and wine on the porch, if you would like to make yourself at home. Dinner will be served at 6:00 o'clock." She smiled again as she gestured towards the back porch.

Good Lord, this beer tastes great, he thought. His near death experience had really been a wake-up call. *Never again will I ignore the simple pleasures of life*, he mused to himself. *The first thing I need to do is find someone to share this life with. Dying alone is the saddest thing I can think of. The second thing will be to get back on speaking terms with my daughter. I also need to do a lot more sailing. There is no place on earth where I feel more at home, in control, and contented than at the wheel of a sailboat. Maybe more friends would be nice, as well.*" As he continued to check over his life's priorities, Agent James returned to the house with a group of young field agents.

"Where is that river rat I left here earlier today?" he asked Maria from the foyer.

"We have patched him up and he is on the back porch enjoying a beer," she said with a big smile. Quinn couldn't help but think, *he even has a way with older women.*

Ken stuck his head out the back door. "There you are. I didn't recognize you all cleaned up. The last time I saw you, you were a nice mellow brown," he said as he laughingly announced, "Hey, guys! I want you to come meet a friend of mine."

Three young agents sauntered onto the back porch, each grabbing a beer. "I would like you to meet Quinn Wilson. He is both a scientist and a field agent for the NCIA. He has a strange knack of being at the center of cataclysmic events. You recall the internal CIA report on the rescue of the UN observers in Africa? Quinn was there and as I understand it saved the day for the squad. Then he led the Antarctic expedition to the meteor impact crater a few months later and, to top that off, he just survived a confrontation with an earthquake, a volcano and a typhoon, while floating down the river. We need to assign an agent to this guy. All we would have to do is wait around and the action would come to us."

A hearty burst of laughter filled the porch as Ken finished his speech.

"It is nice to meet you all," Quinn offered with a feeble toast with his beer and added, "Don't believe half of what he is saying. I'm only a lowly field agent."

"Hell, I have been with the Company for twenty years and my resume doesn't include as much action as yours," Ken added. "I must say though, it does look like you've been badly beaten up. Did Maria and Dr. Chin take care of you?"

"They both were very helpful. Before the local anesthesia wore off, I was enjoying this beer and counting my blessings. I want to thank you for rescuing me. Were you out there looking for me or were you on another mission?" Quinn asked above the jovial discussions between the other agents.

"You were on the checklist of things to watch for and, yes, I took that section of the island hoping I would luck out and find your body. We didn't really think you could have survived when that typhoon swept into the area. Hell, you had to breathe mud just to live through it," Ken said as he reached for another beer. "Your buddy from Washington specifically asked us to keep an eye out for you. They wanted to give you a decent burial. By the way, have you called the home office yet?"

"No, I haven't. Maria and Dr. Chin have been keeping me busy. I need to see if my phone still works."

"That phone saved your butt, man. The GPS unit told us where your body was and once you started moving, we knew that you were at least half-alive. Here, why don't you use my phone?"

"Thanks. Now, if I can remember the number and security codes," Quinn said as he fumbled with the satellite phone. It was early morning in Washington and Quinn was surprised at how quickly he got through to Alex Reager.

"Well, it is good to hear from you. You gave us quite a scare," Alex said cheerfully.

"Yes, it scared me pretty bad as well. It is good to be among the living. For a while, I was sure that my body would never be found under all that mud." Quinn was surprised that his voice sounded so tired.

"How are you doing now? Did you get a chance to see a doctor?"

"Maria here at the safe house called a Dr. Chin who fixed me up pretty well. There were minor scrapes and bruises mostly, with a few puncture wounds for good measure. Over all, I am doing well—nothing a few days of rest won't fix."

"That's good to know, Quinn. You really had us worried there for a while. The entire Pacific basin is hopping and we need your eyes on the ground. Do you think you will be ready to go back to work in a week—or maybe two?"

"Let me get a night's sleep first. Then I'll talk to the doctor in the morning and get back to you. I'll need a new computer and phone—my laptop was impaled by a bamboo spear."

"I'll have them waiting for you when you get back to Sydney. You have to be careful with the taxpayer's equipment you know," Alex said with a laugh.

"Actually, if it had not been for the laptop, I would have taken that bamboo spear through the chest. I hope the taxpayers will understand," said Quinn wryly.

"Well, get better and we will talk again soon. Oh, one other thing—I still need those reports on the incident. The confluence of a volcano eruption and a typhoon is rare, so everyone wants details of the impacts, but I told them that I had a man on the ground. When you feel up to it, email your reports to my attention."

"As soon as I can get in front of a keyboard, I'll work on it. In the meantime, I need some sleep to clear my head. Last night I passed out under a fallen tree in a foot of mud. Now those clean sheets upstairs are looking very enticing."

"Get some sleep, Quinn. Call when you get back into Sydney."

"I'll talk to you soon, Alex."

The back porch had become a party while Quinn was on the phone. A few other agents had returned from the field and the beer was flowing, while light-hearted laughter filled the room.

Marie brought out trays of food for dinner. Ken was in the middle of the celebration and saw Quinn get off the phone. He came over and sat down beside him. "Is everything okay with the home office? Those guys seemed very concerned about you the last couple of days. I wish our bosses cared as much for us."

"I think they were concerned about the computer, not me." Quinn quipped.

"Yeah, that must have been it," Ken said with a smile. "I don't have a ride back to Sydney to offer you, but the commercial flights are operating and there is one out at 1100 tomorrow if you are up to it."

"That would be great, thanks." Quinn replied.

"I'll have Maria set it up. She seems to like you."

"Really, maybe I should stick around awhile. I could use some more friends, especially the female ones."

"Every agent in the Pacific has been in love with her at one time or another. She can afford to be very selective. You should be honored."

"Women have a thing for mortally wounded, helpless men. It brings out their mothering instinct. But seriously, both you and Maria have been very helpful and I appreciate it very much. It's good to be alive. I do have one question though."

"What's that?"

"What are you and all these field agents doing here? Is it just because of the volcano eruption?"

Ken hesitated and looked around the room, as if he were evaluating his response based on security protocol and the requisite "need to know." Finally he responded, "It's more about the effects of the eruption, rather than the event itself. There are several Islamic rebel separatist bands who camp in the interior mountains of the island. They have conducted periodic raids on government facilities in the past and hit some U.S. assets. The eruption has shaken them out of their strongholds and they are on the move and vulnerable. We are here to hunt them down with our Philippine counterparts. Your friend, Caleb, from your African rescue mission, is one of the leaders. You could have done us all a favor by putting a bullet through his head back in Africa. You are the only agent to ever have had him in your sights. So, it's too bad we can't get you back into the field. I am sure your presence would make things happen."

"You can stick with that story and I'll try to stay out of my own way. I can only take so much excitement," Quinn said with a laugh that hurt his ribs. "This near-death thing is *very* tiring."

"I'll be gone when you get up in the morning, so get a good night's sleep and I'll catch up with you back in Sydney. I really do want to see your boat ...and meet that lovely neighbor of yours."

"Sure, come on by. I'm going to be settling into the cockpit recuperating and would enjoy the company. Good night." Quinn was surprised at how stiff he was when he attempted to get up. He hobbled from the room like an old man leaning on his cane.

Maria met him at the base of the stairs with a warm smile. "Good night, Mr. Wilson. I left a bottle of aspirins on the table in your room. Call me if you need anything during the night. I have Dr. Chin coming by in the morning to check on you before your flight."

"Thank you, Maria, you have been very accommodating and I appreciate it very much. Right now I just need to make it to bed before I fall asleep on my feet. Good night."

"Good night, Mr. Wilson," she repeated with a smile.

Sleep came slowly, as always when he was very tired. There were too many images running around in his head for sleep to come. Sometime during the night, he fell into a light and restless sleep, but awoke frequently with visions of fallen trees and muddy current pulling him downriver. He was up at first light for the trip back to Sydney, but found that he had little to pack and no razor to shave with. He hobbled down the stairs on his cane and found the house nearly deserted. The field agents had gotten an early start and Maria was alone in the kitchen.

"Oh, good morning, Mr. Wilson, I was not expecting to see you until later this morning. Did you sleep well?"

"Good morning Marie, I was still pretty restless last night. Apparently, encounters with volcanoes and typhoons are disruptive to sleep patterns."

"Would you like some coffee or tea?"

"Thanks, just point me in the direction of the coffee pot and I'll be okay."

"Would you like some breakfast? I have bacon and eggs or waffles this morning."

"You know, I went to bed without dinner last night and I am pretty hungry. I'll take anything and everything you have left over in the kitchen."

"It sounds like you are feeling better. Dr. Chin will be stopping by shortly to check on you before you leave. I will get you some breakfast going."

"Thank you," Quinn said as he settled slowly into a dining room chair with a cup of coffee. There was a New York Times on the table, with headlines blaring the devastation in the Philippines from the aftereffects of a killer typhoon and volcanic eruption. The pictures looked all too familiar.

Maria was very attentive during breakfast. "It was a pleasure to have you as our guest," she said with a shy smile. "I do hope you come back and see us if you are ever in the Philippines again. Our door will always be open to you."

Dr. Chin arrived after breakfast with smiles and many low bows. He gave Quinn an examination and pronounced him ready to travel. "Thank you both for all the help," Quinn said gratefully.

By 0930, Quinn got stiffly into a nondescript Company vehicle and was on the road heading for the nearest airport. He was booked on a Qantas flight that would take a little more than eight hours to reach Sydney. The ticket agent looked at him with a questioning expression when he said he had no luggage. "I lost my luggage in the storm," he said in the way of an explanation.

The weather was clear enough for him to see the western side of the island after takeoff. The most recent Hibok Hibok volcano cone had created a new island, smoldering just off the coast. The entire western third of the island was brown from the ash created out of the deadly combination of an eruption and a typhoon. The streams and rivers all had new deltas extending out into the Mindanao Sea. It was an impressive sight and a testament to the power of the natural environment.

Quinn took the pilot's recommendation and sat back, completely relaxed during the flight. He noticed that other passengers were looking at him strangely, so he took a quick inventory of his appearance. He had twenty stitches on his jaw and scalp, with another twenty on his right forearm. His clothes didn't match and were a little too large for him. He didn't look like a businessman or tourist and apparently that was raising the curiosity and concern of the passengers and flight attendant. He tried to ameliorate their concerns by smiling back at the stares, but that hurt his jaw and he had to abandon that effort and leave his fellow passengers with their unfavorable impressions of him.

He passed time looking at a magazine in the seat pocket in front of him. There were the usual mix of articles about travel and luxurious hotels, but there was one perfume ad that caught his eye. The woman staring provocatively out of the page was beautiful. *I have got to get back into life. Here I am so desperate for companionship that I am falling in love with a picture in a magazine. How desperate is that?*

Arriving back in Sydney after dark, Quinn hobbled through the terminal on the cane Marie had given him and hailed a cab. He gave the large Samoan driver the address of the marina and they went careening through the city as if on an emergency run. It occurred to him that he had lost his keys and was glad he had remembered to hide a key to his boat in the cockpit locker. Apparently all sailors hide a key in the same location, so that practice offered no security at all. But sailors were a trustworthy group and everyone felt secure in the practice.

The cab driver delivered Quinn to the marina and gruffly accepted the fare and generous tip. The strong wind brought a chill to the air, as Quinn limped down the dock leaning heavily on his cane to stand looking at his boat. The lines were all holding the boat away from the dock, there was no damage to the hull and, despite being a little dirty, the boat looked great. The only problem was the 25-mile-an-hour northeasterly wind whipping across the widest fetch of the Bay, causing the boat to pitch strongly in the slip. It occurred to Quinn that he was going to have some problems getting on board with his injured leg. After watching the movement for a few moments, he took a deep breath and forced his stiff body to sit on the dock. Then with his feet on the gunwale, he waited for the pitching to moderate before painfully jumping aboard, straining the stitches in his thigh in the process. He found himself on his hands and knees in the cockpit, so he took advantage of the position to reach into the locker and retrieved the cabin key. He almost fell down the companionway ladder head first into the cabin and had to pull himself onto the bunk where he lay for a few minutes until the pain subsided. The cabin still smelled of fresh varnish, but it was great to be home.

The only light in the cabin was a red blinking light on the telephone answering machine, which he had installed the day before he left. Although it was probably just the telephone company checking the line, he became increasingly curious to see who had left a message. After about 15 minutes laying in the dark, he forced himself up to a sitting position and fumbled with the answering machine. The voice caught him by surprise.

"Hello, Mr. Wilson …Quinn. This is Meg from Archer Marine. We received some additional parts that we ordered for your Sabra and I wanted to set up an appointment with you to install them. Maybe we could discuss it …hmmm …over lunch? Please give me a call when you get back in. You have my number."

For a second, Quinn's heart skipped a beat as to what this could mean. *If she called me to have lunch and discuss the installation of some additional parts for the boat,* he thought, *perhaps that wasn't the only reason. I wonder how she got this number—I don't even know it myself, yet she went to the trouble of getting it.* Then he reasoned that it had probably been so long since she left the message that she had either forgotten she called or thought he was not interested. *I'll call now,* he thought. *It's already 10:00 P.M. so no one will be there. However, I could leave a message ...yes, a message—where is that number?*

He turned on the cabin lights and rummaged around on the navigation table until he found the Archer business card. His fingers felt too fat to be dialing a telephone so he hung up and then redialed three times before it finally rang through.

"Hello, you have reached Archer Marine. Our hours are 7:00 A.M. to 6:00 P.M. daily except Sunday. Leave a message and your telephone number after the tone and we will return your call at the first opportunity. If this is an emergency please call (07) 4173 9634."

"Hi, Meg, this is Quinn Wilson returning your call. Meg, it's Friday night and I just returned to the boat and got your message. Sorry that it has taken me so long to call you back. I have been ...uh, working out of the country. Yes, I would like to have lunch with you. I was not aware of any additional equipment that was backordered, but look forward to talking to you about it. Give me a ring at ...oh, the phone is so new, I don't know the number yet. Since you called me, I'm hoping you still have the number. If I do not hear from you tomorrow, I'll call you back. I'm going to hang up now before I start rambling. Hope to talk to you soon."

He became aware that the boat was gyrating even more. It was tugging at the mooring lines with a jerking motion that was beginning to feel uncomfortable. It helped him forget about being hungry. But after a couple of hours, Quinn began to feel that uneasy feeling in the pit of his stomach. *Oh, boy, motion sickness,* he thought. *I'm going to have to get off this boat until the wind abates and the seas calm down.* He struggled up the companionway and after some difficulties, was able to crawl onto the dock, only to find that the floating dock was pitching almost as much as the boat. He walked ever so slowly down the dock, crossed the street and sat down on the park bench overlooking the harbor. Out of fatigue, his ankles collapsed and he sat straddle-legged leaning on his cane. He noticed that there was blood on his pants where he had strained the stitches in his thigh.

He was in this position when the black limo rounded the corner and stopped at the end of the dock. He recognized the blond hair and female figure of Betsy Valentine as she stood and talked to the driver for a few minutes. As the limo drove away, she started down the dock towards her boat, then stopped, turned and looked in Quinn's direction. He was sitting in a shadow and felt virtually invisible, so he was surprised when she turned and walked in his direction. He could not help marvel at the female image she cut as she walked into the pool of light from the streetlamp. She was a very beautiful woman.

"Quinn, is that you?" she called.

"Yes. I'm surprised you saw me sitting here. The boats are prancing so much at their moorings that I had to get off for a while."

She sat down next to him with a quizzical look on her face. "Look at you! Have you been in a fight?" she asked with concern.

"I just got back from a mission to the Philippines, where I had a run in with an earthquake and a volcano. So, yes, I guess I have been in a fight. It's been a rough few days."

Betsy placed her handbag on the bench, crossed her legs, smoothed her dress across her lap and looked at him intently. "Well, I have had a hard day at the office as well. I was playing hostess to a small company's Board of Directors and they thought that it was some sort of 'Outward Bound' bonding exercise. They were difficult to handle. Let's forget about that, because I have been wanting to talk to you."

"Oh, about what?"

"I need a sailing partner. I have enough johns in my life, but very few friends—it's an occupational hazard, I guess. I really enjoyed our sail a couple of weeks ago and it got me wondering if we could maybe be sailing buddies?"

"Exactly what do you mean when you say you have no friends? I see a very beautiful and personable woman, who circulates in upper levels of business and society. I would think that you have legions of friends."

"Looks can be very deceiving. My looks mean that men lust after me and women loath my very existence. I have no one that accepts me for who I am. I got into this business to support my sailing passion and from that respect, I have been very successful. My boat is paid for and my bank account is in good shape. I could take off now and sail the world without any financial concerns. But I would need a crew."

"You're planning to circumnavigate?" Quinn asked, a little surprised.

"I have had that thought in the back of my head for some time. I don't know if I am ready to lose the moorings yet, but after a bad day at work, I like to dream. Quinn, I am going to violate one of my principles and be totally honest with you. I told you I was in hospitality, well in a way that is true. I provide certain services to men. In short, I'm an escort, a professional date, a ...prostitute."

"Wow Betsy, I ...I don't know what to say."

"If you want to be friends with me, I have certain conditions. There can never be any romance between us. I will never go to bed with you and I mean never! You probably won't understand, but that would make you a special friend to me. I go to bed with so many men and it is *so* easy. I want something more from a friendship. Does that make any sense to you?"

"Slow down now! You're getting way ahead of me. I ...I think it's going to take me some time to digest this." After an uncomfortable pause, Betsy reached into her purse for a handkerchief, in preparation of a rare rejection of her companionship. Quinn shifted his position towards her on the bench and looked her in the eyes. "Okay, for starters, I am not in a position to turn down any offer of friendship. Also it isn't my place to judge anyone. I have recently been reminded that it can get lonely here without some friendships. My second thought is that you really can't force a friendship. It has to be natural and both individuals have to feel comfortable in the relationship. From our short time together sailing your boat, I think we have some things in common and a friendship could arise from that. We are not there yet and honestly, I just don't know how to make a friendship happen. It just evolves over time. Let's just give it some time and see what happens."

"So, my profession is not an obstacle to our friendship?" Betsy said looking him in the eyes with concern.

"To be brutally honest with you, I don't know how I feel right now about your profession. I would rather think of you as a fellow sailor and neighbor here on the dock. Like I just said, friendships take time to evolve—let's leave it at that."

"I just want to be a person, a sailor and a friend. My profession has destroyed any interest in romance. I want to eliminate that aspect so I can be free from any pretense. It means a lot to me. Do you understand?"

"I think I do. I'm disappointed, but I understand. I suppose us males like to think there is always a potential attraction between a man and a woman. It seems natural and healthy to have some desires for intimacy. Do you understand that?"

"That desire is gone for me. I lost it long ago. Oh, I can turn it on and make a man pay for it, but it's …it's just business."

Betsy shifted on the bench and she and Quinn sat together looking out over the harbor in silence. After a while Quinn spoke, "It looks like the wind is dropping some. Are you ready to head down the dock to the boats?"

They stood up in unison, Quinn leaning heavily on his cane and then headed back towards the dock as Betsy continued, "I am so glad we had this talk, Quinn. You will never know how much I dreaded a rejection. I suppose you men get rejected by women all the time, but I have never begged for friendship before. If you had rejected me, I don't know if I could have taken it. Thanks for leaving the door open."

Quinn stumbled when they reached the floating dock. "Oh, my, you really have been injured. How insensitive of me. What happened to you?" she asked as she reached for his arm to steady him.

"It's a long story. When we have a few hours or days, I'll tell you about it. The short version is that the natural environment can be cruel. I am very sore, but extremely happy to be alive. It's going to take a couple of weeks to recover before getting back to work."

"I am going to take some time off as well. My work can be

equally as cruel. Here, lean on me and I'll help you to your boat."

"Thanks, but I have to get used to navigating on my own. It's part of the recovery," Quinn responded very quickly. They walked together down the dock towards their boats in silence. "Meg Archer called me while I was gone," he said to break the silence. "I don't know how she got my number. I didn't even know it myself."

"I gave it to her," Betsy responded. "Jake told me she called the marina looking for you. I got the number from the telephone installer and passed it on to her. I think she has a thing for you and it's good seeing her interested in someone after her messy divorce. She has been single now for several years."

"Oh, that's right, you do know her."

"I told you that we went to high school, but we also used to sail together when we were younger. We have barely spoken for a number of years now. It is just another example of how my profession can alienate old friendships."

They arrived at their moorings and Quinn was relieved to see that the wind and waves had calmed down considerably. "Betsy, we had better say goodnight here. You do not want to see me getting on the boat. It is not a pretty sight …and it would be embarrassing to have an audience. So, I'll see you in the morning?"

"Oh, but I would be happy to give you a hand if you like."

"Thanks, but no thanks. I just need to negotiate this on my own." Quinn said sheepishly.

"I understand. Perhaps we can talk more tomorrow, so goodnight, Quinn," she said as she headed across the dock to her boat. Quinn followed her progress for a few moments, as he hashed over his conservative reservations.

I hope this is not one of those disasters that Agent James accused me of attracting, he thought as he stepped onto his boat.

CHAPTER 16

Stateside

Nancy awoke with the morning sunlight streaming through the window. There was a clatter of activities in the plaza below their hotel room that reminded her that she was in romantic Paris. Randy was asleep beside her and she studied him in detail while he slept. He was not particularly a good-looking man. He was of medium height, not tall or short, a little overweight with "love handles" that were on the verge of getting out of control. His once blond hair was thinning and almost gray and he snored in a deep baritone that would be very annoying after a while. To top that off, he wears white briefs! How conservative can you get?

She learned the night before that he was not the most accomplished lover, as Roberto had been, but he was comfortable and uncomplicated to be with and that was enough for now. This relationship would only be for a few days and she could easily break it off after they got back to the states. In the meantime, he was paying the bills for the hotel and food.

She tried to push the bad memories of Roberto and his friends out of her mind and think of the present. Today they would go to the Louvre and Eiffel Tower, then have lunch at a sidewalk café and walk along the Seine River, all of which was very romantic. She wished she had more interest in this man, instead of just using him for the convenience and the marginal companionship he offered.

In three days, they would be on the return flight to New York. She had been in France now for almost six months, and with the exception of that one night, it had been a rewarding experience. She thought of Roberto and swore to herself that she would do a better job judging the character of men she let into her life. None of the men she had met on this trip could hold a candle to Quinn. He was strong and caring, a good husband and father. She had totally taken him for granted for too long. She thought back to that morning in St. Petersburg and shuddered to think how she had left him, while hurling as much humiliation and insults at him as she could muster. He didn't deserve any of those insults. How had she changed so quickly when Roberto came into the picture with his smooth talk and words of love and adventure? What kind of a person had she become? She vowed that once she got back to the states she would find Quinn and make amends. Maybe they could still have a life together.

CHAPTER 17

Recovery

Quinn called Archer Marina the first thing the next morning and was disappointed to learn that Meg was in Tasmania, serving as an official for the upcoming Sydney to Hobart Yacht Race. She would not be returning for another two weeks. As he sat stiffly on the bunk feeling sorry for himself, he decided that he must get up and keep moving. He had looked forward to coming home to his boat, but the injuries and stiffness made it difficult to get on and off. He feared he had ruptured some of the stitches on his right thigh and buttock because of the pain and blood stains on his pajamas. He was surprised at how slowly he was moving as he got dressed and climbed the companionway ladder into the cockpit. He looked across the docks and could see that Betsy was up early, supervising a group of delivery boys carrying boxes onto her boat.

She noticed him at the same time and waved. "Good morning, sleepy head," she called out when she saw Quinn emerge from the cabin. "It's about time you got out of bed. I forgot to mention to you last night that the Sydney to Hobart Race starts on Thursday. I still have one berth open, if you are up for it."

"Oh, boy, that's day after tomorrow, isn't it? I'm afraid I would be a liability on this trip in my condition. Can you give me a rain check? Surely I'll be in better condition next year."

"That's a shame. I was looking forward to sailing with you again. The Hobart Race is the social event of the year. It attracts racers from all over the world. I have some extra bagels, would you like one?" she offered with a smile, oblivious to the gawking open-mouth stares of the delivery boys.

"Thanks, I'll take you up on that offer," knowing he didn't want to return to the diner after being ignored the night before. Betsy went below, as he crawled off the boat on his hands and knees. Before he could get the cane under him and regain his footing, he became aware of someone standing nearby. He glanced up and found Steven looking at him with a mocking smile on his face.

"Agent James said you were in bad shape. I had to see for myself. Do you need any help?" he asked.

"No, thank you. So long as the muscles respond to command, I'll keep on doing it the best that I can. What brings you to this part of town?"

"I have your computer replacement. It's all formatted and ready for you to insert your password. You will also find a replacement for your handgun and a new satellite phone. I know yours is still working, but water damage could take it offline at anytime. Agent James wanted me to remind you that you need to be more careful with government equipment," he said with a smile. "He also wanted me to check out your neighbor here at the dock. Do you know which one he was talking about?"

Just then, Betsy came down the gangplank carrying a bagel. "Here you are, Quinn. I hope you like it with cream cheese. I took the liberty of spreading it on pretty thick." She looked at Steven and extended her hand. "Hi, I'm Betsy Valentine. Are you a friend of Quinn's?"

Steven was almost as bad as the delivery boys and he hesitated a few seconds before responding. "Uhh …yes …we are business acquaintances …I guess," he stammered.

"Well, it is nice to meet you," she said with a smile. Quinn chuckled to himself at Steven's response, yet he understood she was something to look at. Betsy was off again, directing more deliveries. Two boxes of fresh fruit and six cases of alcoholic beverages were coming down the dock, along with a small legion of bronzed young men that Quinn assumed were part of her crew. Betsy was in her element issuing orders and keeping account on a clipboard.

"Well, I can see why Striker was interested in your neighbor," he said with enthusiasm, while watching her in action. "Oh, I almost forgot. I am supposed to take you to our Company doctor on direct orders from Marie in the Philippines. Would you like me to get you a wheelchair or can you make it all the way down the dock by yourself?"

"No fair making fun of the cripple. I'm still mobile, so I can make it on my own. You can help by putting the new hardware on the boat for me and locking it up. Getting on and off is a little laborious." Steven jumped onto the boat and almost ran down the companionway ladder. Quinn yelled over to Betsy, "Betsy, apparently I have a doctor's appointment this morning. I also called Archer Marine and they told me that Meg was in Hobart, serving on the race committee, so I missed her."

"I'll probably see her at the end of the race and give her an update on your condition. I know she will be interested." She shouted back as one of her crew members was being hoisted up the mast in a boatswain's chair.

Steven bounded off the boat and landed with a thud next to Quinn. "Are you ready, Pops?" Quinn just shook his head and started walking slowly down the dock, as two more deliveries were being made to Betsy's boat. A large bag of potatoes and of onions, boxes of steak and fish, plus all the makings for salads were being trucked to the boat. "Wow, I wouldn't mind sailing with her at all," Steven said.

The doctor was expecting Quinn and gave him immediate attention when he came through the door. Two hours later, Steven dropped Quinn off at the marina and reminded him, "My nursemaid duties are now officially over. You're on your own. I'm getting back to my real job of protecting the good old U.S.A. So don't call, unless you're on your death bed." With a parting smile, Steven departed in his nondescript four-door sedan.

Quinn smiled and watched him depart. He was feeling better now that he had fresh bandages and was on new pain medication. The activities around Betsy's boat had increased in his absence. A diesel mechanic and marine electronics truck were parked near the dock and the crowd of men taking orders from Betsy was now three-deep.

Betsy and her crew of fourteen young men departed the docks with much fanfare at daybreak the next morning. Quinn walked down the dock as the crew raised the sails and shouted his goodbyes and well wishes. At one point, Quinn found himself caught up in the excitement, waving his cane at Betsy to make sure she saw him. *God, I wish I was going with them,* he thought as the big Oyster joined the fleet heading out of the bay. He stood and watched them as the crowds began to thin and seagull cries could once again be heard over the boat horns and shouts of, “God speed, mates.”

CHAPTER 18

Insurrection

As he ambled back towards his boat, his satellite phone rang for the first time in a week. Quinn fumbled with the holster to retrieve the phone and then answered, "Walter here."

"Walter, this is Alex …how are you doing?

"Alex, it is so good of you to call. I'm recovering slowly, very slowly. Thanks for asking."

"Do you think a cold compress would help with your recovery?" Alex asked, getting right to the point of his call. "Listen Quinn, we are about to have the first civil war on the Antarctic continent and all my advisors tell me that would be a very bad thing."

"Civil war! What are you talking about Alex?"

"Your scientist friends at McMurdo Station are in revolt. Apparently, the NSF supervisor that took your place has caused quite an uproar. It has gotten so bad that the NSF just relieved him of duty. Well, okay—they fired him. This is the first time this has ever been done in the history of NSF's polar efforts. I need you to go back down to the Station and see if you can put things on the right track. Here is the thing, Quinn, not one paper has been published on the meteor strike that you and the team investigated. Every time the NSF asks about the papers, I get a lot of double-talk. Our science program is being upstaged by other nations, and we were there first."

"Slow down now, you're getting ahead of me. You mean to tell me that no papers have been submitted for review or publication?"

"That is correct! No papers have been submitted for review or publication!"

"Some of those papers were well along when I left in the spring! I cannot see how or why they are taking this long."

"You can see our concern here at NSF. Are you well enough to give us a hand on this?"

"I'm still moving pretty slow and have to go to the doctor every day to change the bandages and watch for infections. I'm not sure I'm ready yet, Alex."

"They have a nice little clinic there at the McMurdo Station and the overwinter doctor and nurse are already there. If you can't go now, the winter will be on us and I'm afraid we will lose the entire program, as well as the impact reports."

"Okay, I hear what you are saying Alex. I'll grab my gear and be ready to go in a couple of days. Can you arrange a ride for me?"

"I've already taken care of it. A car will pick you up in one hour."

"One hour—I said a couple of days! You do recall that I am moving slowly. You don't want me to rush packing for Antarctica—it could be life-threatening to forget something in that climate."

"All right, I'll give you an hour and a half, but no more. We have already diverted a plane from New Zealand to pick you up. You have to be at the airport there in Sydney no later than 1:30 P.M. Pacific time. So get packing. And Quinn, I owe you one for this. If there is anything you ever need … well, you know."

Quinn looked at the phone as he disconnected. Then for a second, he scanned the horizon. The fleet of sailboats was well on their way for the starting line and the spectator boats following them with crowds of well wishers. *I had better get my sore butt in gear. Civil War! That has to be an exaggeration,* he thought as he shuffled slowly towards his boat.

Luckily his gear had been cleaned and stowed when he left the ice in the spring and he hadn't needed any of the clothes in the heat of the Australian summer, so he only had to grab some personal items and his shaving kit and he was ready to go. Betsy and her crew had left the dock's handtruck when they departed, so he threw his bag on one and wheeled it down to the parking lot. He left his bag at the Dockmaster's office and had time to make a quick trip back to the doctor before the cab arrived. The doctor just shook his head at Quinn's plans and gave him some extra pain medication and bandages, just in case there wasn't enough at the station. "Oh, well, there will be far less of a chance for getting an infection in Antarctic's cold climate. If you do, however, you'll probably die. I'm fairly sure they will not be equipped to fight a full-blown infection. All I can say is, I hope you have a good trip." Quinn thanked him for his assistance and headed back to the marina to wait for the cab.

The diverted flight added approximately 800 additional miles to the trip and the passengers were not happy about the delay. Most of the passengers were the winter staff of the station and were prepared for the extreme cold conditions of the continent. He was very conspicuous in his Hawaiian shirt and bandages, when most of the passengers had already dressed for the ice. He could tell that it was not going to be a friendly trip.

How did I let myself be talked into this? Once in the air, the temperature in the transport plane forced him to break out a pair of thermal pants and a fleece shirt.

Eight long hours sitting on metal seats left Quinn stiff as a board and glad that he had extra pain medication. He was the last person off the plane and had to drag his bag behind him to get into the terminal. Upon entering, he saw Zeb Palmeri, the recently fired supervisor who had replaced him three months earlier. He approached and introduced himself and found Dr. Palmeri to be very distracted and distant, even aloof. After a few moments attempting to engage him in conversation, Quinn gave up and headed for the station transport.

Once at the station, he checked in at the reception area and was assigned a cubical for his sleeping quarters. He threw his bag on the bed and headed for the cafeteria. On the way, he encountered the first member of the mutinous crew. Dr. Pam Laystrom was standing in the hallway with her fists on her hips.

"What the hell are you doing here?" she asked with a scowl on her face.

"Well, I've come to help," Quinn stated before he was cut off.

"Yeah, sure, your buddies and the NSF have already been more help than we can stand. Your edicts and management style have been in total violation of any scientific investigative principles. You can just get your ass back on the plane and stay out of our f----ing way."

"Pam, can you at least tell me what's going on?"

"As if you didn't know what's been going on! You probably set the whole thing up and handpicked your replacement for his management skills."

"I ...I am truly at a loss. The NSF told me there were conflicts, but nothing more. I really don't know what you're talking about."

"What role are you serving? Are you here to overwinter?"

"I have no official role. I'm here at the request of the NSF to help where I can. And no, I am not here to overwinter. This is a short visit, prior to winter shutdown."

She stood looking at him with distrust. "Christ, as if you could actually do anything in a few days, after your organization has worked diligently to screw this scientific program for the last three months."

"Listen, I just got off the flight from New Zealand and I'm about to starve to death. Come to the cafeteria with me and give me a debriefing over lunch. Okay?"

"Screw you, I'm busy," she said as she pushed her way past him and walked rapidly down the hall, talking to herself under her breath.

Quinn stood stunned for a few moments, and then slowly continued towards the canteen. *This could really be a problem if I can't get anyone to talk to me about it,* he thought. He selected a bowl with the soup of the day and sat by himself, thinking of his next course of action. I guess I'll head up to the NSF office and see what kind of records Dr. Palmeri left that might shed some light on the problem. Before he could finish his soup, a contingent of scientists came through the door. At first, Quinn was delighted to see Mark Raulson, Roy Lynch, and Drs. Randy Worthington and Pam Laystrom again, but their demeanor made him withhold the friendly greeting that he was about to convey.

Mark was the first to speak. "Did you bring any troops with you? You're going to need them to quiet the natives." Quinn laughed out loud at the statement, but noticed that no one else thought it was funny. "Okay," he said, " I have no idea what is going on, so sit down and talk to me. I'm totally in the dark."

There was a moment of silence as the four scientists stood looking at him and his bowl of soup. Finally, Roy Lynch spoke up, "It isn't a pretty story, Quinn, and your timing is terrible. We just rode the last science advisor out of town on a rail and then you show up saying you want to help. We have had it up to our f---ing eyebrows with NSF's help and frankly, we just don't give a shit anymore!"

"Sit down and let's talk! I'm here and I am not going away. You can continue your battles, but I don't even know the issues, so I'm not your enemy. I felt that we were friends and an investigative team when I left in the spring. So one of you, tell me what the hell is going on here."

Dr. Laystrom broke the standoff by turning on her heels and departing the cafeteria in a huff. Mark looked at Roy, took a deep breath and pulled out a chair. Reluctantly, Roy and Randy both did the same. Quinn pushed his half-empty bowl of soup out of the way and waited, looking at one and then the other.

"That bastard, Palmeri," Mark started then stopped and looked around the cafeteria shaking his head. "Well, let me start from the beginning. You remember what it was like when you left the station in the spring. You had delegated the media responsibility to Pam and me. The NSF grant had been approved and a half-dozen technical papers were underway."

"Yes, that is what I recall. Things were going good … and?"

"Well, Palmeri changed all that before you were on the plane. He said that you and the NSF staff in Washington had specifically requested him to serve as Science Advisory because things were being run shoddily and without appropriate attention to scientific research practices. According to him, we were mere amateurs. He wanted to be the primary media contact and none of the papers were to proceed until he approved the outline and content. According to him, he was the only one who could establish the investigative protocol and authorize the expenditure of funds for research. We were cut off from collaborative contacts on the outside and could not send emails regarding the research without his approval. He turned us all into G…D... school kids, bowing to the principal. The final straw was his insistence that he would be the primary author on all papers leaving the Station for publication, all with the blessing of the NSF." Mark was red in the face and was beating the table with his fist with that last reference to the NSF.

"Didn't any of you call the NSF and tell them what was going on? I cannot believe that they would allow this management style."

"Apparently, he beat us to it. He told Washington that we were a group of malcontented mediocre scientists who should not be here and could not be trusted with such an important research program without his direction …and they believed him! According to him, if we were any good, we would be teaching at a university and obviously that was not the case. By the time we got around to calling the Foundation, it was too late. He had won them over completely. So, naturally we have been acting like malcontented researchers and making Palmeri's point with the NSF. There was a time a few weeks ago that we had to physically restrain Pam. She was going to kill him. So what if she would spend the rest of her life in prison—she thought the bastard deserved to die. She still has a lot of anger towards anyone remotely associated with NSF, so you might want to watch your step around her."

"Thanks for the warning. You know I did interview Palmeri in New Zealand. I found him to be a little arrogant, but most professors are. He had sound credentials, even though most of his research had been done based on published literature, rather than primary research. I recommended him, but certainly not for the management role he was apparently playing.

He assumed that himself." Quinn shook his head and ran his hand through his close-cropped hair and asked, "Tell me, what condition are the technical papers in right now?"

"They are a bloody mess. They have been edited to death, reformatted, re-investigated, re-written—you name it. None of us want them to leave here with our names on them. He edited the heart and soul of the research out of the papers," Roy said passionately.

"As I told you earlier, I did not have an official role, but the NSF did send me to help out. They are equally concerned about the papers and their science program here on the continent. I have their authority to work things out, but I'll need your assistance to turn things around. Can we work together?"

The three scientists sat looking at their hands and not saying a word. Quinn could tell that it would take some time to gain their trust. Possibly more time than he had before winter. The problem got even worse. The Foundation had not yet hired a new supervisor for the winter.

Mark finally spoke, "You convince Pam that you are on the up and up and maybe we can work together. But I can tell you that none of these technical papers are leaving here with Palmeri's or your name on them, understood?"

"I have a great respect for each of your research capabilities. As we talked before I left here in the spring, you are in charge of the technical papers under the grant provisions from NSF. I will not be serving as the public voice for the project, and I am not going to dictate the research protocol. I will not expect my name on the papers, unless I have made significant contributions. I would like to discuss the research with you, but I am not going to be the final voice. How is that for starters?"

"Go talk to Dr. Laystrom."

"Okay, I'll do that. Thanks for the word of caution. I can certainly see why she would be upset. I was very pleased with all the efforts on her part before I left last spring."

The evening meal was about to be served and the cafeteria was slowly filling up. Supper was always a social time, as the scientists and support staff lingered over dinner and later and enjoyed the fellowship. Quinn was feeling none of that fellowship as he stiffly rose from the table and headed down the corridor towards the clinic. He stopped outside the clinic door to take another pain pill before entering. The new doctor and nurse sat chatting at the desk as he came in. Both were young women who appeared confident in their new roles at the Station.

"Can we help you?" the nurse asked as she gave Quinn a quick look over.

"Yes, I just flew in this afternoon and need some assistance," Quinn began. "I am recovering from some burns and scrapes and was hoping you could give me a hand with changing my bandages while I am here at the Station." Based on the look of concern on the face of the doctor, he could tell immediately that this request was not being taken very well.

"Who allowed you to come to this station?" she asked curtly. "We have certain health standards for the personnel that will be overwintering here and the rules do not include any physical injuries, most definitely not injuries as extensive as yours. We are just not equipped to handle this kind of care. My advice to you is to catch the first plane out in the morning and get back to New Zealand, where you can receive adequate care. I'm afraid we cannot help you."

"Well, I have pain medication, but I need help with changing the dressings. Can you give me a hand?"

"Did you not understand me? We cannot help you! You would use up all of the supplies we have on stock for the winter, so let me repeat, we cannot help you."

Quinn found himself in the hallway outside the clinic door and he wasn't quite sure how he got there. Inside the clinic, the doctor and nurse shared a laugh at the audacity of the person who would come to the continent in his condition. There was nothing for Quinn to do but head for his sleeping cube and literally tend to his own wounds. Sometimes life just stunk. This was like one of Jack Wolfe's novels where the lead character faced numerous obstacles and had to labor against unbearable conditions just to survive.

He sat on his unmade bunk and stared at the light-green wall and listened to the distant guttural hum of a diesel generator. He removed his jacket and shirt to look at his injuries. It had only been a week since he had lain on the banks of the river in the Philippines. However, all his wounds looked like they were healing, with no infection. Quinn thought he might be able to do without some of the dressings. The problem was that the stitches were supposed to be taken out in about ten days and that was only three or four days from now. Maybe the doctor was right—he needed to get back to civilization. He should never have let Alex talk him into this trip. *Why do the pressures of the job always come before personal needs*, he asked himself? He picked up his computer and left a short email message with Alex.

"Alex, I've made it to the Station and have established a very tentative beachhead with the science team. The conditions here are probably worse than you thought. It sounds like the problems are associated with the overbearing management style of the NSF Science Advisor, Dr. Zeb Palmeri. I will be meeting with key members of the staff first thing tomorrow morning, so hopefully I can help get things going in the right direction. The clinic here informs me that they are not equipped to handle injuries as extensive as mine, so I must leave within the next three to four days to obtain appropriate care.

More later." Walter

Sleep came slowly and with it, a dream of a tall dark angry female scientist sneaking down the hallway holding a long-bladed knife. He awoke with his heart racing. It felt very real at that moment and it took him a long time to fall back to sleep.

He had almost forgotten that morning never really comes at the station. Even if it did, there were few windows to see it. Instead there was just a general consensus among the residents of the Station that it was time to get up and make some noise. Quinn awoke to some distant conversations and hearty laughs, as the staff circulated in the hallway between buildings. He made a quick check and almost laughed to himself by thinking, "*There were no new knife wounds during the night.*" He dressed in a hurry and headed for the cafeteria. That half a cup of soup last night did not stay with him very long and he was starving.

The cafeteria was already busy with a number of people going through the line and filling up the tables. Quinn scanned the room for the members of the science team and saw none of them. *I must be late,* he surmised. *This is not the start I had hoped for. A congenial breakfast meeting would have been a good icebreaker.* The volume of food available at the station was always high due to the amount of calories burned just to stay warm in the Antarctic climate. So with a large appetite, he ended up with far more food than he intended. He found a table in the corner and made a spectacle of himself carrying his tray to the table while trying to use his cane. He placed his tray on the table and headed back for a mug of coffee when he saw the doctor from the previous day standing in the doorway, scanning the dining room. She intercepted him at the coffee urn. "Are you Quinn Wilson?" she asked.

"Yes, I am and I know what you are going to say. I am not going to be bothering you again, Doctor. You made your position quite clear last night. I have work to do here at the station and will only be staying for the next few days at most." He held up his free hand as a sign of peace before she could speak further.

"Mr. Wilson, I need to see you in the clinic right away," she said. "I need to apologize for my response to you yesterday evening. We have gotten several high-level communications from the NSF, CIA, and some place called the NGIA. Can you come with me to the clinic, so we can discuss this further?"

"Well, thank you for the apology. I'll be glad to stop by right after I have my breakfast."

"No sir, I need you to come right now! These agencies are on my back and have expressed concern for your health. I need to give you a complete checkup and respond to their concerns immediately. I understand that you have been exposed to potential topical parasites and infections in the Philippines," she said with some urgency. "I do not want to risk the health of this station to exposure of any potential parasites or infection."

"Well, I don't know what they told you, but I'm well enough to eat breakfast before you take a look at my dressings. Besides, I haven't eaten in almost 24 hours now, and those agencies are just going to have to wait. If you would like to join me for breakfast I can fill you in on the details."

"I'm not talking about just your dressings, I want to do a full examination and medical workup," she said most adamantly.

"I do not have the time for a full physical exam. I think you have gotten the wrong impression from those communications. I'm not here to overwinter. I'm here to assist the NSF on some project reports and will be gone in a few days maybe a week and a half at the most. I may need your assistance for an hour or two during that timeframe. Come and sit down with me, please. Grab a cup of coffee and we'll talk over breakfast, okay?" Quinn said and headed back to the table with a quick glance over his shoulder to see if she was coming.

She stood where he had left her, with her arms across her chest and glared at him disapprovingly, as he shuffled back to the table and sat down. She had been taken by surprise by the phone calls early that morning. Apparently, this badly injured person was on a critical mission and her first response had caused some kind of political problems—something she did not need during her first week at the station. *I do not have time to deal with this*, she thought as she headed back to the clinic.

Quinn watched her go with a measure of resignation. *Nothing was going the way he had planned on this trip*, he thought, as he salted his scrambled eggs.

Dr. Laystrom appeared in the doorway and scanned the tables until she saw him. She walked purposefully to his table and sat down without saying a word.

"Good morning, Pam," Quinn offered with his second bite of eggs on the fork. "I was hoping we would have a chance to talk this morning."

"I'm here against my better judgment. I'm sick of the NSF and their piss–poor management style. How dare them support an irrational manager and take his word over competent scientists? He treated us as children. It was so insulting. I'm only here because we had a good relationship last winter and I thought we should at least talk."

"Thank you for that. From what I have heard since I landed, his management style was inappropriate and overbearing. I do not think the NSF knew what was going on, but his style, in no way, represents their interest." Quinn began hoping to set the right tone.

She impatiently interrupted, "So why are you here? Did they send you?"

"I'm here to help where I can, and yes, they asked me to come," he offered haltingly.

"What were their directions to you?"

"They were concerned that the technical papers had been delayed and apparently saw that Dr. Palmeri was the problem. They took the unprecedented step of relieving him from duty this late in the season and asked if I could fill in until a replacement was found."

"You are not here for the winter?"

"No, I am only here for a week or so."

She stared out across the cafeteria in deep thought. "We were sure that Dr. Palmeri was part of a subversive plot totally supported by the NSF. He was an abusive SOB who would belittle you at every opportunity, demanding to make all decisions and not listening to anyone. He made a mess of the reports, and then wanted his name on them as lead researcher. We are not at all sure that you are not part of that plot."

"Pam, what possible reason would the NSF have to subvert the scientific work here at the station? When I talked to them, they were very concerned about the staff and the reports on the impact."

"Oh they are so innocent! You were not here when Dr. Palmeri relayed messages from Washington, telling us to do exactly as we were told, like good little children. The nice professor knows what is best for all of us."

"No, I was not here. I have only discussed their concerns for the scientists and the program. You know there may be more to these NSF directives than I know about. I would hope that they were just providing long-range support to their Station manager and nothing more. Do you think a conference call with all of us in the room would clear the air?"

"You can call, but I will not talk to them. They will probably plead ignorance of the whole thing."

"Well, I don't know what to do. Are you suggesting giving up on the impact research?"

"I don't care anymore! I just don't care! My interest has been killed."

"Well, I care! You remember that you and I were the first and possibly the only ones to see the meteor and we were the first to the impact area. We were out there on the ice, all of us. And another thing, I've traveled around the Pacific basin since I left the station in the spring. It's amazing how many people followed our expedition and remain very interested in the impact. We have an obligation to report on that event. Science demands the documentation. It is, in fact, one of the biggest scientific events this century!"

"Well, it's going to take more than that to get me interested again, but you have a point."

"Can I see the reports?"

"So, what are you going to do, start editing them?"

"If you are right, I can confirm the condition they are in and help put them back on track for publishing."

"You are not a scientist and should not have input on these reports."

"Pam you're right, I am not a scientist—I am a geographer. I am only trying to help!"

With that last statement, Dr. Laystrom glared at him with dark penetrating eyes and abruptly left the table and walked out of the cafeteria. Quinn sat watching her depart and felt an uneasy feeling of déjà vu. Her piercing look reminded him of that morning back in St. Petersburg when his wife left him. Her departure had left him stunned and he could feel that self-loathing depression coming back despite his efforts to avoid it. *What a fool he was, what a fool,* he thought over and over, as he rose from the table leaning heavily on his cane. He walked slowly out into the hall and looked expectantly in the direction Pam had departed, but there was no sign of her.

He trudged towards the clinic trying to figure out an appropriate course of action. The clinic door was closed with a sign that read, "Examination in progress, do not disturb," on the door. Quinn stared at it for a second and leaned against the wall to wait. He pulled out his satellite phone and searched the memory for Robert Murey's telephone number at the NSF offices in Washington. Glancing at his watch, he noted that it would be late in the afternoon, but Randy should still be there. He pushed the button and listened as the "Big Bang" static sizzled on the line.

"Good afternoon, Mr. Murey's office," came a soothing female voice.

"Yes, good afternoon. This is Quinn Wilson calling for Robert. Is he in?

"Mr. Murey is in this afternoon, but there is someone in his office. May I tell him what the call is about?"

"Please tell him that the call is from Antarctica. He will understand the urgency of the call."

"One moment, please."

Quinn looked up and down the hall and noted that the early morning rush hour was in full swing. The Station personnel were busily moving about talking and laughing in small groups. It was a deceptively happy place. Bob promptly answered the phone, "Hello, this is Bob Murey."

"Bob, this is Quinn Wilson at McMurdo Station."

"So you are already down there? That is good to hear. Alex called me yesterday saying that you were on the way and that I owed him big time for your efforts."

"Yes, I am here and had some talks with the scientists. Things are not very pretty. They claim NSF is involved in a conspiracy to thwart the scientific papers on the meteor impact. They think that Dr. Palmeri was working at NSF headquarters' direction."

"I was afraid of something like that. Highly intelligent people in a closed environment have a tendency of imagining conspiracies like this."

"Imagination or not, they are very upset over the treatment they have been receiving and have essentially lost interest in the reports on the impact. We have to do something quickly or the scientific knowledge will be lost. I suggest that we have a conference call as soon as possible and lay it all on the table. We have to convince them that there is no conspiracy orchestrated from your office and that Dr. Palmeri was operating alone."

"I hate to tell you this Quinn, but that is not entirely true."

"What do you mean?"

"Dr. Palmeri was very effective in convincing us that he was in charge of a group of uncooperative scientists who were not very talented to begin with. Only he knew what was best."

"...and you went along with that?" Quinn asked in disbelief.

"Yes, I guess at first, we all did. I'm sorry Quinn, but you have to understand that McMurdo is a very remote site and we have become used to trusting the advice of our science supervisors. Who else can we depend on?"

"Well, in this case, it has caused an enormous problem, one that may not be resolved in the one- or two-week time frame that I'm here. The science team has lost interest in the reports and do not care to work on them under any conditions."

"You cannot let that happen, Quinn! You know as well as I do that this is the biggest scientific event of the century. It's huge! Our science teams were onsite first and not one paper has been published describing the event and its impact. The single French paper has gotten minimal circulation, but I know it is being translated for publishing in Scientific American magazine. We are losing our advantage! You have got to change that!"

"I know how important it is for us, but do you have any suggestions?"

"Yes, my big idea was to send you to solve the problem and break the log jam."

"So, how am I doing so far? The scientists walked out of our meeting and the doctor here at the clinic has told me to leave the station and go back to New Zealand."

"Quinn, I hate to do this to you but I have to go. I trust your judgment. You tell me what I need to do, anything at all to get the situation under control. Winter will be here in just a few days and the relationship with the scientists and staff has never been lower. Good luck! I'm sure you will work it out."

Quinn stared at the phone as the call was disconnected. Just then the clinic door opened and the doctor stood looking at him with displeasure written all over her face. She stepped aside and motioned with a tilt of her head for him to enter the room. Her disapproval of him filled the room and Quinn made a feeble attempt at amends. "I'm sorry for the delay in getting over here …" he said and received no response. Then with a more direct approach, "Can I tell you about these injuries?" Still there was no response from the doctor.

She unbuttoned his shirt and ripped the dressing from his chest. Quinn flinched at the pain and glanced at the doctor to see a self-satisfied look on her face. Again Quinn grimaced, as she ripped bandages off one at a time. The clinic nurse had returned and watched the process from the door. She could feel the tension and see Quinn bravely enduring needless pain. She crossed the room and opened the storage cabinet. "Doctor, allow me to finish these dressings," she asserted with a hopeful amount of authority in her voice. The doctor looked at her briefly and walked out of the clinic, leaving Quinn and the nurse alone.

"What was that all about?" she asked.

"Actually, I'm not sure. She seems to have taken an extreme dislike to me," Quinn responded sheepishly.

"She came to the Station after serving a year in the war zone and just before you walked in the door yesterday, she told me she had come to get as far away from wounded men as possible."

"Oh, wonderful—and here I thought it was just me."

"Her behavior just now when I came into the clinic was unprofessional. She should never have been that abusive to a patient, no matter what her personal feelings are," the nurse said with concern. "We have a winter tour coming up soon and she is showing signs of being emotionally unstable."

"I'm sure she will be much better when I'm off the ice." However, the nurse's hands were much gentler and Quinn thanked her for her help as he left the clinic and headed for the science lab in the hopes of talking to the team. There Quinn found Dr. Worthington hunched over his computer intently entering data and mumbling at the screen. He glanced up as Quinn entered.

"I'm pissed at you," he offered as a greeting.

"Well, get in line, I seem to be hearing that a lot. So exactly what are you pissed off at …that is if you don't mind me asking?"

"You made a comment while we were out on the expedition to the impact zone and I cannot get it out of my head."

"Oh, what was the comment?"

"You remember! You said that Antarctica did not have any music! I have been racking my brain, trying to come up with a theme or rhythm to work on and I still can't find anything."

"Yes, I do recall that conversation. I remember the sound of silence when we were on the ice expedition. It was so quiet that it sang to my soul."

"Silence?"

"Yes, silence and the wind blowing …that's the sound of Antarctica."

"Silence? You're just going to keep turning the knife, aren't you?"

"Randy, I would love to talk to you further about this, but I really need to talk to the whole science team about their research papers. Do you think we can get Mark, Roy, Tom, Pam and you together for a short meeting?"

"They are far more pissed at you than I am … and right now, I am really pissed."

"Okay, let's get everyone together and have a pissing contest. I'm actually getting pissed myself."

Randy mumbled to himself, turned to his computer and hammered out a quick email.

"Your presence is requested
There is piss in the wind
And we shall have our say today"

With a smile, Randy turned back to Quinn and smugly folded his arms over his chest and waited.

Mark was the first to arrive. "What the hell are you talking about?" he asked.

Roy and Tom came around the corner with blank looks on their faces. Dr. Laystrom was the last to arrive and she stopped after rounding the corner and struck a defiant posture with her hands on her hips.

"I know exactly what you meant by that email," she said.

"Well, you are the only one. How about clueing us in," Mark suggested.

"Thanks, Randy. I asked you all to come because we need to clear the air of any miscommunications, if we can. I talked to the NSF in Washington and they admitted that they were possibly guilty of listening to Dr. Palmeri and following his recommendations. They said that in the entire history of the Station, they have had very trustworthy men—excuse me—scientists, in that role and have become accustomed to taking their advice. They realized their mistake too late, and took the unprecedented step of firing Dr. Palmeri, even though it was too late in the year to replace him before the winter shutdown. They said that this was their mistake and there was no conspiracy, especially against the scientists here at the Station. The NSF director himself wanted me to convey his regrets and his concern for the reports on the meteor impact. He feels that these are very important papers to the scientific community and further stated that he will do everything in his power to put things right and relieve any tension here at the Station."

"Well, it is a little too late for apologies as far as I'm concerned," Pam offered.

"Let me add some personal observations, if I may. Pam, as I mentioned to you this morning, since leaving the station in the spring, I have spoken to several groups of scientists and, on three separate occasions, they asked about this expedition. I was very surprised at their comments. They followed the expedition closely and knew the names of the team members. Pam, I talked to Dr. Styles with the Volcanic Research Laboratory last week and he remembered your name and said you had spoken to his graduate class. He asked when the papers would be published. We owe it to them and the scientific community to document this event. Everyone had indicated that the impact was possibly the biggest scientific event of the century. Personal feelings aside, we are scientists and in our profession, science come first. The process of documenting and supporting a discovery is the test of true scientific work. You all know that. How can we avoid that obligation to our chosen profession?"

"Well, you say 'we' as if you are a part of this. I suppose like Dr. Palmeri, you want to steal our work and put yourself down as principal investigator?" Pam asked in a defiant tone.

"No, the papers are yours …honestly. I would like to be a part of the body of work. We were all on the expedition and all contributed in some degree to the structure of the study and the data collected. But in answer to your question Pam, no, I don't expect to be listed as principal author on the papers. However, if you think I've provided substance to the reports, I would be honored to be a contributing author. The choice is yours."

"I suppose you want to edit them and take out the science like Dr. Palmeri did?" Pam continued.

"I would love to see the papers and I will offer any comment I can to help. I'll review them if you would like, but no, I'm not acting as editor-in-chief."

"Dr. Palmeri took all the science out of the reports and left us with cartoon versions that are not even suitable for the *National Geographic Magazine*. We would have to go back three or even five drafts ago to reclaim the original contents," Randy observed with a noted measure of distain.

"Okay, that is a starting point," Quinn offered as he felt the temperament of the crew of scientists starting to swing in a more conciliatory direction.

"I suppose we still have to publish under the NSF banner," Mark inquired?

"Yes, I think you are correct. We are still working in the respective programs here at the station and are conducting the work under their grant. So, do we have a deal?" Quinn asked.

After a long pause with each scientist looking one to another, Mark said, "Yes, I suppose you are right. We do owe it to the science community. We hated what Dr. Palmeri was doing, but you have to admit, we always intended to publish those papers."

Randy and Tom offered a spark of enthusiasm, as they headed out of the lab talking and waving their arms.

Pam stood alone with her arms crossed, staring at Quinn. At long last she said, "You better not be screwing with me. These papers are just about the most important work I have ever done in my life and I would rather delete them from my computer than allow them to be bastardized."

"Dr. Laystrom—Pam, the scientific world is waiting to hear from you and you have an obligation to respond."

"Oh, don't get sentimental on me now," she said dropping her hands to her side. "You change one word of my text and you had better have a very good—no—an absolute need to do so or you and I are going to have issues ...understood?"

"Understood ...and I'm not kidding when I say the scientific world is awaiting your work. As I said, I've talked to several high-level scientists in various fields and they're all looking forward to reading the reports."

"I hope you're right!" she said as she headed out of the lab.

Quinn sat down in a chair nearby and realized that his right leg was stiff and sore from standing so long. Grimacing, he knew it would mean going back to the clinic for pain medication.

Randy returned to the lab a little while later with a stack of papers and stood looking over them intently. After giving him time to organize his work, Quinn asked, "Randy did they ever find the French crew that was lost on the way to the impact site?"

Randy looked up from his work, as if he had arrived in the lab from a different world. He stared at Quinn for a few seconds before responding, "No, they never found any sign of them. We kept our eyes open and even participated in the search around the impact zone later in the spring but nothing was ever found."

"That is very curious," Quinn said as he rubbed his unshaven chin.

With great formality, Randy straightened the stack of papers and handed them to Quinn.

"This is the report on the impact model. Everything is there from angle of atmosphere penetration to volume of material displaced by the impact. In addition, I've correlated the atmospheric impacts with world modeling experts to show its dispersion and probable impact on climate worldwide. If I don't get a Pulitzer for this work, it will be because the world's scientists are not smart enough to understand a truly innovative investigation."

"Okay, this is a great start. May I read it?"

"I wanted to show you this version for laughs," Randy continued as he pulled out a small stack of paper. "This is what it looked like after Dr. Palmeri finished with it. He cut more than 540 pages of science out of the report."

"I see—it's sort of like an executive summary. I hate to say this Randy, but you may want to hang on to them. If these reports strike the public's imagination, as I think they will, they are going to want newspaper and magazine articles to summarize the work."

"Oh, please … I didn't write this for public consumption. I only wrote to scientifically document this event."

"Believe me Randy, I understand that. But there is a lot of public interest out there right now. It is one of those natural events that grab the interest of almost everyone and they want to know all about it, much like the first moon walk in '69. So, until everything is said and done, hold on to these abbreviated write-ups. Okay?"

"I'm sorry I brought it up. I should have shredded it the minute Dr. Palmeri walked out the door. But, yes, I can see your point and will hold on to this summary. Now will you read the full report and get it out of here? I am tired of looking at it."

Quinn settled painfully onto a stool behind the last remaining drafting table on the continent. It was tucked into a corner of the lab out of the way of the scientific business of the Station, but in clear view of those working in the area. One by one, the scientists dropped their working drafts off for his review, with Dr. Laystrom being the last to make her delivery.

"Your argument about owing the scientific community was lame at best. It would have carried more weight if you were really a scientist. You are only a geographer, so you can't be espousing reverence about the scientific process with any authority. But, I've put a lot of work into this report and would like to have someone other than the bums at NSF in Washington read it. So please, read your heart out, but don't you dare make one editorial remark. You got that?" she queried with a toss of her head and turned and walked out of the lab.

Quinn was left with a stack of scientific reports that was almost two feet tall. As he watched Pam leave the room without saying a word, he turned his attention back to the reports. The first one in the stack was entitled, "The Morphology of Celestial Craters; an Analysis of the Wilkes Land Meteor Impact Zone," by Mark Raulson. He was immediately transported back to Wilkes Land and as he read the report, he could feel the bitter cold he experienced on the expedition. The analysis revealed that the meteor was very compact and actually impacted the ice field, rather than exploding in the atmosphere above the ground. The array of secondary craters indicated that there was minimal deterioration or fragmentation as the meteor approached the impact zone. Those secondary craters that were observed were entrained along the meteor's path, rather than radiating widely from the zone of impact, as would be expected to be in an atmospheric explosion. *Very interesting,* Quinn thought, as he continued to read. Magnetometer readings indicated a large portion of the meteor remained buried under the ice at extreme depths. Much of the meteor had vaporized on contact, yet some material remained just out of reach under a quarter mile of ice, much to the consternation of the scientists. There was a note that future exploration would be needed to retrieve a core sample of the meteor, once a suitable drilling rig could be brought to the continent. There were latitude and longitude coordinates to ensure that future scientific expeditions had the location of the magnetic anomaly. It was an excellent report in structure, research, content and presentation. Pam's report held up to her boasting. It was clean, pure scientific reporting. No edits or corrections were needed.

It had been midmorning when Quinn began reading the reports. He was totally engrossed in the effort and read through lunch and into the afternoon, oblivious to the activities going on around him. On occasion, he would jot down a note in the margin of a report. An action that aroused the curiosity of the scientists, as they would pass closer to the desk to see whose report was being read at the time. Dinnertime came and went as he read on, taking only brief bathroom breaks and grabbing a bottle of water. He was still at it, when the scientists retired for the evening. By that time, their interest in his review had increased considerably. Through the evening, they had inched closer and closer to the drafting table to assess his progress and would then congregate in the hallway to compare notes. The next morning, they found Quinn asleep at the table, with the last of the reports open under his right elbow.

"Hey, wake up! You're drooling on our reports!" Pam exclaimed with a voice tuned for maximum effect.

"Oh!"...Quinn reacted with a start, rubbing the bridge of his nose and looking about the room. There he saw the entire group of scientists, looking more like a class of middle school kids laughing at him. "Give me a minute, scientists. The last thing I remember was looking at the clock, which indicated that it was 3:00 A.M., so I was thinking about heading to bed. Apparently, I didn't make it."

"I guess you didn't. Would you like a cup of coffee?" Pam asked, handing him a cup of Starbucks with a smile.

"Now that will get me oriented back to the Station. Give me a few minutes to go to the bathroom and get my thoughts together and then we can talk."

Halfway through the cup of coffee, Quinn dusted off his hands and began organizing the reports into three stacks. This attracted the attention of the science team and they collected around his desk.

"Well, what did you think? Have you gotten through all of the reports?" Mark asked expectantly.

"Yes, I've done at least a first read-through on every report. You all did an excellent job. They are very thorough. So much so that I think this first pile is ready to go and I mean right now. Pam, your report was especially insightful and well-organized. We should put them on the wire to NSF in Washington and have them published as soon as possible. I have some questions and/or ideas on the reports here in the second stack. Nothing major, but I would like to talk through them before we turn them loose. Randy, as near as I can tell, your report is actually six reports in one. Don't get me wrong, it is very well researched and prepared, all 600 pages of it. You have calculated the size of the meteor, its angle of entry into the atmosphere, probable impact scenarios, size of the crater, amount of ice displaced, the ejecta dispersed to the atmosphere, distribution of material by upper-level air currents and probable impact on world climates. My question is whether you wanted it to go as is, or separate it into individual reports? Now the reports in this third stack appear to be the ones Dr. Palmeri edited. They, for all practical purposes, are each a layman's summary of the more detailed scientific reports. It makes you wonder if he did not understand the depth of the research and was attempting to edit them to his intellectual level."

"So, now that you have read them, I suppose you want your name on them as a co-author?" Pam injected with an aloof tune of voice.

"No, I only wish I had been here during the summer to work on these reports with you. The only input I have had to date was my participation in the expedition along with the fact that some of the photographs from the expedition were mine, which hardly qualifies for a co-authorship, so no co-authorship is warranted or requested. I did notice that Dr. Palmeri's name did not appear on any of the reports. Since he was here all summer, does that qualify him as co-author on any of these reports?"

"Oh, I can't believe you asked that question Quinn! Palmeri was a total ass. He did nothing but obstruct our research and make cartoons of all our reports," Pam said with exasperation.

"Yes, I have heard the stories. Put emotions aside and look at it from an objective scientific viewpoint. Did he have any significant input to these reports that would warrant co-authorship? I have looked over his edits and I believe those reports here in the third stack would be good for newspaper and magazine articles. As I said before, the public is very interested in this event, but there are only a few thousand or so individuals who would be able to digest all of Randy's report."

"We are scientists, Quinn! It is our job to conduct credible research and prepare defensible scientific reports. We do not write for the general public period! You can throw all Palmeri's edits in the garbage for all I care." Randy said emphatically, remembering the 540 pages Dr. Palmeri had cut from his report.

Looking at all the scientists at once, Quinn asked, "Does everyone feel that way? As an objective observer, I think these reports are excellent summaries of the research, gesturing toward the third stack. I would like to hear from the rest of you."

"Pam is right. If those summary reports are sent to NSF, they will think we are an incompetent malcontented group of scientists who can't write their way out of a paper bag. Dr. Palmeri made sure the Foundation viewed us that way," Roy offered.

"Okay then. We will send in the scientific reports and you can hold these summaries in reserve. I guarantee you will receive requests from news publications and magazines for them. Once you do, you can make the decision then to release them," Quinn stated.

"Release them only if it is understood that they are just summaries for the non-scientists," Mark inserted.

"Pam, are you in agreement with that?" Quinn asked.

"I just don't care anymore. You can do anything with them that you want, so long as my primary report is not watered down or edited into oblivion again."

"Are we all in agreement that the research papers in the first stack can go now?" Quinn asked.

"We would have sent them a month ago, if it had not been for Palmeri's obstruction and yes, I'm ready to send them now." Pam said with a more agreeable tone.

"Great, is everyone in agreement then? Oh, and one other thing to confirm. Mark, you and Pam will continue to be the spokesmen for the project, if we get any requests for interviews from the press."

"You mean spokespersons, don't you?" Pam said with a smile on her face.

"Yes, Pam! I meant spokespersons," Quinn said with an added smile.

The next couple of hours were a rush of activity as computer files were compressed and placed on websites. Notices and computer file addresses were sent to NSF in Washington and the floodgates of scientific information were opened to the world. The same process was mirrored in Washington, as the reports were retrieved and read in the hallways and offices at NSF. Before the day was over, the reports were published on NSF website and sent to the presses.

The questions regarding Randy's report were easier to fix than either Quinn or Randy had realized. The files were so large that they had to be sent chapter by chapter. Therefore, six different reports reached Washington NSF with the understanding that they could be stand-alone reports, if the same introductory section was published with each report, to establish the event and location of the impact.

"All the reports are out on the wire and I have confirmation from NSF that they have been received. So, I have another question."

"Shoot."

"The helicopter is still on the flight line. Do you think it would be possible to fly out to the impact site, while we still have an hour or so of daylight left in this afternoon? I would love to see the crater again."

"I don't know—we can check. They usually leave the helicopter in the hangar overwinter. Apparently, there are too many moving parts to freeze up during the winter months, so it's only available for flights during summer months. It's late in the season, but we can ask and see if it is possible to make the flight," Mark suggested.

"The next transport flight out to New Zealand is tomorrow morning, so I have time this afternoon, if the weather cooperates." Quinn continued as Mark picked up the phone to check on the helicopter's availability.

As he hung up the phone, he stated that the pilot was willing to make a quick trip with three passengers, but we would have to go within the next hour to take advantage of the failing light.

After some minor arguments regarding the occupants of the three available seats, Quinn, Mark, and Pam caught the shuttle to Williams Field.

The helicopter was a Bell JetRanger captained by Gene Spencer, a crusty 65-year-old veteran of the Viet Nam War who was more than able to hold his own in the younger man's profession of piloting helicopters. Gene was chewing on a stubbly unlit cigar when the trio reached the hangar. His leather flight jacket sported the patches of his many campaigns, both military and as a pilot for the NSF. He got right to the point, "I have enough fuel for an hour and a half flight. The weather is holding, so load up and let's get this bird in the air."

After a five-minute engine warm-up, Gene lifted off and banked sharply back towards the station. His command of the helicopter and the precision tight turns suggested to Quinn that Gene had been a combat pilot who was used to putting the aircraft through its paces.

"I have to circle the station for a few minutes to gain some altitude, so hang on. There are air-sick bags under each seat. Use them or clean up your own mess, the choice is yours." Gene relayed his well-rehearsed message to his passengers, as he banked sharply in a series of tight circles over the Station.

Once he gained an altitude of 8,000 feet, Gene stood the helicopter on its nose to gain forward speed and headed for the mountain pass. Quinn was struck by the stark beauty of the mountains in the fading light of fall. He checked his watch and knew that in 45 minutes, the sun would partially rise above the horizon and give an hour of increased light before once again sinking back into the twilight of a prolonged dusk. They followed the route of their expedition and half an hour later, Gene laid the helicopter on its side as be began circling the impact site. The maneuver was so abrupt, it elicited an embarrassing scream from Dr. Pam, much to Gene's delight.

Regaining her composure, Pam gave a quick description of the impact zone. "There it is. You can see the degradation around the rim of the crater and that it has been filled in with windblown snow. The crater itself is probably two to two and a half times larger than when we first saw it a year ago. The sides are still calving, as the entire ice sheet seeks equilibrium. In another few years, the crater will be just a depression on the plateau. Our research facilities were closed down and brought back to McMurdo Station last week. We had to move its location three times, due to the decay along the rim. I think any chances of finding the remnant of that meteor are long gone because of the instability. Maybe one day after the crater has been completely filled in, we can come back to these coordinates and drill."

They circled the impact zone in silence as Gene put the helicopter through a series of maneuvers. On a pass north of the crater, something caught Quinn's eye.

"Wait a minute? Did you see that?"

"What!"

"Off to the right there. Gene, can you circle back around?" Quinn asked with a measure of excitement.

"What did you see?" Pam asked, as Gene spun the Ranger around and dove to a lower altitude in one continuous tight maneuver.

"I saw a flash of red off to the right. Was any equipment left on the ice for the winter?" Quinn asked, as everyone strained to see anything unusual on the vast white ice field.

"Not to my knowledge. There were four national teams doing research, but none would have equipment that they would leave out here all winter."

"'There, see it?' exclaimed Quinn, as he gestured along his line of sight.

"Oh my gosh," exclaimed Pam. "It looks like a tractor half-buried in that ice mound."

"See it, Mark?" Pam said with excitement in her voice.

"Gene, can you put us down for a quick investigation?" Quinn asked, as he snapped several pictures of what appeared to be a tractor.

"This is odd. The only piece of equipment that has not been accounted for is the tractor used by the lost French expedition," noted Mark.

"Gene, can you get me a radio link back to the station?"

"Sure," Gene said as he flipped a switch on the dashboard. "McMurdo, McMurdo, come in, please."

"McMurdo Station here, go ahead." Gene gave a thumbs-up sign over his shoulder and Quinn keyed his head microphone.

"This is Quinn Wilson calling for Roy Lynch. Can you track him down and have him call us. We are in the Bell JetRanger over the impact site and need to talk with him immediately."

"10-4 that, hold on."

Only a few minutes passed before the return radio call. "This is Roy Lynch, go ahead."

"Roy, this is Quinn. We spotted a red tractor on the ice north of the impact zone. We could be mistaken, but there's a possibility that it's from the lost French expedition. Do you have any information on their vehicle? Over."

"That area has been searched a number of times with sophisticated monitoring equipment. It cannot possibly be the French tractor. Over."

"We agree, but we are landing to investigate. We will send identification numbers shortly. See what you can find in the reports on the French team. Over."

"You have ten minutes. If you are not back in the copter by then, I am leaving without you. Understood?" Gene said as he maneuvered for a landing close to the partially buried tractor.

"Okay, let's take a lot of pictures, so we can examine them back at the station," Pam suggested as she pulled on her gloves.

The team bailed out of the Ranger as Gene settled onto the ice approximately twenty yards from the tractor. After a short run with Quinn limping in the rear, they came alongside the tractor and started taking pictures. The rear section of the vehicle was encased in a mound of ice. From what they could see, the entire tractor was sitting level, with no observable damage. While Mark and Pam took pictures, Quinn climbed up on the tracks and pried open the frozen door on the driver's side of the tractor. From this vantage point, he could see there were no occupants in the cab. He took pictures of the interior and dashboard before crawling over the driver's seat and into the crew cab. He quickly checked the bunks and head and found no one. But one of the bunks was in disorder, as if someone had just gotten out of their sleeping bag. Quinn got the impression that the occupants had made a hasty departure from the cab. Personal items lay about the cabin and dirty dishes were piled in the sink. Time was getting short as Mark and Pam entered the cab. After a short period of silence, all three began taking snapshots, hoping to capture as much detail as possible for later research.

"I don't think Gene was kidding about leaving after 10 minutes," Pam stated apprehensively. "I, for one, do not want to be left here on the ice. I'm heading back to the Ranger."

"We are right behind you," Mark said as he snapped a last series of photographs.

Gene had his forearm raised dramatically before his eyes checking his watch as the team piled back into the Ranger. "Fifteen more seconds and I would have left your asses on the ice. I'm not going to take a chance of being stranded out here in this climate. I have not run out of fuel in over 40 years of flying and I'm damn sure not going to start now," Gene lectured as he ripped the Ranger from the ground and spun it towards the Station. "Your friend radioed back and said the tractor was built in France and carried the identification number F-186."

Pam raised her head from her camera, turned and handed it to Quinn. There on the screen was the tractor chassis with the number F-186. Their eyes met, as the reality of the discovery and numerous questions it raised ran through their minds.

Gene entered the White Mountain pass at a low altitude and nose-dived the Ranger down the 8,000 feet of elevation to the coastal plain below. He leveled out at 300 feet and raced towards the lights of the Station ahead. This was to be the last flight of the season for the JetRanger before it would be stored in the hangar and he was taking advantage of the flight time to put the Ranger through its paces and to show off a little.

Back at the station, Pam raced ahead of Mark and Quinn and had her camera set up on the conference room's 52-inch flat screen TV when they arrived. They were joined by a number of staff members, who had heard the rumors of the find. Roy and Hank, both members of the first expedition, were among them. Gene Spencer joined the group after he secured the helicopter.

The first series of photographs confirmed that this was indeed the ill-fated French expedition tractor F-186. The questions began immediately.

"How could this possibly be the same tractor?" Roy asked in disbelief. "They did aerial and ground searches for heat sources, metallic objects, and even ground-penetrating radar. All were negative. And here you find it sitting upright, not five miles from the impact! I cannot understand it."

"Roy, we share your disbelief. It just does not make sense." Pam said with equal doubt.

"Let's keep going through these photographs and see if we can make sense of this," Quinn suggested as he stared at the screen.

The next two hours were spent studying each photograph in detail. The evidence was clear. The tractor occupants had apparently exited the vehicle in full dress and had not returned. The physical location of the tractor was ten miles further south than the last GPS coordinates reported by the French. The theory that the expedition had driven into a secondary crater was disproved by the fact the vehicle was in an upright level position. The rear section encased in snow indicated that the vehicle had been driven into the ejecta blanket. However, if the vehicle was totally covered; how did the team exit the tractor?

Quinn's photographs were the last to be put on the screen. It was Gene who noticed an overlooked detail.

"Wait a minute. Can you go back to the last photograph of the dashboard? There, look at that! The ignition key is in the off position. You never turn off your vehicle while you are in this hazardous climate. So it looks like these two experienced individuals left the cab in no particular hurry and turned off the ignition when they left? I don't get it!"

The conference room was silent, as everyone pondered this last piece of information. Finally Quinn spoke, "That key being turned off may well be the biggest mystery we have yet uncovered. Based on our activities on the first expedition, I can see several scenarios that could explain some of the conditions we observed. For instance, we stopped a number of times to investigate the secondary craters. At each stop, a few of the crew members went to investigate. I recall one stop where we traveled up to a few hundred yards from the tractors. We always had the lights on the tractors to find our way back. But if the French team's tractor was in the ejecta blanket, their vision could have been obscured. If they had gotten turned around and somehow headed in the wrong direction away from the tractor, they would only have had 10 to 15 minutes before exposure took its toll."

"How does that explain the ignition key being turned off?" Pam asked.

"It doesn't. I agree with Gene—no one would knowingly turn off the ignition, unless …unless they had some other place to go!"

"What are you suggesting? We were the only other people on the ice and we didn't pick up any hitchhikers."

Quinn was silent in deep thought for a few moments and then asked, "Hank, the tractor was ten miles closer to the crater than reported. Would it have been possible for them to see our lights from that distance?"

"We were lit up like a Christmas tree the whole time we were on the ice. I would say our lights or the glow in the sky could be seen from 20 miles away. We also looked like a fourth of July celebration while we were shooting off the flares. Yes, if they were in the area while we were there, they could see us."

Again, Quinn was in deep thought. "Is it possible they were trying to get to us? Let's say the tractor had mechanical problems, say the alternator went out and it drew the batteries down to the point they could not communicate with their Station or with us. The batteries could have been drawn down so low that the diesel engine shut down and in a last ditch effort, they tried to reach us. So the vehicle was disabled and they turned off the ignition switch on the way out the door, because the engine had already died. One other thing, Hank, do you remember you kept hearing someone or something keying a microphone, like they were trying to contact us? What if that was the French team calling for help on a weak hand-radio?"

"I had forgotten about that. A weak hand-radio—that is exactly what it sounded like! We did not pay attention because we thought there was no one out there but us."

Everyone sat in silence considering this scenario. Mark finally spoke. "That scenario would explain a lot. I hate to think of those two guys racing to get to us as we are pulling away and heading back to the Station."

"Chances are they succumbed to the cold long before they got near us. But, if any of this is true, we have been looking for their bodies in the wrong places. They would have been somewhere between 10 to 20 miles closer than their last reported coordinates. That is why the search came up empty." After a reflective pause, Quinn continued. "We won't have any more answers until the spring, when we can retrieve the tractor and search the areas surrounding it," Quinn said as the meeting began to deteriorate into a series of discussions. "Roy, can you report our discussions to D'Urville Station and talk to them about our suspicions?"

The next flight out was midmorning the following day—weather permitting, of course. There were plenty of seats available since all incoming flights were loaded with last-minute winter supplies and leaving nearly empty. Winter was almost on the continent and it would not be long before flights ceased and isolated the Station from the outside world.

After the meeting, Quinn placed a mission accomplished call to Alex Reager at NGIA.

"Good job, Quinn! We knew you were the right man to send. Rebellious scientists and the threat of the first war on the

Antarctic continent was a little intimidating for the rest of us. Finding the lost French tractor was incredibly lucky. That helps us all close the loop on a major mystery. Give me a call when you get back to Sydney. There is still a lot going on in the Pacific Basin," Alex offered with his usual enthusiasm. Quinn hung up the phone and stared at the handset before turning slowly toward his cubicle and began to pack his few belongings in preparation for the flight out the next day.

He was up early as usual and left his duffle bag near the transport while he went for a quick breakfast. As he looked around, he noticed Dr. Laystrom was sitting by herself over a cup of tea and a bagel. "May I join you?" Quinn asked out of courtesy, as he shuffled his breakfast to the table and was heading back for coffee.

With a nod of her head she said, "Please sit down. Why are you walking with a cane?"

"I've been using this cane since I arrived back at the Station four days ago," Quinn responded. "I had a run-in with a volcano in the Philippines a couple of weeks ago."

"How does one have a run-in with a volcano? Don't you know to stay away from those kinds of things?"

Quinn ignored her comment and added, "I mentioned to you earlier that I met a scientist while I was in the Philippines named Scott Styles. Apparently, he knew you from a lecture you gave back in the states. Does the name ring a bell?"

"Not that I recall, but I talk to a lot of graduate classes during the summer months when I am not here. He was probably just one of many students who heard one of my lectures. By the way, I just wanted to say that we would have gotten those reports out after things settled down and our collective anger subsided. I just don't think you accomplished any great deed. I wouldn't want it to go to your head."

"Yes, I know," Quinn offered. "Believe me I do not have an ego problem. It's not going to my head, but still I'd like to think I helped in some way, even if it was my participation in the expedition last fall."

"You know, Quinn, I kind of hate to admit it, but you really were an asset on that ice expedition to the crater, even if you aren't a scientist," she added with a smile this time. "You held the team together and organized the data collection, while each of us was trying to go off on our own line of research. So, it was good working with you. I have to get back to my research. Have a good flight." She said her goodbyes, shook hands with him and walked away.

Quinn watched her go with resignation. Had the situation been different maybe they could have been friends, he thought as he took a deep breath and returned to his oatmeal.

There was no other chance to say goodbye to the rest of the science team as Quinn shuffled his bag onto the truck for the commute out to the airfield. No one else was leaving the Station this late in the year, so he had the return flight to himself. The plane's engines were running when he got to the airfield and it began to taxi as soon as he was aboard. He was glued to the window as the plane left the ground and flew out over the Ross Ice Shelf. The sea was dark and foreboding in the half-light of this fall day. New ice was forming at the edges of the shelf as it reclaimed the sea. Here and there along the ice shelf were colonies of penguins basking in the last light of summer as the sun barely glowed above the horizon. The drone of the plane's engines had become a familiar transition to the next adventure and soon he was asleep.

CHAPTER 19

Roaring Forties

No sooner had he hit the ground back in Sydney than his satellite phone rang. Once again, he found a jovial Alex Reager on the line. "You did a great job down there at the station, Walter. You have no idea how relieved everyone is here in Washington now that those reports are in circulation. They almost printed them right off the wire, they were that good."

"Thanks Alex, but my part was rather small, compared to the science team's efforts," Quinn offered, to keep the record straight.

"That is not the way it's playing here. Just want you to know your trouble-shooting assistance was greatly appreciated."

"Well, thanks again, but something tells me that's not the only reason you called. Am I correct?"

"Quinn, Quinn, you know me all too well! Things are so busy in the Pacific region that I've asked Hope to come over from the Caribbean and give you a hand. It has been very quiet in her area of the globe and she could use some excitement. She will be coming in about two weeks. That will give you the two weeks of rest and recuperation that I promised you before she arrives," Alex offered.

"You're a prince, Alex. What have you got lined up for us after my ample time off?"

"I'd like both of you to fly over to Banda Aceh on the northwestern tip of Sumatra."

"What is going on over there?"

"We're not sure. Actually, we think we have an anomaly of

some kind. Either that or the land surface is warping. We did an overlay of aerial photographs from last year and there is a minor but notable difference in the location of major land features, including the ridge line of the Pusul Mountain near Banda Acch. There is no way that the location of a mountain can change that quickly. So, we need to rule out the obvious and then work with the satellite photographs to identify the problem. We'll need you to set some targets and take accurate GPS readings to provide additional rectification to the satellite photographs. This will be a fact-finding trip and not as urgent as some of your recent missions. You might even consider it a vacation."

"I'll have to get out my maps and take a look at the location. If my memory serves me right, the area is the location of some of the most volatile tectonic plates on the planet. Wasn't the Krakatoa volcano in that area?"

"Yes, the Krakatoa exploded almost 100 years ago. We know the story, but do not think there is any relationship to what we are seeing on the aerials."

"Can you send those aerials to me? It would help to see what you're looking at."

"I've already thought of that. There are two Mylar prints coming to you via FedEx for delivery on Thursday. Watch for them. It's easier to see with these overlays than with digital photographs. It eliminates the aberrations."

"Send me Hope's schedule when you get a chance and I'll pick her up at the airport. Does she have hotel reservations yet?"

"Don't you have an extra cabin on that yacht?"

"Yes, but it is tight quarters even for one person. I'm sure she would like her own space."

Quinn hung up the phone and looked at the skyline of Sydney. He recalled that the island of Sumatra was on the leading edge of the Indo-Australian tectonic plate that *converged* with the Eurasian plate, a key geologic term meaning that the two plates were colliding and currently in a slow waltz for domination. The more dense Indo-Australian plate was slowly overriding the Eurasian plate, so earthquakes and volcanic eruptions were common along this convergent zone. Theoretically, the plates were moving at 7 to 8 centimeters per year, so a visual diversion of a geologic feature was unlikely. Quinn thought they would have to move a foot, or more precisely, tens of feet, to be perceptible on an aerial photograph. *Unlikely*, Quinn thought. Geologists always say that geologic time is beyond the human capability to perceive. Ten thousand years is like a moment in geologic time.

Quinn was pleased that his recollection of macro-tectonic geology was still there. Still, he needed to bone up on it some more prior to the trip. During his taxi ride across town, he was totally engrossed in his own thoughts about the next mission and was soon surprised to find himself at the marina. He paid the driver and shouldered his winter bag for the hike down the dock, bracing himself on his cane for support.

"Mr. Wilson, Mr. Wilson," the call made him spin around in surprise. He had not heard anyone call his name in a long time. It was Jake coming towards him with one hand raised in greeting.

"Welcome back, mate! Ms. Valentine has called several times, inquiring about your whereabouts. She left this message this morning, asking you to give her a call if you returned from your walkabout." Handing Quinn the message, he added, "Good day, mate, and please give Ms. Valentine my regards when you speak to her. A really fine lass, if I have to say so myself." He gave a two-fingered salute and knowingly winked his eye, before returning to the Dock Master's office singing an Australian tune.

"Huh, I wonder what Betsy wants," he muttered out loud as he reached for his satellite phone and dialed the number. After three rings, Betsy's answering machine picked up. "Hello, you have reached Betsy Valentine! How may I be of service?" The voice was so sexual that Quinn was momentarily taken back. He remembered the conversation they had regarding careers and the message seemed to carry multiple messages. "Oh … Betsy …sorry …I missed you. This is Quinn returning your call. Give me a call back at ....” Just then, Betsy picked up the phone, “Hi, Quinn. Thanks for calling me back. One day you need to tell me where you disappear to,” she said laughingly. “I was hoping you could help me,” she said with a voice only slightly less sexy than her answering machine message. “My crew deserted me after the Hobart Race and I need help getting the boat back to Sydney. It’s about a three- to four-day trip and I think the two of us could handle it. It would be loads of fun sailing with you. Of course, if you know of one additional crew member, it would be perfect. Can you help me?”

Quinn was still standing on the dock next to his boat. He slipped the strap off his shoulder and lowered his bag. As he did, he noticed a familiar figure walking towards him. It was Agent Ken James, who always seemed to know his whereabouts. “I think maybe I can help,” Quinn heard himself say. “I have about two weeks before my next assignment. Let me check on a flight and I’ll get back to you.”

“That would be super ...and Quinn ...I will make it worth your while!” she said laughing out loud.

“Betsy?”

“Oh, I was just kidding. But, I would appreciate your help. Give me a call later.”

He turned to find Agent James standing at the stern of his boat as he hung up the satellite phone. “Agent James, it is so good to see you again. Would you like to go sailing?”

“Hell, yes! What do you have in mind?” replied James.

“A three or four day leisurely cruise back from Tasmania.”

“Whose boat?”

“It’s Betsy Valentine’s 62-foot Oyster.”

“R-e-a-l-l-y ... is Betsy coming along?”

“Yes, she is.”

“When do we leave?”

“Then you’re available?”

“Four days on a boat with a beautiful woman! I’ll force myself to go. I’ve got about two year’s worth of vacation time built up with the Company, so I can leave tonight if you want to.”

“I was going to check on an airline ticket when you walked up.”

"No need, I'll call in a favor and get us a ride. Are you packed?" He asked looking at the bag.

"I'm packed, but not with what I need for a voyage. It will take me a little while to get organized."

Ken was already on his phone and not paying attention to Quinn. "Hey, I need to get down to Hobart tomorrow can you give me a hand? No, this is not business. I'm taking a few days off. Need I remind you of the many favors you owe me? Yeah, tomorrow morning early would be fine. There will be two passengers and I'll see you at, say, 0600? Good and thanks."

"We're all set. Tell Betsy we'll see her midmorning tomorrow."

"Well, great, I'll give her a call right now. By the way, what are you doing down here standing on my dock?"

"You invited me to come down remember? I heard about your work on the ice and knew you would be back in town. So, I thought I would stop by. You have a problem with that?"

"Tell me again, how did you know I would be back in Sydney this afternoon?"

"Hey, I have my sources and I am not at liberty to divulge them to someone of your security level."

"Let me guess, you were just passing by and happened to see me standing here on the dock."

"You can believe that if you like. It would make life simpler. Hey, you want to get a beer?"

"Actually, I could use more than a beer. I've been missing a lot of meals lately. I'm buying."

"Oh no, you aren't. You are somewhat of a celebrity after negotiating an end to hostilities at McMurdo and finding the lost French tractor. So dinner is on me."

"Was that a directive from Washington or are you acting on your own?"

"Give it a rest will you! Let's go eat."

"Let me throw my bag on the boat and I'll be right with you. Why don't you come aboard and look at the boat while you're here?"

"Okay, thanks. I love sailboats, even the ones that are tied permanently to a dock and never sailed."

"Now you can give that a rest! If the physical environment would ever settle down so I could have the time, this boat would be sailing every day."

"So, there is at least a threat of this boat getting under sail?"

"Okay, a threat. I intend to use it for more than a dockside condo."

Quinn clambered aboard and noted once more that canes and sailboat decks don't mix well. Ken, on the other hand, stepped aboard like a professional sailor and made himself right at home at the helm while he waited on Quinn to open the hatch. "Nice boat," he offered after checking out the instrumentation.

"Yes, I had all new wiring and instruments installed. The diesel is new as well. I had a 29-horse Yanmar installed. It's ready for the open ocean," Quinn offered with a blush of pride. "How long will it take us to get to Hobart? I need to let Betsy know we are coming."

"It will probably take two and a half hours for the flight. Tell her we will be there by midmorning."

Quinn dialed the number and Betsy picked up right way. "Betsy, I have another crew member lined up and we can be there by midmorning tomorrow."

"Oh, that would be perfect. I've been watching the weather and we are at the tail end of a front, so the window of opportunity should be about right, that is, if we get underway by tomorrow afternoon. The boat is in great shape, so all we have to do is top off the tanks and untie the lines to get underway. Who is the other crew member?"

"Ken James, an acquaintance of mine and a sailor as well. He's a very resourceful guy and I think you'll like him."

"Quinn, this is a little awkward, but you know my past, and I do not want to mix business with sailing. So tell me, do I know this man or, more specifically, does he know me?"

"Huh …I don't think so, Betsy. Do you want me to ask him?"

"No …if you vouch for him, I think it'll be okay. I'll see you tomorrow morning and thanks for the help. I meant it when I said that I would make it worth your while—just not in the way you were thinking."

"How do you know what I was thinking?"

"Now Quinn, you can't fool a professional. See you tomorrow."

"Oh, one other thing—what marina are you docked at in Hobart?"

"I'm moored at the Royal Yacht Club of Tasmania on the River Derwent. Just ask the cab driver. He'll know where it is. See you tomorrow, love."

Quinn hung up the phone and noticed that Ken was watching him with interest. "We are good to go. She is moored at the Royal Yacht Club and said that we have a good weather window for departure tomorrow afternoon. How much do you know about Betsy?"

"I know she is a lovely individual who runs with the upper social and sailing circles here in Sydney. Why do you ask?"

"She asked if she knew you."

"I don't think I have ever had the pleasure. Certainly I would have remembered," Ken said with a slight smile that made Quinn think that he knew more that he was saying. "Since you asked, how well do you know her?"

"I know her only as a neighbor here at the marina. We sailed once bringing her boat over to Archer's shipyard for maintenance. She is a very good sailor. That's about all I know."

"That's all you know, huh?" Ken asked.

"That's about it," Quinn repeated. "Let's go get something to eat."

HOBART, TASMANIA

Ken and Heather showed up together at the airport the next morning. Both looked like they hadn't slept much the night before. Heather began pre-flight activities on the Lear Jet, while Ken got a cup of coffee and relaxed in the terminal. He wasn't in a talkative mood at 0600 in the morning. Heather rolled the jet onto the runway. Ken flew in the copilot seat, while Quinn found himself uncomfortably alone in the passenger cabin. After a rough start out of Sydney, the weather cleared and Quinn could see the coastline of Australia all the way down to the Bass

Straits. Two hundred miles later, they passed over Flinder's Island and soon began their decent into Hobart, Tasmania.

There was always a certain amount of romance associated with Tasmania. The name alone sounded like the end of the earth. It was a remote and somewhat desolate outpost of civilization made famous by the Tasmanian devil, a rather fierce carnivore with a decidedly bad attitude. The Tasmanian devil was thought to be extinct after early colonies hunted them down for the bounty offered by the government for every carcass. Now after many years, a small population had been found and the devils were now a protected species. Their near extinction evidently did absolutely nothing for their attitude. But now they were loved and tourists came to the island in the hope of seeing one of the devils snarl at them.

Betsy was waiting for them on the dock at the Royal Yacht Club when they arrived. She wore yellow foul-weather pants and boots with a dark-blue European sailing sweater with leather patches on the shoulders. She had again tried to cover her appearance with a baseball cap and baggy clothes, but it wasn't working very well. There were the suggested curves, cobalt blue eyes, and rosy cheeks and lips that could not be hidden. She was most definitely female and a beautiful one at that.

Quinn introduced Agent James, who quickly turned on the charm and ran through his sailing resume in the hopes of impressing the skipper. Betsy listened intently, while maintaining riveting eye contact that usually melted any defenseless male caught in her web. After a few minutes, Betsy turned to Quinn and gave him a surprising hug. "He's a charmer, isn't he?" she asked with a laugh, while Ken stood there with his mouth open. "Does he always talk this much?" she asked with a laugh. "I've finished provisioning the boat, topped off the tanks and checked the weather. Everything looks good. Of course, as it's fall and there could be another front moving up from Antarctica, we need to get underway soon. You just don't want to be caught out in the Straits when a weather front comes through. It's rough enough in good weather, but this time of the year, there's nothing to slow the wind down between here and the ice. We can lose the lines and set out to sea once you two get your bags stowed," Betsy said with the authority befitting a skipper.

At Betsy's request, Quinn took the helm as the big boat moved away from the dock and into the river. Betsy stood in the companionway issuing orders, while Ken served as deckhand. Betsy had set a course almost due east from Hobart. She explained that they needed to clear the island and then turn north once across 150 degree longitude. Then we would hold a heading approximately 35 degrees north until in sight of the Australian mainland. If the weather threatened, they could make it in to Melbourne in about a day and a half. That course would skirt the western edge of the East Australian Stream to avoid the southern flow and possible loss of forward speed.

Quinn was reminded again of how easily the boat handled. At 62 feet in length, it was very stable in the water and did not respond to wind or rip currents in the river. At the mouth, Betsy ordered the sail set. As Quinn came up into the wind, Ken removed the sail's cover. Then Quinn pushed the appropriate button on the control panel and the sail emerged from the mast along the boom track.

"Now this is the way to sail," Ken exclaimed, as Quinn unfurled the Genoa from the helm and eased the boat back to an easterly course. The sail filled with wind as the big boat came alive. "Oh, yeah, she is good to go!" shouted Ken while Betsy took off her baseball cap, smiled at Ken's enthusiasm, and shook her hair loose into the wind. The boat bounded forward on a broad reach through the first waves of the voyage.

Five hours into the voyage, Betsy gave the order to change course to 35 degrees and reef the Genoa for the building southwesterly wind. She also broke out the safety harnesses. "I've got a feeling that we're going to be slogging through these quartering seas all night. Might as well make preparations now," she mused. By nightfall, the big boat was doing 7.5 to 9.0 knots in 20 knots of wind and a building sea. Ken took the wheel for the midnight to 0400 watch, while the weather conditions continued to deteriorate. When Quinn went below, Betsy was on the radio getting an update on the weather.

Quinn could tell that Betsy was concerned. She hung up the radio microphone and updated him. “The weather forecast is still for moderate winds and seas of up to 8 feet. The observer doesn’t believe me when I tell him we have 20 to 30 knots with higher gusts and waves of 25 feet in height. He said that it must be an isolated anomaly and would abate shortly, since barometric pressure cannot support these conditions. Somehow, I just don’t trust those bureaucratic bastards. I don’t think they have ever been out of sight of land. Oh, I’m sorry Quinn. Here you are standing in your wet foul-weather gear and I’m just rambling on. Can I get you something hot? Why don’t you get out of that jacket and I’ll get you some soup?”

“Thank you, but I think Ill keep the gear on until Ken has settled into the watch. We may have to trim sails again if the wind builds any higher, but the soup sounds great!”

Betsy crossed the pitching cabin with the skill of a seasoned sailor. She slipped into a harness attached to the cabinet in the galley to steady herself against the rolling motion of the boat and placed a container of soup into the microwave. “Your friend, Ken, seems nice. How long have you known him?” she asked.

“I’ve only known him for about a year, but he is my oldest friend this side of the Pacific. You are my next oldest friend, and now that I think about it, you two are the only friends I have. So this is definitely a friendly voyage.” Quinn laughed at his poor attempt at making small talk.

“So we are friends now,” Betsy said with a beaming smile. “After our talk at the marina, I wasn’t sure we were going to make it all the way to friendship.”

Quinn was lost in her smile and wasn’t sure what had just taken place.

“What does Ken do for a living?” she asked after an awkward pause in the conversation.

“Hmmm, actually, I’m not sure. He talks about some company and he travels just about as much as I do.”

“Well, he takes time to stay in shape. Something most busy businessmen don’t do,” she said as she handed Quinn a large cup of hot soup.

"Is he married?"

"You know, he has never mentioned it and I never asked. But I don't think so."

"How could you not ask that question? It's one of those basic things you need to know about someone," she asked with a quizzical look on her face.

A gust of wind caught their attention as the boat heeled sharply to starboard and slowly righted itself. "The wind is still building," Betsy sighed. "It's going to be one of those nights."

Quinn took the 0400 watch after little rest and Ken was glad to get off the wheel. Quinn snapped his safety harness onto the stanchion, as Ken gave him the watch update. Shouting in his ear, he said, "It's blowing like hell out here and cold as a well digger's ass. This is a full gale and I can't believe the weather reports aren't picking this up." The wind is gusting to 45 knots and the quartering sea has overpowered the autopilot, so she has to be manually steered, which I have been doing for the last hour. The sails have been reefed to the maximum and only a corner of the main and headsail are showing. Still the boat is making 9.0 to 11.0 knots on almost bare poles." As Ken staggered across the deck and down the companionway, Quinn could immediately feel the pressure on the wheel as the boat surfed the waves and attempted to broach. The waves were now in the 35-foot range, conditions that Quinn had never experienced at sea in his home waters of the Gulf of Mexico. The dark waves were only visible from the white phosphorescence at their crests and seemed to be 20 feet above the boat as they approached from the port stern quarter. As Quinn would brace for impact, the waves would come in and lift the stern and push the boat down the face, while Quinn struggled with the wheel to maintain control and keep the boat from turning sideways into the waves. His legs trembled with each approaching wave. The big boat felt like a toy on the vast expanse of black.

Far to the southeast, another weather front was flowing off the Antarctic ice sheet and 100 mile-per-hour winds were pushing 50 foot waves far out into the South Pacific. These waves traveled for days across the vast empty sea and were strong enough to maintain their form when they met the opposing fetch and wave set off of Tasmania. At repeated intervals, these combined to form a giant wave of over 50 to 60 feet in height that would break under its own weight, sending tons of cold seawater down a steep face with tremendous force. These huge waves slashed through the South Pacific and would pass the 150th longitude by early morning.

The hours passed slowly as Quinn struggled with the wheel and managed to keep the big boat out of trouble during a long cold watch. The dawn was slow to come.

When it did, it broke gray over a cold South Pacific sea. Betsy came on deck at 0600 to relieve Quinn at the wheel. "We'll be working on two-hour watches until the wind drops," she yelled in his ear. "Four hours is too long to fight the wheel. We can't make it to Melbourne, since we would be sailing broadside waves, so we'll continue on to Sydney. Get some rest. I have some hot food in the oven. You're back on watch at1000."

Quinn braced himself in the cockpit and watched Betsy take command of the wheel. She was probably only 5'2" tall, but made up for her slight statue with strong will power, as she braced her leg on the cockpit seats and took command of the wheel. The boat seemed to know she was at the helm. Quinn thought he could feel the boat settle on course and respond to the quartering waves.

"Go below!" Betsy shouted without taking her eyes off the bow.

Quinn waved and ducked through the companionway into the cabin. He shut and secured the hatch to keep the water out. In the background, he could hear Ken snoring loudly. He had just reached for the oven door when a crashing wave shuddered the boat and pushed it down in the stern and toward starboard, which was opposite the current wave fetch. Slowly at first, the big boat listed far to starboard and Quinn waited for it to rebound, but it kept going. His reflexes were in hyperdrive, as he grabbed the handrail in the galley and found himself hanging vertically in the cabin. The boat had taken a full knockdown and was now vulnerable to the quartering sea.

"Shit! What the hell is going on?" shouted Ken who had been hurled from his bunk and not awake enough to react to the situation.

"We took a knockdown! I'm going up to help Betsy. Get your gear on and hurry!" Quinn yelled as he headed up the gangway.

Another wave struck from the port side as the boat began an agonizingly slow effort to right itself. Quinn pushed open the hatch and was hammered back to the floor by hundreds of gallons of ice cold seawater. When the flood diminished, he sprang from the hatch and found himself in the utter confusion of the cockpit. Betsy was not at the wheel and it was spinning as every approaching wave passed under the beam. Quinn scanned the cockpit for Betsy and she was nowhere to be seen. He stumbled towards the wheel and hesitated only long enough to clip into the lifeline. It was then that he saw the taut line over the starboard side. "Betsy!" he shouted, only to have the words shoved back down his throat in the roar of the wind and crashing waves. He grabbed the line with both hands, braced his foot on the cockpit cowling and pulled as hard as he could. "Betsy!" he shouted again as he saw her blond hair raise momentarily from the gray water. He pulled again and reached over the side and grabbed the collar of her life jacket. Had she weighted more than 110 pounds, Quinn would probably not been able to lift her onto the boat. With adrenaline flowing, he brought a limp body into the cockpit. She was not moving. Instinctively, Quinn checked her breathing and began CPR as the waves continued to crash over the broached boat. Her lips were cold as ice and her face was white in the pale early morning light.

Quinn knew that he had to breathe for her. "Breathe, Betsy!" Quinn shouted as he applied five compressions to her chest while tilting her head back, repeating the process again and again. "Breathe, Betsy ...breathe, damn it, breathe!" Quinn breathed again for Betsy as another wave filled the cockpit and he hesitated, leaving his mouth on hers as the wave receded from the cockpit. She coughed then and Quinn shook her as she fought her way back to consciousness. The fear in her eyes seemed to clear momentarily as she focused on Quinn's face only inches from hers. She began to shiver uncontrollably.

Ken finally stuck his head out of the gangway and surveyed the conditions of the boat. "Ken, get her down into the cabin and out of those clothes if you can. She is about to go into hypothermia." Holding her close to his chest, Quinn crawled across the cockpit and pushed her into Ken arms, who disappeared quickly into the cabin. Quinn slammed the gangway shut and turned to see yet another humongous wave approaching the port beam of the boat, filling the cockpit with foaming water. Once it had receded, Quinn pulled himself along the lifeline to the wheel. Grabbing it, he turned it sharply to port in an effort to bring the big boat's bow into the waves. At first there was little response since the boat had no steerage. Taking a chance, Quinn flipped open the engineer control panel and hit the starter switch for the auxiliary engine. After several seconds the panel came alive and Quinn pushed the gear shift to forward and revved the engine to 3,000 rpm. Ever so slowly, the boat began to respond until the bow caught the waves head on. Desperately trying to orient himself and gain control of the situation, Quinn scanned the compass and gauges time and time again. Slowly at first, the condition of the boat became clear. The wind was still blowing from the southwest and the seas were confused with battering waves breaking across the stern and midship on the starboard side. The 62-foot boat had become a pram in rough seas, too small for the conditions and batted about as if it were a chip of wood by the powers of nature.

The compass heading was now 210 degrees or west south west. He was heading back to Tasmania! After gauging the waves, he let the boat fall off and returned to the 35 degree heading. As the reefed sails filled with wind and the boat stabilized on its previous course, he turned off the engine.

Minutes passed and lengthened into hours as he fought the wheel, and still no word from the cabin. How was Betsy doing? The waves were still too volatile to engage the autopilot. Why don't they let me know what's going on? Slowly, Quinn noticed that the wind speed was beginning to drop.

It had been a steady 35 knots, gusting to over 40. Now it was 25 knots, now 22 knots, gusting to 25. When it reached 20 knots, Quinn took a chance and engaged the autopilot and stood exhausted by the wheel to see if it could handle the strain. When it appeared to take control, he quickly crossed the cockpit and opened the hatch. "Is everyone okay below," he shouted. Fearing the worst, he was surprised to find Ken and Betsy cuddled together on the cabin settee.

"She's doing better now," Ken offered. "Everything was so wet below that I was forced to offer my bodily warmth to keep her from going into hypothermia. It took a while, but she finally warmed up and went to sleep. I've checked her out and there are no broken bones. She did take a nasty hit on her shoulder probably from the safety rail. How is the boat doing?"

"The wind is starting to fall, so I engaged the autopilot. Hopefully the waves will diminish soon. I could use some help up here."

"I think that it's more important for me to remain right here," Ken offered seriously. "I think you have the topside under control. The boat seems to be riding a lot better now."

"As soon as you can tear yourself loose, come on deck and help me assess the damage. I could use some relief as well," Quinn added. On hearing no response, he closed the hatch, pulled his jacket tight under his neck and huddled down under the battered dodger out of the wind. The clouds parted momentarily, allowing a streak of sunlight to penetrate the gray around the boat and play on the tops of the blue-gray waves. Out of nowhere the seabirds appeared skimming the waves. Slowly the wind and waves abated as the gale passed and the rhythm of the sea returned to normal. Several times during the morning Quinn increased the sail area as the wind diminished, until the big boat was surging ahead under full sail with a 15-knot wind. The autopilot was doing its job well, as Quinn struggled to stay awake and maintain watch. The wind was coming out of the west now and Quinn sheeted both the main and head sail so that the boat was on a broad reach. He surveyed the deck for damage and found that the starboard lifelines and two stanchions had given way, as had the dodger, but other than that, there was little damage to the standing and running rigging. He removed the stanchions that were banging against the deck and secured a line across the starboard gap.

He was securing the lines when Ken came back on deck and looked around at the sea with a measure of satisfaction.

"How is she doing?" Quinn asked with concern.

"She took quite a beating, but just woke up and is doing much better. She's a trouper—not at all embarrassed about being naked. Getting her warmed up was some of the hardest work I have ever done," he said with a lingering smile as he looked out across the horizon in deep thought.

"Well, the wind has dropped and the seas are back down to a moderate 10 to 12 feet. The autopilot is engaged and we're on course for Sydney. So it looks like we have weathered the storm," Quinn said with a measure of relief. "Are you up here to relieve me? I've been on deck now since 0400."

"Sure, okay, I'm pretty rested. Take a couple of hours," Ken said with a smile.

"A couple of hours, my ass! I'm hungry, exhausted and I haven't slept in a good 20 hours."

"That's a sailor's life, my friend. You can't expect luxuries like sleep when you are at sea."

Quinn stood there for several seconds and looked at Ken to see if he was serious, "Thanks a lot, Ken, for those words of wisdom. I'm going below."

As Quinn slid open the gangway, he could see Betsy sitting on the edge of the bunk wrapped in a blanket.

"Oh, Quinn, how is my boat?" she asked as he entered the cabin.

"First, Betsy, how are you doing? It was touch and go there for a while."

"I'm ...I'm doing some better. I would like to know where the hell that wave came from. I had everything under control, when this wave comes at me from the starboard side against the prevailing wave set. It was huge! I'd say, better than 50 feet in height with almost vertical sides. The boat didn't have a chance of riding over. It broke right on top of me. There were tons and tons of water—God, what a nightmare! Quinn, I remember seeing your face. What happened?"

"Well, as I'm sure you know, we took a knockdown. The boat was lying full over on its port side when I managed to crawl out of the gangway. I couldn't find you anywhere. When I clipped on my safety line, I found yours and started pulling. Thank God, you were clipped in and still connected. You couldn't have been underwater for more than one minute, but you needed CPR to bring you back. I can't tell you how much fear ran through my head while we were out there in the cockpit." Quinn related as his voice broke and he took a wet handkerchief out of his pocket to wipe his eyes, as he tried to compose himself. After a deep breath, he continued, "Once you came around, Ken took you below to warm you up."

Betsy listened and was very much aware of the emotions expressed in his eyes as he spoke. "Yes, I woke up an hour or so ago with this naked man in bed with me. I pretended not to notice …but he was warm, so I lay there for as long as I could."

"No harm done then?"

"No harm done. He was easy to turn off. I pretended to throw up on him and he lost any thoughts he may have been cultivating. You must remember, I am a professional. But Quinn, you saved my life. Another few seconds and I would not have recovered. I don't know how to thank you."

"I'm glad I was there in time and no thanks are required," he said with another break in his voice. To avoid showing more emotions, he changed the subject, "Right now I am about to starve to death. What do you have that I can heat up fast?"

Betsy was aware of Quinn's obvious attempt to lighten the mood and played along, "Try one of those meal packs in the refrigerator. They heat up fast and are nutritious," Betsy said, while looking for some dry clothes. "Quinn, turn your back for a minute while I get dressed. I'm usually not very shy, but for some reason I don't want you to see me naked."

Quinn turned to the refrigerator and found it well-stocked. He grabbed the first package he saw, ripped it open and put it into the convection oven. He was trying to figure out how to turn it on when Betsy appeared beside him and pushed a series of buttons.

"I've got a propane stove on my boat, so tell me, where you're your microwave get its power?" Quinn asked as he watched the oven light illuminate the meal pack.

Betsy slipped on her jacket and leaned against him to steady herself against the roll of the boat as she explained. "There is a small generator under the starboard cockpit seat that starts automatically when you operate the oven. It is one of the nice features of this model Oyster," she lingered in her position near him as their eyes met. "I've got to get on deck and see my boat. Please get some rest," she said as she broke eye contact and looked away.

Quinn ate the meal while braced against the galley sink and headed for the crew's cabin. He stripped off all his cold wet clothes and fell into the bunk. He was asleep before he could get under the covers. At some point, he vaguely remembers someone pulling the covers over him and patting him on the head. For some reason, the gesture brought a ray of hope to his cold, lonely world.

He awoke just before sunset and found Ken and Betsy intently watching something to the port side. "What's going on?" he asked.

"Boat traffic has increased and we thought we could see some coastal lights. The Map Plotter says we are abreast of Cape Howe and at our current speed, we will make port by approximately 1500 tomorrow," Betsy said with a measure of pride.

"It has been easy sailing this afternoon. I haven't touched the wheel all day," Ken said. "Are you ready to take the watch now?"

"Sure, what time is it?"

"It is about 1800. How about taking it for four hours, and I will relieve you at 2200. Betsy will not be standing watch with us, because of her shoulder. So you will have the helm again for the 0200 to 0600 watch."

"I understand and have the watch. Both of you get some rest." Quinn said as he sat down on the deck in back of the wheel.

Quinn scanned the horizon for boating traffic and checked the wind direction and compass. The wind was holding out of the west at 12 to 15 knots and the boat was doing a comfortable 7.5 knots. After checking the sails, Quinn settled back into the pilot seat and tried to relax. *Sometimes you have to stop worrying about something breaking*, he thought as he remembered Betsy's well-stocked cockpit refrigerator. He grabbed a beer and started to enjoy the trip for the first time.

Boat traffic increased during the night and Quinn began checking the radar every 15 minutes to make sure everything was okay in the shipping lanes. Ken came on deck for the 2200 watch and Quinn once again hurried to get something to eat and grab some sleep. He knew the 0200 watch would be on him before he knew it.

By 1500 the next day, the happy crew was all on deck as they entered the Sydney harbor under full sail. Ken was regaling Betsy with his impressions of the trip. "You know, with the exception of that one wave, that storm we went through was really not that bad. I remember sailing in worst weather for four days between Portugal and the Canary Islands. There was just my father-in-law and me. We did two-hour watches for four days straight. But, you know, Betsy, we should have expected trouble with Quinn on board."

"What do you mean?"

"I've always had a feeling about Quinn. Ever since I have known him, he has attracted disaster wherever he goes. You remember that meteor impact in the Antarctic? Well, that was his fault and that volcanic eruption in the Philippines that made the news last month? He was right in the middle of it. So I think that the gale and rough waves were his fault as well," Ken said with amusement.

"Quinn, I did not know you were so powerful." Betsy said with a laugh.

"Powerful and good-looking describes me to a tee," Quinn offered to the resounding laughter of his crew mates.

"Just what do you guys do for a living anyway?" Betsy asked.

"Huh, I am in insurance and Quinn here is one of my clients.

I've got to look after him as much as I can or he would cost my company a lot of money," Ken said with almost no hesitation. "Since you brought it up, what do you do for a living Betsy?"

"I'm in hospitality. I arrange high-end meetings and parties for companies, mostly foreign businessmen. It pays well."

They both lie so well, Quinn thought, as each concocted their stories.

By early evening, they were back in the slip. Betsy had called Archer Marine on the way up the harbor and arranged to have a surveyor look over the boat in the morning. She wanted to get the repairs going right away. "You know," she commented, "I had a crew of 14 in the Hobart Race and the weather was fine. Most of the crew just sat around waiting for me to give an order to change course or reef a sail. I did that a few times just to keep them busy. However, on the way back with just the three of us, we sailed most of the way in a gale. We could have used a few of those crew members, but we did okay, didn't we, gentlemen?"

"I am very happy to answer yes to that question. We are all okay—the boat is a little battered, but the skipper and crew are in one piece. I will carry some haunting memories with me of that knockdown and you surfacing at the end of that safety line, but thank God, you came through it. You are tougher than you look," Quinn offered as a bit of high praise.

"I'll take that as a compliment," she said with a smile as she tugged absent-mindedly on the Velcro pocket tab on his jacket.

CHAPTER 20

Tsunami

Quinn spent the next couple of days hanging around the dock and helping Betsy clean up the boat. He called Meg Archer regarding the phone message she had left in what felt like a month ago. As he feared, her response was cool and she confessed that she could not remember why she called, and no, she didn't have time for lunch.

Hope flew in from Jamaica a couple of days before the field trip. Her Jamaican accent was very fascinating to the Australians. She even drew a crowd at baggage claim as she and Quinn caught up. Quinn showed her the sights of Sydney and they talked again about the events that had occurred during their mission in Africa. She had left for Jamaica soon after Quinn departed on that mission and had not heard all the details. It felt like ancient history to Quinn as he recounted the story. At the end of the tour, he took her by the marina to show off his boat. He was right about Hope. She had no interest in staying onboard, but was looking forward to a cozy hotel room. Betsy came by and Quinn introduced Hope as his associate from work.

"So nice to meet you," Betsy said with her hand outstretched. "Quinn, she is so beautiful and has such a lovely accent and you are going to spend two weeks with this lovely creature? I just might be a little jealous!" Hope may have blushed and all laughed at Betsy's comments. However, Quinn was a little confused and shrugged off the comment as light banter. The day before they were to leave for Banda Aceh, he helped Betsy move the boat to the Archer Shipyard while Hope had her hair done. Meg barely noticed his presence as she coordinated the work order with Betsy.

As they were leaving Archer's, Quinn said, "Betsy, since I have to go on this trip for the next couple of weeks, you're welcome to stay on my boat while I'm gone if you don't already have plans."

"Well, thank you, Quinn. I was going to stay at the Hilton, but I would miss the water. I'll take good care of her and you needn't worry about any parties. I don't work while I am on my boat. My professional life is totally separated from sailing."

"You talk so openly about your work, Betsy. I tend to forget about it and just see you as a person."

"That's what I like about you, Quinn. You're the only person I can talk to like this. It would freak most other men out."

"I must admit some uneasiness about it. I have to restrain any affection I may feel for you."

"Are you saying that you have feelings for me?"

"I'm sure you are used to men falling in love with you. Don't worry. I remember the requirements and limitations of our friendship," Quinn said somewhat seriously.

"Yes, I am used to men acting like fools and saying that they love me. I take advantage of that and they pay dearly. It just feels different when you say it."

"We had better leave this conversation for another time, Betsy," Quinn said as they arrived at the marina and found Ken lounging outside the Dockmaster's office.

"Hey, I was hoping to catch up with you," said Ken. "I wanted to invite my fellow shipmates out to dinner," he said with a huge grin on his face.

"Be honest, Ken. Are you asking both of us or just one in particular?" Quinn asked.

"Oh, since we are being honest here," he replied, "Betsy, I was hoping to have dinner with you. And Quinn, I was hoping you would fall off the dock and drown. Is that honest enough for you?"

"Funny, Ken. Yes that is honest enough and I can take a hint," Quinn said with a laugh. "Betsy, it's up to you."

"I did have one thing I needed to tell you, Quinn. I asked Steven to go with you tomorrow. Call it insurance," Ken said as he put his arm around Betsy's shoulder. "He has your flight information and he will meet you at the airport tomorrow. Now Ms. Valentine, would you be so kind as to accompany me to dinner this evening?"

Betsy glanced briefly at Quinn and said, "Why, Mr. James, I would be charmed to have dinner with you. Am I dressed appropriately?" she asked as she spun out from under Ken's arm and assumed a modeling pose with her hand on her hip.

"Well you two have a good time. Betsy, the offer still stands if you need a place while I'm gone. I'm willing to bet that you know where the cabin key is located in the cockpit. Am I right?'

"Hmmm, let me think. Is it the same place where all sailors keep their key? Hanging from a screw in the cockpit locker?"

"How did you know that?" Quinn said with a false laugh as he waved goodbye and headed down the dock. He could hear Betsy laughing as they got into Ken's car. "Both are liars and they make a perfect couple." Quinn mumbled to himself as he watched them drive away.

The next morning Quinn picked up Hope at the hotel for the trip to the airport. Steven met them at the terminal gate and once again Quinn found himself on a flight to a new adventure. The destination was Banda Aceh on the extreme western end of the island of Sumatra, a coastal fishing village situated between the Indian Ocean and the Andaman Sea. To get there from Sydney, the team flew to Singapore and changed planes from the Qantas Airbus to an inter-island twin-engine turboprop. Altogether, it was nine hours in the air and airport to get to their destination. During the flight, Steven and Hope established the grounds for a relationship. They were about the same age and Quinn felt old as he watched them talk and smile at one another. *Youth is truly wasted on the young,* he thought.

Quinn's first impression on reaching Banda Aceh was that the term, "fishing village," was out-of-date for this place. It was a bustling town of over 200,000 people and at least as many motor scooters. The trip to the hotel was a blur of images and sounds. He who honked his horn first had the right-of-way and it was a necessity, because everyone was seeking that all-important advantage. Quinn and Steven had to run through a gauntlet of women at the hotel. They were either begging or selling and their activities had become so common that they were even ignored by the hotel staff.

Steven and Hope asked if Quinn would mind if they had dinner alone to celebrate Christmas Day. They apparently still had a lot of talking and more smiling to do. Quinn only smiled to himself as he waved them away. "Don't forget, we are here to work. Be downstairs at 0700 tomorrow morning, okay?" This time it was he who got the wave. *Dinner alone on Christmas and maybe some time to look over the aerials and plan some strategy for this investigation*, he thought as he opened his bag.

Sometime during the night he dozed off to the urban clatter outside his open third-story window. Morning came on December 26 way too soon, as did the heat of the tropics. "It feels like 90 degrees and the sun isn't even up yet. It obviously is not going to be a white Christmas." he mumbled to himself. At breakfast, both Steven and Hope asked if they could investigate the beach area.

"What are you going to be looking for?" Quinn asked.

"Well, in part we need to get the lay of the land and see if there is anything unusual—you know, volcanoes, new mountain chains, faults, and the usual stuff," they both said with a round of laughter.

"Okay, if you do see any of that, be sure to make a note and take a picture," he said. Sharing their laugh, he added, "How about looking for more subtle clues, like distortion in the road's pavement or telephone poles out of alignment, docks that are no longer attached to the land, things that may indicate an unstable land mass. In the meantime, I'll head up into the hills and do the same thing there. We will meet back here for dinner at 1900."

Quinn smiled to himself as Steven and Hope headed out of the hotel. It was obvious that they were enjoying themselves and their new-found friendship. "Let them have some fun," he thought. "It must be nice. I'm sure they will settle down to work once they're oriented to the area."

Quinn rented a motor scooter from the hotel vendor and at approximately 0745, he joined the local morning rush hour on the road. He was marveling at the efficiencies of the little scooter as he sped through town and across the bridge when the scooter almost bucked him off. At exactly 0758, he had to brake hard and bring the scooter to a quick stop on the outskirts of town. As he shut the engine down, he was overwhelmed by the rumbling sounds that seemed to come from the very core of the earth itself. Before he knew it, forces beyond his control had brought him to his hands and knees. *Earthquake*, was his first thought as his senses oriented to the forces controlling him. Always the scientist, he began taking inventory of the events occurring around him. The ground rolled as if waves were passing under the ground. He had always thought that earthquakes were a shaking motion and of relatively short duration, but this rolling and thunderous noise continued on for several minutes. He saw people stumbling as they tried to run from these invisible forces. The buildings on the edge of town were trembling and collapsing all around him. People were lying on the ground near these buildings and covered by falling materials. Quinn grabbed his camera from his backpack and began filming. The screams of people in the area seemed to be the only sound that could match the rumbling noise that showed no signs of stopping. The undulations continued as time lost its meaning, a building near him began to collapse and he found himself joining the throngs of villagers as they ran stumbling across the rolling ground away from falling buildings. Finally the rolling subsided, so he was able to gain his footing and survey the landscape through the camera's lens.

Grabbing the satellite phone, he made a quick call to Washington. When the operator picked up, he gave a brief report and requested that word be passed. "There has been an earthquake just moments ago near Banda Aceh on the Straits of Malacca! It felt like a big one with massive destruction to buildings and I think there will be major loss of life. Have Alex give me a call as soon as possible." He hung up the phone and stuffed it into his backpack while looking around the outskirts of the village. What he saw bordered on total destruction. Minutes after the initial quake, an aftershock of almost equal force again struck the area. By the time it subsided, there were few buildings standing, with many disoriented villagers wandering around calling for family members. Quinn rushed to the closest collapsed building and began searching for people trapped in the debris. He was soon surrounded by others looking for family members and begging for assistance from those around them.

In the distance, he could hear the plaintive wails and sobs of people whose lives had just been shaken and turned upside down. While working to find a trapped woman whose screams for help seemed only a few feet from him, he became aware of another sound. There were loud hissing and crashing sounds coming from the area toward town. Quinn turned towards the sound. In the distance he saw a massive wall of water coursing through the streets, consuming buildings, buses, cars and people in its path. Again the screams of agony filled the air, as people who had just escaped the earthquake were once again running for their lives. Many were overwhelmed and disappeared into the ever-increasing pile of debris that was being pushed by this great wall of water.

Quinn stood transfixed by this apparition from hell sweeping toward him. It had only been a few months since he had been caught up in a flood in the Philippines and he knew firsthand the destructive force this wall of water could cause. *Tsunami*, was his thought in a desperate attempt to put reason and purpose to this catastrophic event. The earthquake must have been just offshore, because the waves reached land so fast. A quick glance around told him there was little he could do to help anyone trapped in the buildings. He had only seconds to keep from becoming a victim himself. He raced to the scooter lying on its side nearby and said a fast prayer of thanks as the engine responded to his first attempt to start it. Then he was moving as if in a dream, dodging piles of rubble, downed trees and telephone poles like a running back on a football field. As he concentrated on the broken path before him, the wall of noise seemed to be getting closer with every second. He began to gain altitude as the road entered the foothills of the Pusat Goya mountain chain. At this point, he chanced a glance behind him. There, not more than 100 yards away, was the face of the wall now filled with the carnage from the town. Its speed was slowing down as it pushed a wall of debris. Quinn reached the top of a small hill and found the bridge at the bottom had collapsed, so instead of continuing the racing he decided to make his stand at the crest. He turned the scooter to face the wall and braced himself for the onslaught.

The leading wall of the debris reached the foot of the hill and seemed to work like a damn. A fishing boat, that had been swept up from the coast and pushed before the wall of water, righted itself in the debris field. Instinctively, Quinn sprinted down the slope and dove for the exposed railing on the boat's gunnels. He struggled to maintain his grip, as the rising water tore at his clothing and the debris lacerated his legs. He pulled himself onto the deck of the boat as the wave crested the hill and continued across the open fields until it slowly lost power. With its power spent, the water seemed to hesitate as if rethinking its options and then began to retreat. Residual waves followed the first and left a massive debris field with dead and dying people as the waves subsided. Within minutes, he was out of harm's way. He opened his backpack and grabbed his phone.

This time, Alex took the call. "Alex!" Quinn almost screamed. "That massive earthquake just offshore of Banda Aceh has caused a tsunami. Waves reached as high as fifty or more feet and pushed way inland causing almost total destruction. The waves came ashore no more than a few minutes after the quake. No one could escape this onslaught. I think the casualties will be great. These waves will radiate throughout the Indian Ocean. We have to get word to other coastal areas. The Andaman Islands will be hit next and from what I've seen,

India and Africa are going to be impacted by this event as well. Get the word out if you can."

"Slow down, Quinn. We have not received any reports of an earthquake. Are you okay?"

"I'm okay for the moment. Hope and Steven were looking at conditions on the beach. I have no idea how they are doing. It does not look good for anyone who was near the water when this thing started. I have to go Alex. There are people everywhere screaming for help. I'll call you back when I can."

In the distance, a second wave coursed through the town. Anyone who survived the first waves was again caught in the open as a wave larger that the first rushed forward with devastating force.

"Alex, there is a second series of waves coming ashore from the aftershock. These look even larger than the first! I have to get inside the pilot house and ride it out." At his desk, Alex could hear the onslaught and the screams of people caught in the rushing water, as Quinn was swept along clinging to the railing around the pilothouse. The noise was almost deafening and Alex found himself standing at his desk, as if he was prepared to run for cover.

After several minutes, the noise subsided and Quinn returned to the call. "Alex, are you still there?"

"My God, Quinn I heard that! I can't imagine what you are seeing, but the noise alone sounded like total devastation. Tell me what is needed and I will try to get the relief process going."

"The way it looks now, the area will need everything—rescue operations first, water, food, shelter, medical assistance—you name it. The infrastructure is totally gone. We need to think in terms of rescue, recovery and rebuilding. Right now, it's rescue. I need to get going."

"Quinn, you can do much more for the people by staying on the phone. I'm going to put you online with Admiral Frakes, Commander of the Pacific Fleet. Hold on one moment."

After a few tense minutes and numerous clicks on the phone, a stern voice jolted Quinn back to reality. "This is Admiral Frakes, to whom am I speaking?"

"This is Quinn Wilson, Admiral. I'm a field agent with the National Geo-Spatial Intelligence Agency calling from Banda Arch on the northwestern tip of Sumatra. There has been an earthquake and tsunami that has devastated the area. I fear other coastal areas of the Indian Ocean will also be impacted by the tsunami. Ships in the area should be notified of the tsunami and the populated coastal areas will need all the help we can give."

"The Pacific Fleet cannot be responding to every tremor in that area of the world. There are weekly reports of earthquakes. What makes you think this is any different?"

"Admiral, trust me, this could be one of the most destructive natural disasters on record!"

"Who are you and why should I be taking your word on this? My authority and budget do not allow for arbitrary rescue missions without presidential approval. I have not received any collaborative reports of an earthquake or tsunami anywhere."

"I suspect you will be receiving reports soon. I'm on the ground and providing an up-front description of the devastation. It is NGIA's job to provide intelligence to the military and, Admiral, this is firsthand intelligence."

"You are wasting my time. I need substantiated reports and presidential approval and then, I will see what is needed, if anything. Goodbye."

Quinn was left holding the telephone to his ear, as he surveyed the horizon and the devastation around him. *Politics,* he thought as he dialed Alex's office again.

Alex picked up on the second ring. "Alex, Admiral Frakes needs presidential approval prior to committing U.S. resources to rescue operations …can you send a report to the White House to get the ball rolling?"

"I can do better than that. Stand by to conference in with the president. I'll make the introduction and you take it from there—okay?"

"The president! You have a direct line to the White House?"

"Quinn, you forget NGIA is the natural disaster watchdog for the U.S. government. I have a direct line …but to tell you the truth, this is only the second time I have needed to use it. The first was the meteor impact in Antarctica. So before I call, are you sure this is a global disaster worthy of presidential attention?"

"There is no doubt in my mind! This is a disaster of epic proportions and it is unfolding at my feet as we speak. By now, the tidal wave is coming ashore in the Andaman and Nicobar islands. We need to act fast to notify people of the hazard and get them moving to higher ground away from the coast."

"Okay, I'll ring the White House. Hold on." Quinn's head was swimming as he waited for Alex to come back online. In a surprisingly short time frame, Alex's voice returned.

"Mr. President, I have Quinn Wilson, our NGIA Pacific Field Agent on the line. He is calling from Banda Arch in Sumatra. Quinn, can you give the president a rundown on conditions there?"

"Mr. President, I'm calling from Banda Aceh on the western end of the Island of Sumatra. There has been a devastating earthquake with an epicenter apparently very near shore, causing a tsunami with waves of 50 feet in height or better. These waves have pushed far inland with devastating force. Almost all buildings and infrastructure here in Banda Arch have been destroyed, with substantial loss of life. The tsunami will most certainly radiate out from the epicenter and impact coastal areas all over the Indian Ocean. This is a disaster of epic proportions and these people will need significant amounts of help."

"What is a tsunami?" President Bush asked.

"It's a destructive tidal wave caused by an earthquake near the coastline."

"How long ago did this occur? I have not received any security briefings on this."

"Mr. President, the earthquake occurred only minutes ago. The tsunami followed very quickly after the quake, which means that Banda Aceh was near the epicenter."

"You say there was loss of life in the tidal wave?"

"I estimate there was significant loss of life from both the quake and the tsunami. I watched hundreds of people drown as the wall of water passed through the town. Children look most vulnerable to the flood. They were caught in the open after the quake and were swept away in the water."

"Yes, well, I will need more collaboration of the event before I can authorize any action by the U.S. But, if what you say is true, what will be needed?"

"The coastal areas around the Indian Ocean will need a full range of rescue and recovery assistance, including emergency medical, food and water, shelter, and ... body bags. We should start with reconnaissance flights over the coastal areas to determine what areas were hardest hit."

"I'm told I have a call holding from the USGS. Thank you for your assessment."

There was a click on the line and after a second, Quinn asked, "Alex, are you still online?"

"Yes, while you were talking to the president, the switchboard lit up like a Christmas tree. There are calls coming in from all over. I hope the President remembers where he heard about this first. You were right. The Nicobar Islands have been hit with apparently devastating force. Have you heard from Hope?"

"No, there has been no sign of her or Steven!"

"Quinn, hold on! The White House is calling back."

Seconds later, Quinn was conferenced into the call in progress. "...your agent was apparently correct. The USGS tells me that the quake was almost off the scale. I'm authorizing the Navy to investigate and aid where possible. I want your man there on the island to coordinate with them and be their eyes on the ground during this reconnaissance. I'll call Admiral Frakes at PACOM. You get your man in contact with the skipper of the closest Navy vessel and put them to work. Is that clear?"

"Yes, Mr. President."

"Have him report to the Admiral Frakes at PACOM and the Homeland Security Chief on this. Do not call me directly again."

"Yes, sir," Alex responded.

"Mr. President, thank you for your efforts," Quinn offered in closing.

Within minutes Quinn was online with the captain of the USS Shiloh, a destroyer with the Carrier Strike Group 536. "What the hell is going on?" he asked. "The radio bands have gone crazy and I get this message from Admiral Frakes telling me to expect a call from an agency I have never heard of."

"Captain, this is Quinn Wilson. I am an agent with the National Geo-Spatial Intelligence Agency. I am here in Banda Aceh on the northwestern tip of Sumatra. There has been a devastating earthquake and tsunami. I would place your closest ships on alert immediately for a possible tidal wave in the area."

"Shit!" Quinn could hear the muffled voice of the captain as he spoke to his Officer of the Deck. "Put the ship on full alert and get the crew back to the ship. This is not a drill! Repeat, this is not a drill."

"What did you say your name was?"

"Quinn Wilson!"

"Are you Navy?"

"No, NGIA. I am a former Marine captain, sir, if that helps."

"NG who? Yeah, well, my orders are to coordinate with you on some disaster. In this part of the world, it's good enough that you speak English even with a southern drawl. Where are you located at this time, Marine?"

"I am in the City of Banda Aceh on the northwestern tip of the Sumatra Island, just off of the Straits of Malacca."

Again, Quinn could hear the captain giving orders in a muffled voice. "Find Banda Aceh—it's somewhere near the western tip of Sumatra. Find it and establish a vector to those coordinates and make sure I have a God damn ocean nearby to park this boat when we get there." Back online with Quinn, he barked, "Does this have anything to do with the tremor we felt 10 minutes ago?"

"Yes, sir, it does. There was an earthquake—I'd say about 7 or higher on the Richter scale, followed immediately by a tsunami. I anticipate that the entire Indian Ocean will be affected, based on what I have seen here in Banda Aceh. How long will it take you to get here?"

"My ship will be in helicopter range within 6 hours. I'm 20 hours steaming time from your location. The Lincoln is in Hong Kong. We are getting the entire Task Force underway and the Lincoln should be in flight range within 40 hours."

"Can you helicopter a medical team and supplies to my location from the Shiloh?"

"I'll have the ship's medic and two others with the Marines dispatched. What supplies are needed?"

"We'll need medical assistance for physical injuries, broken bones, and lacerations first. After things are stabilized, we'll need the basics, including food rations, shelter and water—lots of water, since the public supply is surely gone. We'll also need body bags, as many as you have."

"Shit, so much for our tropical cruise," the captain said almost to himself. "How does my helicopter crew find your location?"

"I'll reach a suitable location for the helicopter to land and send you GPS coordinates. Captain, tell the ships to watch their depth finder closely in the Malacca Straits. There is no telling how much the channel has changed from the quake. Also Captain, can you initiate recon flights of the Indian Ocean from the Lincoln?"

"We have the P-3 Orion aircraft onboard the Lincoln that can fly recon. But the Indian Ocean covers a third of the God damn planet. Where do you suggest we start?"

"Let me download some satellite imagery and we'll figure that out. Right now, we need to concentrate on the immediate task of getting rescue operations up and running."

"Roger that, keep your line open. We are on the way."

"10-4, Captain."

Future accounts of the quake and tsunami would report a three-day period of informational fog. Seismic centers around the world were soon reporting an earthquake in the vicinity of Sumatra that ranged upwards of a 9.0 on the Richter scale. However, the reports of the tsunami and the amount of devastation caused were anything but clear. International news agencies at first reported only moderate destruction and an estimated death toll of 13,500. The estimated loss of life suggested a small humanitarian assistance and local disaster relief operation would be sufficient. The lack of information could be attributed to the sheer size of the event and the number of countries that were experiencing the effect of the tsunami. There were a few international journalists in the area and those who were reported on what they saw without having adequate knowledge or communications with other areas. Over the next few days, the estimates were constantly updated until the scope of the disaster became clear.

Quinn disconnected the phone and looked again at the misery and destruction that surrounded his location. People he thought dead were up and walking around in a daze. The calls for loved ones and moans filled the air. His scooter was useless with the streets blocked with so much debris, so he shouldered his backpack and began running back towards town. Less than 50 yards into the trip, he began rescue operations by pulling a woman from a roadside ditch. He collected loose clothing and bandaged her injuries as best he could. He could see she was in shock, just mumbling and moaning about loved ones, pleading to him in a language he couldn't understand, but he could read her request in her eyes. Once he bound her wounds, he clasped his hands together and bowed as he backed away. She protested at first, then fell quiet as if she understood that others needed help.

Quinn continued toward town, helping where he could. His worst fears were correct. It was the children who were impacted the most by the tsunami. Their bodies littered the debris. He was drawn to one small girl who had somehow survived the flood and was now standing naked on the edge of the road crying. She was somewhere between three to five years old. She started to run as Quinn approached and he was forced to chase her. He was unable to provide any comfort, so he picked her up and held her tight as he headed into town. Along the way he picked up stray articles of clothing and dressed her in a droopy tee shirt for protection from the sun. All the while he looked for an area for the helicopter to land and set up the medical tent.

In what seemed like hours, he reached the soccer field near the city's administration building. He could see that the fence surrounding the field had stopped some of the debris. *This is the best place I have found for the helicopter landing area*, he thought. Checking his GPS, he noted the coordinates and relayed them to the captain aboard the Lincoln.

The captain replied, "The Shiloh is steaming at flank speed toward your location. The ship is approaching the helicopter flight range and is expected to be at your location in approximately one hour. There will be three medics and a field first-aid tent aboard. Other ships are in route, so we should have a field hospital in full operation by 1600 today. By the way, we are receiving continuous reports of tsunami waves impacting coastal areas all over the Indian Ocean. The Phuket tourist area was hit hard and we can only guess that conditions are as dire as those you have reported. We do not have enough resources within the fleet to meet all of the needs."

"Have you communicated this to Admiral Frakes at Fleet Command?"

"The Admiral is flying in from Hawaii. In the meantime, the bureaucratic wheels are turning, but I'm not hearing a lot of enthusiasm from the top. The Iraqi and Afghanistan wars have stretched our resources thin. Now if you wanted someone killed, we are set up for that. The ships are fully armed, which leaves little room for rescue supplies."

"I understand, Captain, and I am not sure anyone could have been prepared for this. I think it is one of the largest natural disasters in modern history. We can only do what we can," Quinn offered, as the soccer field continued to attract survivors looking for assistance.

"You should be seeing our copter in one hour. Stay where you are and help them become oriented to local conditions."

"Roger that, I'm standing by."

Quinn was still holding the little girl when he finished the call. He sat her in the only shade he could find and started clearing pieces of roof tin away from the proposed landing site. These were the first recovery actions anyone had taken since the flood and his activities attracted a crowd who stood and watched him expectantly. With a great deal of gesturing, he was able to get the group to move debris and raise a piece of roofing to create a lean-to for shelter. Before he could get the little girl into the shelter, it was full of survivors and some skirmishes were taking place over what little space was available. "Make room! Make room!" Quinn called several times. No one moved. Finally an older woman reached out her hands and allowed the little girl to sit on her lap. That was the last Quinn saw of her.

Softly at first and then louder, Quinn became aware of the whoosh, whoosh sound of helicopter blades cutting through the air. His phone rang as the people in the shelter shouted and pointed towards the horizon. "Quinn Wilson," he said on answering the phone.

"This is Marine Captain Culver, pilot of the incoming helicopter from the U.S. Navy Destroyer Shiloh, requesting landing directions."

"Landing directions, let me see? The wind appears to be out of the northwest at approximately 15 knots. You will need to home in on the coordinates I gave you earlier. Look for a relatively cleared area with a lean-to and a crowd of people. We are a few hundred yards from the mosque, near the center of the city."

"I see your position. Please keep the people back while we are landing."

The whooshing sound of the blades was replaced by noise from the jet engine and the rapid sputter of the blades as the helicopter banked to the southeast and came slowly in for a landing. Two armed Marines stood on the rails outside the cabin with M16s at the ready as the helicopter touched down.

"Stand back! Stand back!" They ordered with compassionate but authoritative voices over the dying sound of the helicopter, as the captain saw that the situation was secure and began shutting down the engines.

In addition to the captain and copilot, there were twelve people aboard the helicopter. All were now on the ground surveying the damages surrounding the area.

"Christ! We had no idea it would be this bad. Are you Wilson? I'm Captain Culver and this is my copilot Lieutenant J.G. Fraser. Where should we unload and set up?"

"First, what do you have?" Quinn asked.

"We have a field hospital and emergency medical supplies, water and a few hundred MREs. I can tell by the severity of damage that we do not have enough. We will unload and return to the ship for additional supplies. There are other naval ships that have been dispatched and you should be receiving additional support by tomorrow morning."

"What have you heard from other coastal areas that may have been affected by the tsunami?" Quinn asked, fearing the answer.

"Preliminary reports indicate other areas have been hit hard without any warning. It sounds like a major disaster. We will be concentrating our efforts here until ordered to do otherwise."

As the Marines stood guard, the tent and supplies were unloaded from the helicopter. Rescue effort was underway with the medics beginning to treat the individuals who were near the landing site. Quinn continued discussions with the pilot about the rescue and recovery process. As they spoke, the Marines cleared away the debris and began erecting the medical tent. Survivors were coming in from all over, after seeing the helicopter touch down in the city square. Many were in urgent need of medical attention with cuts and broken bones. A few were carrying the bodies of loved ones in the hopes of a miraculous recovery. After securing the site, the Marines shouldered their weapons and began searching the surrounding areas for those in need of assistance.

Captain Culver took Quinn up in the helicopter for a recon flight around the city to review the damage to the city and surrounding area. The loss of human lives was staggering. They talked over the intercom in flight.

"Captain, I'm missing two of my field agents who were working towards the beach area. Did you see any signs of Americans during your first over flight?"

"Negative on that so far, sir. There were a few stragglers, but no one acknowledged our passing."

The damage was worse than Quinn had imagined. It looked like the tsunami had swept the peninsula clean. He was surprised that anyone had survived, including himself.

Captain Culver brought his helicopter back in for a landing near the field hospital and they continued their conversation as they walked back to the hospital tent.

"We are going to need more resources," Quinn said. "Are there other nations with ships in the area? I think we need to talk to the Admiral again to coordinate the effort. By now I am sure that everyone is aware that this is a major disaster."

"Feel free to give him a call, sir! I'm only a captain and I do not speak with admirals without authorization."

Quinn reviewed his past calls and found that the admiral's number was still in his satellite phone. The captain took a step back and stood at attention without even thinking as Quinn rang the number. He picked up on the second ring. "Admiral, this is Quinn Wilson from the NGIA, returning your call. I appreciate your dispatching help. The first helicopter from the USS Shiloh has landed and is currently setting up a first aid tent."

"Roger that, let me speak to the helicopter pilot," the admiral said in his usual direct manner.

Quinn looked at the pilot and handed him the phone. "The admiral would like to speak to you."

The captain seemed shocked as he reached for the phone and then took a few seconds to compose himself before he spoke with loud bravado. "Sir, this is Captain Culver United State Marine Corps, sir. How may I be of service?"

"Are you trying to be smart with me, young man?"

"No, sir!" he said with far less enthusiasm. "How may I be of service, sir?"

"Tell me, captain, are the conditions as bleak as the NGIA Agent Wilson has indicated?"

"Sir, yes, sir! If anything, they are worse. I just returned from a flyover and we are looking at total devastation, sir."

"What about fatalities?"

"Yes, sir! There are hundreds, possibly thousands of dead in view from my immediate location, sir."

"God damn it, captain! Am I going to have to play nursemaid in this fucking disaster?"

"Sir?"

"Never mind, does this NGIS Agent Wilson look reliable? Be honest with me, son. Can I commit resources on his recommendation?"

Captain Culver looked at Quinn and turned and walked back toward the helicopter before speaking. "Sir, I have only known this individual for a less than an hour since landing. He has taken charge of a very difficult situation, even though he is wounded and in need of first aid. He has organized the locals in a rescue effort. My crew is also taking orders from him to establish this base station. I think we are lucky to have him here, and yes, sir, I would trust this man and follow his direction, sir."

"Very well, continue your flights and establish an orderly mission there in the area. Afterwards I want you to get that agent's ass over to the Lincoln. We will use him to assess damages in the Straits, Andaman Sea, and the entire Indian Ocean basin. I'm getting reports from Thailand and Sri Lanka as we speak. Do you understand my directive, captain?"

"Sir! Yes, sir!

"Very well, carry on and let me speak to that Agent Wilson."

"Yes, sir, Captain Culver, over and out, sir."

The captain walked back and handed the phone to Quinn as he was organizing groups of four men to accompany Marines into various areas of the town. "Sir, the admiral would like to speak to you."

Quinn took the phone. "This is Quinn Wilson."

"Before we get down to business, I want you to understand that I am responsible for the United States presence here in this part of the world. I command sixteen ships and coordinate with land-based operations for the Marines, Army and Air Force. Therefore, I am in charge of this operation. Is that clear?" The admiral conveyed with authority.

"I do not recall disputing your authority, admiral."

"I want it clear that you will be operating under my authority during this disaster."

"I have responsibilities up my chain of command in Washington as well, admiral, and will have to check with them. In addition, I have spoken twice to the president and he will be expecting an update later today. However, this is an unprecedented disaster and if you are offering to organize the U.S. effort, I will follow your lead, sir."

"That is precisely what I am attempting to do. Now I want you here on the Abraham Lincoln as soon as possible. I am in the air flying in from Hawaii and will be on board the Lincoln within three hours. The Lincoln is already sailing at flank speed towards the Straits. We plan to begin some aerial flights to assess damage throughout the entire region. So wrap up your rescue efforts and get your ass on a helicopter by tomorrow morning. Is that clear?"

Quinn stood mute for a moment surveying the total destruction that surrounded him and the urgent needs of the people in all areas of the city.

"You are wasting my time, agent. You be here as soon as my ship is within range and we will finish this conversation in person." The finality of the metallic click brought Quinn back to reality. He holstered his phone and went back to work.

Quinn was familiar with smaller-scale disasters from his work on recovery efforts after Florida's Hurricane Andrew in 1992 in Miami and Ft. Lauderdale. This tsunami was following similar patterns, although it was much larger and more widespread. The first effort was to rescue those people who were in immediate danger. People trapped under debris or in need of medical attention had to be attended, so they could survive the next few hours. There were also a large number of people wandering the streets in shock looking for their families and the connections to the life they were forced to leave only a few hours ago before the devastating quake and waves swept over the town. The most critical of these were the children who were wandering in tears, looking for parents or anyone that would offer comfort. Everyone, including the aid workers, needed basics, such as water, food, and shelter, all of which either did not exist or was in extremely short supply. The first order of business for the rescue workers was to provide immediate care and start the long process of recovery.

After the first helicopter landing by the Americans, the efforts of the sailors and marines brought immediate help and supplies. Out of total ruin, debris was moved aside, and tent cities emerged, medical aid was offered, and people were brought in and provided immediate shelter, water, and food. These helicopter flights brought body bags as well. So many in fact that Quinn wondered why there were so many available in this region. However, he helped organize an impromptu morgue in the ruins of the cathedral where bodies young and old arrived with tears and wailing from survivors. The hundreds of bodies numbed the senses and challenged the very order and respect for life that all mankind takes for granted.

Quinn knew that after the rescue efforts, the next phase would be recovery. Individuals would have to find sufficient resources to recover and get on with their lives. It was obvious that this was going to take a while before the basic needs of life would allow this community to grieve and begin life again. He saw the young mothers searching for their children, husbands searching for their families, and children searching for their parents. The misery just kept coming, with no end in sight.

He continued working through the night supervising a number of local rescue teams that increasingly became pallbearers for the dead. Helicopter flights continued throughout the night and their search and landing lights had become common sights in the total blackness of the community. By morning, the tired and hungry teams seemed to congregate around the tent city near the cathedral and sought what food and water that might be available before they fell into fitful sleep. Captain Culver found Quinn helping a woman with a bad leg cut hobbling towards the first aid tent.

"Agent Wilson, the Abraham Lincoln is in range. I have orders to transport you to the ship to debrief Admiral Frakes. We will be departing in ten minutes."

"There is still a lot to do here, captain, but I'll be ready. I'll be in the first aid tent, if you need to find me."

Fifteen minutes later, Quinn sat in the open door of the Blackhawk looking at the devastation that unfolded below him. The deadly tsunami had sweep over the entire peninsula, leaving almost total destruction in its path. No building was left undamaged and most were totally destroyed. The scenes of destruction slowly gave way to the emerald-green waters of the Straits as the helicopter moved out to sea. Here he could see the debris and bodies that had been swept out as the waves receded. He looked at them closely, remembering that Hope and Steven's whereabouts remained unknown. He hoped they were alive and helping with recovery in another area of the peninsula. The bodies in the Straits would need no body bags, since they would remain at sea and either sink or be consumed by foraging sharks that he could see under the debris. He fell back into his seat in despair, looked at the ceiling of the helicopter and rubbing his weary eyes. There he fell into a restless sleep.

What seemed like only minutes later, Quinn was roughly aroused and told to secure for landing. As he looked out of the door, he could see the Abraham Lincoln in the distance. The ship was plowing water at flank speed and was an impressive and powerful sight. Despite the circumstances, he was impressed at the sight of this huge American warship. The helicopter circled the ship and came in for a landing in a designed area near the tower.

A Chief Petty Officer met the helicopter. "Agent Wilson?" he yelled over the noise of the helicopter. "Please follow me. The admiral would like to see you immediately."

He slipped down from the Blackhawk and followed the chief petty officer through the tower door and out of the noise of the flight deck. As he glanced back, he could see the flight crew begin refueling and loading the helicopter for the next run back to Banda Aceh. He noticed the captain looking in his direction and gave him an informal salute. He responded automatically with a fatigued salute of his own.

Quinn looked tired and dirty when he stepped through the cabin door into the admiral's office. His pants were ripped and blood-stained and he had not shaved in days.

"It is about damn time you got here. We have got a f---king disaster throughout the entire Indian Ocean Basin and we need to get our arms wrapped around it. I want your ass in the air within 30 minutes to give me an assessment. I am diverting all available ships to this area to assist and I need to know now where to deploy them for best results."

"Admiral, I have not slept or eaten for the past two days and need to get cleaned up before I do anything else."

"Shit, agent, none of my crew has had any sleep. Neither have I for that matter."

There was a moment of silence, as the admiral looked thoughtfully into his cup of coffee. "Look, I realize you and I have been butting heads. They pay me to be a pain in the ass. That is why I wear these stars on my collar. But just between you and me, I have never experienced anything of this magnitude and I need some help getting it under control. You told me on the phone that this is one of the biggest catastrophes in history and I laughed at you. I'm not laughing any more. Now I think you are right, but no one else in my chain of command sees that yet. You have seen this situation unfold firsthand and can speak with credibility to the skeptics in that chain, all the way up to the president. God damn it, agent, I'm trying to say I need your help."

There were a few moments of weary resignation between the two before Quinn spoke. "You got any more coffee?" Quinn asked as he took a seat across from the admiral.

"Sure, how do you take it?"

Two hours later, Quinn was sitting in the back seat of an F-16 as they connected to the steam launchers on the flight deck. The muted chatter of the pilot and flight control filtered through his headphones. The fighter was fitted with long-range fuel tanks and the mission was to survey the islands and coastline around the Indian Ocean. The pilot addressed him through the intercom. "Sir, place your head against the headrest and prepare for launch." Seconds later, the plane surged forward with tremendous speed and they were airborne over the Straits of Malacca. During the short meeting with the admiral, they had reached an agreement. Quinn would be the eyes and ears of the team, while the admiral would direct the resources to the areas Quinn identified as in need. In addition, the admiral promised to listen more and bark less.

Neither would sleep much over the next month. In the meantime, additional resources were streaming into the area from all directions and from a number of nations. Quinn and the pilot surveyed the western edge of the Malaysia Peninsula and the towns and villages of Kelong, Ta Ping and George Town (Pinang) flashed across the GPS monitor. The damage seemed far worse near the resort of Phuket in Thailand, where the waves had pushed far inland destroying the village, derailing a train and ravaging the resort areas in their path. The coastline was severely altered and islands that appeared on the GPS were no longer visible along the coastline.

Quinn had a hunch, "Commander, can I make a satellite telephone call while in the air?

"Not directly, sir, but I can patch you through to the ship and they can connect you." responded the captain as he banked the fighter towards Nicobar Island.

In a matter of minutes, Quinn was on the phone with NGIA headquarters in Washington. "This is Agent Wilson, code name Walter, calling from over the Andaman Sea. We need to get continuous satellite coverage of the Indian Ocean for this tsunami rescue effort. How much coverage do you have and how can I get access to it in a continuous stream?"

"Sir, we have repositioned surveillance satellites to provide photographs on each orbit. As of right now, we have covered half the coastline. Digital orthoimages are available, but we will need a compatible system with sufficient RAM to transmit a continuous stream of data to you. What do you have available?"

"What do you need?"

I can transmit PDFs to an Adobe Reader platform. But interactive use of the files will require a system with at least a Release 9 GIS/ARK INFO software and as much RAM as you can get. This would allow you to view and edit the images on the screen. Of course, you will need a large plotter if you want to download to hardcopy.

Let me call the Carrier Strike Group and find out if their navigational system or weather observation equipment can be adapted to receive and print satellite images. To whom am I speaking and how can I reach you with the information?"

Quinn made a few notes as the fighter passed along the coastline of the Great Nicobar Island. Again there was rack line that extended up to two miles inland. Any developed area in its path was no longer visible. In many areas, it was just a debris field, with homes, cars, buses and boats, all well back from the coastline. The pilot made a low pass over the islands and Quinn could see groups of frantic people on the beach waving in desperation. Everyone on the coastal areas of the Indian Ocean needed help.

The plane was now approaching Sri Lanka. The island had received a direct hit by the waves and the debris field extended a full three miles inland. The pilot reduces altitude and skimmed the beach looking for survivors. Again throngs of people emerged from the debris to wave at the passing plane. Quinn took furious notes of the damage and potential access points to bring in aid. It was now the end of the third day since the tsunami and other aid organizations were finally beginning to access the area. All were looking for places to serve and it seemed to Quinn that few had the facilities to assess the needs and to find areas to begin rescue and recovery work.

The pilot brought Quinn back to the present, "Agent Wilson, the Lincoln's Meteorology Section is on the line." Quinn pushed the lighted button on the communication console.

"Hello."

"This is Lieutenant Nelson, to whom am I speaking?" the headphones crackled with yet another authoritative navy voice.

"Lieutenant, this is Agent Wilson from the NGIA on

mission for the admiral. I'm calling from an F-16 over the Bay of Bengal on recon. Can you tell me whether you have an ArcGIS/ArcInfo computer system with Release 9 or higher on board with the capability to receiving a continuous stream of digital files from satellites?"

"That is priority information and I am not a liberty to discuss technical issues over a non-secured radio frequency," responded the lieutenant with an edge in his voice.

"Well, lieutenant, I suggest you contact the admiral and call me back on a secure line," Quinn responded with an equal edge. "I need to know if you can receive and transmit aerial photographs from surveillance satellites."

Ten minutes later, the lieutenant called back confirming that the ArcGIS system was available onboard the carrier and that it had the capability to receive images and transmit them as PDFs. He also indicated the shipboard systems could print satellite photographs.

"Thank you, lieutenant, we are returning to the ship. I would like to meet with you when we are back on deck." The pilot banked the F-16 over the Bay of Bengal and headed back to the carrier that was now edging its way through the Straits of Malacca to its sea base at Utapao, Thailand, offshore from the Thai Navy Base, Camp Red Dog.

With the assistance of the ship's meteorology staff, Quinn was able to establish a constant download of the most recent satellite aerials and then overlaid the population maps from the CIA World Factbook to show which sections of the coastlines within the Indian Ocean had the highest population that were at risk from the tsunami. These aerials were then formatted as PDFs and transmitted to the growing number of nations who were participating in the rescue mission. By January 3, 2005, a coalition of forces included Australia, Japan, Singapore, Russia, Canada, Great Britain, France and Malaysia. All were directing their operations using the satellite coverage provided by the NGIA. PACOM changed the name of the Carrier Strike Force to Combined Support Force (CSF) 536 on January 3, 2005. Admiral Frakes remained in command of the joint international operation.

Offers of assistance were coming in from around the world. Ships and people were streaming into the region to provide assistance. These included member nations of the Combined Support Force and non-governmental relief agencies, such as the Red Cross, World Vision and the Red Crescent, among many others. Quinn became the ad-hoc traffic controller for the relief effort, much like the fabled Beach Masters during the invasion of Europe during World War II. The commanders of each detachment learned quickly to check with Quinn when entering the disaster area. Quinn would ascertain their resources and direct them to where they could do the most good. All followed his directions and were glad to have the command oversight offered by the Americans. Admiral Frakes was also pleased to have someone in that role. The disaster was so large that it was difficult to know the needs and respond effectively. Quinn had been to each impact area soon after the tsunami and knew what was needed.

By mid-January data coming in from naval ships from various nations reported bathymetric data in the vicinity of the earthquake epicenter in the Indian Ocean, Andaman Sea and the Straits of Malacca. Quinn reviewed these reports with the admiral during one of their meetings between flights.

"Admiral, the changes in the sea bottom along the entire Sumatran coast were striking. The sea bottom has risen as much as 13 to 16 feet along a 750-mile stretch of the fault line. Apparently, the dominate Eurasian Plate vaulted over the Indo-Australian Plate causing the more powerful tsunami. This movement displaced an estimated seven cubic miles of seawater. It was this vertical displacement that triggered the tsunamis. Horizontally, the northern end of Sumatra appears to have moved 118 feet. Can you imagine an island the size of Sumatra moving 118 feet in less than three minutes! This is another fact in the long list of occurrences indicating that the Indonesian earthquake and tsunami was one of the most devastating in history."

"That is remarkable! I do not recall any other changes in ocean hydrodynamics in U.S. Naval history. Will your agency report this data to the USGS, NOAA and other international organizations responsible for changing the nautical charts?"

"Yes, Admiral, these reports are being submitted as they become available. I believe the UN will be conducting detailed bathymetric surveys to record these changes. In the mean time, notices to mariners have been issued and reported regularly on Channel 16 to inform shipping interest of the critical changes near shipping lanes."

Quinn and the admiral stood in silence on the bridge of the Lincoln watching the beehive of activities on the deck below. Helicopters were arriving, being re-provisioned and sent back out to one of the many forward land bases established in the hardest hit sections of the coastline.

"Well, it has not been easy," remarked the admiral. "Look off the starboard bow. You can see the British ships actively ferrying recovery equipment ashore. Off port midship are the Japanese hard at work on their section of the coast. There on the horizon are the Australians and the French. It's truly an international effort."

"It is gratifying to see, admiral."

After another pause the admiral asked, "So what are you going to do now that this recovery effort is well underway?'

"For starters, I'm going back home and sit on my boat and try to get some rest."

"What kind of boat do you have?"

"I live on my 37-foot Sabre. I keep it moored in Sydney Harbor."

"So, you are a rag bagger! I just might come down and spend some time with you. I love to sail."

"That would be great. I have been planning a trip up to New Caledonia along the Great Barrier Reef and could use a deck hand."

"You know I joined the Navy because I loved the sea. But I have advanced so much in rank, all I get to see is the top of my desk. So as soon as I can pass the responsibility of this mission on down to the fleet officers, I'll take you up on that offer. I would be happy to leave command decisions to you and be the deck hand for a while."

"I've got a berth for you whenever you are ready. Hopefully, this is the last disaster we will see for a while and I can cash in on my comp time. So let me know when you can get off and we'll make plans."

They stood in silence looking out across the flight deck like two old combat veterans, who were comfortable in each other's presence.

"There is one other thing I need your help on before you head back to Sydney. I got a call from PACOM asking us to escort a group of scientists who want to see impacts of the earthquake and tsunami firsthand. I'd like you to take them around to the hardest hit areas and give them the support they need. I can assign Captain Culver to fly the team around. He is almost your personal pilot anyway, since you two have worked so much together."

"I would be happy to assist. Where do I meet up with them?"

The admiral looked at his watch and turned to the Officer of the Deck. "Officer of the Bridge, give me a time hack on that Orion due in here with the scientific team."

"Yes, sir," the lieutenant responded as he reviewed a clipboard on the communication console. "It's due in from Christchurch at 1600, admiral."

"Very well, as you were." Turning back to Quinn, the admiral continued, "I'll quarter them here on the Lincoln and give them the chance to see a carrier in operation. We will meet with them over dinner and drinks in my cabin tonight and you can have them at 0600 tomorrow morning after breakfast to start the tour. Excuse me, Quinn, I know it sounds like I am barking orders, but you are the best man for this assignment. Can you help me out?"

"Of course, Tom, you know I'm here to help."

The P-3 Orion arrived at 1530 and discharged a disorderly group of seven scientists. Their nonconformity was in stark contrast to the uniformed crew members working on the flight deck. The scientists' uniforms trended towards Hawaiian shirts and baggy pants. The men sported beards or at least a two-day shadow, while the women wore brightly colored ankle-length dresses and windblown unkempt hair. They stood out among the ship's crew members as if they had landed from another world. "Rainbows," the career navy men would call them under their breath, with a knowing smirk on their faces.

Each member of this scientific team had a different, but interrelated, objective on this field trip. All wanted to see the destruction firsthand. Some were more interested in the geophysics of the tectonic plate movement, while others wanted to study the tsunami and the impact on the human population. Dr. Abigail Rubinstein, from the University of New Zealand, was part of an international effort to study the installation of a tsunami warning system in the Andaman Sea and Indian Ocean. As she explained to Quinn, "Similar systems were operating in the Pacific and Atlantic Oceans, but none had been installed in the Indian Ocean, even though it is one of the most active geological regions in the world. This was due in part to cultural and socioeconomic conditions and the lack of coordination among the nations that share a common coastline."

As the admiral had anticipated; the scientists were in awe of the Lincoln. Landing on a flight deck of an aircraft carrier was a remarkable event, but to be on an operational Nimitz class nuclear air carrier was a cultural shock. At 1,000 feet in length and over 5,000 ship and air support crew members, the Lincoln was a beehive of activity 24 hours a day. While the scientists tried to maintain their learned superiority, they were very impressed by the unity of purpose, as legions of men and women crew members kept the carrier on mission. It was this single-minded dedication to purpose that was largely missing from the academic world.

Despite being a decorated combat veteran of Desert Storm and the Iraqi War, the admiral was a gracious host. He successfully put away his gruff demanding persona, while maintaining the aurora of command and authority as he sat at the head of the table in his dress white uniform. The dinner served in his quarters that evening was worthy of a world-class restaurant. It helped that a seemingly endless supply of rather good wine was served with the meal, and followed by a round of after-dinner cognac.

Quinn sat next to Dr. Rubinstein and they talked about a wide range of subjects over dinner. She was a highly intelligent person with an inquisitive mind. Her thought processes moved so quickly that she seemed almost hyperactive. "Agent Wilson, may I call you Quinn?"

"Of course, and you are Abigail?

"Just call me Abby for short. I understand that you were in Banda Aceh when the earthquake occurred? Can you tell me about it?"

Quinn hesitated for a moment, collecting his thoughts. The events of that day were deeply imprinted on his mind and had taken a profound emotional toll, but he had not yet attempted to put them into words. "We …myself and two assistants, were in Banda Aceh to investigate some anomalies that had appeared between a series of satellite images. We were going to set some targets that could be seen on the satellite photographs and get precise locational coordinates." Quinn hesitated again as he collected his thoughts while Professor Rubinstein read the unspoken emotions on his face. I was on a motor scooter heading southeast out of town when the earthquake hit at 7:48 A.M. It was a deep rolling motion that lasted, seemingly forever, but in reality about two and a half minutes. It was impossible to stand, or to even to stay on your hands and knees. The rolling motion would repeatedly throw you to the ground like a rag doll. All around …buildings were falling and people were dying, crushed by the falling debris." Quinn's voice cracked as he cleared his throat and took a sip of wine before continuing.

Professor Rubinstein was reading volumes in these hesitations and the expressions on Quinn's face, that he was not aware were showing. "Oh, that sounds just awful. We can talk more tomorrow. I don't want to spoil the festivities or hog all of your time."

The scientific team received the tradition reveille call at 4:00 A.M. and was escorted to the Lincoln's mess hall at 5:00 A.M.

The admiral could have had them eat breakfast in the officer's mess, but wanted them to get a better feel for military life by eating in the enlisted men's hall, where over 2,000 sailors preparing for the morning shift. The clink of silverware on bone china plates and the low murmur of almost 2,000 sailors left an impression on the professors.

"Oh, my lord," exclaimed Dr. Rubinstein as she entered the mess hall. "I'm overwhelmed by the size of this ship and this crew. Look at them! There are so many young faces. I can't imagine how you can feed all of these people for an extended time at sea." It took awhile for the scientists to navigate the cafeteria line and get settled at their table. Quinn nursed a cup of coffee and smiled at his charges as they struggled with the giant coffee pots that probably held over 200 gallons of brew.

Once they finally made it to the table, Quinn gave them a summary of the day's activities. "After we finish breakfast, we'll head up to the flight deck, where a Seahawk helicopter will be waiting for us. We'll conduct a grand tour of the coastal impact areas that are in range. First stop will be at the resort area of Phuket in Thailand, then over to Banha Aceh, where the first tsunami waves came ashore and finally, over for several stops on the Nicobar and Andaman islands before returning to the ship. At 1600 this afternoon, there will be a P-3 Orion waiting to take you down to Perth, where you can make connections with commercial flights to your home bases. So when you are ready, we'll get underway."

A half hour later, Captain Culver lifted his helicopter off the deck of the Lincoln and maintained a 500-foot altitude as they flew over the coastal toward Phuket. Dr. Rubinstein and Quinn continued their discussion of the night before. "Quinn, tell me about the tsunami. What did you experience there in Banda Aceh?" Her eyes were riveted on Quinn as he took a deep breath.

"The earthquake had subsided and I was assisting with the rescue of a woman who was pinned under a rafter in a building. The air was filled with screams and moans. People were calling for loved ones and throwing themselves onto the piles of rubble that was once their home, pulling at the debris trying to get to those trapped. I heard the tsunami before I saw it. The noise, even from that distance from the coast was deafening. When I first saw the wave coursing through the city, I was reminded of one of those cheap horror movies that Hollywood makes. The surging water had already picked up boats and buildings from the coast. Buses and cars were swept up in the surge as it passed through town. Everyone around me panicked and ran in all direction. I scanned the surrounding area and saw no higher elevations or standing buildings. So I jumped on the scooter and raced down the road towards the low hills on the edge of town. I didn't make it. As the crest caught up with me, I grabbed the railing on a fishing boat and rode the wave until it lost its power and left me and thousands of dead and dying people in a pile of debris."

"There is something else, Abby, that I have been trying to put to words and have thus far failed to even describe it to myself. If you can tolerate some wandering thoughts, let me give it a try."

"Okay, I'm listening."

"I can see the tension in the people who survived this dual disaster. So, I think they are experiencing the same thing that I am. I can understand what they are feeling and can try to speak for them. On that clear morning in December, the environment that we all took for granted turned deadly. I knew immediate what was happening, but many of the people experiencing the quake had no idea of how destructive the next ten minutes were going to be. The earthquake not only was physically destructive—we could deal with that—but it struck the very foundation of our collective trust in the order of our environment, our sense of well being and our collective emotional stability. You can no longer trust the ground you walk on. It can turn into some kind of liquid in an earthquake and those waves can pummel you to death. You can no longer trust the sea to stay quietly on the shoreline. It can rise up in 100-foot waves and in seconds, wipe out families, villages, cities, and even entire cultures. In a matter of minutes, it took your home and killed your family. You can no longer trust your decision to live on the coastline. It does not matter that generations of your family have lived and died close to the sea. Now you know better … now you know."

Quinn stopped and looked out of the door of the helicopter. Dr. Rubinstein wiped a tear from her eyes and took a deep breath. The other scientists, who were listening in on the helicopter communication system were visible moved and in thought.

Captain Culver broke the silence. "Agent Wilson, we are approaching Phutket. I will be landing near the resort area shortly. To maintain the schedule, we can only remain on the ground for 30 minutes."

"Thank you, captain."

Once on the ground, Dr. Rubinstein and Quinn walked through the resort area as the other scientists spread out to survey the damage. She offered, "Quinn, your analogy of the survivors was very touching and true. My primary job on this visit is to evaluate the potential of installing a tsunami warning system to prevent this kind of human disaster. If the people had been warned, the death toll would have been much lower."

"We thought about that. Once the tsunami came ashore in Banda Aceh with such force, I knew that other areas were in danger. I couldn't convince my agency or the military of the severity of the event, so no early warning was sent. After three hours and several more tsunami landfalls, attempts were made to warn coastal areas. But no one was listening. Look at the situations along this coastline. There are 12 nations, excluding Africa, with different languages, governments and communication networks. How do you bridge those gaps and get a universal timely message out to everyone?"

"You use the universal language."

"What language is that, English?"

"No, a siren!"

"Okay, that would take a lot of sirens and a central control center to monitor conditions 24/7."

"Yes, you see the problem. Getting those 12 nations to agree to the program, set up the control center and install the warning system."

"Who would administer the program?"

"The National Ocean and Atmospheric Administration (NOAA) manages the system in the Pacific from the control center in Honolulu. NOAA has offered to help develop and staff this one until the region can reach an agreement, train staff and take over operation. Would you support an effort to get it started?"

"Me? Why, of course. I'm not sure whether my endorsement would make any difference, but yes, I can see the need."

"Actually, you underestimate your importance to this decision. The NGIA would be an integral part of the warning system and I was told that you were the agency's man on the ground and to talk to you."

"Really? I need to give the home office a call. I've been too wrapped up in this disaster."

"You should do that."

The Seahawk departed Phuket ten minutes late due to the University of Texas professor's interest in some local girls. Captain Culver made up time crossing the Straits of Malacca at 3,000 feet. Quinn noted in crossing, "The tsunami did not affect shipping here in the Straits. The waves passed under the ships without being noticed. We are probably crossing the epicenter of the earthquake now."

There were some cameras pulled from pockets to document the epicenter, even though little could be seen but the blue waters of the Straits. As they approached Banda Aceh, Quinn asked, "Professor Saroma, I understand you are interested in the cultural and socioeconomic impact of the tsunami?"

"Yes, that is my area of specialty."

"I wanted to mention one observation I've made over the past few weeks. Almost every family within Banda Aceh and the other impact areas have lost family members. Women and children seemed to be particularly vulnerable. Survivors appear to be establishing informal family units to support one another and to take care of the children. This appears to be an informal arrangement and I don't know if these will become permanent family units. I don't know what voice the Islamic religion has in these informal family units, but I have to believe they would take exception to unmarried men and women living together. However, this appears to be a vital step in the recovery process—certainly the children benefit by being a part of these family units."

"Very interesting, thank you for bringing that to my attention," he said as he hastily scribbled a note. "Can you tell me if you have observed Islamic Imams participating in the rescue effort and providing comfort with daily calls to prayer?"

"The Islamic clergy have been largely absent from rescue efforts. Those that are still in the area appear to stay in the mosques. I do hear the periodic call to prayer, but they are not out in the field, tending to the physical needs of their people. Now the laymen of that religion were extremely active in the rescue and recovery efforts. Their families and friends were most heavily impacted by the series of events."

"You mentioned that women and children were more vulnerable to the flood waters?"

"Yes, that was just my observation. But, I think an analysis of this disaster will identify the disproportionate number of women and girls killed in the tsunami. I also think there are some cultural and religious factors that contributed to their vulnerability. Women were inside the home when the flood hit. I have been told that some would not leave the home, because they had no male escort or were embarrassed to be seen without their veils or while wet. Also I understand that girls are not taught to swim in the Islamic religion. The men and boys were outside the home and able to swim or climb to save themselves. It was such a terrible tragedy. Almost every family lost members, wives and daughters, husbands and sons."

Quinn grew quiet as Captain Culver circled Banda Aceh and began the approach to the landing pad. These were encouraging signs of rebuilding. However, large numbers of idle men congregated near the landing zone waiting for yet another handout. They surged towards the pad expectantly, as the helicopter was on final approach. Quinn recognized the dependency culture that develops after disasters. People were in shock over the loss of family members and dependent on the resources offered to them, until they could begin to think and act on their own again. Some were always slower to move on than others.

Quinn knew there comes a time in each disaster when no one is left to rescue, all the injured have been treated, most if not all the bodies had been recovered, and survivors are receiving basic care, food and shelter. The helicopter landed at Banda Aceh on January 13th—a little over two weeks since the earthquake. As the scientists spread out to look around the town center, Quinn walked to the first aid compound located near the center of the town square, still at the same location where they had unloaded the first helicopter a little more than two weeks ago. "How are things going?" he asked upon entering the hospital tent.

Navy Lt. Evans was chief medic at the facility. She responded, "Well, sir, things began slowing down about two days ago. The helicopters are periodically bringing in wounded from remote areas of the coastline, broken bones and joint trauma mostly. But, even those flights have slowed down. My assessment is that things have stabilized and people are trying to put their lives back together. They need materials to build shelters and repair fishing boats more than they need medical aid. Our primary efforts right now are to identify bodies, maintain the list of dead and missing, and help console family members who find loved ones on our list of deceased."

"I'm hearing that from other areas as well. I think we are nearing the end of the rescue operation and starting recovery efforts. The nations of the world and their citizens have contributed billions of dollars to rebuild. I think it is going to take a completely different group of people and administrative structure to dispense those funds."

Quinn's last week with the Combined Task Force was spent escorting administrators of the world financial organizations. They included the Indonesian Development Bank, World Bank, International Financial Corporation, the U.S. State Department, and the U.S. Agency for International Development. A number of large non-governmental organizations were also present on the tours, including the Red Cross and World Vision. These organizations had received donations from citizens throughout the world and administered the investments to aid the stricken areas with little or no coordination from the international or respective national governments. Quinn was often asked where the money could be best spent.

His answer was always the same, “Repair and replace basic infrastructure, starting with the water supply and sanitary sewers to help prevent a pandemic diseases from sweeping the area. Next open the trade routes including the ports, airports, railroads, and highways. Give the people the tools they need to get on with their lives and then step aside.”

His advice was seldom heard, as the individual objectives of each agency such as health care, education, power generation, or government reorganization were targeted. All good projects, but in Quinn’s mind, these came secondary to the basic needs of the people. He was reminded of a statement that one of his clients had made back in his consulting days. “People with A-type personalities listen only to themselves. They are incapable of hearing the opinions of others.” *So true*, he thought as he heard these arguments. Individuals who control the money almost always had classic A-type personalities, so the recovery started without a centralized coordination agency and spiraled into disorganization. There was no Beach Master for the recovery process, similar to the role Quinn played during the rescue efforts. Agencies shunned cooperation in favor of expedited implementation of their own favored projects and were quick to report successes to their donors, along with requests for more donations. As the recovery process gathered momentum, over 400 relief agencies were on the ground.

Quinn did what he could to assist in the recovery process, but the effort was beyond the scope of one individual. Quinn and the admiral watched it happen. “Well, Quinn, I think our role is largely over. We need to pull the pieces together into a report, so that others can learn from our experience. There is no one better to lead that effort than you. I've called in a team of U.S. Navy historians and want you to give them the firsthand description of the disaster and rescue efforts. We will leave the recovery process to these disorganized yahoos."

So Quinn joined with the dedicated Navy historians and journalists to research and prepare a chronology of the tragedy and recovery efforts. This report was entitled, "Waves of Hope, the U.S. Response to the Tsunami in Northern Indonesia," and included satellite images and on-site photographs that helped direct the rescue operation.

By February 20, 2005, the preliminary report was sent to Washington, indicating that the initial rescue work was largely completed and the coordinated recovery operation was well underway. On that date, the human death toll was at 157,577 dead, 26,763 missing, and 1,075,350 dislocated and at risk. To date, it was the most devastating tsunami in recorded history. Quinn's review of data coming in from numerous sources was revealing other sobering facts as well. Reports indicated that up to one-third of the dead were children. More girls than boys perished, and as many as four times more women than men died. An estimated 9,000 European tourists died while vacationing in resort areas. Hope and Steven were presumed to be among them, since no sign of them had ever been found.

The U.S. Navy was able to respond quickly to the disaster in large part because of the firsthand reports received from the NGIA. They were also responsive because of the fully manned, all-source operational intelligence capacity of the Joint Intelligence Center Pacific Operational Cell in Hawaii. They were fortunate that the Carrier Strike Group 536 and the 3rd Marine Expeditionary Force were present in the southeastern Pacific in close proximity to the disaster. By January 5, 2005, twenty-five U.S. Navy ships, forty-five fixed-wing aircraft and fifty-eight helicopters were on-station off the coast of heavily impacted areas. By that time, over 610,000 lbs of water, food and supplies had been brought ashore to assist in the recovery.

"Thank you, Quinn. You have been a tremendous aid to the U.S. Navy and the nations surrounding the Indian Ocean during this disaster. You helped us get out of the fog and pointed the direction to the areas of greatest needs. It was a pleasure working with you. Now it is up to others to come in and rebuild with the funds donated from throughout the world. I'm taking my boats back to patrolling trouble spots and fighting wars. That is what we are trained and equipped to do. I've got your satellite telephone number and will give you a call when I can get away. Keep that boat stocked and ready to sail."

"I will, Tom, see you soon," Quinn said as he and the admiral exchanged a hearty handshake.

CHAPTER 21

Home

In honor of his work in the disaster, the U.S. Navy gave Quinn a ride back to the Sydney airport on a P-3 Orion Surveillance plane. He had only slept for few hours a night over the last 35 days, mostly in the Navy helicopters as they traveled from one makeshift camp to another.

He sat in the cockpit of his boat drifting in and out of a light and troubled sleep, with nightmare visions of thousands of victims piled up in the debris left by the flood as he dreamed. These sights and smells would be staying with him for the rest of his life. Each victim was a tragedy by itself and there were thousand, even hundreds of thousands of victims, with numerous children dead and so many families torn apart. No matter how much you tried to help them, it was not enough. There could never be enough to relieve the misery. It would take two or more generations for the population of these coastal areas to trust the sea again and forget the pain of their losses.

A voice penetrated his nightmares and as he slowly came back to this life, he saw a radiant vision of Betsy standing on the dock with her hands on her hips. The sun was setting behind her, sending rays of sunlight streaming through her blond hair and filtered through the white blouse that blew lightly in the breeze. She looked like life itself, bringing images of hope and encouragement to the bleak world that he had been living in for the past month.

"Well, welcome home! Where have you been?" she asked as she brushed her windblown hair out of her eyes. "May I come aboard?"

"Oh, you caught me dozing. Sure, come on board," Quinn said as he scurried to assist.

She needed no assistance as she jumped from the dock and stepped over the safety lines to sit opposite him in the cockpit. She silently looked at him with concern on her face, then with a smile leaned over and kissed him on his cheek. "You look like hell! Where have you been for the last month?"

His barriers were down and he did not feel like maintaining his flimsy cover story, and besides he needed someone to talk to. "I feel like I have been to hell and back, Betsy. I've been attempting to help the victims of the tsunami in Indonesia, Nicobar Islands, Thailand, and Sri Lanka—you name it—and I was on the ground to witness the catastrophe. Also I have slept very little in the last month, so if I fall asleep during this conversation, please do not take it personally."

"Hmmm, so first you have a run-in with a volcano and now a tidal wave? You are not in insurance, are you?" she asked as she reached for his hand.

The warmth of her small hands almost brought tears to his eyes and he realized how emotionally invested he had been during the last month. It was going to be awhile before he was physically and mentally back from the mass graves of the killing fields and he was going to need some help. Her hand moved up his arm to his shoulder. He responded to her jester automatically by reaching for her elbows. Their eyes met and there was an instantaneous exchange of data, like two computers making a wireless connection. There was concern, compassion, friendship, and …passion that passed between them in a matter of seconds. She leaned closer and her lips parted, as she took a deep breath. He responded as if on autopilot, as his hat bumped her forehead.

"Hello, what's going on?" The voice seemed to come from another world and instantly broke the connection between them with a jolt. Betsy jerked away and saw Ken James standing on the dock near the stern of the boat.

"Oh, Ken, you startled me!"

"I see that I did and just in time too. Who is that derelict guy with you? He vaguely resembles Quinn Wilson. I thought he died in the tsunami in Banda Aceh."

"Hello, Ken. No, I am still alive."

"Betsy, we had a date tonight—are you ready to go?" Ken said with a self-confident smile.

"Oh, our date …?" Betsy glanced at Quinn and for a split second, both of them remember the yearning that had passed between them.

Quinn's mind was spinning as he thought, *Betsy don't go! Stay here with me! Stay forever.* Her decision at that moment took on a disproportionate importance in his tired mind, as if the rest of his life depended on which one of them she would choose.

"Okay, Quinn …I …I …will let you get some rest and I'll check on you in the morning. Ken, I'm ready to go."

Postscript

The characters within the novel are all fictional. However, many of their basic personality traits are based on colleagues with whom I have worked over the years. To those, I apologize for any unsavory traits or awkward situations I may have placed them in during the story.

The National Geo-Spatial Intelligence Agency (NGIA) was created in October 1996 from the National Imagery and Mapping Agency with the Department of Defense. NGIA's primary responsibilities are to provide a wide range of geo-spatial intelligence products to the armed forces and U.S. intelligence community. Imagery is obtained from satellites and airborne photography. The NGIA does deploy observers to assist the military in combat situations and to U.S. support agencies during natural disasters. During these deployments, observers will tailor the intelligence products to fit the needs of the situation. As noted by Jennifer Daniel, NGIA Director, Office of Corporate Communications, "In the heat of battle, in the midst of a disaster or during a critical operation, a physical presence and an immediate response are invaluable." (*Pathfinder*, January-February 2010) They are the "eyes on the ground" of the NGIA, similar to the role played by Quinn Wilson in this story.

The events in the book are all based on factual occurrences. The first episode was based on droughts in Saharan Africa where the instability of the government resulted in the formation of rebel factions led by warlords and extremists. These marauding bands of rebels seek to control geographic areas and exploit any opportunity for economic gain through extortion and kidnappings.

The Wilkes Land meteor impact actually occurred approximately 250 million years ago. Needless to say, the timing of the event does not correspond with the story, but the location of the impact was in Wilkes Land of eastern Antarctica as described. The crater was located using gravity measurements, conducted by Dr. Ralph von Frese of the University of Ohio in cooperation with NASA. Gravitational fluctuations were measured by Gravity Recovery and Climate Experiment (GRACE) satellites. The crater or "mascon" is estimated at 30 miles in diameter and is buried under a mile of ice sheet. The debris field associated with the mascon is estimated at 200 miles wide. The impact of this meteor and the resulting worldwide impact are believed to have caused the great extinction of the Permian-Triassic era, when all life on Earth died out, setting the stage for dinosaurs to rise to prominence. There is also the possibility that the meteor impact caused the breakup of the Gondwana supercontinent, causing Australia and possibly India and Madagascar to begin drifting across the Indian Ocean. This led to the speculation in the story that the meteor impact may have caused tectonic plate activities throughout the globe.

The short coral bleaching episode in the French Polynesian Islands is factual. Bleaching has been noted on numerous coral reefs throughout the world. Marine scientists are continuing to investigate these events. While an anthropogenic cause is suspected, climate change and the resultant seawater warming appear to be at least a contributing factor to these bleaching events. While the impacts to the reefs can cause an economic impact to tropical resort areas, the political disruption to the government of the islands was totally fictional.

The combination of volcanic eruption during a typhoon in the Philippines occurred over the island of Luzon in July 1991. The combination of typhoon, wind, rain and volcanic ash may well be one of the most bazaar environmental events on earth. A blanket of sandy wet ash over one-foot thick rained down on Luzon with blinding force, causing buildings to collapse and resulting in over 60 deaths. The devastation of this 1991 event caused the abandonment of Clark Air Force Base, the largest Air Force Base in southeast Asia at the time. The eruption also heavily damaged Subic Bay Naval Base, which in part contributed to its closure two years later.

The sailboat voyage on Betsy's 62-foot Oyster through the Tasmania Sea between Hobart and Sydney was total fantasy. Walter Mitty would have been proud of the voyage. However, this 800-mile stretch of water is part of the roaring forties in the southern latitudes and is subject to volatile weather and wave conditions that were referenced in the story.

The most current episode described in the story was, of course, the Indonesian earthquake and Indian Ocean tsunami that occurred offshore of Banda Aceh on the northwestern end of the island of Sumatra on December 26, 2004. While not the worst disaster to have befallen mankind, it was the most devastating tsunami in recorded history with over 200,000 deaths within 12 countries surrounding the Indian Ocean. As noted in the latter chapter of this book, there were other sobering facts recorded in the aftermath of this disaster. Since over 88 percent of the population within the impacted area were Muslims, culture conditions played a decisive role in the life and death struggle as the tsunami waves crashed into the coastal areas. Reports indicated that up to one-third of the dead were children, with more girls than boys perishing in the flood waters. In addition, four times more women than men died. This is attributed to a variety of physical and cultural reasons. Principal among these is that females are not taught to swim in Islamic nations and most women and daughters were indoors when the tsunami struck. More disturbing are reports that some women refused to leave their homes because there was no man to escort them or that they were too modest to be seen wet or partially dressed in public. This is truly a sad statistic that will have a long-lasting effect on the recovery of the impacted areas. The death toll also included an estimated 9,000 European tourist who died while vacationing in resort areas. ("Waves of Hope, the U.S. Response to the Tsunami in Northern Indonesia," February 2007)

Admiral Thomas Fargo, referenced in the story as Admiral Frakes, was the Commander of Operation UNIFIED ASSISTANCE and the Aircraft Carrier, Abraham Lincoln, was the flagship of the American Joint Task Force 536 that provided humanitarian support and prevented further loss of life and human suffering during the relief effort. I hope that this episode honors the efforts of all the America sailors and marines who participated in this recovery effort.

About the Author:

Roger Anderson is a physical geographer who has worked nationally and internationally as an environmental consultant for most of his career. While *Code Name Walter* is his first attempt at fiction, Mr. Anderson has written numerous technical reports and articles on environmental and land use subjects. He began writing *Walter* as an exercise to hone his writing skills and to escape from the structured demands of technical writing.

He is an avid outdoorsman who enjoys sailing, bicycling, and fishing. True to the lead character in the story, Mr. Anderson is currently working on the recovery of Haiti after the January 12, 2010 massive earthquake.

He and his wife, Rachel, currently live in Jacksonville, Florida.

CPSIA information can be obtained at www.ICGtesting.com
Printed in the USA
LVOW120511161211

259706LV00003B/4/P

9 781614 93072